Mrs Pearcey

About the Author

Lottie Moggach is the author of three previous novels: *Kiss Me First*, *Under the Sun* and *Brixton Hill*. She grew up in Camden Town, and now lives in a slightly quieter bit of north London with her husband, son and dog.

Mrs Pearcey

Lottie Moggach

PHOENIX

First published in Great Britain in 2026 by Phoenix Books,
an imprint of The Orion Publishing Group Ltd
Carmelite House, 50 Victoria Embankment
London EC4Y 0DZ

An Hachette UK Company

The authorised representative in the EEA is Hachette Ireland,
8 Castlecourt Centre, Dublin 15, D15 XTP3,
Ireland (email: info@hbgi.ie)

1 3 5 7 9 10 8 6 4 2

Copyright © Lottie Moggach 2026

The moral right of Charlotte Moggach to be identified as
the author of this work has been asserted in accordance
with the Copyright, Designs and Patents Act of 1988.

Image on p.vii: courtesy of the author.

All rights reserved. No part of this publication may be
reproduced, stored in a retrieval system, or transmitted
in any form or by any means, electronic, mechanical,
photocopying, recording, or otherwise, without the
prior permission of both the copyright owner and the
above publisher of this book.

All the characters in this book are fictitious, and any resemblance
to actual persons, living or dead, is purely coincidental.

A CIP catalogue record for this book is
available from the British Library.

ISBN (Hardback) 978 1 3996 2655 2
ISBN (Ebook) 978 1 3996 2657 6
ISBN (Audio) 978 1 3996 2658 3

Typeset by Input Data Services Ltd, Bridgwater, Somerset

Printed in Great Britain by Clays Ltd, Elcograf, S.p.A.

www.orionbooks.co.uk
www.phoenix-books.co.uk

For Horatio

Gran almon...
toda casa. Atocha, 78, bajo.

Almoneda toda la casa
hay piano Fuencarral 10 pl

Almoneda muebles, col-
gaduras. Sordo, 27, bajo.

Se vende en voluntaria
y extrajudicial subasta la
casa sita en esta corte, calle
de Zurita, núm. 14. El rema-
te tendrá lugar el día 29 del
actual, á la hora de las doce,
en la notaría de D. Juan Zo-
zaya, Plaza del Progreso, nú-
mero 8, donde están de ma-
nifiesto los títulos de propie-
dad y pliego de condiciones.

DINERO
MÁS BARATO QUE NADIE
por el mismo capitalista
á militares de Madrid y provincias y clasque pasen á Ultramar; á empleados de Ha-
cienda, Tribunal de Cuentas,
Ultramar, Diputación Pro-
vincial, Ayuntamiento, fe-
rrocarriles é inmovibles.
Jardines, 24, de 10 á 12 y 5 á 7

PETROLEO de 1.ª, lata, pese-
tas, 95; litro, 75
cénts. Hortaleza, 84, 1.º imp.

BIOSKA
Agente general de negocios
MATRICULADO
Desengaño, 17, ent.º

Esta casa hace las opera-
ciones muy á satisfacción de
sus numerosos clientes, dedi-
cándose con especialidad á
la compra y venta de fin-
cas, trabajando siempre para
elegir de todos precios y condiciones. No confundir esta
casa con otra que se entretie-
ne en copiar mis anuncios.

BAZAR IBO
Leganitos, 63
Tiene gran surtido en Be-
bés de todos los tamaños, ves-
tidos con mucho gusto y que
por tener que trasladarse al
nuevo local de la calle An-
cha de San Bernardo, n.º 18
dup.º, se realizan á precios
baratísimos.

Compras de oro, plata,
platino y galones siempre
bien pagado, Toledo, 7, plat.ª

REGA...
Libros de todas cla...
gantemente encuadernados,
se venden en la librería de
Escribano y Echevarría.
Plaza del Ángel, 12

MAQUI
nas para coser desde 6 á 60.
Compramos, vendemos y
componemos. Carmen, 12.

DINERO
Al 2 por 100
A pasivos, viudas y pen-
sionistas, sueldos y muebles.
Leon, 1, 2.º de 10 á 12, de 2
á 4 y de 7 á 9 noche.

DOY trajes y gabanes que
valen Duros á 14.
Jacometrezo, 63, 2.º

NO
compréis Champagne, Bor-
deaux, Jerez, Manzanilla,
Pedro Ximenez, Málaga,
Moscatel y Cognac, sin antes
ver las partidas que, proce-
dentes de empeños vencidos,
tiene para su venta la muy
acreditada casa de préstamos
MONTERA, 36, segundo
(esquina á la de Jardines).

Para Lisboa, Sr. resp. nece-
sita un joven Palma 46

Coches
buenos y baratos de todas
clases y guarniciones.
REDONDILLA, 6.

1º M.E.C.P
Last Wish of M.E.W.
Have not Betrayed

Libros rayados
Copiadores de cartas, pa-
pel, sobres, tintas y todos los
artículos para escritorio. Esta casa vende más barato que
todos los almacenes al por
mayor. A provincias, franco
de portes. P. Bargueño, Mayor, 30. Madrid.

ORIENTE Hotel, Arenal, 6.
Cuartos desde 2 pe-
setas, pensión desde 7 ptas.

dad, ardor, picazón, irri-
gia, flujos blancos y de san-
gre, etc. Consultas gratis
lúnes, viernes y por correo.
Montera, 33, 1.º

GRIETAS DE PECHOS
50 años de éxito recomien-
dan la pomada de la Farma-
cia de la Latina, de J. Sepúl-
veda, TOLEDO, núm. 62.—
Bote1 pta.—Se remite á provincias por 1'50.

Entredoses
Arañas lámparas para co-
medor juegos de reloj desde
60 ptas. Biombos japoneses
desde 30. Gran surtido en ob-
jetos para regalos. Como fin
de año precios baratos. Mi-
randa, **Carmen, 7.**

18 0[0 annal libre
empleando cantidad en nego-
cio honroso, seguro, nada
molesto y liquidable cuando
RAZÓN Fuencarral, 17,
grabador.

Al detall
Jerez,	desde	1,50 bot.
Champagne,	»	4,00 »
Rhum lardenal »	2,25 »
Cognac superior »	1,50 »
Anis manchego,	»	0,70 »
Casa Taso Colmillo 3 Madr.d

IMPOTENCIA
debilidad y esterilidad
La curan las célebres píl-
doras tónico genitales del doctor Morales. Carretas, 39,
principales farmacias, 30 rs.

Se ceden gabinete y alc.
Sbms. R. Greda, 24, port.

Ceden sala y gabinete
Carmen, 25, ent.º dra.

Venta
de 6 caballos, 2 mulos y 3
mulas en el Regimiento Ar-
tillería, acuartelado en San
Gil, á las once de la mañana
del 29 del actual.

Berlina seminueva Calle
de Duque, 16.

MARTES 23 DE DICIEMBRE DE 1890

OCTOBER 1890

I

Cultivate a smile that is neither too small, which might indicate private displeasure, nor too wise, which may look insincere, and at the very least will distort your features unbecomingly. Aim for an expression of quiet delight, and practise it in the mirror until it becomes second nature.

— Girl's Own Paper

Hannah and Cosmo's engagement dinner was being held at his parents' house in Kensington. Hosting such an occasion was usually down to the bride's family, but Cosmo's mother had insisted, claiming she wanted to show off the pink chandelier they had brought back from Murano, and Hannah's mother had offered no resistance.

'Ma said she thought it might be painful for your mother, hosting a significant family event without your father,' Cosmo explained privately to Hannah, on one of their walks. He paused, and did the adorable squint that meant he was about to be funny. 'But, of course, knowing Ma, it really *is* all about the chandelier.'

Hannah had smiled back, delighted by his disloyalty. It made her feel as if they were already detaching from their families and becoming a gang of two. She considered responding that, despite continuing to wear mourning long after she could have given it up, her mother had never seemed at all pained by her husband's death, but she thought that might be too much – for now at least.

'Well, whatever the motive, it's a grand idea,' she had replied instead. 'It can't fail to be a livelier event than if you came to Camden Square.' She mirrored Cosmo's pause for effect and added, 'But then, a tour of a turnip field would be more fun than that.'

The walk had been a triumph. It was a bright, crisp autumn day and Hannah had felt unusually piquant as they strolled around Camden Square, alone except for whichever of her neighbours was watching from their drawing-room windows. Passing the horse chestnut tree, she'd set her fiancé a challenge: he must pick a leaf and strip out the tender flesh between its veins in order to leave a delicate fish bone, as she had liked to do as a child. Cosmo had tried and failed, as she thought he would, breaking the leaf's veins with the first swipe of his clumsy paw. Hannah had then shown him how it was done, executing it perfectly, holding up the lacy leaf skeleton with a triumphant smirk. It was, she felt, a scene fit for an illustration in a magazine romance: Hannah as the pert, wasp-waisted heroine, her hair piled up like whipped cream; Cosmo, lean in his frock coat, his usual air of authority softened by feelings of tenderness and awe. *Why, Miss Teale!* the caption would read. *Such delicacy, wit and spirit! Just what I long for in a wife!*

That was two weeks ago; now, the evening of the dinner was here. Just before seven, Hannah's brother Will walked to Camden Road to find them a cab, while Hannah and her mother waited for him in the hallway. The scent of boiled potatoes drifted up from the kitchen, accompanied by the muffled clank of pots; the maids were making their dinner. As the Teales would be out all evening, the hallway lamps hadn't been lit, and the wash of evening sun that made it through the fanlight above the front door made little impression on the space. The walls, painted a rich claret several decades ago, had dulled to the shade of old liver, and there were no objects for the light to bounce off.

The Teales had never been ones for ornaments, in any case, but at least there had once been a mirror above the fireplace, and a bucket of brass fire tools beside it; a couple of prints on the walls. But the mirror had been taken down on the day of Mr Teale's death and would not be coming back. Mrs Teale had donated it to her women's refuge, along with the fire tools and prints, and many of the house's other inessential furnishings.

Here was her mother, as light-absorbing as their surroundings. The contrast between them tonight could not be starker, Hannah thought: her, blooming in yellow silk, on the cusp of it all; her mother, bony and dry, in coarse black bombazine. Mrs Teale showed no sign of wishing to speak. This wasn't unusual in itself – the two of them had spent countless evenings together in near silence – but what was unremarkable in the drawing room with a book on one's lap felt awkward down here, loitering in this dim passage. Really, Hannah thought – with her mother in widow's weeds; the heavy quiet; the dusty air, as if they were trapped in a dismal snow globe – the scene was indistinguishable from the last time they had stood like this: waiting for Mr Teale's hearse to pull up outside so they could lay on their wreaths.

'Do I look nice?' Hannah asked, suddenly.

Mrs Teale looked over, surprised.

'Nice?'

Only her mother could make such an innocuous word sound so silly.

'Of course you do, Hannah,' she said, her tone maddeningly even. 'Is it a new dress?'

'No! We got it made for my twenty-first. Don't you remember?'

'Ah, yes.' Mrs Teale paused. 'Oh dear. Perhaps I should have been up there with you this afternoon, helping you get ready?'

It wasn't a real question, and her mother certainly wasn't expressing a genuine regret. Hannah thought of the hours she had just spent at the dressing table – laboriously coiling her hair, buffing her nails, lightly pattering her fingertips over her face to even out her complexion – but in the company of her mother. Such occasions demanded amiable, relaxed chatter; compliments; shared grooming; the passing-down of advice; acknowledgement of the poignancy of the moment. Her friend Emily had this sort of relationship with her mother; they were always stroking the other's hair and leaning into one another, giggling. But for Hannah and Mrs Teale? Impossible!

'What shade of yellow would you say that is?' Mrs Teale continued now, indicating Hannah's dress, as if she'd heard Hannah's thoughts and wanted to prove that actually she was perfectly capable of dull female chit-chat if she was so minded. 'Not quite lemon. Egg yolk? Custard?'

'Well,' replied Hannah, wrong-footed, 'Mrs Didier called it *citrine*, but then she is French . . .'

Her desultory reply was cut short by a loud cackle of laughter coming up from the kitchen. Hannah pictured Ivy and Gwen with their feet propped up on the kitchen table, bowls in their laps, lining their stomachs to see them through the hours ahead. They were going down to Camden Town tonight. This was not that rare an event – Mrs Teale now spent much of her time at the refuge, and Hannah knew they often slipped out during her absence – but there was something special happening tonight at the Bedford. They had been discussing it all week: how they'd do their hair; how they each had just enough money for the entrance ticket and one drink each, and speculating about who might buy them more (Ivy was determined to cross paths with someone called Tom). Hannah knew all this because she'd overheard them. They weren't as circumspect in her company as they were with Mrs Teale. Hannah felt they saw her as not quite one of *us*, but neither one of *them*.

Soon, though, she thought now, she would be the mistress of her own home, and the servants would be careful around her.

Another shriek from below. Hannah realised that the girls must have assumed they were alone; that Will's door slam signalled an empty house. The inevitable next step was for the two of them to come tearing up the stairs to get changed, and for their giddy, delicious mood to puncture at the sight of Mrs and Miss Teale skulking in the hall.

'Shall we wait outside?' she said to her mother, moving towards the front door. 'It's a lovely evening.'

Pulling open the heavy door felt like escaping a mausoleum. Outside, light and warmth – life forces! – were waiting patiently to embrace her. It felt more like summer than mid-autumn, as if an August evening had been kept back in reserve and released just for her. Moving onto the step, she tilted her face upwards, closing her eyes for a moment to better appreciate the melted-butter sensation of the sun.

Before her lay the garden of Camden Square, its blousy foliage escaping its railings like badly pinned hair. The horse chestnut dominated their end of the square, and from beneath it came the sound of squabbling children's voices. The speakers were hidden from view, but Hannah recognised the plaintive tones of the Fletcher twins from Number 4. Rhythmic thwacks issued from the tennis court at the far end of the garden; these players, too, were out of sight, but it was safe to bet that Mr and Mrs Prince had hogged the spot.

Would she and Cosmo play tennis? Did he even like the game? There was so much she had to discover about him. And he still knew so little about her.

The strains of a violin – a scratchy, hesitant Mendelssohn – drifted from an open window on the east side of the square, joining the trills of chaffinches and blue tits, and the distant clanks of the traffic on Camden Road. There was a throb underfoot as a train passed beneath them, bound for St Pancras. The same ambient sounds as all the autumns Hannah could remember.

As well as celebrating the engagement, the purpose of the dinner was to reacquaint the two families. The Teales and the Walters had first met in a very different context: in Naples, back in June, as part of a group of British tourists on a three-day tour of Pompeii and Herculaneum. For Mr and

Mrs Walters, Naples was just one stop on a continental odyssey, and they had continued on to Greece and Turkey. Their son Cosmo had to return to London, to his job as a reporter at the *Star* newspaper, and took the same sleeper train to Calais as Hannah and her mother. In the Observation Car, Hannah and Cosmo had chatted for hours, while her mother sat reading *Villette*, and when they all retired to their respective berths Hannah couldn't sleep at all, buoyed both by the thrilling luxury of the train, with its complimentary chicken croquettes and thick, starched bed linen, so much nicer than theirs at home, and the interest of this lively, knowledgeable young man.

Cosmo's courtship of Hannah began in earnest when they were back home, with letters – *The delightful hours I have passed in your society in Italy have left an impression on my mind as indelible as the ruts of the ancient carriage wheels upon which we walked* – leading to strolls, and within a month, he had fallen to one knee, on the top of Primrose Hill, and offered Hannah his grandmother's sapphire ring.

Now *that* was a significant event, worthy of a magazine illustration. Tonight was unlikely to be, unless there was an unexpected revelation and a woman fainted, or Mr Walters drew out a pistol in the drawing room. However, gazing out over this gilded, familiar scene, in her best dress, waiting for the cab, Hannah felt imbued with a great sense of occasion. She had felt this often since Cosmo's proposal: as if every so often she caught up with the fact that her great turning point was now in motion; that she was about to be admitted into an ancient and profound institution.

The sun was hot on her skin; she imagined freckles eagerly springing up, littering her nose. She should go back inside, but the idea of returning to that dark, cold hallway was impossible, as unnatural as a butterfly stuffing itself back into its chrysalis.

She twisted her engagement ring, stroking the stone with her thumb. The twins had now moved out from under the cover of the tree, identically dressed in their sailor suits, grubby-looking even from here.

She watched as they searched for conkers, inspecting them with the seriousness of Rhodes in his diamond mine. When Cosmo had spotted them in the square, during one of their post-engagement walks, he had remarked, 'Imagine if we have twins!' and Hannah had replied, 'Help!' Cosmo had laughed along, but only belatedly; it was clear she had misjudged the moment.

Now, she thought, considering Cosmo had expressed a desire for three children in total, perhaps it *would* be efficient to have two at once. Could one engineer it, somehow? Her magazines did not address such issues. She would have to ask her friend Emily, already married and occupying a higher plane of wisdom.

She heard the clatter of hooves on cobbles and looked over to see a cab entering the square from the direction of Camden Road. A moment later, Mrs Teale appeared beside her. The cab drew up, wheels rasping against the kerb, and the two of them descended the stairs, in careful little steps, constricted by their skirts.

The driver glanced down at them from his perch.

'Three?' he said. 'Can't take three.'

'Oh no, really?' Hannah said, smiling up to him, her good spirits undented. 'I'm sure we can fit in.'

Uncharmed, the man shook his head. He was old, his face

scrunched and weathered. He looked as if he had been born with a pair of reins in his hand.

Beside her, Hannah heard a small exhalation from her mother, as if she had just caught herself before speaking. Hannah knew – *knew* – that Mrs Teale wanted to say, *Well, perhaps I could stay behind*, but realised that would be too much, even for her.

'It's a special occasion,' Hannah said to the driver – and as a rebuke to her mother.

'Wears out the horse,' he replied.

The horse looked to Hannah to be in fine fettle – sturdy and shiny-coated.

'I am very small,' said Hannah to the driver. She wanted to add, *and my mother is a wraith*. 'I hardly count.'

Now, finally, the driver looked down at her. He didn't smile, but some small part of him must have softened, as he relented.

'Got to charge you extra.'

Hannah smiled and nodded as she opened the door. Will was sprawled across the seat, long limbs filling the space, eyes closed, oblivious to the drama.

'Budge up,' she said.

Will opened his eyes and awkwardly shifted over, his top hat grazing the ceiling of the cab. Hannah climbed in beside him, her cheek pressed against the shoulder of his coat – her father's coat actually, as Will had inherited his wardrobe. It smelt of sweat and cheap lavender oil – the smells of Will's secret Theatreland life. Her mother squeezed in. Hannah sat wedged between her tall, bony relations, in a seat designed for two, her egg-yolk silk sandwiched between their two dark coats. The driver turned the horse around and they set off towards Camden Road.

'I cannot deny, I feel a bit seedy,' announced Will cheerily. 'But I'm sure I'll have rallied by Kensington. What are their names again?'

Will hadn't been on the Italy trip, so hadn't met the Walters at all, and Cosmo only once in passing. He had shown little interest in who was providing his dinner that evening. The prospect of good food and wine – as one would hope for in Kensington – appeared to be enough for him.

Hannah sometimes felt vexed about how Will was going about his life since his sudden lurch to official manhood. Not for the fact that, despite being five years younger, he had so much more freedom than her – that was just the way things were – but for the jejune way he was spending it. Her annoyance was exacerbated by the fact that Mrs Teale seemed unconcerned about his flaws, reserving her judgement for Hannah.

But now, squashed beside him in the cab, Hannah felt more generous towards her brother: his uncomplicated, unquestioning pleasure-seeking seemed a welcome counterpoint to their tricky, censorious mother. And while he may have begun his adult life before her, now, with her marriage, hers was starting, too – and she was leapfrogging over him, going straight to the main event.

The cab fought its way down Camden Road, which at this time on a Friday was at its busiest, clogged with omnibuses and commuters – a quiet, exhausted, black-coated army, making their way home from the city to wives in Kentish Town and Holloway and Finsbury Park.

She and Cosmo hadn't quite decided where they would

live. Cosmo said he was happy to take the train to work, which opened up the whole city. 'Anywhere you like!' he had said, expansively. 'Even Herne Hill!' Her magazine suggested it was wise, if possible, to live within easy walking distance of a husband's workplace, so he did not have any extra trials at the end of a long day and could easily get home to her comforting embrace. So, they had narrowed it down to areas close to Fleet Street: Canonbury, or Islington, or – daringly further east – Hackney. She didn't know exactly how much they would have to spend – in lieu of Mr Teale, her mother had had the required financial conversation with Cosmo – but Cosmo had intimated that rent wouldn't be a problem. Hannah had been poring over the 'Houses to Let' in the *Gazette*. *Large garden, 150ft deep; bays, Venetians; six rooms; nine rooms; hot and cold bath; very comfortable; thoroughly done up; recently papered and painted; a cheerful house; drainage perfect.* Whether the language was bald or evocative, each three-line advert was the invitation to a new life, with one thing in common: wherever they ended up, the 'At Home' cards propped on the mantelpiece would be addressed to Mr and Mrs Cosmo Walters.

They were now inching past the station. Men emerged from the platforms like floodwater, seamlessly merging with those pressing ahead on the pavement. Hannah heard the cry of the sausage-roll coster who was always positioned at the exit and the accompanying waft of warm meat. Her stomach, empty since a playing-card-sized piece of fish at lunch, twitched.

'Quite fancy another one of those,' said Will beside her.

'You've had one already?' she asked, jealous. 'Don't ruin your appetite.'

'There's lots of grog to mop up,' he said. 'Oh, yes – James was at this thing last night. Weren't you mad about him a minute ago?'

Hannah's goodwill towards her brother fell away.

'Don't say that!'

She glanced over at her mother, but Mrs Teale didn't appear to be paying attention, engrossed in picking stray hairs from the sleeve of her jacket.

'Oh, sorry,' Will said blithely. It made it worse that he didn't care. He wasn't being mischievous or malicious; he had punctured her mood without any thought at all.

James was the older brother of a schoolfriend of Will's, the only other contender in what Hannah had innocently imagined would be a heady period filled with multiple suitors jostling for her hand. He was a trainee architect with very thick dark hair swept high off his face, and a stern, uncompromising manner. He didn't take sugar in his tea, because of indentured labour, and when Hannah had mentioned that she liked reading George Eliot, he had told her not to be parochial and given her a French novel about a man who killed women in states of delirium.

He was awful, really, but Will was right: she had found James oddly thrilling, sleeping with the book under her mattress, even if she couldn't bring herself to actually read it, ready to sign up for a life of being educated and reprimanded by him. But it turned out he'd been auditioning a number of young women and had chosen one of them instead.

'What I feel for Cosmo is completely different,' she said to Will now. 'Completely. It's like comparing a – I don't know – a penny sausage roll with a beef wellington.'

Was it, now? If anything, Cosmo was the sausage roll

– straightforward and available. She felt even more cross with Will for making her scrabble for a nonsense comparison. She registered her annoyance by attempting to turn her back on him.

'Just going to have a quick snooze,' he announced, and leant his cheek against the window, his hat askew.

They had now reached the bottom of Camden Road, where it joined the high street. In fact, five thoroughfares met here, in a permanent tangle of traffic. Heading west, towards Regent's Park, their cab soon came to a stop outside Brown's dairy.

Leaning out over her prone brother, Hannah saw their horse reach over to touch muzzles with a nearby cart horse; they were unbothered about the delay. Hannah looked past Will, down the broad sweep of the high street. She was no stranger to the streets of Camden Town – she often made a point of coming here to shop for food, even when one of the maids could do it, to fill her hours. But she only knew the place in the daytime. Normally at this hour, she'd be eating dinner in Camden Square, before heading upstairs to read in the drawing room. This, then, was the second wave of commerce, tailored to the working people just released from their grind.

The atmosphere felt more febrile than it did during the day; all the sellers seemed to be bellowing at double the pitch. There was the fishmonger, Mr Harwich, standing in the door of his shop, fringes of small fry strung up above him like bunting. During Hannah's interactions at the shop, she'd always found him cloyingly respectful, hands clasped behind his back as he praised her choices: *Ah, the plaice, very good. What I'm having for my own dinner, as it happens.* Now, his apron was heavily soiled, and he was having an emphatic conversation, clutching a man's shoulder as he leant close to his ear. On the pavement outside the baker's sat several large baskets, presumably containing baked goods now going cheap; a handful of people were on their knees, rooting through them.

Outside the Mother Red Cap, a street band was tuning up and men were leaning against the wall, jackets off, talking at each other in loud Irish voices. As she watched, a man shouted, 'He's betwattled, so he is!' and pushed his companion over, to shrieks of laughter from onlookers. At the curve of the road, just in view, were the flickering lamps of the Bedford Music Hall: where Ivy and Gwen were heading, to see where the evening took them.

When Cosmo had first learnt they lived in Camden Town, he had cried, 'Ah, the tradesman's entrance to London!' When Mrs Teale had raised an eyebrow, he'd explained, with feeling, 'No, no, Mrs Teale, it's a compliment! Raw, real life – how the masses live – *that's* what interests me.'

Captive in their cab, the Teales were besieged by gutter-merchants: a flower seller offering wilted old marigolds, a muffin man with his tray balanced on his head, who, wincing, carefully lowered himself to their eye level to display his wares. A musician playing a dreadful, wheedling tune on his pipe came right up to the window and leant close to Will's sleeping face, trying to wake him up. A moment later, the cab jerked forward, decisively this time, and picked up pace, pulling free from the junction and carrying them up the slope of Park Street. Soon the fever of Camden Town was behind them, and they were trotting briskly around the hushed outer circle of Regent's Park. The sky was now streaked the colour of damsons. On one side of the road stretched the Nash terraces, their stucco glowing arrogantly in the dusk, and on the other lay the park, as still and dark as a lake. The air carried distant howls and calls from the zoo, beyond the black expanse. For the rest of the journey Hannah and Mrs Teale were silent, and Will remained asleep, Hannah feeling on one side her brother's chest languidly expand and contract and, on the other, her mother's shallower breathing.

As her in-laws-to-be had only just returned home from the continent, this was the first time Hannah had been to their home. The houses on Milton Terrace were similar in size and style to those in Camden Square – about twenty years old, five storeys high, Italianate – but had a more assertive air, she thought. They weren't set back, so the front door was right on the pavement, and on the lower floors bay windows jutted out, claiming air space. At Number 15, this effect was magnified by large glass cases fixed to the bays, which even in the darkness Hannah could see were stuffed with greenery – Mrs Walters' famous ferns?

As their cab pulled up, the front door opened to reveal a glowing hallway and the silhouette of a man, arms aloft like a maestro's as he emerged to greet them. Cosmo! Hannah's heart made the requisite flip. It was only when she had carefully climbed down from the cab and was gliding towards the door, smiling, that she saw how the streetlamp illuminated the man's bald temples and registered the belly straining his waistcoat. It was not Cosmo, but his father. She persevered with her smile, not wanting to betray her mistake.

Mr Walters was in full evening dress and had the air of a man well practised in greeting dinner guests on his front step. Waving away Mrs Teale's apologies for their lateness, he squeezed first her fingers and then Hannah's, before glancing over Hannah's shoulder to where Will was discussing with the driver the price of the ride.

'Go in, go in!' he instructed them, before dashing over to the cab. 'Oh, no, don't be silly!' Hannah heard him say to Will. 'Really, let me!'

Following her mother into the hallway, Hannah saw that its blaze didn't come from gasoliers, as you'd expect, but rather ranks of candles – a dozen, at least, on each wall. Their heat warmed her cheeks as she passed; the scent of wax was as strong as at church at Christmas. She was glad she was behind her mother and unable to see Mrs Teale's reaction to such extravagance. They passed a maid pressed against the wall, as discreet as a coat stand. The girl smiled wanly at Hannah, without making eye contact.

Candlelight glinted off every available surface: the gilt overmantel mirror; the glass of the dozens of prints crammed together on the walls; the large brass gong in the fireplace; the Tiffany lamp on the sideboard. Several pairs of antlers jutted out overhead. A bunch of tall white flowers, as fluffy as foxes' tails, stood in a waist-height vase. A trio of oval domes contained delicate preserved birds. A dozen walking sticks sat in a stand, curved heads all turned the same way, like a parade of flamingos. Ahead of her, on the half-landing, a stained-glass window lit from behind sent soft red and yellow beams down the stairs.

So busy was Hannah taking it all in that she only then noticed the two figures standing to the right of the stairs. Mrs

Walters – and Cosmo! Hannah smiled and stepped forward to accept her beloved's hand. Like his father, he was in his swallow tails, the collar a good three inches tall, so he had to keep his chin up to accommodate it. His hair was darkened with oil and slicked back into one solid mass; the cheeks of his wide, expressive face were freshly shaven.

Hannah turned to his mother. In Italy, Mrs Walters had tended towards unstructured linen outfits, but tonight she wore a sheeny green silk with a wreath of fabric leaves looped around her plump, sloping shoulders. Her mouse-grey hair was arranged in a vast bun that was nearly the same size as her head. Behind them, the door to the dining room stood ajar, and Hannah glimpsed a lavishly laid table beneath what must be the new chandelier – a heap of pink and white glass, like suspended confectionery.

Mrs Walters was holding Hannah's hand; now, she twisted it and brought it close to her face to inspect the engagement ring.

'Oh, beautiful. Splendid! Charles, do look at Gigi's ring!'

Mr Walters, who had come up behind them with Will, dutifully leant over to inspect the sapphire. The engagement ring had once belonged to Mr Walters' mother, known to all as Gigi, who was still just about alive in Tonbridge.

'How beautiful it looks on you!' Mrs Walters went on. She was the daughter of a Welsh industrialist, and a slight lilt was still present in her voice.

Hannah smiled demurely. Her married friend Emily had told her that engagement parties could be seen as a sort of rehearsal for the wedding, where the bride's role was to be a mute object of admiration. 'Of course, you can gas away, if you want,' Emily had said, 'but I rather liked not, for once.

You just sit there looking adorable and sphinx-like; you don't have to bother being clever or amusing or anything.'

'If only dear Gigi could see it!' Mrs Walters continued. 'But – you two are visiting her soon, is that right, Cozzy?'

'Yes, Mama,' replied Cosmo patiently. 'Next weekend, I thought. If that's convenient for Hannah, of course.'

Over his mother's head, Cosmo met Hannah's gaze and did his squint. With it, she felt him communicate that he, too, saw this evening as a performance in which they would both diligently play their parts as the Young Engaged Couple. Soon, when they were married, they would be able to shrug off these costumes and become fully themselves.

'Now, we daren't leave Catherine waiting,' said Mrs Walters, glancing theatrically down towards the kitchen, 'but I think we can squeeze in ten minutes upstairs.' She led the way up to the drawing room, her corset so tight that her shoulder blades almost touched.

The L-shaped drawing room occupied the entire first floor but was still not nearly big enough for its contents. There seemed to be at least three of each piece of furniture – chests, chiffoniers, writing tables, commodes, side tables, plant stands – and at least a dozen chairs. The floor was overlapped with carpets and the wallpaper had the appearance of embossed leather. Many more pictures were on display, and encircling the whole room was a high shelf laden with blue and white china. No surface was free from ornament and trinket: gilded nymphs were even welded into the frame of the chimney glass. On top of the grand piano were dozens of framed photographs.

When the front door had opened to reveal Mr Walters silhouetted against that blazing hallway, Hannah had felt intensely thankful that this event wasn't taking place at Camden Square. Now, standing in the drawing room, she felt it anew. For a start, the furniture in the Teales' drawing room consisted of a piano, a bookshelf, one small sofa and two cane chairs. No family photographs or ferns, no velvet, no figurines, no silver cigarette boxes. She imagined Mrs Walters trying to compliment the interior, but what could be said about a room that had been decorated just the once, in 1870, by a woman who couldn't have cared less about her surroundings, and who had since stripped the place of almost all extraneous objects?

'Gosh, what a lot of beautiful things you have,' Hannah said, forgetting to be sphinx-like. 'I don't know what to look at first!'

'Did you hear that, Edna?' replied Mr Walters, on his feet. 'Hannah thinks you too profligate!'

'Oh, no, I didn't mean—' said Hannah, dismayed, before Mr Walters chortled and patted his wife's shoulder.

'Just ribbing,' he said. 'You're completely right! We always joke that my wife has excellent taste – just rather too large an appetite.'

The Walters both laughed, and Hannah smiled, uncertain about the tenor of the exchange. She looked over to Cosmo, in the hope that he might give her some direction, but he was busy at a side table, pouring hock into glasses, as Will watched on eagerly.

Mrs Walters asked after their journey, offering sympathy for the traffic and confessing her horror at the monstrousness of the city.

'I cannot bear all this development, can you, Mrs Teale?' she said, with feeling. '"The relentless march of the unsentimental builder." Red bricks at every turn. All the old charm lost.'

'I suppose charm is something of a luxury,' replied Mrs Teale.

'How so?'

'Well, those in desperate need of four walls and a roof probably don't care about the colour of the brickwork.'

'Ah, yes, of course!' said Mr Walters. 'Your sanctuary for fallen women!'

'We don't tend to use that term,' replied Mrs Teale.

'Oops!' said Mr Walters, pulling a face, like a naughty schoolboy caught out.

Hannah took a sip of sour wine and looked away towards the wall. From this angle, she could see that the expensive embossed wallpaper didn't reach all the way behind the picture frames; it had been carefully cut to be used only where it was visible.

Back in June, over the course of three dinners in their Naples guesthouse, the two families had covered the basics of their lives: Mrs Teale's refuge; Mr Walters' work as a publisher; Cosmo's job at the *Star*; the three older Walters daughters, happily planted with families in the country. They had delicately dealt with Mr Teale's tragic accident on the Kentish Town Road. But mostly they had talked about Italy – its rich history and visceral present. They had revelled in the sensations of the holiday: the butter-soft figs; the stiff, salty ham; the startlingly strong coffee; the pistachio ices; the constant racket in the streets that was somehow more poetic than it was in London; the scraggy cats winding around their feet; the fierce heat; the relentless insects. In that place, wonder and novelty had united the two families. And surely,

Hannah thought, the marriage would draw them closer in due course. But in this moment, in this over-stuffed drawing room, it felt as if they were strangers once more. Even Cosmo, his hair slicked with some mysterious ointment from a cabinet in an unseen bedroom, seemed unfamiliar.

Mrs Walters changed tack.

'Have you been to the Pears shop recently? The one in Oxford Street?' she asked.

Mrs Teale shook her head.

'You simply must go! It's completely extraordinary. I won't ruin the surprise – all right, I can't bear it, I'll tell you! They've turned it into Pompeii! Columns, mosaics, frescoes, vines . . . It's most wonderful. I was walking around and telling everyone that I'd actually been to the real place. I'm sure they all thought I was quite mad.'

'They left out the casts of bodies convulsed in agony, I assume,' said Mrs Teale.

Mrs Walters laughed, too loudly. She must have hoped that harking back to their time at Pompeii would soften up Mrs Teale, Hannah thought. Although it had never been explicitly acknowledged, there was something about the place that had bound the women of the tour group together. For a start, they were segregated by sex for much of the visit, the men taken off to see the erotic murals and the women left sharing parasols, passing around glasses of lemon water and reading aloud from *Pictures from Italy*. But it was more than that; it was the place itself. After all, tourists from all over the world didn't flock there to admire the vast forums where Roman men laid down laws. Rather, it was the city's domestic life that most enchanted people. They came to peek into the inner sanctums, the women's realm: the secret bathhouses; the ovens where the bread was made; to pity the cast of the housekeeper with the keys still clutched in her fist.

In Pompeii, there had been a sense of sisterhood. But that was then. And now, Mrs Teale was being too rude for words.

'That sounds wonderful!' she said to her future mother-in-law. 'Did you know that I wrote an article about Pompeii?'

The two women looked at her with surprise.

'*Did* you, Hannah?' asked her mother.

'Well, yes,' she said, already regretting speaking up. 'Not an article, really. Just a little record for myself.'

The truth was that on returning from Italy, she had sent an account of their trip to the *Girl's Own Paper* but had not heard anything back.

'Well, some women are writing little things for the papers now, aren't they?' said Mrs Walters. 'Maybe Cozzy can help you get it published.'

Cozzy. Hannah wondered what her own nickname for her husband would be. So far, they hadn't got further than the generic *darling.* She glanced over to where he was standing beside the piano, talking with Will and his father.

'Hannah's written an article about Italy!' called his mother to him. 'You must read it!'

'Nothing would give me greater pleasure,' he replied sincerely.

Hannah gazed over at him. The fact that her fiancé so looked like his bumptious father didn't bother her. Indeed, she thought, there was something honest about it; before committing to Cosmo, she was being shown what awaited her in three decades' time. Less of his hair; more of his belly. Reddened ears and spider veins on that characterful, flat-bridged nose. His twinkly blue eyes disappearing when he smiled.

She was denying Cosmo a reciprocal glimpse into the future, because she looked absolutely nothing like her mother. She took after the late Mr Teale: small, dark, thick-eyebrowed and rather sturdy, if she wasn't careful. But however much Cosmo resembled his father – and she hers! – they were different inside. A new, evolved generation.

'Hannah, come here and look at these,' Cosmo said.

Obediently, she went over to the piano, where he showed her photographs of his three sisters, their husbands and children, reeling off a list of names that immediately escaped her. How odd that these strangers were about to become her family. The Teales were a small, denuded lot, both sets of grandparents dead, aunts and uncles living in far-flung places, cousins near-strangers.

Alongside the family portraits were a number of more informal photographs. Mrs Walters featured in playfully dramatic poses – a hand to her forehead, or balancing on one leg – as well as other women. Will leant in to peer at one.

'Is that Clara Llewellyn, the actress?' he asked. 'I like her.'

Mr Walters smiled proudly.

'She's a rather likeable person,' he said. 'Past her prime, of course, but still good value. We had lots of fun at that shoot.'

'What,' said Will, 'you mean, you took these yourself?'

'Yes, indeed,' replied Mr Walters. 'I'm just an opportunistic amateur, really. A keen student of the human form. I've been so self-indulgent as to install a studio upstairs. I'll show you later.'

'I'd like that very much,' said Will. 'And if you're a theatrical man . . .'

Hannah knew what was coming next.

'. . . perhaps I could talk to you about a show I'm involved with. A jolly good investment opportunity, I think.'

Hannah winced, but Mr Walters replied genially, 'Why not? We'll talk after dinner. As it happens, in the not-too-distant future I'm going to have some money to play with—'

'What's this?' Hannah interrupted, before Will could continue with his pitch. She pointed to an unusual photograph of a couple walking along the street, heads turned towards each other in conversation, seemingly unaware that they were being photographed.

'I have this ingenious camera, which you wear under your coat to take pictures incognito,' replied Mr Walters. 'I like capturing unstudied moments.'

They were interrupted by the wan maid summoning them for dinner. Mr Walters led the way downstairs, with Mrs Teale and Hannah behind him. When Hannah entered the dining room, she gave the gasp of delight that she knew was expected of her, but the room really did look splendid. Under the chandelier, the hexagonal table was laid with a white cloth that glowed against the olive-green panelling of the wall. At its centre sat a tower of wax flowers and figs, twisted together in an embrace and bound with a length of ivy. A trio of silver dishes held real figs, raisins and nuts, carefully piled into pyramids. Each place was set with multiple pieces of flatware, a menu card in careful calligraphy and a napkin folded into the shape of a lotus flower, in which a bread roll was nestled.

'Aren't they fun!' said Mrs Walters to Hannah, indicating the napkins. 'Gigi taught me how to do it. Come over for tea soon and I'll show you.'

The first course was artichoke soup. A highly polished tureen sat on the sideboard, the girl stationed beside it. The moment they had all taken their seats, she carefully picked it up and placed it in front of Mr Walters, her lips tight in concentration. As Mr Walters served them, the conversation began with the full story of finding and purchasing the chandelier in Murano.

Hannah listened, smiling, while she stroked the silky beige soup with her spoon, dipping her head for the occasional sip. After a few minutes, Mrs Teale set down her spoon, her bowl scraped clean. In contrast to her restraint and ascetism in other areas of her life, her mother had a good appetite and always ate up her plate; one could even call her greedy, although, maddeningly, she never put on weight. She had no interest in wine, however, and her glass sat untouched. Mr Walters hadn't noticed and kept topping her up as he went round the table, so now the liquid was nearly at its brim.

Meanwhile, Mrs Walters was tearing her bread roll into little pieces and dipping each one in the soup before popping it into her mouth, as if to eke out the course for as long as possible.

The conversation was still on the chandelier; the Walters' anxious moment after it finally arrived in England after its sea voyage, and how they unwrapped it expecting carnage but miraculously found it still intact. Hannah smiled in the right places and observed Will as he watched his glass being refilled, actually licking his lips in anticipation. He was well loosened up, seemingly recovered from last night, chortling over-animatedly at the story. Beside her, Mr Walters shifted around in his chair and stretched out his legs, revealing swollen, hairless ankles.

The soup bowls were cleared and the girl brought in the fish, a thick, glistening white fillet in a puddle of red sauce. Mr Walters stood to serve it.

Mrs Teale was asking Cosmo about his work at the *Star*.

'So, reporters can choose the subjects they cover?' she asked.

'Well, reporters, no, they generally have to do what they're told by the editor,' replied Cosmo. 'But it's a bit different for specials.'

'You're special?' said Mrs Teale, with a chilling smile.

Cosmo laughed. 'Oh, no! Apologies – I've lapsed into shop talk. What I mean is, I'm what's known as a special correspondent, or a "special". That means I do more in-depth investigations, and so forth.'

'And what sort of investigations might they be?'

'I suppose I'm getting a bit of a name for myself as someone who is willing to go to the places others won't. Social investigations around the East End, exposing ills and injustice. Quite recently I spent two days—'

'Oh, please don't talk about your sojourn in the dosshouse,' Mr Walters cut in jovially. 'Your mother will become hysterical.'

Mrs Walters gave her husband what appeared to be a fond glance, and addressed Mrs Teale.

'Mrs Teale, you understand,' she said, laying her hand on her heart for emphasis. 'You'd feel the same if it was your Will, I warrant. I was on the verge of combustion for the whole time Cozzy was in there.'

Hannah knew about the dosshouse: Cosmo had told her the story during their first walk in Camden Square. He had spent two days undercover in Spitalfields, pretending to be a street man and sleeping at a notorious lodging where he witnessed despair and degradation almost beyond description. Now, he obediently relayed the story, pretty much word for word as he had told it to her.

Hannah listened, while delicately prising apart the plump flakes of fish on her plate. She wondered, with a purely novice curiosity, whether a man should apologise to his fiancée for repeating a story in company that she had heard before, or at least acknowledge the fact. She didn't know. She was sure, though, that her job now was to support him, and so she reacted as if she was hearing it for the first time.

'One must be careful not to be seen as just a slum tourist,' said her mother.

'Of course!' said Cosmo. 'I admit that one cannot fully comprehend the reality of a desperate situation in just a few days. But I do believe that such reports can do good. They give readers some insight.'

'Personally, I think it's the middle classes who most deserve our pity, not those wretches on the street,' said Mr Walters. 'At least the poor have freedom of a sort. But those in the middle — I'm talking the clerk class here — they have neither the liberty of the poor, nor the opportunities of the rich. Their lives are just weary, tedious work and then a dreary round of supposed relaxation on their days off. Visiting relatives. A walk in the park on a Sunday. A week in Broadstairs in August. Honestly, I'd rather be out on the street!'

He smiled, pleased with his provocation. But Mrs Teale didn't react; indeed, she ignored him entirely, and addressed Cosmo.

'So, you don't involve yourself with the salacious stories? The murders?'

'No, that's not my beat,' said Cosmo. Hannah saw a shift in his expression, a tightening of his brow, and he added, 'But I suppose I do support the right of the paper to run them.'

'Ah!' said Mrs Teale triumphantly. 'So, you approve of how they covered the Whitechapel killings, for instance?'

'Well, I only joined the paper last year,' he said, 'so I wasn't working there in 1888. But the plain fact is, murder sells. So, I suppose what I think is that there is a space for both sorts of journalism. Give them what they want, the juicy stuff, to get them to buy the papers. Then, when you have their readership, you can also give them what they *need* – which is the sort of thing I do.'

'Titillate, then educate,' said her mother crisply. 'I see. And do you agree with those false news stories, when journalists wrote letters pretending to be from the Whitechapel man, and so forth, just to keep their readers excited?'

'Of course not, Mrs Teale!' said Cosmo. Face flushed, he bent his head to take a forkful of fish. Hannah interjected.

'Mama, he said he wasn't even there then!' She turned in the direction of her fiancé. 'Tell us more about being a special, Cosmo. It sounds fascinating.'

Cosmo smiled gratefully at her, and she modestly returned the smile. Taking her husband's side against her mother, in public! She had never felt more like a wife.

'Well, two days are never the same—'

But Mrs Teale hadn't finished.

'Which paper was it that had an editorial wondering why the Whitechapel murderer had such poor taste in victims?' she interrupted. '*Gin-soaked drabs* was the phrase, I think? Was that the *Star*?'

Cosmo laid down his knife and fork. 'I don't know, I'm afraid, Mrs Teale.' His voice was loud and tight; Hannah hadn't heard it like that before. 'As I say, it was before my time. Look, I'm not saying we don't make mistakes. By "we" I mean Fleet Street as a whole, of course.'

'But do you not think the reporting was beyond irresponsible?' Mrs Teale went on. 'That sort of coverage . . . it threatens to unravel bonds of sympathy. It inures people to horror. The fact that they may want it is no excuse; it's just base, salacious entertainment.'

'Mama, please!' pleaded Hannah. Her collar was strangling her. She looked down at her hands on her lap, neatly placed together, as pale and dead as a pair of chicken breasts.

'No, don't worry, Hannah, this is a worthwhile debate,' said Cosmo, his gallantry partly restored. 'Your mother is hardly the only person to have such concerns.' He focused back on Mrs Teale. 'I believe that Stead said—'

'Ah,' said Mrs Teale. 'Of course, you are a disciple of Stead.'

'Well, I've never worked for the man, but, yes, I admire him, as an editor. Most of us do.'

'You admire what he did with the Eliza Armstrong affair?'

Now Will paid attention, roused by an unknown female name and the whiff of impropriety.

'Who's that, Ma?'

'You must remember, Will,' she said impatiently. 'A few years back. William Stead, the editor of the *Pall Mall Gazette* – he claimed to be exposing the vice trade and bought a thirteen-year-old girl to show how easy it was. Then he kept her hostage, in some degradation, before splashing all sorts of foul details all over the paper. He got arrested.'

'Well, that was a complicated business,' said Cosmo evenly.

'W.T.S. – that's what we call him – he's a complicated man. A maverick. He makes mistakes. But he's trying to change things. And he cares. He says that the job of the press is *to afflict the comfortable, and to comfort the afflicted.* Expose wrongdoing. That it's our duty to interpret the knowledge of the few for the understanding of the many. It's a new form of government . . .'

'You got into a spot of trouble with little girls, didn't you, Charles?'

The interruption was from Mrs Walters. Startled, the rest of them turned to look at her; she was addressing her husband with an odd smile. Hannah realised she'd been uncharacteristically quiet for a while now. On her plate was a decimated wax apple from the centrepiece, and beside it a pile of feathery shavings from where she was scraping at the surface with a fingernail.

'It was rather funny actually,' she continued, her voice high and tinkly. She wasn't looking directly at anyone, but rather into the air above the table. 'With his special camera under his coat, he was taking pictures of schoolgirls, and the teacher at St Saviour's spotted him and really didn't like it. Did she, Charles?'

Hannah glanced at Mr Walters. He was still smiling but clearly uneasy, his eyes narrowed.

'So we've agreed it's best for him to make sure his pictures are only of adult women, haven't we, darling?'

Hannah glanced at Cosmo. He was smiling, too, but his eyes were blank, as if he wasn't really listening. Perhaps he was still stuck in the argument with her mother, or perhaps he'd learnt to switch himself off when things got tense with his parents. She didn't dare look at her own mother.

Hannah took a slug of wine, more than she would ever normally take in one go, and said decisively, 'Mrs Walters, I've been wanting to ask about the sideboard. It's so splendid. Did you get that from your travels, too?'

It was a crude intervention, but it worked. After a moment, Mrs Walters gathered herself and explained that the sideboard had been a wedding gift from the famous Gigi, and the dull exchange seemed to deflate the tension in the room. The whole table – even Mrs Teale – surrendered to harmless topics again: the latest Gilbert and Sullivan; the new Electric Railway (apparently Will had already travelled on it, in his secret life); the crisis at Barings Bank; the latest events in the Congo.

Will, now very drunk, was leaning heavily on the table and telling Mr Walters in detail about the plot of the theatrical production he wanted him to invest in but getting it muddled. 'And so then the first woman says, "Oh no, you don't, mister, I know your game!" Wait – actually, no, it was the second woman, the one with the hair, who said that . . .'

Over the fruit, during a pause in conversation, Mrs Walters leant over and clutched Hannah's arm.

'Can you believe it – we've been having so much fun, we've forgotten to talk about the wedding!'

Mr Walters hooted and banged his palm on the table.

'Now, what are we doing about the announcement?'

'I'll deal with that,' slurred Will, as if he placed notices in *The Times* every week.

'A standing toast!' said Mr Walters, getting unsteadily to his feet. 'To your Hannah and our Cosmo!'

Hannah saw her mother glance at her brimming wine glass and make the calculation that it could not be safely lifted. Instead, she raised her water glass and gave a quick smile.

After the toast, Mrs Walters told them that she'd recently attended a friend's daughter's wedding at the new Savoy hotel on the Strand, and the famous French chef Auguste Escoffier had personally prepared the wedding breakfast.

'*Sole Veronique* and *tarte au citron* for a hundred and twenty!' she said. 'And so many waiters that it felt like we were all served at exactly the same time . . .'

Hannah saw her mother open her mouth to speak, but Cosmo got there first.

'Actually, Mama, Hannah and I were imagining something more intimate. Just family and a couple of friends.'

'Being small will make it even more special!' added Hannah.

'Well, in that case,' said Mr Walters, 'why don't we just host the reception here?'

'A wonderful idea!' said Hannah. She smiled across the table at Cosmo, admiring their teamwork, and then glanced at her mother, but if Mrs Teale was feeling grateful for being saved from having to awkwardly spell out her financial constraints, she was keeping it to herself.

There was further discussion about possible local churches, and it was decided it would be lovely for them to get married on New Year's Eve. Then, they all went upstairs, and Hannah played them the piano piece she'd prepared, and Mr Walters took Will to see his studio on the top floor. At eleven, Cosmo found them a cab back to Camden Square. As soon as it pulled off Will fell asleep, while the two women sat awake but silent. In the dark cab, Hannah relived the evening, and looked forward more than ever to the wedding, when she and Cosmo would be relieved of their families, like shrugging off sodden greatcoats, and scamper, unburdened, into the future together.

2

The power of a literary man is doubled when he gets a clear-headed, sensible wife, who shields his sensitiveness against disagreeable things; who acts like one of those cushions that sailors put down the side of a vessel to keep it from jarring too roughly against the dock.

— Girl's Own Paper

Two days later, Hannah received a note from Cosmo asking her to lunch near his office on Fleet Street. Hannah briefly considered walking there: the weather was still mild, and the distance didn't intimidate her. Only, who knew what type of restaurant he would be taking her to? In any case, the first meal alone with her fiancé surely deserved impractical clothes: an ostrich feather in her hat, and her grey satin shoes.

She couldn't justify a cab, and so at midday Hannah walked down to Camden Town to catch the omnibus. Sitting on the open top deck, her feather fluttering above her like a cavalier, she pictured herself as she must look from the street, imagining pedestrians speculating about this elegant lady, and where she was heading. Sitting at the same height as the plane trees lining the road, Hannah felt almost godlike, gazing down at the small people below, as they strolled, chatted, shopped; her subjects obediently going about their business on a fair October morning.

Passing through Mornington Crescent, she spotted someone she knew on the pavement below: Mrs Sawtell, the wife of the inspector at Kentish Town Police Station. Mrs Sawtell had been brought in to attend to the family after Mr Teale's accident, sitting with them in a cramped side office at the station while the paperwork was being done. She'd had some problem with her hip, and kept on shifting around on her chair, apologising as her knees came into contact with theirs, eyes glistening with pain, unable to overcome her discomfort and provide the solemn solace the occasion demanded.

Mrs Sawtell's hip was clearly still causing her trouble; she was walking with a limp, and grimacing as she went. Hannah felt sorry that the woman was still afflicted after all this time, but also had the urge to shout down to her: *Look at me, Mrs Sawtell! I'm off to lunch on Fleet Street with my fiancé!*

As the omnibus lurched east towards St Pancras, Hannah fantasised about the meal ahead. She saw silver cloches being lifted to reveal lamb chops capped with paper frills; discreet waiters appearing at her elbow exactly when needed. As they ate, she and Cosmo would laugh about the dinner at Milton Terrace, acknowledging their parents' various foibles and distancing themselves from them. Or perhaps they wouldn't mention it and just talk about each other, filling in the gaps in their histories and looking forward to their shared future.

She alighted at Temple Bar. To her right stretched the Strand, leading to the familiar terrain of the West End, but she turned left into the City, that foreign land of male endeavour. Her father had worked here as a barrister for years, but she could only recall coming to the street once before, on a family outing to see the brand-new law courts. She remembered thinking at the time that the building's Portland stone was the same pale straw colour as her hamster's fur. Now, eight years later, the façade was heavily streaked with coal dust, as if stained by the sin that had passed through it since.

As Hannah started up Fleet Street, it seemed that the rest of London was coming along with her. The pavement was thick with pedestrians, mostly men, and a blend of classes – although most visible were bowler-clad clerks, clutching reams of paper to their chests as they darted into alleyways and slipped behind ornate, important-looking doors.

A smart, middle-aged man cut across her path, hand raised in apology, leaving a trail of cologne in his wake. Hannah paused to watch as he ducked through one of the stone gatehouses that led to the Inns of Court. In age and bearing the man could have been Mr Teale – as she continued on it struck her that her father had come to this street most days for nigh-on thirty years, and she didn't even know the Inn he had worked for. Which of these gatekeepers in their little boxes had bidden him good morning and farewell each day? Where had he eaten his lunch, and had his hair cut? It hadn't seemed odd at the time, this complete separation of his work from their home life, but now, the thought that she had no idea where or how her father had spent his days was rather sad. She could ask her mother, she supposed, but that missed the point.

Fleet Street curved gently to the right, bringing into view the dome of St Paul's, faintly visible through the sooty air. She caught the waft of an unusual smell – hot and sweet and oily – and noticed that on the buildings she passed, the names of legal chambers had been replaced by the titles of newspapers. *Lloyd's*; the *Telegraph*; the *Daily Chronicle*; the *Globe*. And not just London papers, or national ones: provincial titles, too – the *Hull Advertiser, York Chronicle, Dundee Courier* – although these smaller papers appeared to be sharing space, piled on top of each other, sometimes four to a building. Then, there were all the supporting industries crammed in around – engravers, press cutting agencies – as well as the services meeting the everyday needs of an army of men: the hairdressers, boot makers, restaurants and cigar shops. Some of the frontages were so busy with written signs, they looked like news pages themselves. The rattles and thumps of the traffic on the road were joined by the clanks of hidden machinery, chuntering away out of sight behind the offices. It was one of those places where there was as much happening behind the scenes, down the side streets, as on the main drag.

The crowds around her had changed, too. Now, rather than harassed clerks darting about with piles of legal documents, it was young newsboys, clutching piles of papers with blackened hands and expertly threading through the crowd.

Passing by the office of the *Illustrated Evening News*, Hannah saw that a group had gathered in front of its window, gazing in as if it were the Christmas display at Fortnum & Mason. She stepped closer and saw that the object of their attention was an enlarged poster of that day's front page. A drawing showed a young woman leaping off a bridge into the Thames, hair flying and hand clamped over her eyes. MAIDEN FALLS FROM LONDON BRIDGE, read the headline. From somewhere in the crowd behind her, she heard the trills of young voices: *Who's for today's paper? Paper, gentlemen! News, news! Paper, paper, paper!*

A church opposite sounded the hour, and Hannah sped up; they were meeting outside the *Star* office at 1 p.m. She found the building easily; the name was emblazoned high up on the façade in stark capitals, each letter on its own stalk. The building was vast and vaguely Romanesque, with columns flanking a short flight of steps that led up to double doors, trimmed with highly polished brass. And there, standing at the top of the steps, hands tucked into his pockets, was Cosmo.

He spotted her at once and loped down the steps two at a time.

'Look at you!' he said, as he reached her. 'What a splendid feather.'

He held her gloved hand and they stood, smiling at each other. His coat collar was turned up and she noticed that he had a pencil tucked behind his ear – his hat was cocked to allow easy access to it. He looked the very embodiment of the successful young pressman – or how she imagined they would dress, anyway – and far more attractive today than he had at dinner, trussed up in his tails.

'What an impressive building,' Hannah said.

'It *is* impressive, isn't it?' said Cosmo, doing that pleasing thing where he repeated what she had just said as if it were insightful and original.

'Will you show me around?'

'Oh – really?' Cosmo frowned. 'Thing is, there's really not much to see. Just lots of anxious people scribbling away and barking at each other and trying to either catch the eye of the editor or avoid it.'

'But at least I could see your desk,' she continued, thinking of her father's regretfully mysterious job. 'So I can picture where you spend your days.'

He grimaced again. 'Well, I don't actually have a desk, as such. Specials are out and about the whole time, so it doesn't really make sense to have a permanent spot. We tend to just find a perch wherever we can.'

'I see,' she replied, giving up. 'So, where are you taking me?'

'I thought we'd find somewhere together. Lots of choice around here. What are you in the mood for?'

She felt a momentary deflation that he hadn't planned where they would go, as well as foolish for being so dressed up.

'Where do you usually go?' she asked.

'Oh, we tend to just grab a pie at the Cock or Cheshire Cheese.'

'Well, let's do that.'

'What? No!'

'Why ever not?'

'Well, for a start these places are frightfully rough.'

'I'd like to,' she said firmly. 'I want to.'

He looked at her, surprised. 'You're serious?'

She was. She wanted to see where he usually ate, and she didn't mind if he felt uncomfortable about it: it served him right for not making a plan himself. He acquiesced and they started walking.

The Cock Tavern was just a few doors down from the *Star* office. It was an old-fashioned place with a narrow, wonky façade and small, mullioned, steamed-up windows. Hannah had peered into public houses before, but only the gin palaces in Camden Town, with their high ceilings and ornate bars and mirrored walls. This, in contrast, was the kind of establishment that had no need to appear inviting or advertise for its custom. The kind of place that she would never have considered entering before now.

Even from the pavement, the din inside was palpable, and when Cosmo pushed open the door, a roar of noise was released. As Hannah followed him through the doorway, she felt her feather catch on the low door frame and ducked down.

'Golly, it's even worse than usual,' said Cosmo. 'I can't see anywhere to sit, can you?'

Hannah craned to survey the crowd. The place had a fuggy, subterranean air, with little natural light, the walls unadorned except for dark panelling and coat pegs. Men sat squashed together at long communal tables or stood packed into every last foot of floor space, clutching glasses of beer and sucking on pipes and cigarettes. They all appeared to be engaged in animated or secret discussions, either whispering furtively or haw-hawing with laughter. The men standing closest to them turned to inspect her before returning to their discussions. She could see no other women at all.

At the back of the room Hannah spotted a doorway, with a drawn green curtain, leading into another, equally dim room. Inside she glimpsed a white tablecloth and caught a waft of hot meat.

'Perhaps . . .' she began, and then shrieked as something flitted past her face.

'Oh!' cried Cosmo. 'Polly! I should have warned you.'

Breathing hard, Hannah stared after the green parrot as

it continued its flight across the room and settled on a hat stand.

'Shall we try somewhere else?' said Cosmo, and this time she nodded meekly, her earlier bravado having seeped away.

But as they turned back towards the door, a voice cried, 'Not so fast!'

Although the room was full of bellowing male voices, this shout seemed directed at them. They paused and turned to see a young man weaving his way through the crowd.

'You're not escaping like that,' he said as he reached them. 'The famous Miss Teale!'

The man was around Cosmo's age, tall and narrow, with flushed cheeks and dense, dark curls. He wore a baggy tweed sack jacket.

'Please come and join us,' he said. 'Save me from Ovilry's theories on why we lost the Test Match.'

'This is my colleague, John Timmer,' Cosmo explained to Hannah. 'We certainly don't have to join them. In fact, I'd strongly caution against it.'

John Timmer smiled. 'He's probably right,' he said to Hannah. 'But please do come anyway.'

Here, then, was her chance to learn more about Cosmo's life at work and meet people who appeared to be his friends.

'I'd like to,' she replied.

Cosmo shrugged. They followed in Timmer's wake as he weaved back through the crowd, stopping at the end of a long table beside the fire. Another man sat there, leaning back against the wall, his chair balanced on its hind legs. As they approached, he tipped himself upright and rose to his feet.

'And this is Ovilry,' said Cosmo. 'Winston Ovilry.'

Ovilry took her hand and gave it a quick, hard squeeze. He was of a similar age to the other two but seemed an altogether different breed: broader and better nourished and far more dapper, with a neat parting and a gold watch chain on his waistcoat. He, too, was dressed for a restaurant with silver cloches and discreet waiters – not this place, with its gobbets of saliva on the floor.

'Let me get you a drink,' Timmer asked her. 'What would you like?'

What would she like? Not beer. One couldn't drink wine during the day. Water was too cheerless.

'A lemonade, please,' she replied.

'And the usual for you,' Timmer said to Cosmo, a statement rather than question, before wading back through the crowd towards some unseen counter. There was a small space on the bench, and Hannah and Cosmo sat, wedged together. She felt a solid pouch of flesh above his hip – a secret piece of him that surprised her – and clenched up, unnerved by this prematurely intimate contact. But after a minute she relaxed. It felt rather thrilling to be here in this room full of fizzy young men.

'Young Walters has talked much about you,' said Winston Ovilry, opposite them. Although his seat was nearest the fire, he didn't seem at all overheated or flustered. Rather, he had a knowing, amused expression, as if always on top of any situation. He stretched out his legs and crossed one foot over the other; his brogues had very pointed toes. 'You're already famously too good for him.'

'You're a special correspondent, too?' she asked.

'Ovilry's recently joined us,' replied Cosmo quickly. 'Poached from *Lloyd's*. He's quite the brilliant new thing.'

There was a disingenuously light note to Cosmo's voice: perhaps he felt that by declaring Ovilry's status, rather than it being revealed by the man himself, it somehow reduced its potency.

'Well, that is far too flattering,' said Ovilry.

'He's certainly our top blagger,' Cosmo continued. 'Aren't you, Ovilry?'

'Top what?' asked Hannah.

'Sorry, shop talk. A *blagger* is someone who dishonestly talks their way into somewhere.'

'Well, that's rather blunt!' said Ovilry. He was leaning back in his chair again and smiling, as if amused to observe Cosmo's ill-concealed jealousy.

'What's the most interesting place you've . . . gained entry to?' asked Hannah. She didn't know how to use this new word in a sentence.

'Well, I suppose it has to be the mortuary for the Annie Chapman autopsy. She was the second Whitechapel victim, if you remember.'

'How on earth did you manage that?'

'Oh, I shouldn't really say,' he said smoothly. 'It's all rather sordid, I'm afraid. I'm not trying to make the world a better place, like your fiancé.'

'But the editor certainly values you more,' said Cosmo, with a dry laugh. 'You've got the bulging purse to prove it.'

'Well, he values what the public want to read,' replied Ovilry, 'and that appears to be murder, the gorier the better. Anyway,' he continued, 'you know I'm envious of your shorthand, Walters. I could have used it in the Bailey this morning.'

Cosmo gave a pained smile. Hannah knew that she

shouldn't encourage this Ovilry man to show off at her fiancé's expense, yet she found herself asking, 'Why were you in the Old Bailey?'

'Covering the trial of a housekeeper and her husband accused of murdering her mean employer when she wouldn't give them a pay rise,' Ovilry replied. 'Quite interesting, actually – the trial hinges on this note from the woman to her old man. Whether it shows intent, you see. If there's intent, it goes from manslaughter to murder, and then they hang.'

He reached into his breast pocket for his pad, and then, without asking, plucked the pencil from behind Cosmo's ear. He wrote something and then turned the pad around so Hannah and Cosmo could read it.

'This is what the note said.'

Written in capitals, it read: MRS B DUE BACK NOON. LET'S GO TO GET HER.

'Well, that's pretty damning,' said Cosmo.

Hannah stared at the words, frowning. 'But perhaps that last part is meant to read TOGETHER, not TO-GET-HER,' she said, after a moment's thought. 'If they're domestics, they might not be confident with writing. She might have spelt out the syllables of that long word. Maybe all the note shows is that the woman wanted her husband to come with her to ask her employer about a pay rise, for moral support.'

Ovilry smiled at her. 'Well, aren't you clever! That's exactly what the defence is arguing.'

Beside her, Hannah felt Cosmo twitch. His irritation with Ovilry had stymied him, she thought, blinding him to something quite obvious and putting him even more on the back foot. Feeling for him, she looked down at the table, noticing all the crumbs collected in the seams of the wood, and resolved to keep quiet.

Thankfully, just then John Timmer returned with their drinks, in rather smeary glasses. As there was no room for him on the bench, he leant awkwardly against the fireplace. She saw that he had a book stuffed into the pocket of his jacket.

'What do you do on the paper, Mr Timmer?' she asked.

'I'm terribly boring, I'm afraid,' he replied. His face was long and fine-boned, like a red setter's. 'Not on the front line, like these two. At the moment I'm busy taking the world's great novels and reducing them to a form that can be digested by your average clerk's wife from Finchley.'

'What do you mean?'

'The editor has a sideline, a small publishing venture that turns novels into, well, pamphlets. Making them accessible to the common man. I'm halfway through *Jane Eyre*.'

'Timmer's a literary chap,' explained Cosmo. 'His spiritual home is the Reading Room of the BM. This is a rare sighting of him outside it.'

'I rather feel like the enemy of literature at the moment!' said Timmer. 'Charlotte Brontë would certainly agree.'

He took a swig from his glass. Hannah could see him already starting to sweat from standing so close to the fire. She liked Timmer; unlike Ovilry, he seemed to have no side to him.

'But it's a step up from your last gig, isn't it?' said Cosmo, before addressing Hannah. 'He used to write stories for women's magazines.'

'Oh!' said Hannah, trying not to betray the extent of

her interest. Cosmo didn't know about her *infra dig* reading habits.

'Actually, I much preferred writing them,' said Timmer. 'They didn't involve butchering masterpieces. Quite fun, too. I could write one in two hours with a fair wind.'

How amusing that this rangy, diffident man might have been behind some of the stories she read! Perhaps one day, over dinner in her and Cosmo's future house, she could ask him all about it.

'You've a literary bent, too, haven't you, Walters?' said Ovilry now, addressing Cosmo. 'I mean, some of your turns of phrase! Miss Teale, did you read his dosser story?'

'Not yet,' Hannah replied. 'But I've heard a lot about it.'

'Like Dickens on a good day!' continued Ovilry. 'What was that line, Walters? The East End is akin to *a dark continent that is within easy walking distance of the General Post Office . . .* The editor just loved that one, didn't he?'

'Stop it,' Cosmo said, smiling.

'Oh, yes,' Ovilry continued. 'And how was it you described that woman you met, who draped herself all over you? *A hideous hag, clutching a half-inch of candle, muttering with a voice as melodious as the croaking of an asthmatic frog.* Or was it *an antiquated donkey* . . .?'

'All right, enough,' said Cosmo. His smile had disappeared, his lips now a tight line. Hannah moved away from him, as much as she could on their confined bench; she couldn't bear feeling him vibrate with anger and humiliation.

'No, don't tell me – your name is Polly?'

Hannah looked up to be met with a blast of whisky fumes. A man was looming over her shoulder, his bulbous drinker's nose a few inches from hers.

'Or have you eaten Polly?' the man went on.

She felt an odd sensation above her head and realised that the man was batting the feather on her hat.

'Oh, do stop,' she said quietly. The batting continued.

She turned to Cosmo. He was looking at the intruder, but in a slightly dazed way, as if he was still so furious with Ovilry that his reaction was delayed. In that moment, Ovilry got to his feet.

'Move on now, would you?' he said, his tone firm.

Hannah heard a hiss above her head, as if the intoxicated man was about to respond, but he stumbled away without protest. There was a moment's silence, and then she felt a release of pressure at her side as Cosmo stood up from the table.

'What was I thinking, bringing you here?' he said. 'Come on, Hannah, let's find some lunch.'

Hannah got to her feet and bid the other two goodbye. Timmer clasped her hand with his, while Ovilry nodded at her from his seat.

'It was an honour,' he said.

Hannah followed Cosmo as he fought his way out through the crowd to the door. After the fug of the tavern, Fleet Street seemed as fresh as a spring field.

'I'm so sorry,' said Cosmo, walking briskly away.

'Cosmo, it was completely fine,' said Hannah, trotting to keep up. 'Honestly. Your friends – colleagues – are nice. Well, Mr Timmer is, anyway. And who cares about some silly drunken oaf?'

'Now, you must be ravenous,' he said, still walking and still not looking at her. 'Where shall we—'

Somewhere overhead, a church bell struck two. Cosmo stopped in his tracks.

'Blast it,' he said. 'And now that's lunch hour gone. Never mind – I'll take another hour. What's the worst they can say?'

Hannah shook her head.

'No. Really. It's fine.'

The lunch had been a failure; there was no reason to draw it out. And it was her fault. She shouldn't have demanded to peek behind the curtain of his working life; she had intruded on a male space and stirred up competitive instincts. At least she could spare him from feeling obliged to attempt to regain his pride; to undo the damage done by Ovilry.

Cosmo was standing still, arms dangling at his side. She noticed that the pencil was no longer behind his ear; Ovilry must still have it.

'I do love you, you know,' she said.

He looked up at her in surprise, eyes bright. 'Well, that's a jolly nice thing to hear at 2 p.m. on a Tuesday.' He smiled. 'And I love you, Hannah.'

He turned back towards the office, before adding, 'Remember, we're going to visit Gigi on Saturday. She's going to love you, too.'

Hannah watched until he was absorbed into the crowd before turning and heading back to Temple Bar. On the bus home, seated on the lower floor this time, she went over their farewell. She had baldly professed her love for Cosmo not because she had felt it like an arrow to the heart, but because he looked so pathetic and she wanted to make things all right. To restore him, after his humiliations at lunch. But did it matter where the declaration sprang from? After all, as his wife, it would be her job to bolster him. And of course, the statement may have been impure, but it wasn't untrue. She *did* love him – she was about to marry him!

Back at home, she told Mrs Teale that they'd had a very nice lunch in a very pleasant restaurant, and for once was pleased that her mother didn't press her for details.

The next day, Wednesday, Hannah sat beside the drawing-room window with a nightdress on her lap and needle in her hand. Aside from Ivy down in the kitchen, she was alone in the house. Mrs Teale was out calling on someone; Will was back up at Oxford; Gwen was shopping.

Nightdresses and undergarments for a wedding trousseau had to be embroidered. This was traditionally undertaken by mother and daughter, but of course Mrs Teale had better things to do, so Hannah was tackling them on her own. She had decided not to embroider a forget-me-not or butterflies, or any of the standard motifs, but rather an octopus – a reference to an ancient floor mosaic she and Cosmo had admired together in Italy. She had been pleased with her originality at first, but now, on the fourth leg of only the first octopus, it didn't seem such a clever idea. In a pile beside her were five more nightdresses, all still to be worked on. The prospect of the task ahead made her feel like a puppet with snapped strings. It was an enervating, bloodless sort of day to start with; outside the window, the square was quiet, the sky as blank as the expanse of linen spread before her.

Then, a pleasing thought came to her: Wednesday was publication day for the *Girl's Own Paper*. She still wasn't properly dressed, so took a penny from her purse and went downstairs to ask Ivy to run out to the newsstand on Camden Road to buy a copy.

'It's just for a recipe for the wedding,' she said, as if Ivy was her mother and would think less of her for reading it.

Once Ivy delivered the magazine to her in the drawing room, Hannah took it up to her room. Her bed was where she read her magazines. Underneath her mattress were secreted dozens of past issues, mostly the *Girl's Own Paper*, but also *Princess*, the *Girl's Realm*, the *Female's Friend* – anything she could get hold of, hidden away from her mother's scorn and disappointment. Every night, she lay on top of layers of sediment that formed her: not only the romance stories, but articles on the language of flowers, mosaic for beginners and painting on ivory miniatures; the history of salt, heraldry and the life of Handel; dress patterns and sheet music, and instructions on how to construct a pair of paper bellows and make pineapple fritters, care for maidenhair ferns and kid gloves; appreciations of Longfellow and Beethoven; the florid, sentimental poems; accounts of travels in Norway and Lausanne; the advice for lissome hands and pretty feet. And, of course, her favourite section: 'Answers to Correspondents'.

This page did exactly as it stated: printed the answers to letters received by the paper, but without the original enquiry. The advice was wonderfully eclectic, moving seamlessly between the prosaic and the lofty, covering moral issues, housekeeping, etiquette, educational matters and general miscellany. Often the nature of the original enquiry was obvious from the answer, but sometimes not at all, leaving Hannah's imagination to fill the space. Answers ranged in length from a pithy single line to a few hundred words and, because they could address several questions in one, often contained non-sequiturs. Each of these snippets of one-sided conversations, addressed to a first name or pseudonym, was a tiny portal into the head of another girl in the country, and reading it made Hannah feel part of a huge sisterhood, connected by tiny threads of curiosity and anxiety.

The editor's tone was that of an all-knowing mother: prescriptive, no-nonsense and often tart, slapping down vanity and pretension, but also fair and benevolent when warranted. This 'magazine mother' of hers was rather too religiously minded – the Teales were not at all devout – but Hannah loved the fact that she was someone for whom nothing was too trivial to mention, unlike the real Mrs Teale, for whom almost everything was too trivial to mention.

Now, propped up on her stomach, she turned straight to it.

MURIEL – If you eat buttered bread or hot buttered cakes, we advise you to remove one glove, unless you have a new pair in your pocket, or one duplicate glove ready for use when your afternoon tea is finished.
INDIGO – Yes, you are quite right, there was a manufacturer of stained glass in Hampstead.
FELINE LOVER – You had better clean the long fur of the Persian cat by rubbing it well with flour and then cleaning it off with a soft handkerchief.
JULIET – We do not enter into nor discuss subjects of the kind about which you inquire.
AVID READER – Use tweezers, and accept our good wishes for your success.
GERTIE – We only said just what we meant, and regret that you are unable to comprehend our plain-speaking.

STOCKING KNITTER – You ask too many questions. We will answer one: the rule for a well-made stocking is that the foot should be one third of the length of the leg.

A third of the way down the second column, she caught her breath.

CAMDEN GIRL – We found your account of your holiday to Pompeii informative and poignant (particularly the description of the poor dog 'frozen forever in contortion, forelegs raised as if in supplication to Vulcan'). We are sorry we have no room to include it here.

Warmth flooded her face. She read it again, tracing the text with her finger. Never mind that her account hadn't actually been published. She didn't really expect that, assuming that the articles were written by professional writers. But to get such a positive reply – what joy! The correspondents at the paper were notoriously tough on writing submissions. She had read comments such as, *Your story has no special merit or originality. It is no use to us. You do not express yourself correctly or clearly. The composition is of the usual schoolgirl kind.*

And actually, some of her article *had* been published! Just a line, but still. To think, all over the country, the readers of *Girl's Own Paper* would encounter her words! That thought compensated for the fact that she couldn't tell her mother about it, for risk of Mrs Teale sneering. Perhaps she *would* tell Cosmo . . .

Three floors down, the doorbell rang.

Hannah ignored it, expecting Ivy to answer, but when, a

minute later, it rang again, she realised that the maid must have gone out. Reluctantly, she laid down the magazine and went downstairs herself. Opening the door, she exclaimed: her second surprise of the morning.

On the doorstep stood Cosmo. His head was lowered, one hand clamped on his neck, and his expression was abject. Thoughts of her *Girl's Own Paper* triumph evaporated.

'What happened?' she cried.

'I'm very sorry to just turn up like this,' he said meekly, avoiding her eye. 'May I come in?'

Hannah stepped back so he could enter the hall. As she led him upstairs, she glanced fruitlessly towards the mirrorless patch of wall. She was wearing a particularly voluminous and comfortable sack of a morning dress, and her hair was undone. She was barely decent enough to open the door to the knife sharpener, much less her fiancé. But Cosmo seemed too distracted to notice her. Once in the cheerless drawing room, he sat heavily down in the chair that held her pile of nightgowns.

'Is your mother at home?' he asked.

'No,' said Hannah. 'Cosmo, what is it? You look desperate.'

He took a deep breath and then slowly expelled the air before turning to her.

'Gigi has died,' he said.

'Oh! Oh dear. How terrible,' said Hannah. 'Was she – a good age?' She must have been ancient, she thought, if she were Mr Walters' mother.

'Eighty-six,' said Cosmo. 'She went yesterday, around lunchtime.'

'I'm so sorry,' she said. 'Were you particularly close?'

Although she was being sympathetic and saying the right

sort of thing, Hannah couldn't help but feel that there was something disproportionate about Cosmo's desolation. Rushing across London in order that Hannah comfort him over an elderly relative she'd never met?

'Close? Well, no,' said Cosmo. He had raised his voice; in fact, he sounded almost angry. 'No. Apparently not.'

Confused, Hannah stared at him. He continued, 'Truth be told, Hannah, it's left me in rather a pickle. You see, there was a hope – no, a promise! – that Gigi would leave me a substantial amount. She always assured me it was coming. But in the last year or so she was rather annoyed with Father. Didn't approve of his photography and whatnot.' He shook his head. 'Anyway, I'm afraid that I seem to be a casualty of this grave disappointment. Her will was sitting there, on top of her bureau, so Papa had a peek – and my uncle has got the lot.'

He gave another great sigh.

'She'd have been so delighted with you, Hannah. She'd have seen that I'm on the right path and things would have gone differently, I'm sure. Anyway. No point in *if onlys*. That's the situation. Nothing for our side at all. Father and mother are most distraught; they don't have much at all, no savings or investments. Just the house, really. They say they're going to have to start selling the furniture.'

'How dreadful,' said Hannah.

'No, it really *is* dreadful,' said Cosmo emphatically. 'You see, Hannah – during the financial discussion with your mother, what I stated as my income included what I had been told I was guaranteed to receive from Gigi. And so, the bottom line is, we are now facing marriage with far less than was anticipated. *Far* less.' He paused, to let the words sink in. 'May I ask, darling – and I'm sorry to do this – is there anything else at your end?'

Hannah shook her head. 'I don't think so. Mother is giving us fifty pounds as a wedding gift, you know about that, but I don't think she's sitting on much more.'

'I thought, as you were holidaying in Italy, that might have been indicative of a reserve fund . . .'

'I'm afraid not. Father's legacy left her with a small yearly income, and then there was a lump sum, but most of that went to the refuge, and then we had the holiday with the rest. So, it's basically gone now. I did wonder whether it was wise to spend it like that, but she wanted to. She doesn't really believe in possessions, you see.'

Cosmo slumped in the chair and rubbed his hand over his mouth. Downstairs, Hannah heard the front door open and close; someone had come in. If it was a maid, they'd go down to the kitchen. If it was her mother, she'd soon appear at the drawing-room doorway, which would be most unwelcome now.

'It's all right, Hannah,' said Cosmo, trying to rally. 'We mustn't panic. It's just a setback. Albeit a rather large one.'

Hannah strained for footsteps on the stairs, but there were none. It must have been one of the maids.

'Does the paper not pay you very much?' she asked.

'Barely nothing!' he replied bitterly. 'Unless you're a sensation-merchant like Ovilry, of course.'

His spirit from a moment ago seemed to have lapsed again. Hannah felt it was her turn to be upbeat.

'Don't worry, darling. Wherever we live, it'll be an adventure!'

Her vision of their future dissolved from a newly papered,

six-roomed Canonbury townhouse to a modest rural home. A little cottage to the west, somewhere on the Thames. Ramshackle but still charming. A riotous garden. Beehives. Chickens. Perhaps a little desk in a corner for her, where she could do some more *informative and poignant* writing . . .

But Cosmo immediately took the wind out of her sails.

'We certainly won't be able to set up a home together yet,' he said. 'We'll have to wait a bit.'

'Oh! Do you mean . . . you want to postpone the wedding?'

'What? Oh, darling, no, no!' Cosmo tipped out of his chair and came to kneel in front of her, clasping her hands between his. 'Don't even say such a thing. I cannot wait to marry you. It's just – I think it would behove us to live with my parents.'

Hannah froze, her hands dead in his.

'They'd be delighted to have us,' Cosmo continued, 'or we could stay here, of course, if your mother could bear it. Either will be fine, won't it, as a temporary measure? Just for a year or two.'

Hannah couldn't speak.

'And meanwhile, I'm going to try to get some really good stories,' he went on. 'Some big hitters, you know? I was thinking of infiltrating a lunatic asylum. Pose as a madman, expose the conditions from the inside, that sort of thing. Seems an obvious progression from the dosshouse, don't you think?'

'It sounds rather alarming!'

'Don't worry, darling,' he said, putting his hand over hers. 'I'll be all right. And if it gets rough, I'll just tell them who I am and they'll let me out.'

Hannah nodded weakly. 'And the editor will pay a lot for that story, do you think?'

'Well, probably not a lot, to be honest. It's no murder. But readers do like madhouses, and it'd show him that I'm capable of intrepid things.'

'Has no one ever done such a thing before?'

'Well, apparently someone in America did it for ten days. So, I think it'd have to be at least that long to get the editor's attention. Prove my chops.'

He looked at her imploringly, and she mustered a reassuring smile, her fingers still limp in his.

When she saw her mother later that day, Hannah told her about the death of Cosmo's grandmother, but not about the will and its consequences. She'd have to, sooner or later, but she couldn't yet bring herself to say the words out loud, to make the situation a cold fact. Instead, the disappointment swilled uncomfortably inside her, like indigestion. Her future life at Milton Terrace was horribly vivid. Cosmo would go out to work and leave her there, a captive audience for Mrs Walters' every thought and flutter and ailment. Then, in the evening, Mr Walters' suggestiveness. She would have to absorb the tension between them, and hear over and over again about Gigi's betrayal. She'd exist in a permanent state of indebtedness, condemned to voicing continuous praise and gratitude, and be slowly drained of her life force as you are when around people who aren't really your sort. They'd all have to make conversation over breakfast and then lunch and then tea and then dinner – every day. And coming down to breakfast the morning after the wedding night! She could already hear Mr Walters facetiously enquiring as to whether they'd slept well.

The only prospect more unappealing than moving into Milton Terrace was that of Cosmo coming to Camden Square. Every day would provide numerous opportunities for him to clumsily attempt to please and entertain, and for her mother to cut him down. Not only would this be agonising to witness, but however much she was on Cosmo's side, her mother's lack of regard for him might start to poison Hannah's own feelings towards her husband. And then, the practical arrangements! Hannah pictured her mother waiting outside the bathroom for him to complete his ablutions. There was only a single bed in her attic room; she imagined the embarrassment of having to install a bigger one there, the furniture men getting stuck with it on the narrow stairs. Alternatively, they'd take Will's larger room on the floor below, with only a thin wall between their quarters and Mrs Teale's. Impossible!

She tried to console herself with the fact that Cosmo was proving himself to be a spirited man of action with his asylum plan. It did bode well, didn't it? And whatever he was paid for it would take them a few steps closer to renting their own house.

The following day, a letter arrived.

My own true Hannah,

Regarding the enterprise I mentioned to you yesterday – I am resolved to see it to fruition. I will pretend to be a madman, get admitted to the asylum at Friern Barnet, and spend a full ten days there to expose the conditions for the poor unfortunates condemned therein.

From casual enquiries, it seems that there are two routes to admission: either being recommended by one's doctor or being found making a show of yourself in a public place and getting taken in by force. The latter seems the obvious choice.

It is to be a secret to everyone but you. I will tell my colleagues at the paper I am taking a holiday in the Lake District, walking with a friend. My parents will hear the same tale – I know my mother will worry and try to talk me out of it. I confide only in you, my dear future wife, as I know you will appreciate the reasons for my endeavour, and have faith that I can fulfil it.

I do not know what the situation will be vis-à-vis communications once inside – perhaps letters will be forbidden or monitored – so please do not worry if you don't hear from me, although I will do everything in my power to write to you. For this mission I have decided to take an assumed name, Charles Winterbottom (initials the same as mine so I cannot be caught out by any monograms on my clothes).

I aim to be admitted this weekend. I will spend Saturday gibbering in Trafalgar Square and proceed from there.

Wish me luck, my darling.

Your Cosmo

P.S. My mother mentioned you two are having tea on Sunday to talk about napkins. Don't let the cat out of the bag!

3

A good and loyal wife takes upon her a share of everything that concerns and interests her husband. Whatever may be his work, or even recreation, she endeavours to learn enough about it to be able to listen to him with interest if he speaks to her of it, and to give a sensible opinion if he asks for it.

— Girl's Own Paper

At 7.30 a.m. on Saturday, Hannah was in bed, in no rush to begin the day that yawned ahead. Later she would visit her friend Emily, who was loaning Hannah her wedding dress, but that was not until five.

'Hannah?'

It was her mother, outside her bedroom door.

'I'm going to Somers Town in a bit. Would you like to come?'

Several times a week, Mrs Teale went to the slum to talk to the women and advertise her refuge. Hannah had occasionally joined her. But the place was so bleak, with its courtyards full of damp fog, the broken windows, the shoeless, staring children.

'I don't think I can,' she called, from her bed. 'I've got so much to do for the wedding.'

Her mother's light footsteps retreated down the stairs.

Hannah supposed she did have things to do for the wedding. She should leaf through the recipe books downstairs for ideas for the wedding breakfast to discuss with her future mother-in-law at tea tomorrow. Take yet another trip to Bowman's and pretend to the assistant that she could appreciate the difference between Maltese and Lille lace. Sew more blasted octopuses' legs. But none of this could be less appealing – especially now that on the other side of her wedding day lay not a little place of their own, but a terrible limbo at Milton Terrace.

She let out a long, silent sigh, her cheek pressed against the clammy eiderdown. The congealed atmosphere of the house was most pronounced up here, in this high little room she had slept in for two decades, unchanged in all that time, with its chipped washstand and bookcase and worn, sludgy floral carpet. Out of the corner of her eye, she noticed the darkened halo on her pillowcase, from the soot in her hair. She should wash it, but that seemed too great an effort. She turned her head the other way, towards the window. A feeble rain shower had spattered on the glass.

Her delight over her mention in the *Girl's Own Paper* already seemed a long time ago. The issue of the magazine was now under her mattress, mixed in with all the others. Perhaps she'd tell Cosmo about it, one day.

What was he doing right now? Perhaps at this very instant he was in Trafalgar Square, bellowing and flailing about, splashing in the fountains. She imagined him being tackled to the ground by a passer-by, folded into a straitjacket and then pushed into the back of a cab bound for Friern Barnet. She rather envied him the excitement.

There came a creak from next door, from the room shared by the maids. Hannah heard Ivy announce she was going to have a rest while Gwen went to the baker's. Gwen must have silently acquiesced, as Hannah then heard her go downstairs; she could always tell when it was Gwen on the stairs because the girl wore her skirt too long and was always treading on the hem and stumbling. Hannah felt Ivy's continued presence just a few feet away on the other side of the wall. She, too, would be lying on her bed, perhaps thinking about this Tom person, or turning over some family issue, or another of the excitements or worries of her life that Hannah wasn't privy to.

Minutes passed, static and silent. She must have drifted off, as she was suddenly bolted awake by a loud noise very close by, like a door being flung open. And then, a terrified voice out on the landing.

'Ivy, oh my God, Ivy!'

Gwen. Hannah sprang out of bed and opened the door to the landing. The girls were standing at the entrance to their room, Gwen clutching Ivy's forearms. Gwen was panting, her long face pale and her eyes huge. Ivy looked bewildered.

'What's happened?' asked Hannah.

They both looked over, blankly. They were too upset to be surprised to see Hannah.

'You won't believe it,' said Gwen, turning back to Ivy. 'I was in the queue at Macaulay's, and this man rushes up – Mr Macaulay's son's friend, you know the one, with the orange hair? – so, he's just been up in Hampstead and apparently there's a body found there. A woman, all torn up. Just like in Whitechapel. They say it's *him*. The Ripper. Back again.'

'Stop it!' said Ivy.

'Apparently, a man who fitted his description was seen fleeing the scene.'

'I don't believe you!'

'It's true,' Gwen continued. 'They found her on Crossfield Road.'

'Where's that?'

'Near the Swiss Inn, apparently.'

'My God!' shrieked Ivy, hands flying to her cheeks. 'I was drinking there the other week, with Tom. It could have been me!'

'Well, he only goes after lone women, doesn't he?' said Gwen, in a reproving tone. 'So it wouldn't have been you, if you were with Tom.'

'Who is it?' Hannah asked from the doorway. 'The woman? Do they know?'

Gwen glanced over and shrugged. 'A young woman. That's all they said.'

'Were her guts out and everything?' asked Ivy.

'I think so,' said Gwen.

'Oh God, it's so horrible!' cried Ivy, throwing herself onto the bed. 'I'm never going out again!'

Hannah turned away unnoticed, quietly closing their door behind her. Back in her room, she sat down on her bed, conscious of her heavy breathing. An idea had come to her – one that was so stupendously bold, it seemed to have materialised from somewhere outside of herself.

She would go down to the murder scene near the Swiss Inn, see what was happening, and write a story for the newspaper.

Who knew how much they would pay her, but it would be a good amount, surely? Cosmo and Ovilry had made it perfectly clear: newspapers wanted murder, the gorier the better. And what could be a bigger, bloodier story than the return of the Whitechapel monster?

That unthinkable *year or two* at Milton Terrace might become six months. Maybe even less.

Ideally, of course, Cosmo would do it. By alerting him to this news, through a note to his home or workplace, Hannah would have gloriously fulfilled her role as his helpmeet. But he was not at home or work. He was, most likely, gibbering in Trafalgar Square, or *en route* to the madhouse.

Somewhere outside, a dog barked; it could have come from the front step or from five miles away. She stared blankly into space, fleshing out the plan. She knew where the Swiss Inn was, on the Finchley Road. As for writing the story – well, how hard could it be? She thought of the magazine under the mattress beneath her. CAMDEN GIRL's article was *informative* and *poignant*, and they regretted not being able to publish it. She was sitting on her qualification certificate.

The memory came to her of something said by that awful, thrilling would-be suitor James. He'd been fond of quotations, and, as with everything he'd said, she had taken them to heart, earnestly writing them down after their meetings. This one was by Goethe: *at the moment of commitment, the entire universe conspires to assist you.*

Abruptly she stood up, galvanised, and quickly got dressed. Beside the bed was a notebook she'd bought to write lists for the wedding. She slipped it into her pocket and, passing the maids' closed door, crept downstairs.

The most direct route to the Swiss Inn involved cutting through Kentish Town and taking the Prince of Wales Road, but instead Hannah found herself on the long way, heading towards Camden Town, her natural centre of gravity. The weather was drab and, although the high street was as busy as usual, the place felt low-spirited, as if people were quickly resupplying rather than making a morning out of it.

Turning right at Brown's dairy, she headed north towards Chalk Farm. Approaching the canal and railway, the environment noticeably changed, from commerce to heavy industry. The shops thinned out, replaced by huge warehouses and depots; the horses on the street grew stockier, from glossy cab horses to shires with yellow-stained forelocks, wrenching impossible loads.

Now, on her left, was the high wall of the railway complex. Blackened with coal dust and running for a quarter of a mile, it was baleful and forbidding, better suited to Newgate. Walking close to the wall, Hannah could hear the whinnies and snorts of the horses housed in the stables behind it – eight hundred of them, she'd heard, tons of dense, damp muscle, just a few feet away. Unlike the blank sky elsewhere, above the railway swirled thick dark smoke and wisps of steam – its own private weather system. Hannah remembered why she didn't often come this way. The racket was horrendous – the jarring clunks and screeches of metal on metal, the rough bellows of the workers, in their flat caps and grubby shirt sleeves – and the defining stench of London, the acrid smell of coal dust and horse sweat, was at its most concentrated.

She passed a boy crouching to laboriously scratch his name on the wall – T-O-B-Y – his marks revealing the original yellow brickwork underneath the soot. She thought of the graffiti in Pompeii, and how Cosmo had attempted to translate the inscriptions for her, stopping short when he realised the message was indelicate.

How proud he was going to be of her! What a team they were! She walked faster, propelled by nerves and admiration for her own boldness and quick thinking.

The gloomy wall came to an end at the circular gin warehouse. The surrounding air hung with that juniper scent, on the breath of the poor women who beseeched her from doorways – the kind of women who fell victim to homicidal maniacs. The smell chastened her. This was not just a jaunt; this was about the appalling murder of one of these unfortunates.

Soon enough she was at Chalk Farm. Her father had once told her that when he was young this area was wild country, famous as a site for duels. Throughout Hannah's own childhood, the area was undeveloped, and walking through here would leave your shoes heavy with thick red mud. But like everywhere, in recent years it had been built up, and was now an enclave of white stucco. After the rawness of the railway district, Hannah felt back on home turf.

Turning left onto England's Lane, she found a busy little high street, with the requisite butcher, fishmonger, baker and haberdashery, and a Saturday-morning shopping crowd. In their dark coats and hats, the female shoppers looked just like Hannah: anyone noticing her, should they care to think about her at all, would assume she was there to browse gloves or buy pork cutlets. Being in such decent surroundings quelled her trepidation and again she felt emboldened and frisky, enjoying her secret, as she asked one of the women the way to Crossfield Road.

As directed, she walked on into Eton Avenue. The street appeared to be purely residential, and the houses brand new and elaborate in design, with ornamental glass and pitched roofs. Some had signs of occupation, such as hangings in the window and prams by the door, but most appeared empty. There were still undeveloped sites in between the houses – mounds of rubble; timber scaffolding – and from somewhere unseen she heard the repeated *clink-clink-clink* of builders' trowels, London's birdsong. From nowhere arose the long-buried memory of a builder exposing himself to her as a child, when she was playing alone one day in Camden Square. She had just stared, frozen, not screaming for help, as he had smiled, enjoying her shock.

Unnerved, and feeling profoundly alone, she slowly continued along Eton Avenue. Any thrill she had felt passing the shoppers on her secret mission had evaporated. Her saliva tasted sour in her mouth. It was so very quiet, and she was so alone. This felt like Ripper territory. *Wild country*. Up ahead, she spotted the small figures of a woman and two children, and felt a trickle of relief, but the trio immediately disappeared into one of the houses. A stray dog raced past her, frantic, as if being chased.

Hannah wanted to flee, too. Instead, she told herself not to be silly, and to continue onwards, until, finally, she was at the corner of Crossfield Road.

Like Eton Avenue, the street was not finished: between the new buildings were sites in various stages of construction. But it was not quite deserted. A hundred yards up on the left, just past a large pile of bricks, stood a policeman, hands behind his back, staring into the middle distance. He was the only sign that anything untoward had happened here.

This was it? Hannah felt both relieved and wrong-footed. Was she expecting a mutilated body to still be lying there, exposed, like in the lurid drawings of murder scenes on the front pages? Perhaps she was.

It felt somehow unseemly to approach the policeman directly, but really, she had no choice: there was no one and nothing else around. She strolled towards him, casual as anything. As she drew near, she noticed he was guarding a rectangular wooden board lying on the ground, like a marker. A-ha – was this something?

'Morning, constable,' she said, and then glanced down at the board, as if just noticing it. 'Oh – what happened here?'

The policeman, an older man with a baggy, kind face, appraised her. She felt him noting her respectability.

'An incident, miss,' he said. 'I can't say any more, but it's nothing for you to be concerned about.'

Hannah smiled and thanked him, then continued walking. Of course, she thought, as she made her way up Crossfield Road, the policeman's answer proved nothing. If it was suspected that this was indeed the work of the Ripper, moved from the East End to a more salubrious hunting ground, he wouldn't want to alarm her. His *nothing for you to be concerned about* could have been a reference to the fact that the man famously preyed on women of low repute, not women like her. Or perhaps Gwen's source in the baker's had got it entirely wrong, and there had just been some common-or-garden altercation here. Perhaps there was not even a murder at all.

Hannah felt she should make some notes on the scene, although there wasn't much to say. At the far end of Crossfield Road, far enough away from the policeman, she stopped and took out her pad, as if jotting down an impromptu shopping list. *Genteel suburb. Quiet, tree-lined street. Building site.*

Sensing movement nearby, she glanced up, before starting with alarm. A man was standing just a few feet away, staring at her.

'Heard about it, did you?' he said. 'Terrible business.'

He was young-ish, about the same age as Will, and although respectably dressed he looked crumpled, and his eyes were red. Before she could reply, he continued.

'I was the one who found her, you know? The woman.'

Now it was Hannah's turn to stare.

'What was that?'

'I'll tell you all about it, if you like.'

Hannah found herself taking a step back from the man, as if to accommodate this extraordinary turn of events.

'You want to report back to your friends? Give the ladies the gossip?' he said. He had a sing-song voice, with a rising inflection. 'I don't blame you. A hell of a thing, if you'll excuse my language.'

Trying not to sound too eager, Hannah replied, 'Yes, why not?'

She glanced around furtively. The policeman was still the only other person around, stationed at the other end of the street. He didn't seem to have noticed their encounter. Hannah turned back to the young man.

'I'm going to be honest, miss,' he said, with a wince. 'I'm still a bit shaken up. Haven't slept at all, and I'm meant to be at work today. I had to skip it, to talk to the police and all, and that's a day's wages.' He paused, and then when she didn't immediately respond, added, 'I'm embarrassed to ask, miss, but would it be at all possible for you to spare a little change for my time?'

Hannah smiled, flustered.

'Of course.'

Was this how these things were done? If only Cosmo were here to advise her. But, of course, if he were here then she wouldn't be doing this at all. How much should she give him? She dug into her pocket and felt three coins.

'I can give you – two pence?'

He shrugged and she passed him two of the coins, which he pocketed. His hat and the shoulders of his coat were speckled with brick dust. She opened her pad and stood poised with her pencil, ready to write.

'You're keen, aren't you?' said the man, indicating the pad.

'Just so I get all the facts straight,' said Hannah. 'For when I tell the ladies.'

The man shrugged and began his story. As he spoke, he made sporadic eye contact with Hannah, but mostly kept his gaze fixed over her shoulder.

'I live just up there, you see, and I was coming home from work last night – this was around seven o'clock – passing down the road, just here. It was a dark, dull night, there was no moon, if you remember, and I could just distinguish the outline of a woman's figure lying down. Her head was covered with something – a hat, I thought. I assumed she was intoxicated and passed on. But then, I reached the end of the street, and it struck me as queer – you don't often get drunkards around here, and she was lying in this odd position, you see – and so I thought that maybe she was ill, or had had a fit, and so I returned to her, and she definitely didn't look right, so I ran for help . . .'

'Wait, how did she not look right?' said Hannah.

He looked surprised by her interruption. 'Well, it was like one leg, her right one, was straight, and the left one was sort of bent and under her body. And her right arm was straight and her left one sort of bent under her shoulder.' He demonstrated the posture and then continued.

'And her head was covered in a brown thing . . .'

'A brown thing?'

'You know.' He pointed at her jacket. 'Like a wool jacket.'

'A cardigan?'

'Perhaps, yes.' He sounded irritated now.

'And what else was she wearing?'

'I don't know, a black skirt, and, um . . . I don't know . . .'

Perhaps he wasn't familiar with women's clothing. She reframed the question.

'Were they decent clothes?'

'Fairly decent,' he said. She scrawled this down, and he continued with his story. 'So then I went immediately to Swiss Cottage station to find help, and on the way, on Upper Avenue Road, I spotted this policeman, and he came back here with me . . .'

'What was his name?'

'Constable Gardiner, it was. He felt the woman's pulse and found nothing, and then he unwrapped the thing around her head and that's when . . .' He hesitated, glanced at her, then looked off over her shoulder. 'We was greeted by the most gruesome sight. A woman, aged about thirty, with her throat cut ear to ear. Face smeared with blood.'

From being reasonably animated when he first approached

her, the man's voice had flattened, and his face was drained and blank.

'It looked to me like she was taken from behind, like this' – he raised his arm, bending his elbow, as if gripping around someone's neck – 'like the Ripper did, but then it was—' Now, with his other hand, he mimed someone wrenching a knife across a throat. 'Her head was nearly clean off. It was only a little bit of skin at the back that was keeping it on.'

Hannah grimaced. *Nearly clean off,* she wrote.

'So then the constable blew his whistle for assistance and told me to go and fetch a medical man; it just happens that I know one in Belsize Park. So I ran off to fetch him and when he came back with me to the scene, he tested her skin with his hands to decide how long she had been dead for. Her legs were still warm, and he decided that she had not been dead for more than an hour.'

He paused, taking a deep sigh. Hannah was grateful for the break; her hand ached. He had been talking so fast, she had resorted to a sort of shorthand to keep up, sometimes just jotting single words.

'Was there a lot of blood on the ground?' she asked, after a moment.

He shook his head. 'None, really. It was all on her.'

'And then what happened?'

'By now a couple of other constables had responded to the whistle, and word had spread, so there was a small group of men . . .'

'What time was this?'

'About half past eight. They went through her pockets to find something to identify her but no luck. They found a handkerchief and a brooch, but that's all. They searched the area for a murder weapon and again no luck. And then they took the body away.'

Hannah thought for a moment. 'Wouldn't you imagine that she would have a latch key?' she said. 'I mean, if she was . . .'

She trailed off. She meant *if she was taking men back home* but couldn't quite say it.

The man looked at her, not helping her out. She sensed he was getting irritated by her interjections and questions.

'All I know is what I told you,' he said. His tone was stiff now. 'Look, I'd better be going.'

And with that he scuttled off, shoulders hunched and hands stuffed into his pockets, in the direction of Belsize Park.

It was an abrupt termination, but Hannah didn't mind. The man had told her a lot – surely enough for a story. Now, she must get back and write everything down before she forgot the meaning of her rushed notes. She realised she hadn't even asked the man's name; hopefully that wouldn't matter. Stuffing her notepad into her pocket, she started walking briskly homewards.

Retracing her route up Eton Avenue took what felt like a fraction of the time it had to get down it. She felt like a wholly different person. Her feet were barely skimming the pavement, such was her excitement at having executed such a bold plan so successfully.

England's Lane was still busy, shoppers innocently queuing outside the butcher's, chatting, listening to a one-man band outside the public house. Weaving anonymously through the crowds, Hannah smiled as she felt the weight of her pad in her pocket, a pad that by rights should contain a shopping list of lettuce and turbot and ribbons but instead held the gruesome details of a murder.

And then, she heard a cry: 'GHASTLY DISCOVERY IN HAMPSTEAD!'

She stopped in her tracks. For a mad, confused moment she thought the cry had unconsciously come from her. She turned to see a newspaper boy, stationed a few feet away. He was holding up a paper and flapping it around.

'MURDER MOST HORRID!' he shouted. 'HAMP-STEAD SLAYING!'

As Hannah stared at him, she heard another cry, from a different direction, and swivelled to see another boy holding up a different paper on the other side of the road. 'RIPPER RETURNS!' he shouted. And then, a little way up the street, another one: 'BUTCHERY ON THE STREETS!' In fact, it seemed that in every direction she turned, a ten-year-old boy was bellowing out her story.

After a long moment, Hannah started walking again, even more quickly than before, but this time her head was bowed in shame. How could she have thought she was the first person on the scene? That's why the young man had looked so weary: he had already told the same story to a dozen different reporters. And those reporters had then gone to their respective offices on Fleet Street and written up the experience, the paper had been printed, and now it was already out on the streets. It was too much for her to absorb, how in just a few hours this situation had gone from a woman lying dead on a muddy road, alone except for stray dogs, to the story being printed in dozens of newspapers, to be read by hundreds of thousands. All this in the time between Hannah innocently eating her salmon last night, and her toast and marmalade that morning.

She upped her pace, breathing hard, desperate to get home. Thank goodness no one else need know about her foolishness. But she felt something else, too, she realised: a faint but unmistakable sense of being personally wronged. When walking down Eton Avenue, she'd felt as if she inhabited this poor woman on her final, lonely journey. It was ridiculous and unjustified, she knew, but she had felt the story was *hers*. And now it was everyone's, and everywhere. Common knowledge to be picked over.

This time, when she reached Chalk Farm, Hannah took the direct route home, turning left onto Prince of Wales Road. It was a long, ordinary residential street, with no thronging shoppers or yelling paper boys to broadcast her humiliation, and as she progressed down it, she found herself growing calmer, her sense restored. Indeed, by halfway down, she was composed enough to wish there *was* in fact a paper boy about, so she could buy a copy of a newspaper and read the full story of the lonely body in Crossfield Road.

Approaching the Kentish Town Road, the pavement became busier, and Hannah spotted some costers offering toasting forks, blackleading, beetroot and artificial flowers. No newspapers, though. Then, she spotted a woman approaching, holding a small stack of papers, flat in both hands, like a tray, so the front page was visible. It was the *Star* – Cosmo's paper. The woman was whistling to herself, and when Hannah put out her hand to waylay her, she abruptly stopped.

'Could I buy one of those?' Hannah asked.

The woman frowned.

'But they're mine,' she replied.

She fanned the papers out, as if she needed to prove she wasn't a seller, and Hannah saw that she was holding half a dozen issues of various publications, not only the *Star*.

'Forgive me,' Hannah said, lifting her hand in apology.

She walked on, but had only taken a few steps when she heard the woman say, 'Help me.'

Hannah stopped and turned back. The woman hadn't raised her voice; she wasn't calling out. Rather, it was as if she was talking to herself, but from her direct look it was clear she was addressing Hannah. She was about Hannah's age, and pleasant looking, if no beauty: medium height, average build, heavy-lidded blue eyes. She wore a blue hat with a small, bent feather; underneath, her hair was the red-brown colour of new bricks. But what struck Hannah now was that the woman was clearly petrified. It was obvious from her pupils as she stared at Hannah; from how her front teeth were clamped on her lower lip; from how she was now clutching the pile of papers to her chest, in a white-knuckled grip. Hannah stepped back towards her and put her hand on her arm.

'Don't worry.'

She remembered what the policeman had said to her at Crossfield Road and, although his reassurance had clearly been an evasion – an 'incident', indeed! – she repeated it now.

'It's terrible,' she said, 'but there's nothing for you to worry about.'

The woman gave Hannah an odd look, then, to Hannah's surprise, she smiled and gave a bark of a laugh.

'They'll catch him soon enough,' Hannah said blandly.

'Are you sure?'

Hannah nodded, slightly uncomfortable now. She had no authority to reassure this poor woman about anything.

'What if there's more than one culprit?'

'You mean *victim*?' said Hannah kindly. 'I honestly think they'll catch him before he strikes again . . .'

The woman looked at her steadily for a moment, with her pale-blue gaze, and then she did something surprising. She took the top paper in her pile and held it out to Hannah.

'Take it,' she said.

'Are you sure?'

The woman nodded. 'I don't need to read it.' She gave that strange bark-laugh again.

'Well, let me give you this.' Hannah dug into her pocket for her remaining penny, but by the time she'd found it, the woman was already off down the street, hurrying in the direction of Chalk Farm.

'Here!' called Hannah, but the woman didn't turn back. 'Thank you!'

Hannah repocketed the coin and continued her journey, resisting the urge to open the paper straight away. There was something exposing about devouring such a story on the street. On reaching Camden Square, she considered smuggling the paper in under her skirt, to avoid Mrs Teale seeing it and commenting, but decided against it. Why should she be ashamed at reading her fiancé's newspaper?

But her bravery had no witness. When she called out hello from the hallway, only Ivy answered, from the kitchen. Glancing at the grandfather clock on the landing, Hannah was astonished to see that less than three hours had passed since Gwen had thumped upstairs, panting with her news. Time was behaving very oddly today.

She went up to her chilly bedroom and shut the door before laying the paper on the bed, kneeling on the floor beside it and starting to read.

It wasn't stated who had written the leading article about the Hampstead murder – it was ascribed only to *our correspondent* – but the man was certainly intrepid. He had even somehow got inside the mortuary where the body was being held, to give readers a graphic description of its condition. Was it Ovilry, she wondered, doing a blag?

The grisly account tallied broadly with what the young man had told her. As well as suffering terrible head injuries, the victim's windpipe and upper spinal column had almost been separated from her body. The report also contained quotes from the young man who had discovered the body – almost word for word the same story he had given Hannah.

There was also a detailed description of the victim, which the police had provided at a press gathering late the previous night – again, Hannah marvelled at how fast real life transmuted to newsprint. She was around thirty years of age, fairly tall at five feet six inches, with dark hair and blue eyes, and what was described as a swarthy complexion. Unlike Hannah's interviewee on Crossfield Road, the police had a grasp on women's clothing: they stated that the dead woman was wearing an imitation Astrakhan jacket, black cashmere dress, red and yellow striped petticoats, blue woollen stockings with suspenders and white linen drawers. The final item had the initials P.H. embroidered on them.

The paper reported that the police already had a suspect for the killing: a man *aged forty, nearly six feet high, with a dark moustache and wearing a light suit and a peaked cap* who had been spotted in Crossfield Road the previous evening. This description was apparently strikingly similar to some descriptions of the man believed to be Jack the Ripper.

Hannah paused in her reading, feeling unsavoury. How awful for this poor woman, having her most personal garments peeled off and inspected, her body exposed to all these cold male eyes. Although, she supposed, if the victim was a woman of the night, then she would be used to such invasions.

She was interrupted by an unbidden memory, of seeing her father in the morgue, when she and her mother went to identify the body after his accident. They pulled down the sheet and, as Hannah gazed at his peaceful face, she realised she'd never had the opportunity to properly inspect him before. She hadn't spent much time in his company – he'd always been working, or out, or, if at home, he'd usually leave the room as she entered it. In those times when she was around him, she'd been too shy to stare at his face for any length of time; it would have felt impertinent somehow. Only now, in death, did she have the chance to see where her own features came from: the tea-coloured skin and thick eyebrows, the full cheeks, the hint of darkness under her eyes that she'd had even as a baby. Just as they were leaving the morgue, out of nowhere it struck her that she had never seen his bare feet before, and her chance would soon be gone. She had run back and asked the policeman to lift up the sheet at the other end of the body, just for a moment. His feet were surprisingly delicate, for a stocky man.

But wait, Hannah thought, coming back to the present,

to the story in front of her — what was there to say that the woman was a prostitute? The crime was suspected to be the work of the Whitechapel man, so the dead woman was assumed to be the same sort as his victims. But why, after a period of two years, would he attack on the other side of London? From the description, the woman's clothes sounded perfectly respectable — similar to what Ivy or Gwen would wear on a day out. That's what the man at Crossfield Road had said, wasn't it, when she'd asked him to describe the victim's clothes: *fairly decent*.

Furthermore, Hannah thought, the way the body appeared bore few similarities to the Whitechapel women. Everyone knew that they were slashed to bits in the most horrific way, killed on the spot where they were found. According to her witness, there was no blood at the scene, which suggested that the death did not occur there. Surely the Ripper wouldn't have wrapped up her head like that with the brown cardigan, regardless of whether this move was motivated by shame or pity, or from wanting to conceal her injuries. The Ripper had not tried to hide his work, nor shown any remorse. Quite the opposite.

Hannah read the newspaper report carefully again, to confirm her suspicions. Indeed, it appeared that the only clue that this might be the work of the Whitechapel killer was the sighting of this supposedly suspicious man in the vicinity. While his description may well have matched that of previous Ripper suspects, it also sounded like every second man on the pavement.

Hannah slid the newspaper under her mattress and went downstairs to the drawing room. Gwen was on her hands and knees, blowing the fire to get it going.

'Are you all right, Gwen?'

The maid sat upright on her knees. Hannah expected to receive the usual nonchalant shrug, but instead, Gwen said quietly, 'Bit shaken about the Ripper being back, to be honest.'

'I honestly don't think it's him,' replied Hannah. 'Don't worry. I think it was just a sad, common, domestic argument.'

Gwen looked unconvinced. 'I reckon it's him.'

Frowning, she leant back into the fireplace and gave the fire one final great blow, before abruptly getting back to her feet and leaving the room. By the time Mrs Teale arrived home twenty minutes later, the fire was established and Hannah was in her chair by the window, the mound of white linen nightdresses on her lap, but her hands were still and her mind elsewhere as she sifted through each moment of her extraordinary morning.

Later that day, Hannah went to see her friend Emily. She and her husband Stan lived in Stoke Newington, but following the birth of their first child, they had temporarily moved back in with her parents so that her mother could help with the baby.

The house was on Gloucester Crescent, a ten-minute walk from Hannah's, on the other side of Camden Town. The area was dominated by piano factories and the workshops serving them: veneer makers, ivory carvers, stringers, French polishers, key loaders, bench upholsterers. Whenever Hannah walked through here, the banging and twanging and the smell of glue and sawdust happily transported her back a decade, when she and Emily would come back to

Emily's house for tea and Garibaldi biscuits after a day at the North London Collegiate School for Girls.

Reaching Emily's parents' house, Hannah noticed that the road outside was covered with straw to muffle the noise of passing carriage wheels. She thought of that plank of wood on Crossfield Road, indicating the spot where the body was found: a horribly banal marker of the end of a life.

'I hope your parents aren't unwell?' Hannah asked Emily, once she was ensconced on a sofa in the drawing room, a tin of biscuits on the table in front of them.

'The straw, you mean?' said Emily. 'No, it's for me. Stan did it, so I could get some sleep. I'm just so tired all the time now, and I wake up at the slightest sound, thinking it's her.'

She reached for a biscuit with her free hand. With the other she held her daughter, so tightly swaddled she resembled a matchstick, a big red face atop a narrow white body.

'And so hungry all the time, too,' Emily said, passing a biscuit to Hannah. 'And you're encouraged to eat! One of many lovely things they don't tell you about this business.'

Hannah took a bite but for once she didn't want it. The mouthful tasted gritty, the raisins as hard as lead.

'Em, did you hear about this murder?' she said, after swallowing. 'Just up the road, near the Swiss Inn. This poor woman. At first they thought it might be the Whitechapel man, but I don't think so . . .'

'Han, please.' Emily put out a hand, her tone uncharacteristically serious. 'Sorry, I just can't stomach it. I feel quite squeamish at the moment. It's like I've had a layer of skin taken off.' She lowered her voice. 'Between us, I think I might be *enceinte*.'

Astonished, Hannah stared at her. 'Again? Already?'

'Well, obviously I won't know for sure for months. But I feel very similar to how I did with Beatrice.'

Hannah adjusted her tone. 'Congratulations!'

Emily smiled. Her friend had changed physically since becoming a mother. Before, she'd looked rather mousy and bloodless, and younger than she was. Her appearance hadn't reflected her strong character. At school, where the other girls spent their playtimes writing poems to their future husbands, Emily had read natural history books and joked that she was hoping to end up at the home for friendless girls of good character on the Hampstead Road. When asked by their teacher to write an essay on their hero, rather than choose the queen, or Florence Nightingale or Isambard Kingdom Brunel, Emily had chosen that scandalous Mary Wollstonecraft, until she was forced to pick another.

Now look at her: a woman of substance and experience, her hair as glossy as tar, her colour high, expertly cradling her baby with one arm in the pose that united the Virgin Mary and a wretch on the Ratcliffe Highway. The fact that they were in the drawing room – an adult realm smelling of linseed oil, filled with mahogany cases of artefacts from Emily's father's time in Ethiopia, which previously Hannah had only scuttled past on her way up to Emily's bedroom – only enhanced the impression that Emily was now a fully-fledged grown-up.

'Now, there is the dress,' said Emily, indicating an armchair, in which sat propped a cardboard box, as long as a torso, emblazoned with *Russell & Allen, Dressmakers*.

Hannah opened it to glimpse folds of gleaming vanilla satin nestled in tissue paper.

'I didn't include the veil,' said Emily. 'That's the most intimate thing, isn't it? I know you'll want to get your own. Or the gloves or shoes, because we're different sizes. But you'll have enough for those, won't you?'

'It's so kind of you,' said Hannah, peering into the box. The bodice looked frightfully narrow; Emily had bigger feet but was altogether slighter than her. 'I only hope it'll fit.'

'You can get it altered,' said Emily generously. 'Honestly, it's not like I'm going to use it again. I briefly had this notion that Beatrice might want to wear it, but she won't, will she? Fashion will have moved on in twenty years and she'll shriek at the sight of the puffed sleeves, or whatever.' She chuckled. 'Are you very sad not to be having your own dress?'

Hannah looked up from carefully replacing the box lid.

'Not really. I mean, it'd be nice, I suppose. But I had one made for my twenty-first, and – you know.'

'Yes, I know,' said Emily. 'And your mother's quite right. Fifty unfortunates could be fed for a year for the price of that thing. The dress doesn't matter, anyway. I'd have happily married Stan in a flour sack.'

Hannah sat back down on the sofa, and Emily reached for her hand.

'Oh, Han, I'm so pleased it's happening for you!' she said with feeling.

'And it's all down to you,' replied Hannah.

'Yes! My magic bouquet! Thank goodness Matilda didn't catch it instead of you. She was really trying, wasn't she? She almost knocked you to the floor as she lunged for it.'

On the sofa, the two friends smiled at each other. Hannah recognised the moment as being lovely and poignant, although a part of her mind was still elsewhere. Was P.H. married? Was her husband missing her?

'Maybe I should give you my baby list, too,' Emily went on. 'All the things you'll need. If you're getting married at the end of December, yours will come in September – the same month as Beatrice! Wouldn't it be funny if their birthdays are exactly a year apart?'

'But – it doesn't always happen right away, does it?'

'Oh, I think so,' replied Emily. 'Almost always.'

'But what if you don't want it to happen straight away?'

Emily laughed. 'Why would you not want it to happen?' She gave the baby a delicate peck on the nose.

Hannah looked away to where a stuffed antelope's head was mounted on the wall. Its dark, liquid eyes gazed back pityingly: *You poor humans, having to dance around such acts of nature.*

'So, Em, come on,' she said. 'What's it like?'

'I must say, Han, it's kind of bliss!'

'What?' Hannah frowned. *'Really?'*

'Yes! You'll remember, at first I was quite worried about it, becoming some worn-down, small-minded martyr, but actually it doesn't have to be like that, if you get a decent, modern husband. Stan comes home from work, and he's had to deal with money, and knows all about politics, and all these things that I am actually quite interested in, and I can ask him about them if I want. But you know what? Mostly, I *don't* want!'

It had taken Hannah a while to catch up with the fact that Emily was talking about the general joys of marriage.

'The world out there doesn't impinge on you,' Emily continued, waving her free arm towards the window. 'You're protected from it all. All you have to do is create a nice ambience at home, look after the servants, have a lovely time with your baby, be pleasant to a man you're fond of when he comes home from work—'

'Em, come on,' Hannah interrupted. 'You know what I'm asking.'

Emily did know. She pursed her lips and clutched her daughter more tightly to her shoulder and laid a protective hand over her ear – *Not in front of the baby!*

'Oh. That.' She gave Hannah a maddening look. 'The thing is, Han – it's all very well giggling over books and whatnot, but when you're married, it feels wrong to talk about it. It's sort of . . . sacred. You'll understand soon enough.'

Hannah looked away, hurt and disconcerted. Marital relations had been a hot topic when they were younger: the girls had surreptitiously borrowed Emily's parents' books on the subject, winkling out whatever information they could from under the delicate phrasing and euphemisms. *The bridal night is the most important turning point in a woman's entire life*, they had intoned portentously. Emily had found a copy of a pamphlet called *The Art of Begetting Handsome Children*, which instructed husbands on the importance of *allurements to venery* and ensuring a woman's *tinkling pleasure* for the conception of a child. Such mystery!

And now, such coyness!

Emily gave a conciliatory smile and put her hand on Hannah's arm.

'Oh, remember that time with your father, and his colleague who had given a woman a child?'

Despite herself, Hannah smiled. The incident *had* been funny, in its excruciating way. It occurred when Hannah was around ten and had overheard her father in the drawing room, holding court with a group of barrister friends. The story he was telling involved a colleague who, at a loss as to how to defend a woman accused of killing her employer, had 'given her a child' so she could plead her belly and avoid the gallows. Hannah hadn't fully understood the story and assumed the barrister in question had found a child from somewhere and handed it to the woman. She had said as much to her mother, who then had to awkwardly explain the truth.

'Stop!' said Hannah. 'It makes me shudder to think of it.'

The baby woke up and started crying, and Emily's focus turned to comforting her daughter. After watching for a minute, Hannah stood up and bent down to kiss her friend, before picking up the dress box.

'I was hoping to come to the Foundling Hospital service tomorrow,' said Emily. 'But I suspect I'll be too tired. My parents will be there, though.'

Hannah nodded, distracted, as she moved towards the door. Her thoughts had preceded her exit and were already far from Emily's cosy world, back with P.H. on the mortuary slab, her head wrapped in a brown cardigan by someone acting from warped tenderness, or shame.

4

Cunning is a weak imitation of wisdom, and is liable at any time to merge into fraud.

— Girl's Own Paper

Hannah liked attending the Sunday-morning service in the chapel of the Foundling Hospital, and so did much of the rest of London. For years, the service had been hugely fashionable and over-subscribed, with no guarantee of a seat. This fact should have been enough to put her mother off going, Hannah felt, but no. Every week without fail, Mrs Teale made the journey down to Bloomsbury.

They set off at 10 a.m., their route taking them down York Road and through King's Cross. It was another heavy, blank-skied day, and York Road felt particularly low-key and Sunday-like. The industries that defined the wide street – the great cattle market and its attendant slaughterhouses; the tile factory – weren't operating today, but their stale odours laced the air and seagulls wheeled and cawed above them, impatient for opening time.

A fair number of street people lived here in the shadows of the factories, in tents made from old garments. As the

Teales walked, an ancient man approached them, trembling, the legs of his trousers in tatters and long beard matted like felt. Hannah dug into her pocket for a coin, and he accepted it, but his hands were shaking so much it dropped to the ground. Hannah bent to pick it up for him at the same time as he fell to his knees. Being so close to his scrunched, agonised face and fierce odour, and hearing his laboured breathing, made her remember Cosmo, up with the madmen in Friern Barnet.

As she and Mrs Teale walked on, Hannah worried that she hadn't been thinking about her fiancé enough. True, their future life together had been the catalyst for her decision to go to Crossfield Road yesterday – but then the visceral experience of her journey and the horrible facts of the murder, and her humiliation over the newspaper stories, had flooded her head. She had barely considered his current reality: under an assumed name, cheek by jowl with lunatics, in that vast, terrifying place.

'Do you know anyone who's been in the Friern Barnet asylum?' she asked her mother as they continued down York Road.

Mrs Teale looked at her sharply.

'Why do you ask?'

Hannah sighed.

'No real reason. I was just looking at that poor man and wondering whether he'd be better off there.'

'I see,' said her mother, her tone softer. 'Well, yes, I do. A lot. About half of the women in the refuge, I think. And almost all of them shouldn't have been in there.'

'Mother, you know what you were saying to Cosmo at our engagement dinner?' Hannah said. 'About him being a slum tourist? I don't think that's fair. Your poor women, or that man back there – no one is listening to them. Whereas journalists like Cosmo, they have some power. They can raise consciousness. Do good.'

'Hmm,' Mrs Teale said.

'Why do you think so little of him?' Hannah cried.

'Hannah, I have no animosity towards him as a person,' said her mother. 'But I do strongly dislike his newspaper. And yes, I know he writes supposedly campaigning journalism, but what that actually entails – swooping into a godforsaken place, spending a few hours gawping at the unfortunates, and writing a lurid account – it's almost as distasteful as the front-page murders.' She was hitting her stride now. 'It's perfectly possible to expose the ills of our society without sensationalising or exploiting. If you're interested in asylums, there's a book you can read, called *Ten Days in a Mad-House* by an American journalist who went undercover in one. It's very sober and sensitive. The library will probably have it.'

Ten Days in a Mad-House. Was this the story Cosmo had referred to, that he was trying to emulate with his stay at Friern Barnet?

'I'm sure Cosmo is capable of following in this American chap's footsteps,' said Hannah, enjoying her secret.

'It's not a man, actually. She's a young woman.'

A young woman! This fact pleased Hannah, while also confirming that she must never tell her mother about her unedifying expedition to Crossfield Road.

Approaching King's Cross now, they heard the racket of a street market ahead. These Sunday-morning affairs were an encore of the markets held on Saturday evening, and the Teales soon found themselves stepping around piles of twelve-hour-old rubbish: cabbage leaves, nut and mussel shells, orange peel, slicks of animal effluvia. The pavements had filled up with makeshift tables and sacking laid with heaps of random things – cracked vases, used stockings, bits of wire, heaps of coal and hills of muddy turnips, every last part of a sheep laid out in bloody pieces. The trill of a hawker, his *Hi-Hi!* as piercing as an amateur opera singer's, shot through the muddle of everyday noise: the dog barks and donkey haws and back-slang of the street boys, the wincing scrapes of the knife-sharpener's cart.

Amid the mêlée came a piercing shriek, loud enough to stop them in their tracks.

'No, you don't!' screeched a female voice. 'No, you don't!'

The altercation was just a few feet away, between a little boy and a woman. The boy was trying to grab something the woman held tightly in her arms – it looked to Hannah like a loaf of bread – and she was resisting as violently as if it were her newborn.

'No, you don't!' she repeated. 'No, you don't!'

The boy gave up and disappeared into the crowd. The woman stood panting. Mrs Teale stepped forward.

'Mrs Aversham!'

Still agitated, the woman looked at Mrs Teale blankly, before her face cleared and she nodded in recognition. She might have been in her twenties, and had clearly once been pretty, but her face was now etched and her fair hair stringy.

'He was trying to steal Harry,' she explained. Now, Hannah saw that the object the woman was clutching was actually a tortoise. The woman lifted up the animal horizontally; its limbs were retracted, giving Hannah a view of its cavity, and she saw that there was indeed an animal in there, its scaly legs framing the little nodule of its head, embedded in the loose wrinkles of its neck. The sight was unsettling – obscene, somehow.

'You poor thing,' said Mrs Teale, rubbing the woman's upper arm. 'These awful, feral boys! Are you all right? Will you go to the refuge tonight?'

Calm now, the woman nodded and then started striding away in the direction of King's Cross, clutching the tortoise to her chest like a tiny shield.

Hannah and her mother continued walking.

'That was one of them, actually,' Mrs Teale said. 'One of the women I was talking about. She has epilepsy and was in the asylum for months.'

As the Teales walked by, the costers called out to them, but their entreaties lacked vigour; the women were clearly not going to buy a broken picture frame or an apron-full of trotters. As the church bells began to peal, signalling half an hour before the morning service started and the market would have to pause trading, the industry around them noticeably upped its pace, the transactions more hurried, the cries louder.

Of course, it was almost entirely women doing the shopping, while their men stood around chatting, or having their weekly shave in the makeshift barber shops set up in the front rooms of the houses that lined the road. As they passed one such place, Hannah glanced through the window and saw a man sitting with his head back, his exposed throat covered with soap, while beside him another man was reading a newspaper. He was holding the paper up in a way that made it possible for Hannah to read the headline.

HAMPSTEAD TRAGEDY – VICTIM NAMED!

Hannah flinched and looked away, as if she had glimpsed someone in a state of undress. Even some minutes later, when they were clear of the market, she was still feeling unsettled. Did she really crave more details? After all, the name of the murder victim would mean nothing to her. Why did it matter if the poor P.H. was Peggy Hines, or Patsy Hawton, or Polly Hilton, or Pamela Higginbottom?

As they approached the ornate hulk of St Pancras station, the newsboys were out in force, each with a foot-thick pile of papers clamped under one arm, shouting over each other in Cockney monotones.

'Hampstead slaying latest!'

'Hampstead tragedy – terrible new details!'

'Hampstead murder – shocking update!'

Mrs Teale marched on, chin raised, pointedly ignoring them. A few steps behind her, Hannah felt as she had done on England's Lane the day before: as if she were running a gauntlet of newsprint, and the boys were taunting her, each cry further escalating the drama.

'Hampstead Murder – killer revealed!'

Killer revealed? Hannah came to a halt and looked over at the newsboy. He was about ten feet away, and from this distance she couldn't make out any words on the paper he was selling, beyond its headline. *HAMPSTEAD MURDER – KILLER REVEALED.* She glanced at the back of her mother some way ahead and thought of the pennies in her pocket, intended for the chapel's collection plate. It would take seconds to dash over and buy one. No way to read it now, but she could fold it and stuff it in her pocket, then excuse herself when they got to the hospital and devour it in the WC.

But, if it was now believed that the murder was indeed

linked to Whitechapel, the sellers would be making that explicit, wouldn't they? They hadn't been shy about bellowing a possible connection yesterday. No. As Hannah had concluded herself the day before, this story was not about the dramatic re-emergence of the Ripper. It was to do with a pathetic Peggy, Patsy or Polly killed by a lowlife William, John or Thomas. A tragic end to a drunken argument, fuelled by debt or infidelity. A mundane tragedy, sensationalised by the ghastly, immoral press. Hannah started walking again, briskly now, to catch up with her mother.

They reached the hospital with a few minutes to spare. The building's austere lines were in stern contrast to the extravagance of St Pancras station. A handful of people were still trailing into the chapel, and the Teales hurried to join them, pausing just inside the door. The room was packed, as it always was. Under a field of best hats was a happy, genteel hum as people greeted each other and congratulated themselves on being at *the* place to be on a Sunday morning. They spotted the Olivers, Emily's parents. Mrs Oliver waved them over to their pew, where she had saved a space.

As the two families exchanged pleasantries, Hannah glanced up at where the foundlings sat in rows in the gallery, white bibs gleaming, their grave silence a rebuke to the chatter below. She knew that those children seated in the first row were blind, but from here they all seemed to be sightless, with the same fixed, glassy stare. Shafts of sunlight shot in through the chapel's windows, highlighting random faces in the congregation.

The minister climbed to the pulpit and cleared his throat. The room hushed, and after a long moment of silence, the children started singing.

It was Tallis's 'If Ye Love Me', a staple of these services. Hannah closed her eyes, awaiting transportation. God may not have been a presence at home in Camden Square, but this place, with its grand columns and delicate stained glass and Handel's famous organ flanked by those solemn, neat-haired angels – how could it not fail to stir? Now, as an adult, listening to the harmony of the foundlings' immature voices was the closest Hannah got to surrendering herself to the moment.

Today, though, it didn't seem to be working. Her mind would not clear; dark shapes lurked at the edges. She opened her eyes and shifted on the hard pew. Up in the gallery, the children stood with their arms plastered to their sides, only their mouths moving in song. Some looked as if they were miming, while others broadcast with great feeling, enunciating each note. Watching them, Hannah thought how odd and sad it was that the people who had given these children their looks and personality traits – had made them tall and reticent, or an enthusiastic ginger-haired performer – were not here in the audience to watch them.

After the opening song came the sermon and prayers. Hannah fidgeted, just wanting it to be over. Beside her, Mrs Oliver's woody scent seemed to be getting increasingly more pungent, like rotting herbs. On her other side, her mother was discreetly removing stray hairs from the arms of her coat, pinching them between thumb and forefinger before dropping them to the floor with the disdain of a giant disposing of a troublesome child in a fairytale. At last, the service ended with the foundlings singing the hospital song, the lyrics of which baldly reminded the congregation of their obligation to open their purses on the way out: *Blessed are they that considereth the poor* . . .

Duties complete, the children filed out, one row at a time. Mrs Oliver gave a deep sigh, as if emotionally wrung out. No awkward memories had ruined the service for her.

'Now,' she said, once recovered, 'girls or boys?'

It was a moot question; the answer was always girls. Following the service, the congregation were allowed to observe the foundlings as they ate their midday meal. Visitors could choose which sex to follow – the boys were based in the west wing, the girls in the east. The girls were by far the most popular, not least because they were housed with the babies: new arrivals who would soon be sent off to live with foster mothers for the first five years of their lives, before returning to the hospital for their education.

The Teales and Olivers stood up and followed the crowds from the chapel to the east wing. Once in the refectory, the spectators stood to the side as the children were seated, grace was sung and orderlies began to move between the tables, doling out dinner.

Hannah actually found the refectory visit the least enjoyable part of the whole outing, and not just because the smells of a hot lunch – roast pork today – always made her ravenous. Watching the children eat felt awkward and prurient, as if they were a set of eerily well-behaved chimps at London Zoo. Initially, she was surprised that her mother, always so alert to the feelings of the underclasses, did not feel the same. But then she realised that for Mrs Teale, this was another opportunity to do good, and to promote the refuge. After the children had eaten, the visitors were allowed to converse with them, and Mrs Teale always went to talk to the older girls, presumably alerting them to the fact that there was a place for them, should things go wrong when they left this institution and tried to make their way in the world.

The older children ate quickly, and once the lunch plates were cleared, Mrs Teale headed over, approaching one of them – a short, saturnine-looking girl with dark hair cut into a heavy fringe like theatre curtains. Hannah recognised her from previous visits; she was Mrs Teale's favourite. Hannah stood near the infants' table, along with most of the other female visitors, all of whom seemed to be clutching either their hearts or their mouths in rapture at the sight of the six bibbed infants still finishing their dinner. The babies were making more noise than the rest of the room combined, eating with their fists, batting at each other, gurgling and generally being blissfully unaware that soon they would have to stop being childish.

Hannah tried to imagine actually possessing one of these creatures: the weight of it on her lap, the smell of its head, spooning orange mush into its mouth and wiping its chin in the brisk, expert manner of the matrons here. Mrs Oliver appeared by her side.

'Oh, they're just too heartbreaking, aren't they?' she said, sighing again. 'Especially after the news of the baby.'

Assuming she was gushing about her new granddaughter, Hannah smiled and nodded.

'Yes, she's adorable,' she said. 'You must be so proud.'

'I mean, really – can you believe a woman was capable of such evil?'

Hannah looked at her, confused.

'What do you mean?'

'The Hampstead tragedy. Dear, didn't you hear? The poor woman had a baby daughter, and they found it perished, too. Unspeakable.'

Hannah gazed at Mrs Oliver, then glanced over to check that her mother was out of hearing range. It was safe; Mrs Teale was still talking intently to the dark-haired girl.

'I don't understand,' Hannah whispered. 'Are you saying that the dead woman first killed her baby, and then – slit her own throat?'

'No, no!' Mrs Oliver flushed, excited to be the one breaking the news. 'How can you not know? It's been all over the papers. They have arrested a woman, for murdering the mother *and* child.'

'A woman?'

'A young woman! She killed them in her house and then used the baby's pram to dispose of the bodies. And she lives near us! Well, nearer you, I suppose – just behind Camden Town station.'

Hannah stared at the scuffed floorboards as she attempted to absorb the news. Her skin felt thick and numb, as if slathered with a layer of cold lard. Seconds passed; she looked back up to where Mrs Oliver awaited her reaction.

'Heavens,' said Hannah, her voice emerging small and reedy. 'How dreadful.'

'Too appalling for words!' cried Mrs Oliver, as if disapproving of her muted reaction.

'What's her name? The woman who did it?'

'Mrs Pearcey. Believe it or not.'

Mrs Pearcey. The woman who pierces people.

A bell rang, signalling the end of the visit, and the two broke off their conversation. Within a few minutes all the guests had been flushed outside into the hospital grounds. The Olivers offered the Teales a lift home in their cab.

'I think I'll walk,' said Hannah, adding, 'Mother, you go with them,' although there wasn't a chance of this. Mrs Teale didn't like being squashed in a carriage with her own children, let alone Emily's parents.

'No, I'll stay with you,' said Mrs Teale.

Mother and daughter said their goodbyes and set off back towards King's Cross.

'Shall we go a different route, up Great College Street?' asked Hannah, and her mother silently acquiesced; they bore left towards the gasworks.

Hannah was grateful for her mother's lack of chit-chat, although neither did she particularly want to be alone with her own thoughts, swirling around what Mrs Oliver had told her, alighting every few seconds on the image of a mother and her baby stuffed together in a pram. How could they even fit? She squeezed her eyes shut, trying to dispel the image. As they passed through the sulphurous cloud around the gasworks, she felt a lurch of nausea.

As they neared the bottom of Great College Street, she tried to distract herself by singing 'If Ye Love Me', which was nothing without the harmonies. To her surprise, her mother joined in, but even two voices weren't enough to stop the song sounding terribly weedy.

'Oh dear!' said her mother. 'Tallis is twitching in his grave.' Hannah smiled, surprised. These flashes of her mother's larkiness were few and far between.

They were now at the bottom of Great College Street. Like much of the area, this was a piano district, and the street was lined with factories, hoists patiently waiting outside the large windows for the working week to begin. In fact, the largest place on the street actually produced playing cards; the reek of sulphur from the gasworks was replaced by a sweet inky smell that reminded Hannah of Fleet Street. And at the top of the road sat Camden Town station, behind which, according to Mrs Oliver, was the murder scene.

Hannah knew that her primary motive in coming this way was morbid curiosity, and she should acknowledge that, rather than try to dress it up. Yet, she felt there *was* something else driving it, perhaps particular to her, after her expedition yesterday to Crossfield Road. She had stood at the spot where this whole awful business had ended for P.H. Now, she was drawn to where it had begun.

Yet again, she wondered: how could it possibly be that in just a little over twenty-four hours, all this had happened? A body found. The victim identified. A dead baby discovered. The suspect arrested. A *woman*. Two people's lives gone; several more shattered and changed forever. It was as if the story was unfolding in a different time frame to normal life, sped up like a zoetrope.

Approaching the station, the buildings lining the road became smaller and more domestic, factories replaced by ordinary terraced houses and shuttered shops. Just ahead of them, an omnibus pulled up and disgorged several passengers, including a large, middle-aged woman. As the bus moved on, the woman remained where she was on the pavement, glancing around, clearly not sure where to go. As the Teales passed by, she called to them.

'Where's Priory Street?' She spoke in a blunt Cockney accent. 'Where *she* lives.'

Hannah felt a little detonation in her chest. Mrs Teale, meanwhile, had on the patient smile she reserved for the poor and chaotic.

'I believe Priory Street is just up there, behind the station,' she said, pointing.

'Just there?' repeated the woman, looking over.

'Wait,' said Hannah, seizing the opportunity. 'I'll show you.'

'It couldn't be easier,' said Mrs Teale. 'Just straight on past the station—'

'It's fine, I don't mind,' said Hannah over her shoulder, already trotting to catch up with the woman. 'I'll see you at home.'

Without looking back, Hannah reached the woman, who gave a grunt of surprise at her unsolicited companion.

'It's just up here,' said Hannah superfluously.

Within half a minute they had reached the road, the station just opposite. It was too busy to cross immediately, and so they waited awkwardly for a gap in the traffic. Overhead, on the railway bridge, a man was suspended from a rope, brush in hand, giving the finishing touches to a newly pasted advert, a cure for chapped hands that replaced the one for toothpowder that had been there for weeks. The woman stared fixedly ahead, intent on her mission, not wishing to chat. She had tarnished skin and unnaturally black hair, dyed so dark it had a bluish tinge.

Opposite, people were pouring out of the station exit, and even from across the road the general air of excitement was palpable – Hannah was reminded of the scene at Hampstead Heath station on the days of the bank holiday funfair. When there was a gap in the traffic, the two women crossed over, and Hannah's companion immediately left her side, unceremoniously disappearing into the mêlée.

'This way!' shouted someone nearby.

'Priory Street?' cried another. 'Up here!'

The crowd was moving as one, streaming north past the station, but this army didn't have far to march. As Mrs Teale had said, Priory Street was very close, only a hundred feet or so away. It was a short, unremarkable terrace that Hannah had passed many times, the spot marked in her mind by the intimidating public house on the corner, which always seemed to be hosting a raucous sing-along. Approaching now, Hannah saw a crowd gathered at the top of the road, giving the impression that the entire street was packed to overflowing, but as she drew near she saw that the house at the focus of attention was just next door to the public house, and so the crowd was concentrated here.

Except for the fact that a policeman was stationed outside the front door, arms folded across his chest, Number 2 Priory Street was unremarkable. About twenty years old, three storeys high, flat-fronted with grimy stucco, a few steps leading up to the front door and, beside it, a small area enclosed by a black railing, in which sat a number of healthy-looking pot plants. There were nets at the lower windows, and behind them, the curtains were drawn, as they were in all the upper windows, too.

There was nothing to see, yet Hannah stared rapt at the house, as if something extraordinary or shocking would reveal itself. Around her, everyone else was doing the same. She felt validated in her curiosity, knowing that all these other people – many perfectly respectable-looking – had also chosen to come here on a Sunday afternoon.

Their conversations washed over her. 'Did you hear the woman's head was almost clean off?' 'And not a scratch on the baby . . .' 'Apparently, she's quite comely . . . no, not the victim, the murderess. The victim was plain and mannish, I hear . . .' 'It's the first magistrate's hearing tomorrow, down at Marylebone – will I see you there?'

Nearby, an enterprising boy was selling toffee apples, weaving through the crowd holding bunches of them overhead. She could hear the strains of a violin; perhaps someone had tumbled out from the public house, trying his luck at busking.

A sudden noise made her jump, and only then did Hannah notice that the railway sliced across the bottom of the street, running over a brick arch. In a few seconds the train had disappeared on its way west, the low-level thunder receding with it. Looking around the crowd, Hannah noticed a familiar-looking dog tethered to its owner a few feet away. It was a pug who was often snuffling around the gardens of Camden Square. His owner, Hannah's neighbour, noticed her, and the two exchanged smiles, but of a different kind from the ones they would on a normal day. They were embarrassed, but also collusive: *I won't tell if you don't.*

Hannah turned again to the house, to its unyielding façade. And then – incredibly – there was movement. A female figure appeared at one of the upper windows, drawing back a curtain to peer out before pulling it closed again. A wave of excitement passed through the crowd, and Hannah, too, before it dawned that of course this woman couldn't be *her*. She – Mrs Pearcey – had been arrested and was currently in a cell somewhere. This must just be a neighbour.

The sighting of the figure, producing that intense, brief

thrill, served to break Hannah from her trance. The crowd she was part of now seemed less a congregation of like-minded souls than a mob of prurient ghouls, grossly over-excited by proximity to gore and evil. Surely, she was better than this.

Head bowed in shame, Hannah retreated, pushing her way through the crowd. Once clear of them, she allowed herself one final glance back at the house and then paused in her tracks. A familiar man was on the front steps, talking to the policeman. It was Winston Ovilry.

Even from this distance, it was clear he was trying to win over the policeman, addressing him intently and waving his hands about. The policeman gazed at him impassively from under his helmet.

As Hannah watched, Ovilry seemed to give up, shaking his head as he returned to the pavement and made his way through the crowd towards Great College Street, just as she had done. She turned and started walking away, keen not to be spotted, but he moved quickly and was soon level with her. He glanced over and immediately recognised her.

'Well, hullo!' he said. 'I didn't think you were the sort to be here, gawping at the house of horrors.'

'I live nearby,' she replied primly, as if this excused her.

He nodded and smiled graciously, as if to say, *Yes, I'm sure you do*. He was shorter than she remembered – but then, in the tavern, he'd hardly been on his feet. He was dressed smartly again, in a dark-blue three-piece suit complete with watch chain, highly polished shoes, a tie-clip on his high collar and a silk handkerchief in his breast pocket. No pencil behind the ear for him. He looked like he was off to run a bank, not grease up to a policeman outside a murder house.

'Where is your fiancé, by the way?' he said. 'He wasn't in the office yesterday.'

'I don't know,' she replied, pleased to be keeping Cosmo's secret from Ovilry, then belatedly remembered his cover story. 'Oh, yes – he said something about visiting an old friend, going walking up a mountain somewhere.'

Ovilry wasn't interested. As she talked, he couldn't keep still, lightly bouncing on the balls of his feet, his gaze flitting around.

'Were you disappointed that this wasn't the work of the Ripper?' she asked him.

'Not at all!' he said, looking at her again. 'Well, perhaps for a tiny moment, at first. But, you know, I'd almost say that this is a better story than the return of the Ripper. A *female slasher*! Women poison, but they're hardly ever violent like this.'

'Are you interviewing people already?'

He nodded. 'The upstairs neighbour said she didn't see anything but heard a commotion and noticed the baby's pram blocking the hallway. But it's not enough. It's not an exclusive. Everyone's talking to her. Look.'

He gestured to the edge of the crowd, where Hannah saw another smart young man talking to a short, drained-looking woman. By 'everyone', then, Ovilry meant other pressmen – and now he'd pointed this one out, Hannah spied what might be more of them among the rubberneckers: young men with darting looks, scanning the crowd, scribbling away on tiny notepads hidden in the palms of their hands. She noticed several other men on the sidelines drawing rapidly in sketch books balanced on their forearms, glancing up at the house every few seconds. Illustrators for the papers, she guessed.

'Where is she – Mrs Pearcey?' she asked Ovilry.

'Kentish Town Police Station.'

'Was it you who got inside the mortuary on Friday night?'

Ovilry smiled and shrugged: *Yes, of course.* 'My luck's run out, though. That policeman won't budge. Shame. A description of the murder scene would be most winning. Apparently, she did it in the kitchen. But hey ho, etcetera.' He held up his notebook. 'Must go and write this up. Give my regards to your energetic fiancé.'

Hannah said goodbye and watched as Ovilry trotted down Great College Street towards the station. She should have moved, too, but she didn't. Instead, she looked back over at the house and thought of this woman, this Mrs Pearcey, currently held at Kentish Town Police Station. And Hannah *could* vividly picture the scene, because she had been at the station herself, on the night of Mr Teale's accident, after the inspector had knocked on the door at Camden Square to break the news.

She and her mother had been placed in a little room off the station's lobby, which wasn't a cell but might as well have been, with its clammy cream brick walls and hard chairs and tiny, barred interior window through which they could clearly hear the slurry, self-pitying tones of a drunk being reprimanded at the desk outside. And then, of course, there was the inspector's wife, Mrs Sawtell, with her bland expressions of female sympathy, but unable to stifle her own discomfort with her hip.

This memory now connected with her sighting of Mrs Sawtell, just the other day, from the top deck of the bus on the way to Fleet Street. The poor woman still limping, several years later.

A thought took hold. Hannah kept looking towards the house, but now her breathing was suspended as the idea started to unfurl.

She knew, immediately, that she mustn't overthink this. No working through all the possible consequences. If she did that, it wouldn't happen. She just had to act.

She threaded her way through the crowd to the house and, without breaking stride, took the steps up to the front door.

'Hullo,' she said to the policeman, with a quick smile. 'I've been sent to collect some belongings for the prisoner.'

Her tone was the one she used to address the fishmonger: friendly yet brisk. The policeman was young, with a moustache that was too thick for his slight face.

'Sent by whom?'

'Mrs Eileen Sawtell,' she replied, and then, when he didn't immediately respond, she continued casually, 'Her hip is giving her trouble, and she asked me to come instead.'

She resisted the urge to say more – to entreat and persuade as she'd seen Ovilry do from afar. Instead, she just cocked her head, hoping she was communicating suppressed impatience. She felt hundreds of eyes on her; the crowd had gone quiet as they strained to hear what was being said on the doorstep.

The policeman's eyes were barely visible under the lip of his helmet. *Come on, come on*, she thought. Then he nodded and raised his hand, but instead of placing it on her shoulder and arresting her for blagging, he leant over and pushed the front door open. Just like that.

Behind her, the crowd stirred and murmured. Coolly, Hannah nodded her thanks and stepped across the threshold.

The moment she was inside, the door was pulled firmly shut behind her.

The slam brought sudden darkness and an abrupt cut-off from the hubbub outside. And with it, her earlier poise was ripped away. Adrenaline bubbled up and overflowed, like boiling milk in a pan. Trembly and nauseous, she clutched at the wall to keep herself upright, and listened to the sound of her erratic breathing.

As her eyes adjusted to the dimness, she saw that she was in a narrow hallway. Ahead of her, to the right, was a staircase going up. Straight on, the hallway led to a closed door. On the left were two more doors, also closed. On the wall to her right hung a foxed, frameless mirror and a print – some sort of brown landscape. Beside the door stood an empty coat stand. There was a faint whiff of mildew.

It could not have been a more ordinary space, where the most dramatic thing you'd imagine happening would be someone shaking out their umbrella. But Hannah recalled what Ovilry had said, about the baby's pram blocking the hallway, and had a powerful sense of its bulky presence. She even found herself pressing up against the wall to accommodate it.

Then, a startling sound from above: scraping, as if someone was moving a chair on the upper floor. Her heart juddered, even though she knew that the house was divided into several lodgings, and there were other people living here. She had seen one at the window; Ovilry had talked to one outside. She felt another thump of alarm, because she didn't know which of these rooms belonged to Mrs Pearcey. What a disaster to get it wrong and burst in on innocent neighbours, cowering in their rooms. It would instantly uncover her.

Had Ovilry mentioned which floor she lived on? Hannah tried to remember, but her thoughts had scrambled in her panic.

Calm down, she instructed herself. *Quickly!*

What did she know? That the murder had taken place in the kitchen. In Camden Square, and the other houses she was familiar with, the kitchen was situated in the basement. But – and she thought back to the view of 2 Priory Street from outside, the little front area covered in pot plants, the lack of a cavity – this place didn't have a basement.

In that case, the kitchen would be on the ground floor. But this didn't necessarily mean that Mrs Pearcey lived there. Presumably all the occupants of the house shared the kitchen. So, it was possible Mrs Pearcey and her victim came down to the kitchen from the upper rooms, perhaps to have a cup of tea . . .

Come on! She must act. In a sudden, decisive move, she stepped towards the first door to her left, turned the handle, pushed it open and slipped inside.

With its curtains drawn, the room was almost as dark as the hall, but Hannah could see that she was in a front parlour. She had been in poor people's homes before, but only the *really* poor, on slum visits with her mother, where there was a foul bucket in the corner and the floor was covered with drying matchboxes, so that every step you took risked damaging the inhabitants' pathetic livelihood. This room was in a different league, with the trappings of respectability. Hannah made out the shape of an armchair, and then an upright piano against the wall, its lid closed. She walked closer, and noticed the indentation on the piano stool, suggesting the piano was well played. She peered at the music, propped up on its stand: Schumann's *Forest Scenes*.

Hannah shivered. She herself played this — in fact, it was what she had performed at her engagement dinner at Milton Terrace. Then she told herself off; the piece was so common, every second woman in London must have it in their repertoire. She mustn't be silly about things.

Near the window was an aspidistra, caught by a thin shaft of light from where the curtains didn't quite meet. The plant's leaves shone as if they'd been polished. Outside the window, she could hear the hum of the invisible crowd just a few feet away — that crowd she'd just been a part of, shifting and snorting like the horses in the railway stables. On a little side table beside the chair sat a candle and a couple of books. Hannah bent close to examine them: one was a penny romance titled *A Bride in Belgravia* and the other a slim volume, *Bradshaw's Complete Anglo-Spanish Phrase-Book*. Hannah picked up the phrase-book and opened it; inside was inscribed, in clumsy italics, *From Your Eternal Cherished Partner.*

She carefully replaced the books and straightened up. On the wall opposite the window was a set of double doors, slightly ajar, leading into the adjoining room. Hannah went through, expecting to find a back parlour, as was the layout at Camden Square, but instead found herself in a bedroom. Of course — this was an apartment, not a house. This room was far better lit than the front one; the window here looked onto a small back garden and its curtains hadn't been drawn. Hannah noted striped wallpaper; a single bed with a rose-coloured eiderdown; a rather scratched dresser; a cabinet. A black shawl hung from a nail beside the door. There was a strong scent of mothballs. The room was in disarray, the bed linens rumpled and drawers open, disgorging clothes, and revealing glimpses of flowery sprigged lining paper. Hannah presumed this mess was a result of the police search; judging from the front parlour, Mrs Pearcey was houseproud.

Slowly, Hannah walked around the small place, mentally logging details. On the dresser sat a small screen, decorated with a paper collage of butterflies, birds and cherubs, cut from magazines. A trinket bowl on the dresser contained a few small effects: a plain ring; the stub of a pencil; some hair pins. Beside it sat an unmarked glass jar, its lid undone. Inside was an unctuous white substance – home-made cold cream, she guessed. A sheet of pink blotting paper, shiny from use, lay discarded beside it.

The search can't have lasted long in here, Hannah thought. This was not a squalid, or unrespectable life – just a meagre one. Hannah couldn't see any evidence of a man's belongings at all. Despite her title, Mrs Pearcey appeared to live alone.

Among the tangle of dark garments on the floor, Hannah spotted a chemise and a stocking, bunched up just like hers were when she didn't bother smoothing them out. Perhaps Mrs Pearcey did have her slovenly moments after all. The fireplace grate hadn't been swept, and there was a fair build-up of ash. On the wall above hung a framed picture, a shampoo advert featuring the requisite golden-haired, pensive-looking child, which also looked like it had been taken from a magazine. On the mantelpiece sat a few cheap china ornaments, the kind one might get as a souvenir on a day trip. A miniature porcelain shoe; a dog; some glued-together seashells. A mug commemorating the queen's jubilee. Propped up among them, displayed as reverently, was a creased business card.

She picked it up to examine it more closely. It advertised a furniture-removal service in Castle Road, Kentish Town, and on the back was written, in crude capitals, FOR GIGGLE-MUG. Carefully, she replaced it.

Seeing something draped over the bedhead, Hannah moved towards it. It looked like a shawl, but when she reached out to touch it, she recoiled at its unusual softness. It was a sealskin. The tip of her finger traced the fur back and forth, velvety in one direction, coarser in the other. She was familiar with sealskin made into muffs and jackets, but had never seen a full pelt like this, opened up like a kipper. Her finger reached an interruption in the fur and, peering closer, she saw that the skin had two holes in it, marking where the animal's flippers had once been. Suddenly repulsed, she retreated from the bed.

Come on, Hannah told herself again. She was here to gather information and must be quick about it. Should she open drawers and search pockets? No. Even if others had done so before her, it felt too invasive. Besides, she had a vague sense that, were she to be caught by the police, she would be in more trouble if they found that she had actually interfered with the woman's belongings.

She crouched down to peer under the bed. A chamber pot and some boxes, and then, a familiar object caught her eye. It was a magazine: one of the *Princess* series that Hannah herself read. Not only that – pulling it out for a closer look, Hannah saw that this edition was from the previous month. Hannah had read it.

Of course, Hannah also kept her magazines under her bed, secreted under the mattress. But her copies were hidden because her mother would disapprove, whereas this one, Mrs

Pearcey's, was splayed as if it had just slipped from her hand as she fell asleep or been carelessly kicked under the bed while tidying up. Hannah supposed she was just the sort of woman these publications were aimed at and would have no reason to hide it.

Despite being published recently, the magazine looked well read, pages worn and spine broken. The main story was entitled 'A Fatal Promise', the text accompanied by an illustration of a dark-haired woman in a wild state being restrained by a man in evening dress. The plot was just the usual convoluted formula centred on the tussle between forced marriage and true love, with lots of altercations in drawing rooms. Its only distinction was that the wilful heroine had a man's name: Bertie.

Hannah and Mrs Pearcey played the same piano piece. They read the same magazine.

Hannah straightened up and found herself facing a small wall mirror that hung beside the dress cabinet. She looked at her reflection for a moment, her eyes dark and glistening, cheeks flushed. A faint bellow came from the direction of the street, reminding her of the crowd outside. How long had she been in here? Three minutes? Longer? She had no idea. She hadn't even been into the kitchen yet, the scene of the crime.

She opened the bedroom door and entered the hallway. The closed door to her left, which must lead to the kitchen, was just a few feet away. But as she faced it, she was overcome with sudden, profound trepidation. Her heart battered at her chest, and she heard herself make an odd gurgling sound. The front door behind her, and the fresh, free world beyond, pulled at her like a magnet.

She made herself step forward until she was in front of the innocuous, white-painted kitchen door.

Only when the door had swung open did she realise she had been holding her breath; now, she exhaled deeply. At first sight, the kitchen could not be less remarkable. Like the other two rooms she had seen, it was a cramped, low-ceilinged space, modestly furnished but all in apparent order. The walls were painted custard yellow. On the right was a small range and beside it a built-in cabinet piled with tableware. Opposite her was an open door, through which Hannah glimpsed a sink. The scullery. On the wall to her left, a window looked out into the yard, its green blind pulled up. In front of it sat a small round table, clean but with a couple of old circular burn marks from a pot, and three wicker chairs. There was the very faintest trace of cooked fish in the air.

Hannah moved into the middle of the room and looked around more closely. Above the range, a shelf held a red teapot and a chipped glass vase. A colander hung from a nail on the wall, some of its little holes clogged from use. On the ledge of the dresser, beside a pile of plates, sat half an onion. Its exposed side was brown and tired, as if it had been cut a few days before. Beside it stood a full cup of tea. Hannah dipped the tip of her little finger in the pale-brown liquid. Stone cold. Then, she recoiled as what looked like a white worm bobbed to the surface; it took her a moment to realise that it was an extinguished cigarette.

Next to the scullery door sat a sewing machine and a dress stand, with a tape measure draped over it. Ah, thought Hannah – perhaps this woman lived by her needle. Through the window, she could see the small garden, half paved, half lawn. Some well-tended dahlias and geraniums in pots. The privy.

It was so quiet back here, the sounds from the street muffled. Hannah was struck with a profound sense of aloneness, adrift from the rest of the world. *Snap out of it*, she told herself.

She kept looking around. At her feet was an ordinary rag rug. At first, she hadn't registered it, but glancing down at it now, something about it seemed wrong. Crouching down, Hannah saw that a section of it was missing, and the remaining fibres were oddly stiff. She leant down and sniffed it. Paraffin. That was odd.

Frowning, she straightened up, and now, as she looked around the room again, it was as if a veil had been lifted. With escalating unease, she realised that there was something unusual about two panes of glass at the bottom of the window, partly obscured by a chair. Moving closer, she saw that they were smashed. She noticed that the chair was broken, its wicker seat caved in. And then – her insides clenched – she saw that there were dark speckles on the wall around the window. Her gaze skated frantically over the yellow paint as, with a sense of mounting horror, she registered more and more of these tiny dark-red marks. It was like when the ladybirds infested her bedroom in winter – once you'd noticed one, you started to see them everywhere.

Bile rose into her mouth, and she stepped backwards into the middle of the room. This little kitchen wasn't just the stage for the modest, solitary life of Mrs Pearcey, who had used half an onion for her dinner. Now, there was another presence here – a woman with the initials P.H., who was sitting at the table on a not-yet-broken wicker chair, drinking a cup of tea and chatting to her host, all the while listening out for her baby, who was asleep in a pram in the hallway. And then, something terrible had happened, right here, where Hannah stood.

Her chest felt as if it would rip open from the pressure of her heart. She turned and ran out of the kitchen into the hallway, and in a second was at the front door, pausing just long enough to take a deep breath, before turning the latch.

Stepping out onto the doorstep, she stopped short, wincing at the brightness. A sea of faces had turned to her, hushed and expectant, as if she were a performer bursting onto the stage at the Alhambra. She closed her eyes for a moment to compose herself, and when she opened them, there before her was the policeman.

'I was beginning to think you'd been bumped off yerself,' he said. He had removed his helmet and was roughly rubbing his hair. Now Hannah could see how tired he was. 'Only that?' he added, with a downward glance. 'What is it?'

Hannah looked at him, confused, and then followed his gaze to her left hand, which she saw was clutching the magazine. She hadn't realised she had taken it into the kitchen. It was tightly rolled up, as stiff as a baton in her fist.

'Oh,' she said, trying to hide her surprise. She unrolled it so he could see the cover.

'Lot of fuss for a magazine,' he went on. 'That's all she wanted?'

In her rush to get out of the house, Hannah had forgotten her story about collecting belongings for Mrs Pearcey, but it seemed that she had inadvertently backed up her own tall tale. This stroke of luck galvanised her; she was no longer a terrified, stammering girl, but a cool, artful blagger.

'She was in the middle of reading it apparently,' she replied casually. 'Said it'll keep her calm.'

'Let's see how calm she is as she's led to the noose,' replied the policeman, replacing his helmet. His eyes hidden again, he was back to being impenetrable.

Hannah raised a wry eyebrow – *indeed* – and slid the magazine into her pocket, before flying down the steps. Her feet barely touched the ground. Weaving through the watching crowd, not meeting the curious gazes, she was almost at Great College Street when she felt a tap on her arm. She yelped and turned to see one of the newspaper men she'd noticed earlier. His pad was out, pencil poised.

'Will you tell me what you saw inside?' he said, rather desperately. 'Do you know Pearcey? Please let me interview you.'

She shook her head, and kept walking onto Great College Street, feeling a sense of pleasure at this little moment of power, as well as charitable pity for the young man, who lacked a story when she had pulled off such a coup. If only Cosmo could see her now!

Turning left onto Camden Road, she started to run, and kept up the pace all the way home, pounding the York stone in her unsuitable boots, as if charged by a supernatural force. Only when she reached the steps of her house did she pay the price, bending double and gasping for air.

Once recovered, she went inside and flew straight up to her bedroom, calling hello to her mother in the drawing room as she passed. In her room, she hid the magazine under her mattress, alongside her own copy. Then, she took her wedding notebook and, lying on her stomach on the bed, wrote down everything she remembered from Mrs Pearcey's home. Like a house remover making an inventory, she started with the big things, the likely evidence of the crime that the newspaper would want: the horrifying ladybird speckles of blood; the smashed windowpane; the broken chair; the sticky, sawn-off rug. Next, she recorded minor details that weren't horrifying in themselves but spoke of Mrs Pearcey's domestic life. The polished aspidistra. The piano. The collage screen. The home-made cold cream.

She didn't write down everything. Initially she noted down the sealskin draped over the bed, but then the image of the unsettling flipper holes came back to her. She paused, then, and heavily crossed it out. It felt too private, too unsettling a thing to reveal. Neither did she mention the tiny, everyday domestic details – the half-onion; the cold cup of tea with its soggy cigarette end; the clogged colander. Such things surely weren't worthy of inclusion in a newspaper.

She didn't mention the magazine.

Two hours later, she laid down her pen, her account complete. Now, she must get it to a newspaper – but how? Time was of the essence, she knew, but it was Sunday afternoon. She couldn't think of a plausible excuse for her mother that would give her the time and space to go down to Fleet Street at this time of day. Come to think of it, were newspaper offices even open on Sunday?

It would have to wait until tomorrow. She'd go first thing.

Hannah slid the notebook under the mattress but didn't immediately retract her hand from the tight space. Instead, her fingers searched until they found the edge of Mrs Pearcey's copy of the magazine. She pulled it out and, lying back on the bed, started to read 'A Fatal Promise'.

After a few lines, the whole story came back to her. Bertie

Verner, the impoverished young heroine, was of course captivating – *tall, slender, curly masses of chestnut hair, soft fair skin and the great, liquid, dark-grey eyes with their sweeping lashes that are laughing, pathetic, arch – what you will – by turns or all at once.* The hero of the tale was Captain Errol Cameron of Lochmohr, possessor of *finely cut features, very brilliant, dark hazel eyes and a soft brown moustache shading his upper lip.*

He, too, was a hoary old stereotype, of course – dashing, commanding, yet understanding of female yearnings and emotional volatility. Nonetheless, Captain Cameron had had an effect on Hannah when she had first read 'A Fatal Promise'. She supposed they all did, these romantic heroes: unconsciously or not, each played his part in forming her idea of what a man, and what love, should be.

It really wasn't that odd that she and Mrs Pearcey owned the same story – there must have been tens of thousands of copies printed. Yet, she couldn't help but feel unnerved by the connection. That she and this woman had inhabited the same fictional world, for the twenty minutes it took to read that silly story, and had felt and thought similar things.

Hannah opened another page at random. It was the part where Captain Errol Cameron of Lochmohr had found his twin flame in Bertie, but was bound in an unwanted betrothal to the undeserving Miss Juliet Marling. *Lochmohr stood still a moment, with heaving breast and glowing eyes. His heart was thrilling with the touch of the girl's soft lips; the wine of a new life was mounting through his veins. Alas for him! For his honour was pledged to another woman! Ah, Bertie! You need never know what such sacrifice as this means. A woman can break the chain as if it were a thread; a man – if he values his honour – must lay down far more than his life for a promise once given.*

'Hush, child, hush! I cannot make Juliet Marling my wife when my every thought, my whole soul, belongs to you!'

She turned over again. The climactic scene had the heroine confronting her love rival, Juliet, in a genteel drawing room. Bertie had a flashing temper. After Juliet belittled her, *Bertie sprang forward with a bound like a panther, and grasped Juliet's wrist, with a grip so fierce and strong that the other was powerless.*

'Stop!' she said; 'stop! Or I will kill you!'

Hannah shuddered histrionically. Tempers lost; two women fighting. Was this not eerily similar to what appeared to have happened in the kitchen of 2 Priory Street?

Stop, she told herself. People did not commit murder because they were inspired by the melodrama of a penny magazine. If so, every second parlour in London would be speckled with blood.

She turned the page, away from the story. 'Some Ways of Cooking Fresh Boiled Beef'. An article about the precious jewels in the treasury of the Sultan of Turkey. *At the French seaside places, dresses of crimson foulard, with small white spots, will be much worn this year.*

She turned again – and stopped. There, nestled in the pages, was a scrap of paper with handwriting on it.

Without removing it from the page, as if it were a fragile archaeological discovery, Hannah peered at the paper. It appeared to be a shopping list, written in blue ink in a round, girlish hand.

Sprats
Treacle
Pots
Bread

Onions
Bacon?

The innocent banality of it! Extraordinary that the same mind that one minute was occupied with whether or not to buy bacon could the next be consumed by a murderous fury.

'Miss?'

Hannah started. Gwen was standing in the doorway.

'Tea's downstairs. Mrs Teale is there.'

As the maid turned back down the stairs, Hannah shut the magazine and slid it back into its hiding place before following her down to the drawing room. It was only half an hour later, as she sat absently holding a cup of tea, her mind spooling over her extraordinary day, that her mother mentioned that they should probably invite her Aunt Bea to the wedding, and Hannah remembered, with a start, that at that very moment she was meant to be in Kensington, being taught how to fold napkins by her future mother-in-law.

5

We would say to our girls one earnest warning word about what they may not do. They may not do anything of those things that make them imitators of men; they may not try to break down the God-appointed fence which divides their department in the world's great workshop from the department of men.
— Girl's Own Paper

The next morning, just before 9 a.m., Hannah boarded the bus to Fleet Street. Today there were no feathers in her hat; rather, she had on her drabbest outfit, the one she'd wear to go to the butcher's. She grabbed the last free seat on the bottom deck where she sat hunched in her coat, as inconspicuous as possible. Yesterday, when she realised she had stood up Mrs Walters, she'd written a lavishly apologetic note explaining that she'd been taken ill and had fallen asleep, and begging to rearrange for the following weekend, when she'd surely be recovered. It was very unlikely that Mrs or Mr Walters would happen to spot her in town, but she felt uncomfortable enough about the lie — coming so soon after her illicit trip to Priory Street — to want to lay low just in case.

Besides, she was on a covert mission.

The omnibus colluded to make her invisible, stopping every few hundred yards to let on even more workers. By the time it reached Mornington Crescent, it was packed, the seated Hannah swallowed up in a sea of coarse black coats. Some people lit pipes, and soon smoke had filled the confined space. A man was squashed so close to her he was almost sitting in her lap, the tip of another's umbrella pressed into her foot and, just behind her, close to her ear, someone sniffed loudly over and over again. Hannah stared out of the window as the bus jerked and rattled its way to the City.

Would it be sensible, she wondered, to resist the draw of the familiar, and instead try to sell her account of the murder scene not to the *Star*, but to another publication? She thought of the vast bales of blank paper she had seen being carted ceremoniously down Fleet Street, needing to be filled. She would surely be welcomed at any of the dozens of newspaper offices there. Going elsewhere would reduce her chances of bumping into Winston Ovilry or that other bookish chap whose name she had forgotten, and having to come up with yet another lie about what she was doing there.

No. She would bear the risk and stick with the *Star*. After all, when Cosmo came out of the asylum and she told him what she had done, he might think it disloyal of her to have gone to a rival. Besides, she could not deny a little pleasure at the thought of Ovilry's face draining at the sight of her story in the *Star*'s pages, losing his *savoir faire* at the fact of someone else on his turf.

She got off at the Royal Courts of Justice and hurried up Fleet Street; now she was part of the street's distracted, harried workforce. At the *Star* building, she didn't hesitate before bounding up the steps, remembering her success at Priory Street yesterday, when she didn't allow time for nerves to bite.

The building's double doors were heavy, their brass handles highly polished, as if hers were the first fingermarks of the day. Inside, the lobby was built to impress, with a pale-pink marble floor, a high ceiling hung with ornate gasoliers and a large gold clock positioned above a mahogany desk. Bulging mail sacks lined one of the walls, each one the size of a well-upholstered man. The walls were hung with framed posters of the front pages of the *Star*.

But the space was oddly deserted. She'd been expecting the same sort of buzzy uproar as in the Cock Tavern, but this scene was quite the opposite. In fact, the only other person there was the man behind the desk, who had short, neat grey hair and epaulettes on his jacket shoulders, and who was observing her with polite interest. Hannah remembered the time she had turned up for a party on the wrong day and found the hostess drinking hot chocolate in her armchair. She approached the desk, her earlier certainty draining away.

'I'd like to see the editor, please,' she said hesitantly. Inside her pocket, she clutched the folded sheets of paper.

'I'm afraid Mr Grieves isn't in yet,' he replied in a deep, theatrical tone. 'One never spots him before midday, as a rule.'

'Oh.'

'He works until the early hours, you understand, and a man has to rest.'

'Is there anyone else I might see?'

'May I ask your matter?' the man said, his fingers tented on the desk.

'I have a story,' she said, and then, because that sounded feeble, added, 'an exclusive one.'

The man smiled and cocked his head.

'What kind of story?'

His tone was one of polite interest, but she just knew he was expecting her to reply, *I've invented a new recipe for oxtail soup*, or, *I've composed a tale for children about a family of squirrels* – or, indeed, *I've written an account of my recent trip to Pompeii.*

'It's about the murder that's on your front page,' she said. 'And on all the other front pages in London.'

The man blinked at her and laughed. How pleasing it was to surprise him!

'In that case, there'll definitely be someone in to see you,' he said. He glanced to his left and raised his voice a notch. 'Sam?'

Following his look, Hannah was surprised to see that there was someone else in the room: a scruffy chap leaning against the mail bags, apparently asleep, his cap pulled over his eyes, like a farm boy on a haystack. He levered himself upright and yanked up his cap.

'Would you be so kind as to take this lady over to editorial?'

The desk man's tone was so unctuously polite that Hannah realised this must be a little game between them: the gentleman deferring to the messenger. The boy nodded and darted towards the double doors to the right of the desk, holding one open for Hannah but not looking at her. She followed him through into a spacious, unlit and seemingly unoccupied room. The space was dominated by a long table with some twenty chairs around it, a few pulled out at an angle, as if the occupant would be back any minute. The table was laden with piles of newspapers, and as they passed by she saw they were not just editions of the *Star*, but publications from all over Britain and the world. The *Rochdale Observer*, the *Liverpool Daily Post*, *Allgemeine Zeitung*, *Le Petit Parisien*, the *New York Herald*. Around the edges of the room were ranks of high, slanted desks; most of them, too, held an open newspaper. The odours of ink and dust and stale tobacco hung in the air. The place had a similar sort of vacated feeling as York Road had on a Sunday.

The boy led her to the far end of the room, and she saw that it wasn't entirely deserted. One of the tall desks was lit by a small gasolier, and standing at it was a man in his shirt sleeves, fiddling with a pipe. The boy pointed at the man, then turned on his heel and dashed off, all without having said a word.

Seemingly unsurprised, the man looked over at Hannah.

'May I help you?' He was much older than Cosmo; his large, square face was pallid and his wispy hair slicked to one side. A half-eaten slice of pie sat on his desk.

'I have a story for your paper,' she said, confidently this time.

The man cocked his head, inviting her to go on but still concentrating on patting down his tobacco.

'It's about the murderess – the alleged murderess – Mrs Pearcey. The one who killed the mother and child. I went into her house, you see.'

Now, the man's bearing changed. He laid down his pipe and looked at her properly, his face lifted, like a tired cut flower placed in a vase of cold water.

'Go on,' he said. Even his voice now had a different, deeper timbre.

'Well, I went inside yesterday. The murder scene. By myself. And I wrote this.'

Hannah produced her folded account from her pocket and handed it to him. He opened and read it, his head bowed to reveal a bald spot, and when he straightened up, his eyes were gleaming.

'Well, this is rather interesting. How did you get in?'

Hannah hesitated, and then said simply, 'I was a blagger.'

The man looked at her for a second, bemused, and then chuckled. His gaze returned to the page as he reread her account.

'How much do you want?' he said to her, and, when she didn't immediately reply – she should have thought about this! – he answered his own question. 'I might be able to stretch to five shillings.'

Was this a good rate? She had absolutely no idea. If only Cosmo were here to guide her.

'Six?' she replied tentatively.

The man shrugged his acquiescence. Hannah smiled, triumphant. This was the first time anyone had paid her for anything she had produced – unless you counted the penny someone had once given her for an embroidered thimble-box cover at a school sale.

'Thank you,' she said.

'Thank *you*!' he replied. He stepped over to another desk

and unlocked a drawer, from which he drew six coins. Then he paused and, instead of handing them over, laid them down on the desk.

'One more thing,' he said. 'I was going to do this for you, but actually I think it'll be useful for you to see how it's done.'

He picked up Hannah's article, holding it so they could both see it.

'This is good material, but it needs to be rephrased. At the moment it's far too quiet and measured. You need to inject some drama, grab readers around the throat.'

'Oh!'

'Here, you see, you've written, *Entering the narrow hallway, one can't help but recall the fact that the victim's pram was stationed here during the fateful afternoon . . .* Well, that should be phrased like this: *On entering the hallway at 2 Priory Street, I was immediately overcome with a profound sense of horror. In the half-light, I sensed the presence of a bulky pram, and lying within it a babe, cheerily gurgling, innocent of the fact that soon her brief life was to be snuffed out in the most unimaginably vicious fashion. A shudder runs through me, but far worse is yet to come . . .*'

'Oh!' said Hannah again. The man continued scanning the paper.

'And here: you write that her lodgings are *modest but well kept*. We're going to change that to *Mrs Pearcey's lodgings were pitiful, wretched and dismal and imbued with a sense of most sinister oppression*. You write that the lower windowpane was broken – how about, *it was a jagged hole through which the breeze eerily whistled*? Don't say the rug smelt of petrol; it *reeked* of it. You mention that the rug had been cut; why not add that this is *highly suspicious*? It's nice you compare the blood splatters to ladybirds, but it's not strong enough: the blood splatters were *as vile and horrifying a vision as one could ever conceive . . . A back-room slaughterhouse in Seven Dials might come close.*'

'Gosh,' she said. 'I see. It's all very . . .'

'It's all about going for the jugular,' he said. 'Much like your woman Mrs Pearcey did.' He smiled and folded up the paper. 'Ovilry will be most put out by this.'

'Is he the reporter following the case for the paper?' Hannah asked innocently.

The man nodded. 'Our official correspondent. Done a perfectly decent job so far – but he didn't get this. I greatly look forward to telling him when he's back from Marylebone later.'

'What's happening in Marylebone?'

'It's a magistrate's hearing today,' he said. 'For Pearcey. Now, what name shall we put on it? I didn't catch—'

'Oh, no,' said Hannah quickly. 'No name. Please. Can you just say *from our correspondent*, or something like that?'

Again, the man gave her a quick, bemused glance, before shrugging. 'As you wish.'

Hannah heard a noise and, looking around her, saw that another man had entered the room and was hanging up his coat on a peg. In fact, there were several men in here now, putting away their things or already at their desks. The working day was beginning.

'If you have anything else like this, don't hesitate to come back,' the man said as Hannah made to leave. 'And if you can't get to the office, feel free to write to me.' He handed her card bearing the name Mr Alfred Summersdale, which she put in her pocket beside the six shillings, then said goodbye and hurried back out to the lobby. A man entering the building held open the door for her, and she hastened down the front steps and merged back into the anonymous, fast-moving flow of Fleet Street.

When Hannah was young, the area of Marylebone carried a great charge, as it was the home of Madame Tussauds. The waxwork showroom had not only been a site of wonder, but the primary source of her history education. Whenever she heard mention of, say, the Magna Carta, it was the Tussauds' tableau of Runnymede meadow that came to mind: the blazing gas lamps overhead replicating the afternoon sun; the mannequin of King John with his poised quill, looking trapped and irritable. Then there were the dramatic set pieces, like the elephant hunt in India, and the unnervingly intimate groups of the current child Royals, little wax demi-gods in their lace collars. Even the ostensibly dull scenes, such as a meeting of ecclesiastical representatives or the endless ranks of French nobility, thrilled her.

Of course, Mrs Teale had always refused to pay the extra sixpence required for entry to the Chamber of Horrors. Once, though, on Hannah's birthday, she compromised by paying the supplement for the museum's other special adjoining room, where possessions that once belonged to Napoleon were displayed, including the camp bed on which he died.

Staring at the bad waxwork on the rickety, faded canvas stretcher, the young Hannah had asked, 'Do you think the people in history knew they were in history?'

To her credit, her mother had known exactly what Hannah meant.

'I'm sure people like King John and Napoleon did,' she replied. 'Important people who signed decrees or won battles. And perhaps people who did things that went against the grain. But I think most people were too busy thinking about what they were going to eat that day to think about how the future would view them.'

Now, fifteen years later, Hannah approached the Tussauds showroom once more. A long queue of people waited for entry, and, passing by, she caught snatches of conversation – they sounded largely from the countryside and overseas. 'Goodness, what a queue!' 'Is it even moving?' *'Apparemment la guillotine de Robespierre est ici . . .'* 'Quite dear, isn't it, for a whole family . . .'

Hannah paused to ask the doorman the way to the Police Court. He gestured west and told her to turn left at Seymour Place. Continuing along the Marylebone Road, buffeted by the traffic funnelling into the city, Hannah felt small and vulnerable. The road had always been somewhat busy, but she remembered people living on it, in a normal way, with plants on their doorsteps and children and pets wandering freely. Now, although there were still a few residential buildings left, interspersed between the new red-brick hotels and institutions, it was essentially a thoroughfare, given over to vehicles.

When she reached the junction with Seymour Place, she didn't need any further directions to the courthouse. Halfway down the street, outside an elegant, pale-stoned building, a crowd had gathered, its thrum audible even from this distance. It was as if the scene from Priory Street had been transplanted wholesale to this more formal location. Indeed, as Hannah approached, she spotted among the sea of heads the unnaturally black hair of the taciturn woman from yesterday, the one whom Hannah had accompanied to Priory Street.

As Hannah slipped into the crowd, the awkward feelings that had brewed during her journey – her sense of prurience; nervy anticipation at what lay in store – began to dissipate. Look, she was not alone in her interest – there were so many people here! As at Priory Street, the crowd was mostly female, but there were some men at the front, near the courthouse door, their clothes and stance signalling that they were here to work rather than spectate. Among them, of course, was Winston Ovilry. He was wearing the same blue suit as yesterday and talking to another man, but Hannah noticed that he was not giving his companion his full attention; rather, his gaze skated over the crowd as he spoke.

She quickly turned away, so as not to be seen by him, and for good measure crouched down, pretending to scratch her ankle. At that point, when she was still bent down, she heard a voice cry, 'Hold up, here she comes!'

Hannah quickly straightened, losing her balance in her haste. A Black Maria had turned the corner onto Seymour Place and was slowly making its way towards them. A sound like a whooping gasp, a collective intake of breath, passed through the crowd, as it parted to allow the carriage through. Straining for a view over the heads in front, Hannah could see only the top section of the windowless, highly polished carriage. It came to a halt and immediately the back door opened. The crowd went dead still and silent. First a policeman emerged, and then a woman. Her head was bowed, so all Hannah could see was her dark hat. Another policeman appeared and took her other side, and the two of them whisked her into the building. The journey from carriage to courthouse door took all of ten seconds. Seamlessly the crowd followed, funnelling into the building behind them. The scene reminded Hannah of a wedding – the woman arriving flanked by men, face covered, remote and untouchable, an object of fascination.

Hannah joined the procession inside and found herself in an ornate lobby, like that of a theatre. She couldn't see the prisoner and could detect from the lack of tension in the crowd that she was not in the vicinity. She must have been taken to another room. People now seemed to be focused on an ordinary-looking door off to one side, roughly forming a queue in front of it. How did everyone know what to do?

Joining the back of the line, Hannah watched as Ovilry marched straight to the front, opening the door just wide enough to slip inside. Pressmen must be allowed in first.

'Didn't we sit beside each other at Adelaide Bartlett?'

The woman in front of Hannah had turned to address her. Her accent was Cockney. She was thickset, with bushy strawberry-blonde hair, and was wearing an almond scent, as strong and sweet as marzipan.

'I don't believe so,' replied Hannah, although the name was somehow familiar. Within a moment it had come to her: Mrs Adelaide Bartlett was the subject of a famous murder trial a few years back.

'No. I certainly was not there,' she added firmly, wishing to differentiate herself from these ghoulish tourists. Then, worried that she'd been rude, she continued, in a softer tone, 'But I'm curious to see how the criminal justice system works. It's important for us women to understand the mechanics of these things, even if we don't actively participate in them, don't you think?'

The woman looked at her askance. Her wide, handsome face was heavily powdered, as if she really was off to the theatre.

'If you say so, pet,' she replied, and winked.

Hannah looked away and shifted on her feet, now uncomfortable in a way she hadn't felt outside. The woman was right to tease her: she could no longer claim to be a curious passer-by. She could tell herself she was here in a journalistic capacity – except that she wasn't, was she? She wasn't one of those smart, hungry young men who had already slipped through the door to take their seats at the press table. In this place, with its marble floor and varnished walls, the unsavoury excitement of the crowd was now amplified.

Still, she didn't quite have the will to leave. A part of her hoped that she wouldn't be allowed in and so the matter would be decided for her. There appeared to be at least thirty people ahead of her in this rough queue – surely there wouldn't be seats for all?

A few minutes later, the door finally swung open and the queue pressed in, and Hannah was ushered into the courtroom along with them. At first, all she registered was a mass of seated people. Every place in the room appeared to be occupied. But then the woman with the marzipan perfume tugged at Hannah's coat sleeve, indicating a space at the end of a bench.

'Come – we can both squeeze on.'

Hannah smiled her thanks and followed her.

'I'm Moira, by the way,' said Hannah's new friend, before

instructing the woman already on the bench to move up. After she grudgingly shifted an inch, Hannah and Moira sat down, squashed together in a space barely big enough for one. But they were lucky to get a seat at all. Other spectators stood at the back of the room, three persons deep.

Now, Hannah could properly take in the room. It was largish and grand, with high ceilings and curlicued plasterwork, and half of its floor space divided up by mahogany panels. In fact, the scene reminded Hannah rather of the Foundling Hospital Chapel concerts – the audience packed into hard wooden pews; the bubbling anticipation – although the crowd here was far less smart. At the front of the room, on a platform, was a large desk flanked by cabinets filled with important-looking leather-bound volumes. Near to the desk were several raised wooden compartments. A clock above the desk told her it was coming up to 1.30 p.m.

All the women were in the spectator seats, while the great majority of the men were in the panelled compartments or front benches – they must be legal men, clerks and the like, and, of course, pressmen. Ovilry was up there, on a bench that appeared to be reserved for his kind; she watched his shoulders dip as he leant over to whisper something to his neighbour. Instinctively, she sank into her chair, but she didn't really think he would spot her; his mind must be on his job, and she was just one in a mass of women.

Hannah got the impression that most of her fellow spectators had done this kind of thing before. They all seemed far more relaxed than her, as she shifted about, twisting her hands in her lap.

'So,' said Hannah, turning to Moira, 'what will happen today?'

Despite her father's job, she realised she knew next to nothing about the legal system. Her father had never talked to her about his work, and such things weren't taught at school.

'It's a magistrates' court,' replied Moira, pleased to be an authority. 'And this is a hearing to decide whether there's enough evidence for the case to go on to a criminal court. There'll be a coroner's inquest, too.'

Hannah was about to ask another question when a court official entered and motioned to the room to stand.

'Here we go!' said Moira happily, as they got to their feet.

'Mr William Major Cook,' the man announced.

A door at the back of the room opened to reveal a compact man, who stepped forward and planted himself at the desk without acknowledging his audience. Hannah could see a balding head and small wire spectacles on an old, fleshy face. He examined the papers on the desk and then glanced up at the clock.

'Could you please bring in the prisoner?' he asked the official.

The official nodded and glided to another door to the left side. His was the only movement in the room, which had fallen into a tense silence. Hannah felt a squeeze on her hand, and, surprised, looked down to see that Moira had taken it and was grasping it tightly, seemingly unconsciously, her gaze fixed on the door.

The door opened and a policeman entered, followed by a young woman, her head lowered as it had been outside the courthouse. She'd removed her hat, and her hair showed a reddish tint as it caught the light. She was wearing a dark, shabby dress and shawl. Pauper's clothes. She was led to one of the compartments near the judge's table, and it was only when she was in position in the dock that she finally raised her chin and looked straight ahead, so her face was fully visible. The moment managed to be both understated and dramatic, the silence in the room broken by the furious rasping of pencils on paper as the journalists and illustrators on the press bench captured their impressions.

Mr Cook coughed, and then said, in a flat tone, 'The prisoner, Mary Pearcey, is charged with the wilful and felonious killing and slaying of Phoebe Hogg on the twenty-fourth of October past, and further charged on suspicion of the killing and slaying of eighteen-month-old Phoebe Hanslope Hogg.'

Moira leant over and said, in a loud whisper, 'She looks so hard and *masculine*, doesn't she?'

Hannah could only stare at the prisoner.

Mrs Pearcey defied easy categorisation. She appeared neither tall nor small, strongly made nor delicate. Was she attractive? She had blue eyes and good skin and thick hair, but there was something off about her mouth. The jaw was weak, and her top teeth stuck out slightly, making her look as if she was constantly biting her lower lip.

Hannah craned for a better view and then froze. She had seen that mouth before. That face. It belonged to the woman Hannah had talked to on Prince of Wales Road, on Saturday morning. She had been carrying a pile of newspapers with headlines about the murder, with Cosmo's paper on the top, and that wonky mouth had been whistling a tune.

'Loosen up a bit, love,' came a whisper beside her, and she looked down to see that it was now she who was tightly squeezing Moira's hand.

★

Hannah was so thrown that she barely registered the first part of the proceedings; all her mental and emotional energy went into digesting the fact of her close encounter with the woman in the dock. She felt a compulsion to stand up and declare their meeting to the court – but to what end? What did she have to contribute to the evidence? What could be extrapolated from Mrs Pearcey's behaviour on the Prince of Wales Road, the day after the murder? Her whistling might have been a sign of insouciance or arrogance, but perhaps it was an unconscious nervy habit. She'd given Hannah one of her newspapers. Was that out of kindness, or because she was proud of her notoriety? *Help me*, she'd said. Did she know her actions were catching up with her? Or had she become entangled in a living nightmare through little fault of her own?

There's nothing for you to worry about, she had told Mrs Pearcey that day. Now, in the courtroom, Hannah closed her eyes to register the innocent irony of that moment.

The usher called a witness to the stand: a Mr Frank Samuel Hogg. A square-shouldered, brown-haired man sitting on the front bench slowly got to his feet and stepped up to one of the elevated compartments. Addressing the court, he announced that he was the husband of the dead woman and father of the dead child, and that he had been married for two years. Hannah felt a shift in the room; the collective realisation that, since the child was known to be eighteen months old, she must have been conceived out of wedlock. Then Frank stopped and started noisily weeping. Hannah and the court silently watched this pathetic sight for a long moment, before the magistrate spoke up to ask him, more gently, if he would run through the events of the day of the murder.

Frank Hogg roughly rubbed his face with his palm, ostensibly collecting himself. He was decidedly unprepossessing, Hannah thought, with stiff, greasy-looking hair like a pigeon wing, a prominent brow and small eyes too close together. He started to speak, and in contrast to his display of histrionics, the voice that emerged was flat and nasal, and his account unengaging. He gave pedantic levels of detail about what sounded like a wholly unremarkable day – saying goodbye to his wife and child before going out to work as a furniture remover – that made it hard to engage with his account. Hannah tried to listen, but her gaze was fixed on Mrs Pearcey. The prisoner turned to look at Hogg, before leaning forward to whisper something to a rather debonair man sitting directly in front of her. Her lawyer, presumably. Then, Mrs Pearcey straightened up and gave her attention back to the magistrate. As Hannah watched, she reached up with her left hand to stroke the back of her neck.

It struck Hannah that she had never before been in a position to observe someone like this. She supposed she judged people all the time, by their dress and the way they spoke and how they behaved – the normal, everyday things that everyone surely noted. But never had she been invited to inspect someone, standing silently on display before her. And not just anyone, but someone accused of doing something truly horrifying, the worst thing a human being could do.

A policeman stood up, interrupting Hogg's droning testimony, and addressed the magistrate.

'Sir, could I suggest that you ask Mr Hogg whether he had

called at the prisoner's house on the night of the murder?'

Obediently, the magistrate turned to Hogg.

'Do you know the prisoner?'

'Yes, she had been very friendly with my wife,' replied Hogg.

'Did you go round to the prisoner's house on the night of the murder?'

'Yes,' said Hogg. 'I went there a little after ten o'clock on the twenty-fourth of October, shortly after I got home.'

'Did you find the prisoner at home?'

'No, sir.'

'You did not see her?'

'No, sir,' said Hogg. 'I found that she was out, and so left a note for her.' He rubbed his hand over his beard.

Hannah felt on high alert, sitting tall and still, like those African mongooses in London Zoo. It wasn't just her; the atmosphere in the court felt charged, as if proceedings were inching closer to some important truth. The magistrate continued.

'When did you see the prisoner last?'

Hogg replied that he had seen her briefly on Wednesday afternoon, two days before the murder.

'Had there been any quarrel between the prisoner and your wife?'

'No.'

There was a pause. Hogg looked down at his hands, clutching the rail of the witness box. Again, the policeman stood up and said something to the magistrate, which Hannah couldn't catch.

'Do you have a latch key to the prisoner's house?' the magistrate then asked.

Hannah glanced at Mrs Pearcey. She was looking at Hogg with a steady, unreadable gaze, her mouth ajar, as if on the verge of answering the question herself.

'Can you speak up, please?' asked the magistrate.

'Yes,' Hogg said, so softly he could barely be heard.

Then, to Hannah's surprise, the magistrate told Hogg he could step down. The tension in the room abruptly deflated.

'Ooh, so they was clearly having a leg-over,' said Moira, too loudly, as Hogg returned to the bench. 'Him and her.'

Although Hannah had been thinking the same thing, she was embarrassed by her new friend's language and didn't know how to respond. Then, it was too late, because the next witness was called: the policeman who had interrupted and spoken to the magistrate during Hogg's testimony. His name was Inspector Bannister.

In the witness box, Inspector Bannister cut a far more impressive figure than Frank Hogg – admittedly, not a hard act to follow. Hannah thought he looked like a policeman from a picturebook, with good bearing and a fine black moustache; immaculately turned out, even though he must have been working all through the weekend. His account was also full of detail, but from him it came across as gimlet-eyed and thorough. He often referred to a notebook he held open in his hands. As he spoke, Mrs Pearcey didn't look at him, as she had done with Frank Hogg, but gazed towards the ceiling, front teeth grazing her lower lip.

Bannister described the events of Saturday, when he'd first met Mrs Pearcey. She and Frank Hogg's sister, Clara, had turned up at Kentish Town Police Station just after 11 a.m. Clara had told the policeman on duty that her sister-in-law and her baby had been missing since the previous day. Her brother Frank had grown worried and that morning, at his suggestion, Clara had gone round to Mrs Pearcey's home on Priory Street to see if Mrs Pearcey knew of their whereabouts. Mrs Pearcey had claimed that she had not seen the pair. Then, Clara said, they had learnt from the newspapers that a woman had been found slain in Crossfield Road. From the descriptions of the victim, she believed it might be Phoebe Hogg.

The newspapers. Hannah was again transported back to the Prince of Wales Road, some time after 10 a.m. on Saturday, when she had faced the woman now standing in the dock. Just the two of them. She thought of how Mrs Pearcey held the pile of newspapers, carefully, with both hands, like a full tea tray. Now, listening to the inspector's account of the day, she realised that their encounter had occurred just before Mrs Pearcey and Clara Hogg had gone to the police station. It must have been during one of her last minutes of freedom; a secret moment that occurred just before the beginning of the official account of the day; the account that was witnessed and was now being relayed in an open court, hastily scribbled down by journalists to become news in tomorrow's press, transcribed for the records to become the facts of the case forever more.

'I accompanied them to the mortuary,' Inspector Bannister continued, 'where the prisoner's behaviour struck me as strange.'

'How so?' asked the magistrate.

Bannister described how the coroner had drawn down the sheet covering the victim, so the two women could get a better look. The deceased's face had not been washed and was disfigured by purple, green and yellow bruises; her black hair was matted with blood and dirt. Her mouth was hinged in an unnatural way because of the deep cut to her throat. On viewing her, the prisoner became agitated, exclaiming, 'Oh! It's not her!' and trying to drag Clara away from the body, crying, 'Oh, don't touch it!' But when the corpse's face was washed, Clara Hogg positively identified the victim as her sister-in-law.

Mrs Pearcey subsequently calmed down, said Bannister, but her reaction had aroused suspicion. Wanting to keep her under observation, he agreed that the women should now go and inspect the child's pram, which had been found abandoned in St John's Wood the previous evening. While they were doing this, Bannister went to the Hoggs' home at 141 Prince of Wales Road to interview Frank Hogg. He was searched, and a latch key to 2 Priory Street was discovered on his person. When Clara Hogg and Mrs Pearcey returned from identifying the pram, all three were taken to the police station to be questioned further.

At the station, Bannister had said to Mrs Pearcey: 'I think it desirable to search your lodging. I suppose you have no objection?'

'Oh, no, not in the slightest,' she'd replied, handing him a set of keys. 'I should like to go with them because I don't think they'll be able to get in.'

By now it was 3 p.m. on the Saturday. Two policemen, Sergeant Edward Nursey and PC Parsons, accompanied Mrs Pearcey to Priory Street. In the kitchen, Sergeant Nursey pulled up the window blind high enough to observe that two panes of glass were broken. Mrs Pearcey explained that she had smashed them while trying to catch mice. When he pulled the blind fully up, and his eyes adjusted to the light, he noticed droplets of blood on the glass and surrounding walls and ceiling.

Again, Hannah felt something of an out-of-body sensation, overcome with a visceral memory of being alone in that cramped kitchen, with the half-drawn green blind. The smell of paraffin and the stiff, cut-up rug. Half an onion and that clogged colander. The caved-in chair. Those speckled walls . . .

On the stand, Bannister continued. When asked about the blood in the kitchen, Mrs Pearcey again claimed that it was due to her killing mice. '*Killing mice! Killing mice! Killing mice!*' Bannister said, quoting the prisoner, the repetition of the phrase in his even, quiet tone underlining the ludicrousness of the excuse, and the nervousness of the person who made it. His colleague, Sergeant Nursey, said to Mrs Pearcey, 'I believe you saw Phoebe Hogg yesterday,' and now the prisoner changed her story. 'I know,' she replied. 'I should have told you before this. She called about six o'clock and asked me to take care of the child. She wanted some money, but she did not come inside.'

After this exchange, said Bannister, Nursey left Mrs Pearcey in the parlour and went to telegraph Inspector Bannister. Alone with the other policeman, PC Parsons, Mrs Pearcey talked about 'poor dear dead Phoebe', whom she 'loved so much', and the baby who was 'just beginning to prattle, oh so prettily'. Then she sat at the piano and played some popular tunes, 'rather well', before telling Parsons the same feeble story she had told Nursey: that Phoebe had called the previous day asking for money and for Mrs Pearcey to mind her child, but Mrs Pearcey had refused. As for the blood marks in the kitchen, she now claimed that they were from a nosebleed on the Thursday evening.

'Huh!' said Moira, *sotto voce*. 'A nosebleed like a fire hydrant!'

At this point, Bannister himself arrived at Priory Street. He inspected the kitchen and picked up the poker by the fireplace. Its end was oblong, and he remembered the coroner telling him that the murder weapon would be something that could strike a hard blow and had an oblong shape. The poker had traces of blood on it. In a kitchen drawer, he found two large carving knives, one stained with blood, and he also discovered a black skirt and white apron, both of which appeared to be bloodstained despite attempts at washing them.

Bannister went back into the front parlour holding the knives and poker. Mrs Pearcey was sitting in an armchair, and when she saw the items she began to whistle to herself. She had, he said, a pose of 'perfect indifference'.

The whistle, thought Hannah, with a shudder. She wondered if it was the same tune Mrs Pearcey had been whistling on the Prince of Wales Road, just earlier that morning.

Bannister continued his methodical report. When he told Mrs Pearcey he was going to arrest her, she had jumped out of the armchair. 'You can arrest me if you like,' she said. 'I am quite willing to go with you, but I think you have made a great mistake.'

Now, for the first time since he started speaking, Bannister paused for long enough for the room's gaze to turn to Mrs Pearcey, looking for a reaction to this damning account. The prisoner did not oblige, holding her dull stare, as unreactive as a Tussauds dummy. Hannah wondered whether the inspector had deliberately paused to allow the court to consider whether her inertia was an illustration of that 'perfect indifference' he had seen in her.

Bannister was not quite finished. 'One more thing I would like to add for the record,' he continued. 'Although the prisoner represents herself as married, she is not. Her real name is Mary Eleanor Wheeler. She had been living with a man named John Charles Pearcey, who came forward of his own accord yesterday. She likely adopted his last name for the sake of respectability.' He coughed neatly. 'And I would like to request the prisoner stay in remand. I have also taken statements from neighbours who will attest to seeing her wheel the pram from Priory Street on the night in question.'

The magistrate agreed to a week's remand and ordered an inquest for 9.30 a.m. the following morning, to be held at Hampstead Drill Hall.

Finally, Bannister stepped down and the debonair man seated in front of the dock got to his feet. He introduced himself as Freke Palmer, the counsel for Mrs Pearcey. Hannah was struck that this was the first time he had spoken during the proceedings. Did he not want to interrogate the witnesses? But perhaps that wasn't the form at this initial hearing; all the cross-swording would come at a later date. Now, all Palmer asked was that his client might be able to exchange her workhouse clothes for clothing more befitting a woman of her station. The magistrate granted his request, and then banged his gavel, abruptly bringing the hearing to a close.

Hannah looked at Mrs Pearcey. Now, for the first time in the proceedings, it appeared that the prisoner was properly surveying the room, turning in her chair to inspect those who had been inspecting her. Hannah missed a breath as the woman's slow gaze reached her – would Mrs Pearcey recognise her, and pause? Perhaps even exclaim? But her gaze passed smoothly over Hannah, without the faintest ripple of recognition. Hannah felt a shameful pulse of disappointment. But of course, she told herself, she wouldn't be recognised: Mrs Pearcey's memory of their slight, meaningless encounter would surely have been obliterated by the crushing events before and after it. Besides, she didn't *want* to be singled out by this monster, did she?

Two policemen approached Mrs Pearcey's chair; she stood up and was led out. As the door closed behind her, the room erupted into noise and action. The legal people urgently conferred as they gathered up their documents. The pressmen self-importantly rushed out of the room, clutching their pads, Ovilry leading the pack. Meanwhile, the spectators loudly shared their thoughts as they gathered up their things and moved towards the door.

'*Juicy*,' exclaimed Moira happily. 'I don't like the look of the bloke, do you?' She picked up her bag and got to her feet. 'They can only try her with one murder at a time. I wonder which one they'll go for, mother or child? Whichever has the strongest evidence. They barely mentioned the child so sounds like the mother, doesn't it? Guess we'll find out more at the inquest tomorrow.'

'I won't be there tomorrow,' said Hannah, over her shoulder, as she was already moving towards the door. 'Nice to meet you, though. Thank you for the seat.'

She made her way through the crowd in the lobby, pushing open the courthouse doors and emerging onto the pavement just in time to watch the Black Maria reach the end of the street, turn the corner and disappear east onto Marylebone Road. Half running in its wake were the group of pressmen – heading back to their offices, she supposed, to turn the hearing into a story. Hannah recognised Ovilry's broad back among them.

She should go, too, but she remained standing there, deep in thought or sensation, intensely aware of the smells and sounds around her. Manure, smoke, the smell of soap from the washhouse next door to the court. The scraping of wheels and jolting carts passing over cobbles; whinnies and barks; the yells and clunks of building work; the cries of costers. Just the unremarkable impressions of an average day. But if even half the evidence presented that afternoon was true, Mrs Pearcey would never again be able to stand on a pavement and experience such things.

Hannah watched a woman heading to the washhouse, her laundry in such a heavy and cumbersome bundle that she was reduced to dragging it behind her. Just as one would go about disposing of a corpse, thought Hannah. Was she now condemned to find horror in even the most banal of scenes?

The church bells began to chime three and broke the spell. She started walking towards Marylebone Road, on her way home, in the wake of the Black Maria.

Back at Camden Square, Hannah quietly let herself in with her latch key. From the hallway, she could hear the sounds of the girls preparing dinner downstairs. At this time, her mother would most likely be reading in the drawing room. She crept up the stairs, hoping to get to her room without being noticed, but as she reached the first-floor landing, she heard a sharp, 'Hannah?' followed by another female voice, crying, 'Oh, thank goodness!'

Her mother had company? Hannah's heart sank. She would not be able to avoid some polite chit-chat. Fixing on a smile, she pushed open the door.

The smile did not last long. There, in her usual chair, was her mother – and sitting next to her, in Hannah's spot, still wearing her coat and an elaborate purple hat, was Mrs Walters. At the sight of Hannah, Mrs Walters leapt to her feet.

'There she is!'

Hannah's first thought was that something terrible had happened to Cosmo, and she cried, 'Is he all right?' But even as she said it, in genuine alarm, a part of her recognised that jumping immediately to such a conclusion was a result of the dark world she had been inhabiting that day, where people did horrific things to each other.

'Cosmo?' replied Mrs Walters. 'It's *you* we're worried about, my dear.'

Hannah closed her eyes as the picture fell into place. Mrs Walters had received her note about being ill, got worried, and rushed to the house. The two women had been sitting here, trying to make conversation for goodness knows how long. Would her mother have hidden the fact that Hannah's grave illness was news to her? Had Hannah been caught out or might she be able to . . .? Eyes still closed, she felt for the support of the door frame.

'Oh, you do look very pale,' she heard Mrs Walters say. 'Are you faint?'

Hannah realised that she really was. Her head felt horribly tight, as if it had been clamped, and she couldn't seem to draw air down into her lungs. It was as if the minor shock of

Mrs Walters turning up here had broken a seal, and made her body finally register all of the major tremors of the past few days. Someone touched her arm, and she realised that both women were now at her side. Supported between them, she drooped.

6

Is there any work done by men as useful as that which is done by a good mother? The work of the Prime Minister or chief servant of England is no doubt very great, but it may be that the best mother of England, whoever she is, serves her country more.
— *Girl's Own Paper*

Hannah woke to near-pitch darkness, and almost immediately understood, from the contours of the mattress and scent of the linens, that she was in her own bed. Her hand flew to her chest — yes, she was wearing her chemise.

Almost as quickly, she realised something else. She was not alone in the room. From somewhere close to her head came quiet, regular breathing.

She didn't gasp or scream, but rather lay still for just a moment and then, in one sudden movement, pushed herself out of bed and to her feet, braced to run or attack.

'Who's that?' she said, intending to sound strong and fearless, but her voice came out as a croak.

'Only Ivy, miss.'

Only Ivy. Hannah's muscles softened, and she sat heavily back down onto the bed.

'Sorry,' she said, between deep breaths. 'Why are you here?'

'Your mother asked me to sit with you while she went out.'

Hannah fumbled on the cabinet for the box of matches and lit one of the candles beside the bed. Ivy was sitting on a chair a couple of feet away. She was taking her vigil duties seriously, sitting unnaturally straight, hands piously clasped.

'Sorry for being rude,' said Hannah. 'I'm just disorientated. What time is it?'

'A bit past seven.'

'On Monday?'

Ivy nodded.

'What, so I've been asleep for' – in her befuddled state, she couldn't do the calculation – 'for a little while.' She frowned as earlier events floated back to her. Lying about being ill in a note to Mrs Walters. Selling her article to Fleet Street. Going to court in Marylebone. Seeing Mrs Pearcey. A worried Mrs Walters turning up in Camden Square.

'You're unwell, miss,' said Ivy patiently. 'Don't you remember?'

'You know, I don't think I am that ill.'

In fact, she felt fine: alert and clear-headed.

'Where is my mother, do you know?' Hannah continued.

Ivy shrugged. 'Maybe out with her . . . *unfortunate women.*' Hannah wondered what Ivy and Gwen called the slum women in private. 'Is there anything you need?'

Hannah considered.

'Actually, there is something,' she said. 'Would you nip over to Camden Road and get me a copy of this evening's *Star*?'

'The newspaper?'

'Yes.'

'Oh. I was thinking more of a cup of arrowroot, or a compress . . .'

'And if that woman is selling sausage rolls by the station exit,' Hannah continued, 'could you get me one?'

Ivy left, and a minute later Hannah heard the front door slam. She reached again for the matches and then lit the other candle to create enough light to read by.

She was startled to see that her story was on the front page of the paper. *INSIDE THE HOUSE OF HORROR!* shrieked the headline. Actually, the story itself was on the inside page, because the whole front page was taken up with illustrations. Sitting up in bed, the paper laid out on her lap, Hannah studied them as she wolfed down her sausage roll. The main picture showed the exterior of Number 2 Priory Street, and the crowds gathered outside. Dotted around this, in smaller panels, were a succession of more dramatic scenes telling the story so far: the discovery of Phoebe Hogg's body on Crossfield Road, followed by the pram in St John's Wood, and the baby in some scrubland on Finchley Road. There was also a line portrait of Mrs Pearcey in court, her expression distant and unreadable, illustrating that 'perfect indifference'.

The portrait was actually a fair likeness, Hannah thought, with the prominent eyelids and sloping nose and that small, fleshy lower lip, although as the mouth was firmly closed the artist hadn't captured her overbite – her most distinctive feature. How very odd – and thrilling – it was that she, Hannah, was one of the few people who knew the real truth behind these crude line drawings reproduced all over London. Who had actually seen the flesh and blood, the bricks and mortar.

She licked her fingers clean of grease and turned the page to her story, holding the paper closer to the candle.

Our correspondent managed to get exclusive access INSIDE the house where these most horrible deeds occurred. Their chilling account now follows . . .

As promised by Mr Summersdale at the *Star*, her story had been luridly transformed, her original words whipped up, like an egg into a meringue. This impression of her visit to Priory Street — read by candlelight, like a ghost story — felt divorced from the murky truth of how it had really felt to be there, alone in Mrs Pearcey's world. The truth was a more complicated and unsettling blend of dread, isolation, revulsion, prurience, intimacy and banality that was difficult to describe, or to digest.

Reading it, Hannah was reminded of a time, years ago, when she and Emily had made crude cosmetics from things around Emily's house — burnt cork, carmine food dye, flour — and Emily had insisted Hannah not look in the mirror while she applied them to Hannah's face. When she was finally allowed to see herself, Hannah was greeted by an apparition with slugs for eyebrows, heavily powdered cheeks and smeary red lips, as if she'd been eating a jam tart with her hands tied behind her back. The person in the mirror was based on her. It wouldn't exist without her. But it wasn't *her*. Reading this story felt the same.

So, it wasn't the truth — but it *was* wildly effective. The hyperbolic language swept her up in the ghastly thrill of it all and, by the end, when the author crept out of the house *thoroughly disturbed, and certain that a peaceful night's sleep was now a luxury of the past*, she felt quite wrung out.

The article ended with a statement that the inquest would take place at the Drill Hall in Hampstead, at 9.30 a.m. the next day.

Hannah remembered her pious response when the marzipan-scented woman had mentioned the inquest in court yesterday: *I won't be there.*

Well, she thought now, *a woman is allowed to change her mind, isn't she?*

'Hannah?'

The thin, dark shape of her mother filled the door frame. Hannah instinctively swept the paper onto the floor, where it lay splayed and visible, but as Mrs Teale approached the bed, she didn't appear to notice it. She sat down in Ivy's vacant chair, her features just visible in the candle-light.

Hannah laughed. 'Am I on my deathbed?'

'I hope not,' said Mrs Teale. 'But I was worried.'

'Really?'

'Well, you're never ill. If you were the sort of woman who constantly fussed about your health and thought she was too delicate for the world, it would be different. But you're not, so, yes, I was concerned.'

'Well, I'm not ill now, I don't think,' replied Hannah. 'Or if I was, I feel completely better.'

'What do you think it was? A sort of fainting fit?'

'I don't know,' said Hannah. 'But I feel perfectly fine.'

After a pause, Mrs Teale said stiffly, 'How are the wedding preparations coming along?'

Hannah smiled with surprise.

'Thank you for asking,' she replied, as formal as her mother. 'I think it is under control. I've got Emily's dress; I just need to get it altered.' As she spoke, she felt a wash of guilt about quite how far the wedding had been from her mind recently, and then, immediately in its wake, came the realisation that she had just given herself the perfect excuse to get out of the house for the inquest. 'I've actually got an appointment with Mrs Didier tomorrow morning.'

'I'll come with you,' said Mrs Teale.

'Oh, no,' replied Hannah quickly. 'That's such a lovely thought, but I wouldn't bother. She'll just take some measurements. And all the while that silly dog nipping at your ankles . . .'

'I'd like to.'

'Please,' said Hannah, her tone too desperate. Why now, of all times, was her mother trying to be close? 'I'd much prefer to do this part alone. It'll be too dull for words.'

They fell silent. Hannah looked down at her hands lying on the eiderdown, at the glint of Gigi's ring.

'Of course, perhaps you'd prefer Mrs Walters to accompany you,' Mrs Teale said.

Hannah stared up at her mother, and instinctively pulled the eiderdown up around her shoulders, protection against this sudden change in weather.

'What do you mean?'

'Mrs Walters tells me you and Cosmo are going to live with them,' continued Mrs Teale. 'After the marriage.'

'Oh.' Hannah winced. She had forgotten about the meeting between the two mothers – all that time together waiting for her in the drawing room.

'I was going to talk to you, of course,' she said now to her mother. 'I'm still a bit in shock myself. Obviously, I'd really rather not . . .'

Hannah continued to blather away, explaining the situation with the inheritance. From what she could see in the semi-darkness, her mother looked genuinely hurt, her forehead pinched, flashes of that tight, unsuccessful smile. It was an expression of vulnerability that Hannah had never seen on her before and wouldn't have guessed she would ever see. She wanted to say, *Don't worry, all this is moot because we're going to have a place of our own – I'm seeing to it.* But of course, she couldn't, and in her fluster, she heard herself saying instead, 'Of course, we'd much prefer to live with you . . .' At that, she realised she must stop, before she made things worse.

The two women sat in silence for a moment.

'I was thinking, it's been a long time since I came to help at the refuge,' Hannah said. 'I'd like to. Shall I come along tomorrow?'

'That'd be nice,' replied Mrs Teale, appearing sufficiently mollified. 'I'm going there now, but I'll also be there tomorrow. I'll leave you to get some sleep.' She stood up, and at the door added, 'By the way, Will's downstairs, so don't be surprised.'

Hannah thought to herself: *My bar for being surprised is set quite high these days.*

When her mother left the room, Hannah picked up the *Star* from the floor and secreted it under her mattress, then blew out the candle and lay back in the darkness. She closed her eyes, but remained awake, buoyed by the fact of the article lying beneath her. Yes, it may have been rewritten, but it was still her doing. She felt quite amazed at herself. Only a few days ago, she had been thrilled by a two-line mention in the

Girl's Own Paper praising an account of her holiday. Now, she had done something unimaginably bold, gone where men had failed to access, and was being read by hundreds of thousands of people.

As the minutes went on, and she sank a little deeper towards sleep, darker thoughts intruded. She had the sense of a figure sitting in the chair, just by her head. One moment the figure was that of her mother, wearing that awful, pained expression; the next it bore the impassive profile of Mrs Pearcey, eyes glassy and mouth ajar. Then, somewhere behind them, barely visible in the dark corner of the room, was Cosmo, silently writhing in a straitjacket.

She opened her eyes and stared into the darkness. Her beloved, to whom she hadn't been giving nearly enough thought. He was locked in a madhouse! She should be consumed with worry for him; he should have been at the forefront of her mind. It was true that contributing towards their future life together had been the reason she started this Mrs Pearcey business – but it was also true that this motivation, and the fact of Cosmo's own money-making mission in Friern Barnet, had been somewhat buried under all the drama and excitement.

Cosmo, forgotten in the asylum. Her mother, hurt by the revelation of Hannah moving to Kensington. Now, guilt lay upon her, as heavy as a winter eiderdown.

Sleep was impossible. She lit the candle again, swung herself out of bed, got dressed and went downstairs. Her brother was sitting in the drawing room, clad in his tails, leafing through Mrs Teale's copy of *The Bostonians* without any real interest.

'Sis!' he said, putting it down. 'I thought you were at death's door!'

'But that wasn't enough for you to come upstairs to check on me,' she said genially. She was pleased to see him; it always took a while for Will's blitheness to become annoying. 'Why are you home?' she asked, sitting down.

'Going to the Gaiety,' he said. 'It's the opening night of my friend Cee-Cee's play.'

'Cee-Cee?'

'You don't know her. She's an actress!' he said proudly.

He reached for his hat, which was sitting on the side table. Under the overhead light, Hannah saw that the moleskin was looking a bit worse for wear, as if much handled by greasy fingers.

'What's the play?' she asked.

He frowned in thought. 'Can't remember, actually.'

'Can I come?'

He looked surprised, then gratifyingly pleased.

'Why not?' he said. 'When did we ever go out on the town together?' He hesitated. 'I won't be able to talk to you all the time, because of my friends, but if you don't mind that?'

'I would expect nothing more,' she said, smiling.

'Right, well, I'll go and find us a cab,' he said.

'And I'll get changed.' It was only then that she glanced at the little carriage clock on the mantelpiece. 'Oh, it's so late! Won't it have started already?'

'We're not going to the actual play,' Will explained, halfway out the door. 'Just the party afterwards.'

It turned out that the play was called *A Needle in a Haystack*, and Hannah and Will arrived at the theatre in time to see its audience emerge onto the Strand: a glamorous, strongly scented crowd of fur stoles and bright-white starched collars. Standing among them as Will paid the driver, Hannah overheard snatches of conversation – 'I quite enjoyed the song in the second half . . .' and 'Gosh, what did you think of that?' and 'Do you think there's a play in London in which the actors *don't* masquerade as the opposite sex?' – which made her think that perhaps it was just as well that they had missed it.

As the audience hailed cabs or hurried off down the Strand, Will led Hannah around to an alleyway at the side of the theatre, and in just a few steps she felt far away from the most glittering street in London. The alley smelt of urine and rotting vegetables, and was so dim she could only just make out the shapes of a couple of men loitering against the wall. There was one single source of illumination in evidence: a little way down, underneath a feeble, flickering lamp, was a scruffy entrance marked *Stage Door*. Stationed beside the door was another rather shifty-looking man, the worse for wear. As they approached, he straightened up, with some effort.

'Cee-Cee is expecting me,' said Will authoritatively.

The man was in no state to argue, even if he wanted to. Hannah followed Will down a corridor with brown, peeling walls, up the stairs and down another corridor, similar to the lower one, except this one was lined with doors, each with a hastily painted-on name. *Arthur Tilley, Victoria Summers, Betsy Alderswood* – and then, *Cecilia Leno*. Will knocked once, loudly, before pushing the door.

The action was like prising open an automated music box. Into the drab, quiet corridor burst a plume of jolly noise, bright lights and warm, smoky air, as if all the gay life of the theatre had been compressed into this one little room. There were perhaps twenty people inside, of both sexes, packed into a space not much bigger than a scullery. A couple were perched on chairs, but most were standing, one hand clutching a wine glass or champagne bottle, the other leaning against a wall or another person's shoulder. A handful turned to look at Hannah and Will in the doorway and then returned to their chatter – except for one man, who whooped, 'It's Willy!' and thrust out an arm to thump Will on the shoulder. 'Come in, for God's sake!' the man continued.

Hannah and Will obediently advanced into the room, although the space was so packed that once over the threshold there wasn't really anywhere for them to go without pushing.

A couple of the men were in conventional evening dress, like Will, but most looked flamboyant, as if they'd each been allowed to choose an item from a dressing-up box. One wore a peacock-blue suit; another a fur cape; another had a long velvet scarf looped over his shoulders. And here there were women. *Actresses!* Will pointed out Cee-Cee, but so surrounded was she by men that Hannah could only glimpse silky black hair and a thin, ivory-pale arm.

Now, Will pushed forward to join the circle around her.

'Cee-Cee!' Hannah heard him cry. 'How magnificent you were tonight! Such a privilege to see you up there on stage. Wouldn't have missed it for the world.'

Hannah waited for him to introduce her, but the circle around Cee-Cee swallowed Will up, and he didn't look back. Hannah retreated to the relative safety of the wall. She was wearing her egg-yolk dress, which now seemed horribly prim, and she noticed a dirty smudge on the skirt, picked up from the cab or the theatre. Head bent, she licked her fingers and rubbed at the silk. Why on earth was she here? Her cold little bedroom and a book didn't seem so unappealing now.

'You need a drink,' said a voice on her right.

Hannah looked over to see a woman she hadn't noticed until now, sitting on a chair against the wall. Her blonde hair was curled and laced with strings of paste pearls, and her small face was heavily painted. She was wearing what Hannah supposed was her stage costume: a doublet and stockings, her crossed legs on display. Beside her, a tall young man was leaning on the wall, with a thin little moustache and wearing an extravagant feathered hat, like a cavalier's. His eyes were closed, and a bottle dangled from his hand. The actress noticed Hannah looking curiously at him.

'He *doesn't* need a drink,' she said, and eased the bottle from his limp fingers. 'Now, a glass might be useful.'

The actress got to her feet. She was a similar height to Hannah. Up close, Hannah could see that under the paint, the woman had rather cherubic features. Along with her curled blonde hair, it gave an unsettling effect, as if she were the child star of a defaced Pears advert. Beside them was a narrow side table, cluttered with objects – unguent bottles and jars, a candlestick, a newspaper – and from it the actress picked up a glass, held it up to the light, squinted. Deeming it clean enough, she filled it with champagne from the man's bottle and passed it to Hannah.

Hannah thanked her and took a sip. The wine tasted half flat and too sweet; still, she took another, deeper gulp. Beyond the offer of the drink, the actress didn't appear to feel the need to chat with Hannah, preferring to look around the room, clocking the scene. The black paint around her eyes gave her the air of a watchful animal. Feeling she should say something, Hannah introduced herself.

'Dolly,' said the actress in return.

Hannah had never met a real actress before. They were regularly cast in the magazine stories, occasionally as a temporary role for a poor heroine who, desperate to support her aged parents, had taken to the stage as a last resort, and suffered repeated indignities before being rescued by the man who would marry her; or, more commonly, as a superficially alluring, deceitful creature in line for a comeuppance.

'Were you in the play?' asked Hannah stupidly.

Dolly gave the question the raised eyebrow it deserved and took a sip. 'Do you know why it's called *A Needle in a Haystack*?' she said.

'No!' said Hannah, pleased that they were continuing the conversation. 'Do tell me.'

'Because this little prick appears in it.'

The actress jabbed her elbow into the ribs of the man still dozing on the wall beside her. He started awake and stared at them both in confusion.

'Everything all right, darling?' he said, blinking.

Hannah laughed, more from shock than anything else. Dolly gave the man a challenging look, and Hannah realised she was in the middle of an argument, albeit a one-sided one, considering the man was comatose. She looked across the room to see a couple plastered together, rocking back and forth; it was a shockingly intimate moment, and she looked quickly away, back down at her skirt – the only safe place in the room. It was all desperately uncomfortable, but she also felt privately gratified that this evening was so far conforming to her wildest expectations of an outing behind the scenes at the theatre. Insouciant painted women; indecent writhing; risqué remarks; the terrible racket; drinking bad champagne out of someone else's glass.

'Will this happen after every performance?' she asked Dolly.

'God, no. Can you imagine? No. It's the opening night.'

'Did you enjoy it? Being in the play?'

Dolly shrugged. 'It's all right. Feeble script, but at least I can walk home.'

'Where do you live?' said Hannah, hating herself.

'Soho,' said Dolly, waving towards the West End. 'You know Kettner's restaurant?'

'No,' said Hannah. 'I mean, I think I've heard of it, but I've never—'

'Well, I live next to there.'

They lapsed into silence again. It was clear Dolly wasn't going to ask any questions herself.

'Is it difficult playing a man?' Hannah went on desperately, gesturing to Dolly's costume.

'Not at all,' replied Dolly. 'They are pretty basic creatures, aren't they? Hardly difficult to work out.'

Hannah smiled and nodded.

'Don't you think?' said Dolly challengingly.

'Well, I suppose everyone is different . . .'

Dolly gave her a pitying look. 'They are so easy to manipulate,' she said airily. 'I can make any man do whatever I want.'

They stood in silence for a few moments longer, Hannah horribly conscious of her dullness amid the shrieking crowd. She could tell she had lost Dolly's interest, failed the test, and felt caught in an unhappy space between feelings of annoyance at Dolly's self-absorption and lack of interest, and her own sense of inferiority.

The violin was getting louder and louder; where once it played a jolly tune, now it screeched discordantly, as if trying to stay one note above the pitch of the partygoers, whose laughing and chatter had slurred into one ghastly sound. Glancing around, she saw that another couple were now entwined in a corner, pressed hard into each other, her hands clamped over his behind, his dug deep into her hair. Or was it her behind, and his hair? She flinched and looked away, hot and mortified. Panic bloomed in her chest. What on earth was she doing here, in this sordid, deafening cupboard?

She looked over at Will and managed to catch his eye, but when she pointed towards the door he pretended not to see her and turned back to Cee-Cee.

A stocky young man with shoulder-length hair came bowling over and snatched up the newspaper from the side table, before pushing his way to the door. Dolly sprang after him.

'No!' she said. 'You can't take that. It's mine.'

The man turned back to her with a pleading look.

'But, Dol, we need it for the lav,' he pleaded. 'It's run out of paper.'

'Not that one,' she replied. 'I haven't read it yet.'

She reached over to him and plucked it from his hand.

When Dolly turned back towards her, Hannah saw that the paper she was holding was the *Star*. She couldn't resist.

'I wrote something in that paper,' said Hannah.

Now, finally, a flicker of interest, but only a flicker.

'What was it?' and then, before Hannah could answer,

she added, 'I'm afraid I'm only really interested in the murders.'

Hannah paused. How often did life provide moments such as this? In a few words, she could shock Dolly out of her blaséness. Such power, and such temptation! Even if she didn't admit to actually writing the article, she could at least lead Dolly into a discussion about the thrilling account of the crime scene at Priory Street.

Yet, something held her back. Yes, she wanted to prove to this superior woman that she was interesting. Yes, it would be gratifying to observe Dolly gasp over the Priory Street details, while hugging her little secret. But stronger still was her desire to get out of the party.

She turned to Dolly.

'Can you really make a man do whatever you want?'

'Pretty much.'

'Prove it then,' said Hannah. She pointed at Will, who had his back to them.

'Him, over there. Persuade him that it's time to leave.'

She could see Dolly was intrigued. 'Is that your lover?'

'Oh, no!' said Hannah quickly. 'Just my brother. But I want to go home.'

Dolly smiled. 'You and me both.'

Still holding her glass, Dolly pushed her way over to Will and laid her hand on his shoulder. Hannah watched him as he turned, annoyed, expecting it to be his tiresome sister, then his brow softened at the sight of Dolly. He bent his head to hear what she was saying. Watching his glazed look as Dolly whispered into his ear, Hannah realised quite how drunk he was. He must have been continuously pouring wine down his throat while in the Cee-Cee huddle.

Whatever Dolly said, it worked. Will detached himself from the group and unsteadily followed Dolly back to Hannah.

'Time to go, sis,' he said, his voice thick.

Dolly folded up her newspaper and tucked it under her arm, then raised her eyebrows triumphantly at Hannah. Hannah smiled her thanks, bade goodbye and supported her little brother's arm as they made their way downstairs, out into the alley and back onto the Strand. It was past eleven, and chilly now; her thin cloak wasn't nearly warm enough. Cabs went by but didn't stop. She waved at them, ever more desperately, as Will sat on the kerb, head bent.

'Where's your money?' Hannah asked him, and when he didn't reply she dipped into the inside pocket of his jacket and found a shilling, which she held out to the passing cabs like bait.

When eventually one stopped, she pushed Will inside before climbing in beside him. The cab pulled off and, safe now, she gazed out of the window. Those still out on the street appeared to be either intoxicated – shouting, stumbling, wheeling about – or taking advantage of the intoxicated. Opposite, Hannah watched a woman lead a man, almost bent double, into a door marked *Beds to Let*. Another man jumped out of a cab nearby and raced down the stairs into the basement of a nearby building, as if his coat was on fire. The theatres and shops might be dark, but the more Hannah looked, the more she noticed lights burning in high-up windows and heard the faintest strains of noise from somewhere. The sleazy nocturnal city. The inverse of polite daytime society. It had been a thrill for a brief moment, but she now just wanted to get home, retreat to her own world.

Once they had turned right at Charing Cross and were safely heading north, she relaxed somewhat.

'What did she say to you, that blonde actress?' she asked Will.

But she wasn't really expecting an answer, and when she turned to him, she saw that he was asleep. The cab jostled the champagne in her belly, reactivating it and making her feel horribly sick. Her eyes closed, too.

7

One way in which girls often thoughtlessly offend against good taste and good manners is by asking questions. Very few like to be examined as to their feelings, affairs or intentions, and believe me, no habit is more likely to render you unpopular. Mind your own business, and leave your neighbours to mind theirs.
– *Girl's Own Paper*

Hannah had plenty of reasons to travel up to Hampstead Village the next morning. There were several shoemakers up there; she could enquire about wedding slippers. She hadn't been up that way for a couple of years and knew the fields around the high street were being developed at a furious rate. It would be interesting to see all the changes. And then there was the prospect of a walk on Hampstead Heath. It was as good a place as any to while away a few hours, before heading down to Somers Town to help her mother, as promised.

She reached the high street just after half past nine, short of breath from the long climb from Chalk Farm and the brick dust in the air. Her timing was deliberate, to miss the shameful, exposing milling-about on the pavement outside the Drill Hall. She didn't know the venue, so asked a street sweeper, who directed her to an alley tucked away at the top of the high street, where she found a newly built institutional building with a knife-sharp steeple.

It appeared her plan to avoid the throng had been too successful. The street outside was empty, except for normal pedestrians. If this inquest had attracted a crowd similar to that of the hearing in Marylebone, they had all been fully absorbed into the building. The hall door was ajar. Tentatively, Hannah pushed at it, and found herself in a bare, empty lobby, facing a staircase. The place felt dead. She crept up the first flight of stairs, stopping at the landing. There were now several doors ahead of her, none of them marked.

All she could hear was some muffled street noise. Whoever was in the building must be now firmly, quietly ensconced in a room beyond one of those impenetrable black doors. Still, she lingered. On her right, the staircase twisted to continue up another flight. It was a tight turn and, standing still as she was, Hannah noticed that a small chunk had been chiselled from the side of the upper flight, to ensure that those running their hands up and down the banister of the lower one did not graze their knuckles. She was gazing at this thoughtful little groove when she heard a sound behind her and turned to see the front door open. A group of men entered and made their way purposefully up the stairs; she stood back as they filed past, not acknowledging her. They were ordinary-looking, but too silent and solemn – and male – to be spectators. Yet neither were they smart enough for lawyers, and certainly neither fashionable nor lively enough for pressmen. Then, two policemen entered, bringing up the rear and having a discreet conversation. As they passed

Hannah, she heard one say, 'Yes, let's hope the family don't want an open casket.'

She couldn't resist. As the last policeman passed her, Hannah seamlessly joined the back of the group, following them across the landing to one of the doors. The men went through first, then one policeman, but the second one noticed her behind him and put his arm in her way.

'You're too late,' he said. 'Everyone has to be seated before the jury enter.'

He went through, closing the door decisively behind him. Hannah stood there for a moment, listening, but she could hear nothing at all from the room beyond. She felt that if she flung open the door, it would be an empty cupboard, the people vanished like a magician's trick.

She turned back down the stairs and out onto the street. Walking briskly away from the hall, she thought: this was all just as well. It had been one thing going to Priory Street, finding a story there that no one else had and selling it to the newspaper, but the inquest wouldn't be like that. Like the hearing in Marylebone, it was a controlled public event, with dozens of pressmen present, recording it for their papers. She would be there purely as a spectator, part of the prurient mob. She had inhabited that role in Marylebone, and it hadn't felt comfortable. This wasn't who she really was. Perhaps her subsequent fainting fit at home was proof of that.

Nonetheless, for the next few hours she chose not to walk on the Heath, or to explore the new streets on the periphery of the village, but rather to stay on the high street, within a short distance of the Drill Hall. She compared too-expensive boots at Lilley & Skinner and J.G. Ferrin, and looked at oil paintings of naval battles in the window of the art dealer, and knife cases in the cutler's. At the draper's, she was given a presentation of a new grip to hitch up her skirt, safe from the mud. As she browsed, she thought of the actress she had met the previous evening, and how she made it clear how dull and conventional she thought Hannah was. Presumably, Dolly was spending this morning lounging around in her garret, perhaps still drinking that bad champagne, making some man do whatever she wanted. And, listlessly trailing around the shops, Hannah was doing exactly what Dolly would expect of her, if she spared her a thought at all.

All the same, Hannah felt she was enacting an alibi, keenly aware of the church clock. How long would the inquest last? The Marylebone hearing was less than two hours. By midday, she was sitting at a table for two in the front window of a coffee house directly opposite the Drill Hall, feeling as if she was waiting for a badger to emerge from its set. Her patience was rewarded at around quarter past, when a Black Maria pulled up outside. Hands unsteady, she carefully put her coffee cup down on the table.

The hall door opened. First to emerge was a policeman, followed by a woman – not her, but a chaperone Hannah recognised from Marylebone. Then there she was, with another policeman close behind.

Her head was not covered or bowed, as before, presumably because the street was empty. The mob was still indoors. No one was watching Mrs Pearcey – except Hannah.

The collar of her dark dress was a freshly laundered white – she must have been given the respectable clothes requested by her lawyer at Marylebone – and her hair was looking stiffer and oilier than it had before. The group did not immediately board the carriage, as a policeman was having a word with the driver, and for an unguarded moment, Mrs Pearcey looked out over the street before her, turning her head to take it all in, as if wishing to capture what she could of innocent street life before being taken back down into darkness. Her gaze landed on the coffee house, and Hannah looked back at her confident that she couldn't be seen behind the painted sign on the window. A second of one-sided contact with those milky blue eyes before the policeman beckoned, and Mrs Pearcey bent down to climb into the Black Maria.

Hannah had no time to digest the moment, as no sooner had the carriage pulled away than the door of the hall opened again. This time, it was the group of men she had passed on the stairs. The jury. They didn't linger on the pavement but scurried off in different directions, heads down. Then, like the contents of an uncorked bottle pouring onto the street, came everyone else: the female observers (there was Moira), the older male officials, the young pressmen. Ovilry, of course. She watched as he talked briefly with another man, before skipping across the road, towards her coffee house. She assumed he was en route down the hill, back towards London, but instead he stopped at the window, in front of where she sat, and rapped on the glass.

She jumped, jolting the table. So she was visible, after all. Ovilry pushed open the door of the coffee house and poked his head in.

'You again!' he said. 'Did you know the Pearcey inquest was just there?'

'Really!' Hannah affected surprise. 'I'm just up here doing some shopping.'

Whether Ovilry believed her was dependent, she realised, on whether he had spotted her among the crowds at Marylebone. Passing by Priory Street was one thing, but three Mrs Pearcey-related coincidences would be hard to swallow. It appeared he was in too much of a hurry to care.

'Can't stop,' he said. 'I've got to get to . . .' – he looked at the pad in his hand – 'Prince of Wales Road. The Hogg house. Do you know which omnibus is best?'

'It's not that far to walk,' she said. 'It'd be quicker, probably. Just keep on down the hill for about a mile, then turn left at the bottom.' She hesitated and looked around, in case someone she knew had somehow sneaked into the coffee house and was listening. 'I'm going that way, actually. I'll show you.'

She fished in her pocket for a penny, laid it beside her cup and got to her feet.

They started off down the hill, at a march.

'So, what happened in there?' she asked.

'Oh, all sorts,' he said. 'Fairly juicy. Actually, it'd be useful to tell you, I can compose my article out loud. Firstly, Miss Teale, I need your womanly advice. May I read you my description of Mrs Pearcey, in there, and you tell me what you think?' He added hastily, 'I don't mean about the quality of the writing, I don't need reassurance about that. Just about whether the sentiment will wash with readers of the fairer sex?'

Without waiting for her response, he opened his notepad and began to read, all the while keeping up his urgent pace. '*She is striking, with all the assets of youth,*' he intoned. Hannah noticed he had a grey mark on his lips, presumably from sucking his pencil. '*Tall and slim, but not too thin; fresh, clear skin; thick, russet-coloured hair; lively blue eyes . . . indeed, it is hard to imagine an appearance more at odds with the hideous acts of which she has been charged . . .*'

'No!' Hannah interrupted. 'That's not true at all! Her eyes are pale, and heavy lidded. Her mouth is too big. And her teeth! To describe her as beautiful will make you look foolish!'

Ovilry looked rather taken aback by her vehemence.

'Sorry, it's me who is being foolish,' she said more quietly. 'You know, I think she is neither handsome nor plain. She looks just like . . . an ordinary young woman. Someone you could meet in the street and not remember the next hour.' Belatedly, she remembered that she wasn't meant to have seen Mrs Pearcey in person and added weakly, 'I mean, going by the illustrations in the paper.'

Of course, she knew the cause of her outburst: the secret fact that she was the only one, out of Ovilry and his pals, who had actually been face to face alone with the accused. The woman they were all trying to pin down – Hannah felt she had a claim on her.

Ovilry was now looking ahead, with a thoughtful expression.

'Perhaps you are right,' he said. 'Maybe I should go down the monstrous line . . . *masculine and brawny, with a deformed mouth . . .*'

'Can you tell me what happened in there?' asked Hannah again, cutting him off. 'Why was there a jury when it wasn't a trial?'

'They were just a bunch of men rounded up from the nearest building site,' said Ovilry. 'It's essentially to judge if there's enough evidence to go to trial. Which there is, in abundance.'

'People gave evidence?'

Ovilry nodded. 'First up was Hogg. He started off giving his alibi for the murders, which was that he had been working with his brother on that fateful Friday. He assumed his wife and child had gone to visit her father outside London, and then on Saturday, when he didn't find them at home, he dispatched his sister off to Pearcey's house to see if they were there.'

'But why did he think that Phoebe might be with Mrs Pearcey? Were they friends?'

'Apparently so. Which makes it all the juicier, because then Hogg confessed that he and Pearcey had been in an illicit relationship.'

He consulted his pad for Hogg's words, which he read in an approximation of his rough nasal accent. '*I'm going to speak the truth, sir. It's for the best. I confess I was on intimate terms with Mrs Pearcey. I visited her two or three times a week. I don't think my wife knew about it.*'

'Gosh!'

'It wasn't a surprise as such. I mean, we could all guess that. But to hear him say it like that was rather a moment. And that wasn't the end of his dramatics, as they then wheeled in the baby's pram – rather gratuitously, I thought – and he fell to his knees weeping in front of it. It was all a bit much.'

'Do you suspect him?'

'Well, I wouldn't be at all surprised if he had a hand in it. He looks like such a rotten apple – heaven knows what Pearcey saw in him. He has an alibi – claims he was working all day helping his brother Edwin move furniture – but the only people who can corroborate that are his brother and some casual labourer in their employment. Hardly impartial.'

Hannah absorbed all of this, as much as she could while walking at such a lick. They were at Belsize Park already, only a few minutes from Crossfield Road. Hannah thought of her experience there on Saturday morning – impossibly, only a few days ago.

'And then what?' she asked.

'The coroner gave rather gruesome details of the injuries inflicted on Phoebe – very violent – and on the baby, thankfully less so. In fact, there were no marks on little Tiggie at all, which is good; people don't like reading about injuries to children.'

'But mutilated women are fine, are they?'

'I'm afraid so,' he said, before continuing. 'Then there were a number of witnesses from Priory Street, including Pearcey's doughty upstairs neighbour, who shared the kitchen. She said she went down for breakfast on the Saturday morning after Phoebe's disappearance and was surprised to find the scullery waterlogged and the zinc bath containing the kitchen curtains, which appeared to be stained with something.'

I've been in that kitchen, thought Hannah. Their downhill trot, combined with Ovilry's lively account of all the drama, was making her feel bold and energised.

'That reminds me,' she said. 'I saw the *Star* article about getting into Priory Street. You did it in the end!'

Ovilry glanced at her but didn't miss a beat. 'Yesterday's news,' he said. 'It's all about today's story. And so, yes – another neighbour gave evidence that she saw Pearcey wheeling a *heavily laden perambulator* just after 5 p.m., her head bent over the cobbles. She was wearing a flower in her hat. Then came Martha, the sister of Phoebe. Mousy-looking but quite good value. Said that Phoebe had received a note on Friday morning asking her to tea. It read, *Dearest, come round this afternoon and bring our little darling. Do not fail.* It was unsigned but apparently Phoebe could tell Pearcey's handwriting. So that's major, as it could show premeditation.'

He briefly paused to cough, before continuing.

'Next came Lizzie Styles, who was Phoebe's niece. Dressed in mourning. A giant, strapping lass but not unattractive, once she'd lifted her veil. She said she was very close to Phoebe – they had both worked as domestic servants and saw each other a lot. Clearly loathed Frank Hogg, intimated that he was lazy, but didn't really get a chance to say much, as she was asked to step down after only a few questions.

'Finally, there was Clara, Frank's sister. Rather unfortunate looking; pugnacious features, like her brother. She said that after she went round to Priory Street to look for Phoebe, she spent the whole of Saturday with Pearcey, and they travelled together to the police station and then to the Prince of Wales Road.'

Not quite the whole day together, thought Hannah, recalling her encounter with Mrs Pearcey with the newspapers. She knew she was at risk of blurting out the fact of their meeting to impress Ovilry – a fact that he would grab and take down to Fleet Street to process before doling it out to the public domain. She must keep it to herself, deep in her pocket. For now, at least.

'And then the last witness was the best – Mr Pearcey!'

'Her husband?'

'Well, actually not – they weren't married but she took his

name to look respectable. He's a carpenter and joiner, lived on Camden High Street. Met her when she was eighteen and working at a sealskin factory.'

A sealskin factory. A frisson passed through her. That pelt over Mrs Pearcey's bed. A leaving present from her grateful employer? Or did she steal it, sticking it under her skirt as she was leaving work one day?

'What was he like, Mr Pearcey?' she asked.

'Ginger hair, freckled, a bit crumpled. Could not be more unassuming. They lived together elsewhere in Camden Town for a while, and then when they separated she moved to Priory Street. He said he'd been sore about the separation but had spoken to her civilly when they bumped into each other. Anyway, he claimed that the cardigan found wrapped round Phoebe's head was actually his. He had given it to her. He identified it from a burn mark on the pocket. Oh, and there's another man in the picture, too – one Charles Crichton. Their arrangement seemed to be that he paid the rent for Pearcey's rooms at Priory Street, in exchange for a visit or two each week.'

Hannah nodded, trying to mirror Ovilry's matter-of-factness. Really, though, she felt rather shocked. Did this mean that Mrs Pearcey was effectively a prostitute? Her vision of such people didn't extend beyond the wretches plying their trade on slum corners. Was it possible to be a respectable prostitute, who owned a piano and a polished aspidistra, or was there a different term for such women? She couldn't ask Ovilry.

They could now see Chalk Farm. Some building works were blocking the pavement, requiring them to cross over to the other side of the road. A gnarly crossing sweeper was there to give them unsolicited assistance, and when, having escorted them safely across, he put his hand out for a reward, Ovilry distractedly dug into his pocket.

Extraordinarily, it was only then, twenty minutes into their journey, as she tried to absorb these new, unsettling details about Mrs Pearcey's life, that it struck Hannah that anyone who saw her and Ovilry together like this would naturally assume they were together. And if Cosmo could see her, walking, deep in conversation with his nemesis!

This realisation made her slow right down, as if her shoes had been turned to stone. Ovilry didn't notice, and carried on down the hill, a man in a hurry. Hannah watched him forging ahead of her. She could stop this whole thing now, shout after him that she had to go home. He would probably just put his hand in the air, and not even slow down.

Then, she thought of what Dolly might say. *Why are you bothered about what some random crossing sweeper thinks? Your fiancé is locked up in a madhouse in Friern Barnet, so he's not going to see you. You know whether you're doing something to be ashamed of. And if you're not – who cares?*

Hannah knew she had no inappropriate feelings towards the overconfident Winston Ovilry. The Mrs Pearcey case – well, that was another matter. But she could think that through properly later. She felt in thrall to a momentum that was propelling her towards the next stage of the story, as inexorably as if she were on a long playground slide.

She ran to catch up with Ovilry. Oblivious to her moment of reckoning, as soon as she drew level with him he continued seamlessly with his account.

'And then, finally, the coroner summed up the case. He

said, the affair served as motive, and there was evidence of a struggle in the kitchen, although what precipitated it was unclear. And then Phoebe's body was taken out of Priory Street in the perambulator and dumped at Crossfield Road. And whoever wheeled the pram also murdered the child. The evidence clearly pointed to the guilt of one party, and one party only. The jury didn't even leave the room, just put their heads together for a minute and came up with a verdict of wilful murder. And that was that.'

They were now at the corner of Prince of Wales Road.

'And here we are,' said Hannah, coming to a halt and indicating the road sign. 'What are we doing here, by the way?'

'I need a quote from Frank. Or one of his nasty family. They're all we've got now, the Hoggs.'

'How do you mean?'

'Well, she's in Holloway Prison now, so there's no getting to her. And he's clearly a wrong one, isn't he? The question is, whether he played a part in it.'

He lifted his hat to Hannah. 'Thank you for getting me here, and for being my sounding board. And my regards to your fiancé, whenever he returns from his holiday.'

He started off down the road.

'Can I come with you?' called Hannah, coming after him. To end her journey now, so close to the target, felt almost perverse.

He turned in surprise.

'Really? Well, all right,' he said. 'You might be useful. But please let me do the talking.'

The Hoggs' house, Number 141, was a hundred yards up the road, in the middle of a long Georgian terrace, all wrought-iron balconies and small front gardens. The paintwork was blistered, but overall the house appeared well kept, the window glass clean and the nets bright. It was a step up from the humble Priory Street. A small group of pressmen were gathered on the pavement outside. Opposite, on the other side of the road, a row of ancient men sat outside their almshouses, rugs tucked over their laps, with the air of being permanent street furniture. They must have had a lot to gawp at this weekend, Hannah thought, as she and Ovilry approached the group. More drama in one weekend than the rest of their lives altogether.

'They not back yet?' said Ovilry to one of the other journalists.

Even as the man was shaking his head, his gaze was fixed over Ovilry's shoulder and Hannah saw his face brighten. She turned to see a hansom approach from about twenty feet away. The pressmen around her sprang into action, digging into their pockets for their pads as they rushed towards the cab. Before it had fully come to a halt, Frank Hogg jumped out, followed by two women, one old and one younger. His mother and sister. Behind them, another cab pulled up.

'Frank! Clara! Frank! Frank!' the men called, like desperate lovers.

The journalists swarmed around the Hoggs, and while the two women pushed through them to go straight inside the house, Frank stayed behind on the pavement. Hannah glimpsed him rest one leg on the wall of the front garden, ready to talk, before the pressmen encircled him and he disappeared from view.

Ovilry stood beside Hannah, surveying the scene.

'Right, which one is the brother?' he muttered, loud

enough for only her to hear. She watched his gaze alight on a man who had disembarked from the second cab and was now loitering a few feet away from the huddle around Frank. He looked similar to him – compact, with squashed features, heavily bearded – although he lacked Frank's style in dress. There was no cravat; his hands were stuffed into his stretched waistcoat pockets.

Ovilry stepped towards the man and thrust out his hand. Hannah followed.

'Winston Ovilry, from the *Star*.'

'Edwin Hogg,' said the man, nodding but not offering his hand.

Ovilry gave a quick smile, pleased to have identified him correctly.

'Can I have a few moments of your time?' he said to the man. 'Hear your side of things?'

Edwin Hogg gave a nonchalant shrug as Ovilry flipped open his notebook. Edwin didn't appear to mind Hannah's presence, or indeed to register her at all.

'How was the marriage of your brother and his wife?' asked Ovilry.

Hannah was surprised he began so bluntly, but Edwin didn't seem nonplussed.

'My brother and his wife lived upon the most amicable terms,' he replied. He had the same nasal voice as Frank. 'Several times my wife and myself have spoken to her and asked, "Phoebe, are you perfectly happy?" and she has replied, "Yes, perfectly happy."'

'But they separated, did they not, in February?' said Ovilry. 'Why was that?'

'It was over them letters, the letters Phoebe sent and

received, but hid from Frank,' he replied. 'That's when she went to Mill Hill. To stay with her father.'

Ovilry nodded, scribbling away. Hannah couldn't help herself.

'But what *were* these letters?' she interjected.

Edwin stared at her, as if noticing her for the first time. He addressed his reply back to Ovilry.

'I don't know, really. It weren't much, the argument. Then the next morning, myself and Frank went to Mill Hill and retrieved her. Persuaded her to come home, like.' His tone shifted slightly, and he stood up straighter. 'I personally managed the reconciliation,' he said. 'Frank stayed in the other room as I spoke privately to Phoebe. I said to her, "Phoebe, do you wish to see your husband?" And she replied, "Does Frank want to see me?" "That is not the question," I replied. "Have you thought of what you are doing by leaving him? You have only been away for a day, but you must know the longer you are away from him the more difficult will be the reconciliation. I have come to ask you whether you wish to see him and return to him." Phoebe relented, put her head on my shoulder and burst into sobs, before agreeing to return home. I then called Frank into the room, and the pair were immediately reconciled.'

He smiled for the first time, revealing a strip of bright-yellow teeth. Hannah was surprised at how unguarded he was, but she could see that he was proud of his role in the drama.

'Are you sure there wasn't another, perhaps more secret, reason that Phoebe didn't want to return here?' pressed Ovilry.

Edwin's smile dropped. 'No, no. She was embarrassed

she'd acted so childishly. Especially as there was nothing in the letters, really. They were just between her and her niece, Lizzie.'

It was then that Hannah noticed that someone else had joined them, standing just behind Edwin. It was Frank Hogg himself.

He was only about two feet away from her, openly listening to what was being said. Instinctively, she took a step backwards, repulsed. At best, this man had been in Mrs Pearcey's bed, acting adulterously beneath the sealskin. At worst, he was involved in the murder of his wife and child.

And now, unlike his brother, Frank Hogg noticed her. As Ovilry's attention was trained on Edwin and his notebook, Frank Hogg looked at Hannah over Ovilry's bent head, holding her gaze with small, curranty eyes. He didn't smile, but slowly rubbed his lips, his look steady and challenging. *And you are?*

Flustered, Hannah looked away. When she glanced back, Hogg's stare had moved away to something over her shoulder, and his expression had changed. Now he was clearly annoyed: frowning, lips pressed tight together. Instinctively, Hannah turned to see what he was glaring at, but the only people on the other side of the road were the almshouse men, harmless in their chairs, and a tall female pedestrian.

The sound of Frank Hogg's voice pulled her attention back to her group. He was speaking to Ovilry, in that peevish tone familiar from the court room.

'My brother quite agreed with me that it was only my right to insist that my wife's letters should be shown to me,' he said. 'I had my suspicions, and they were warranted.' And with that, Frank Hogg unceremoniously terminated the interview, turning and pushing open the gate to the front garden. Edwin followed in his wake. Hannah watched as the two men walked up the path, and Frank opened the front door. Just before ducking inside, he turned to glance back, but again, he appeared not to be looking at Ovilry and Hannah, but at something, or someone, beyond them.

'Better hotfoot it to the office to write this up,' said Ovilry beside her, stuffing his notebook into his pocket. He nodded goodbye before hurrying off towards Chalk Farm. The other pressmen had melted away and the patch of pavement outside the Hoggs' house, so busy and charged just a few moments ago, was now deserted. Feeling exposed and foolish, as if she were the dupe in a childhood game, Hannah turned to head back to Camden Square. But something nagged at her. Why had Frank been glaring across the road towards the almshouses? Looking over there now, she saw only the same innocent scene as earlier: five ancient men planted in their chairs, a woman in black walking past.

But wait. The woman wasn't moving. Rather, she was loitering directly opposite the Hoggs' house. And it was the same strikingly tall woman she had noticed earlier.

Now she was giving the woman her full attention, Hannah could see that she was in mourning, her face veiled. *Dressed in mourning. A giant, strapping lass.* Hannah recalled the account Ovilry had given of the inquest. On instinct, she ran across the road to where the woman was standing.

'Excuse me,' Hannah asked. 'Are you Miss Lizzie Styles?'

'I am,' said Lizzie Styles, in a loud voice, and lifted her veil.

Ovilry was right: Lizzie was rather beautiful, her eggshell skin fair and poreless. But Hannah could see that her cheeks were smeared with tears.

'I'm so sorry about your aunt,' Hannah said, chastened. How easy it was to forget that there was a human tragedy at the heart of all this.

Lizzie acknowledged the courtesy with a nod. 'Did you know her?' she asked.

Hannah just shook her head. 'I just – I'm interested in the story.'

'Are you a reporter?'

'Oh,' said Hannah. 'Not really. I mean, I'm just . . . I'd love to hear your views on these terrible events.' Her voice had no conviction in it; she felt horribly embarrassed and intrusive, and even as she spoke she was backing away, in the direction of Camden Square, where she belonged.

But Lizzie said, 'I'm happy to talk.'

'Oh!' said Hannah again, wrong-footed. As she dug into her pocket for her paper and pencil, it occurred to her that this must be precisely the reason Lizzie had come to the Prince of Wales Road, to stand prominently opposite the Hoggs' house. She wanted to be noticed and asked for her side of the story; to say what she hadn't had the chance to at the inquest.

The two of them perched on the wall of the almshouses, and Hannah rested her pencil on her pad, ready.

'Mr Hogg over there mentioned some letters sent by Phoebe, which he took objection to,' she asked Lizzie. 'Do you have any idea what was in them?'

'Of course I do,' said Lizzie. 'They were mainly addressed

to me, as well as members of my family. We were very close, all of us.'

'Was Mr Hogg right to be suspicious of them?' Hannah asked, writing this down. 'The letters, I mean?'

'He was indeed,' said Lizzie.

'Were they . . .' As Hannah hesitated to think about how best to phrase the question, Lizzie jumped in.

'No, no,' said Lizzie. 'She would never have had any dealings with another man. She was far too demure. She wouldn't even talk to people on the street, let alone strike up an intimacy with a stranger.'

'So why was Frank Hogg right to be suspicious of the letters?' asked Hannah.

'They often contained expressions not favourable to him or his family. You see, whatever impression *he* likes to give, the fact is that their marriage was not a happy one. Phoebe hated living here. In fact, it was a perfect misery for her.'

'No sitting on the wall!' came a voice, and they both turned to see one of the old men, red-faced, waving his stick at them. Lizzie raised her eyebrows at Hannah and then the two of them got to their feet.

'Why was that?' Hannah said, once they were standing.

'He just isn't a nice man. Prickly. He wound my aunt up. Like, with Tiggie, he would hold her wrong, say, and even when my aunt corrected him, he wouldn't stop it.'

'What?' Hannah caught her breath. Was this proof of Frank's history of violence towards his daughter? 'Are you saying he was harsh to the baby?'

'No,' said Lizzie, and to Hannah's shame she felt a pulse of disappointment. 'No, he loved Tiggie, I think. But he wanted to punish her – my aunt – for criticising him. He couldn't bear to be criticised, you see.' Lizzie paused. 'And then there was their financial situation. They were in very narrow straits. Sometimes, my aunt even had to go without food in order that her baby might have essentials.'

'But Frank – Mr Hogg – he worked, did he not?' said Hannah. 'At the hearing they said he worked for his brother Edwin's furniture-moving business . . .'

Lizzie gave a mirthless laugh. 'Well, the work was there. But he worked when he wanted.'

'You mean he was idle?'

Lizzie shrugged her agreement.

'Was his family also a matter of contention in the marriage?'

'I admit that both families, the Hoggs and the Styleses, interfered in the marriage,' replied Lizzie. 'That's why Frank asked Phoebe to stop the letters. He also asked that her friends and family did not visit unannounced, only when they were invited. He meant me, really.' She paused. 'He thinks I am a troublemaker, because I am on my aunt's side of things.'

'And did your aunt agree to this ban?'

Lizzie nodded. 'On the proviso that he also did not let his friends come here,' she went on. 'Specifically, *her*.'

Another interruption came in the form of a fire engine, rounding the corner into the road at breakneck speed, the horses foaming at the mouth. A gaggle of little boys chased after it, whooping.

Hannah waited until they had gone past before continuing.

'So, Mrs Hogg was aware of her husband's relationship with Mrs Pearcey?'

'Oh, I firmly believe she knew but decided to stay quiet,'

replied Lizzie. 'And that's why she begged Frank to find them somewhere else to live, far away from his family – and from *her*. But Frank never did. If he had, she might still be alive.'

Lizzie watched as Hannah wrote down her words, Hannah trying to keep her hand steady in her excitement. *This* was a story.

'She never liked Mrs Pearcey and I never did. I know my aunt was afraid of her, for when she told me once that Mrs Pearcey had invited her on a day trip to Southend, my aunt said to me, "No fear of me going to Southend. Why, I might be thrown over the cliffs and none of you would know anything about it here."'

'But why,' asked Hannah, 'if Phoebe was so afraid of Mrs Pearcey, would she have gone to visit her at Priory Street?'

'This I cannot tell,' replied Lizzie. 'There must have been some very strong inducement in the letter she received from Mrs Pearcey on Friday morning.'

Ovilry had mentioned the contents of this letter being relayed at the inquest. Hannah frowned, trying to recall the wording.

'Didn't it just say something like *come for tea, and bring the little darling*?' she said.

Lizzie shrugged. 'All I know is that she didn't like Mrs Pearcey, and was scared of her.'

'But Mr Hogg sent Clara round to Mrs Pearcey's house on Saturday morning, so he must have known, or suspected, that Phoebe had gone there,' said Hannah, talking to herself as much as to Lizzie. 'It was the first place he thought of looking. It just doesn't add up.'

Hannah noticed Lizzie glance across the road to the Hoggs' house and saw the girl's posture change; she stood straighter, lifting her chin defiantly. Hannah turned to follow her look and was startled to see the shape of a figure at one of the first-floor windows, facing them. The figure looked male, but it wasn't clear whether it was Edwin or Frank, or someone else entirely.

'I suppose I'd better get back to Albion Street,' said Lizzie, turning back to Hannah. 'I get on the train just down the road.'

She shook Hannah's hand before gliding off eastwards towards Kentish Town – purposefully not hurrying, Hannah guessed, for the benefit of whoever was watching from the window. Hannah was heading in the same direction, but she waited to allow Lizzie to get a good head start and to save them both the awkwardness of meeting again after saying their goodbyes. She silently counted to twenty, examining her fingernails, affecting nonchalance. She didn't look up at the Hoggs' house, but she felt the weight of the unknown person's eyes upon her.

Ossulston Street, the site of Mrs Teale's refuge, was the main artery of Somers Town but had the air of a remote backwater. The whole slum was silent and desolate, as if its inhabitants were too low to even make noise or move beyond the bare minimum required to keep them alive until the next day. When Hannah had first come here, she'd expected a sort of feral industry and a ribald sense of community and was surprised to find such barrenness, the streets deserted except for the odd, staring child in a doorway, the air thick with the particular dank fug that comes from burning damp wood and the smell of open sewers. The houses were on the verge of collapse, walls visibly sagging, windows broken and splattered with mud. Even the dogs there didn't act like dogs, but rather lay flattened in furry puddles on the pavement, enervated to the point where it was unclear whether they were actually alive.

Hannah didn't have time to register the gloom as she hurried down Ossulston Street that evening. She was late. After Prince of Wales Road, she had gone home and written up what she had got from Lizzie, and by the time she had finished, found a stamp and addressed the letter to Mr Arthur Summersdale at the *Star*, it was already past 5 p.m.

The refuge was in a narrow, four-storey old house with a forbidding exterior like its neighbours, its brickwork blackened with soot and windows and doors wonky with subsidence. Inside, though, the place was oddly familiar, on account of it being furnished with things she had grown up with in Camden Square. On the wall to the right was the mirror from their hallway, and on the floor a purple and pink runner that once lay on the corridor outside the maids' room. And there was a dining chair with a faded floral tapestry seat, which had for years been in Hannah's bedroom, the spot where she used to lay her clothes at the end of the day.

Now, the chair sat further down the hallway, at the bottom of the stairs, underneath the single ceiling light, and on it sat her mother, spotlit, as if on London's most low-key stage.

'I'm sorry . . .' Hannah began, still short of breath.

'Don't worry,' replied Mrs Teale, standing up, and gesturing to Hannah to take the seat. 'They generally don't start coming until six. Would you like some supper?'

Hannah smiled and nodded, pleasantly surprised at the lack of rebuke. Mrs Teale disappeared into the back kitchen, reappearing a moment later with an enamel mug of sweet tea and a piece of bread and dripping. Suddenly starving, Hannah demolished the bread in seconds, taking another bite before she had finished chewing the last. In this place, she felt released from the need to be refined. Hannah was grateful for the smell of warm fat under her nose, which went a little way to masking the unpleasant smell in the hall, a blend of damp and the tang of mouse urine. To her right, the door to the front room was ajar, and from behind it she could hear the crackling of a newly lit fire.

'So, how was Emily's dress?'

Hannah started and twisted in her seat to see that her mother hadn't in fact gone back into the kitchen but was still standing there, a few feet away. Putting her hand over her mouth as she swallowed the bread, Hannah scrabbled around for something to say about the wedding dress, which she hadn't inspected or tried on since bringing it home from Emily's. She couldn't even conjure up a picture of it from Emily's ceremony.

'It's nice,' she said. 'It's cream silk.' Triumphantly, she remembered what Emily had said about it. 'And it has puffed sleeves.'

'It does sound nice,' said Mrs Teale placidly. 'Does it fit?'

'Not quite,' Hannah said. 'Mrs Didier will have to work her magic.'

After a pause, Mrs Teale said, 'I feel we haven't spoken enough about all of this. Not about the dress, I mean – other marriage-related matters.'

Hannah flinched and looked away, down at the rug.

'I wanted you to discover things by yourself,' her mother

continued, 'but I think perhaps I was wrong, and that there are some things I should discuss with you.'

'There's no need,' said Hannah quickly. 'So . . . how are things here? Busy?'

But Mrs Teale would not be deflected.

'Is there anything you'd like to ask? About the rights of husbands, and so on?'

Hannah made herself look up at her mother. The unforgiving overhead light exposed the web of shed hairs clinging to her mother's shoulders. A memory came to Hannah from when she was young, of sneaking into her mother's bedroom when she was out and going through her trunk, unearthing her undergarments – not out of prurience, or even curiosity, but rather in an attempt to feel some sense of connection with the body that was so mysterious to her, but from which – extraordinarily – she had emerged.

She'd once so longed for a close relationship with her mother, but now that intimacy had been sprung on her, and her mind was so much elsewhere, it felt quite unwelcome. Shifting with discomfort, Hannah looked over to the front door, willing it to open and for them to be interrupted. She could ask her mother the same simple, broad question she had asked Emily: *What is it like?* Her mother certainly wouldn't give a bland, gushy response; that was beyond her. Her answer would even reveal things about her own marriage, that opaque arrangement.

But then another question came to her, which felt more pressing at that moment.

'Actually, there was something I was wondering,' she said. 'Is it a husband's right to read a wife's letters when you are married?'

Mrs Teale raised her eyebrows. 'Oh. Well. I don't know whether there's a firm answer to that. That specific point is certainly not in the marriage contract, but I suppose it would come under the oath to "obey".'

'Would Father have read your letters?'

Mrs Teale gave a dry laugh. 'Your father wouldn't have been the slightest bit interested in my letters.'

The front door banged open and cold air shot down the hallway. On the doorstep stood a group of three women. The evening was beginning.

Mrs Teale was already halfway back to the kitchen. 'Now, it's a penny entrance, remember,' she called to Hannah. 'And if they say they don't have it and you believe them, let them in anyway.'

The trio of women bustled down the hallway towards Hannah, rummaging in their pockets for change. The first time Hannah had sat in this chair, she'd been struck dumb by the parade before her, from the broken, reeking old souls, with brown teeth and frizzy grey hair, string holding up their skirts and men's carpet slippers on their feet, to younger ones still with some life to them, with keen eyes and truculent airs. Of course, she'd passed unfortunate women on the street, in doorways and on kerbsides, but she'd viewed them almost as another species, akin to horses; all around her yet completely distinct. It was quite another thing to interact with them like this, up close. In here, it was she who was the minority, sitting down, physically positioned lower, easily overlooked or barged into.

Now, the three women – one old and two young – barely registered her as she smiled and received their pennies, directing them to collect their supper from the kitchen. They were regulars and knew what to do. After returning from the kitchen with mugs and bread in hand, the trio filed into the front room to eat in front of the fire. Even with the door closed, their conversation was quite audible to Hannah in her chair. 'Let's get a drinky, you brought a diddle for me? Ah, aren't you sweet.' 'That was a big gulp, you bugger, give it back.' 'Now don't say something like that, don't even think it!' 'Are you finishing that?' 'Lend us a penny, I'm gasping.' 'Bloody hell, don't touch it, it hurts.' The front door banged open again, delivering another blast of night air, and over the next hour there was a steady trickle of women. Hannah greeted them, received their pennies and pointed to the kitchen, and the front room filled with more voices: fond greetings; complaints about being cheated by local pawnshops or barred by bad-tempered landlords; grumbles about arthritis and chilblains; enquiring after each other's children; gossip from the streets; comparing the quirks of some of their male customers and warning about the violence of others; crude expletives and impenetrable slang.

As she continued to smile and greet, and the din in the front room grew louder, Hannah's thoughts slid back to the afternoon, to those uneasy encounters on the Prince of Wales Road. She had found it much harder to write up Lizzie's interview than to compose her account of Priory Street. Odd, really, as it should have been a case of simply transcribing what the girl had said, then throwing in a bit of lurid language, as she'd been taught by Mr Summersdale. But as she'd lain on her stomach on her bed, committing Lizzie's words to paper, Hannah had had the curious sense that she was creating facts – or, at least, what amounted to facts in the eyes of the *Star* readers. The things Lizzie had said might be disqualified later, at the trial. But right now, her statements had weight, and when – if - they were printed, they would be absorbed by thousands of people across London.

Perhaps, Hannah thought, Lizzie's statements weren't actually that shocking or important. Lizzie clearly loathed Frank, but beyond bolstering an unfavourable impression of him – something the papers had already established by describing his appearance and demeanour at the hearings – what did she say, really? The fact that the Hoggs' marriage was unhappy was no surprise, considering the fact that Frank spent half of his week with another woman. As for Lizzie's harsh words about Mrs Pearcey – well, of course she wouldn't think fondly of the woman who was interfering in her beloved aunt's marriage.

Hannah had met Frank, and his aura was undeniably dark, wasn't it? That impression must mean something. She thought of the hard stare he had given her on the pavement, and how it had made her feel. It was a look of . . . what? Suspicion? Warning? Curiosity? Those short, thick fingers rubbing his lips as he looked at her. And the thought came to her, not of what those fingers *might* have done, but what they definitely *had* done. Touching Mrs Pearcey. Touching the things that she, Hannah, had touched, in Mrs Pearcey's bedroom.

'I said, hello?'

Hannah jerked to attention. A young woman was standing in front of her, hand outstretched, a penny between her fingers. Hannah took the coin and started to instruct the woman to collect her supper, but the woman was already moving towards the kitchen. Another old hand. As she passed, Hannah saw that she held something under her right arm: a large tortoise, carried on its side like a dispatch case.

'Hey!' Hannah said. The woman turned, a few feet away. 'I saw you before on York Road. You talked to my mother.'

The woman looked at her blankly. Today, her thin blonde hair was in a complicated style, with lots of tiny little plaits, as if a bunch of fairies had been to work on her. She wore a red plaid shawl pinned tightly around her neck.

'When that boy tried to steal your tortoise?' Hannah prompted.

'What are you saying?' the woman replied. 'Who stole Harry?'

'No one. But a boy tried to. On Sunday, on York Road. You can't have forgotten!'

But it was clear from the woman's expression that she hadn't a clue what Hannah was talking about. Perhaps, despite her youth, she already had some drink-related brain rot. Hannah smiled, with the intention of releasing the poor woman from this failed exchange, but the woman kept standing there, looking at her, as if expecting more.

'Tortoises are extraordinary, aren't they?' Hannah said genially. 'Like little dinosaurs.'

The woman nodded, and Hannah saw the twitch of a smile. Encouraged, Hannah remembered something she had been told at school, the only fact she could remember about tortoises, and went on, 'I heard that when Charles Darwin and his crew were coming back from South America—'

'Who?'

'Oh – he's a scientist,' said Hannah. 'They brought back with them lots of rare giant tortoises, and they just kept them on their backs, and they survived for months like that, without any food or water . . . until they were needed.'

'Needed?' frowned the woman. 'What do you mean?'

'Well . . .' and Hannah hesitated, sensing it was unwise to continue. 'Oh, it doesn't matter.'

'What do you mean?'

'Well – the crew ate them.'

The woman stared at Hannah. Her eyes and mouth hardened, and Hannah felt she could see her growing larger, her chest puffing up with fury like some exotic frog. She was taken back to that moment on York Road with the boy, just before the screeching and hitting started, and was just about to call for her mother, when suddenly the woman's shoulders dropped and she deflated, as if someone had pricked her with a pin.

'Some people just don't deserve to live,' she said quietly, and then she turned and headed into the kitchen. Emerging a moment later with her cup and bread balanced in one hand, to accommodate the tortoise under the other, she went into the front room, but Hannah did not hear her voice join the mêlée.

It turned out the tortoise lady was the last guest of the evening. The refuge shut its doors at 8 p.m., and not long after, the women were ushered upstairs to their beds, in rows of coffin-esque cots. Mrs Teale emerged from the kitchen, pink-faced from her hours bent over the stove, and told Hannah she could also go up to bed; it was too late to return to Camden Square, and so Hannah should sleep in one of the two box rooms in the attic of the refuge.

The rooms were tiny, far smaller than the maids' quarters at Camden Square, and even more sparsely furnished, with the same wooden cot as the women downstairs were given, and a washstand. The smell of mice was intense. There was a small window, but the view of the night sky was obscured by a splatter of mud; it even got up here, four storeys high.

The cot's eiderdown was thick and smelt relatively clean – a pleasant surprise. Hannah undressed as much as she could bear to, climbed in and pulled it tight around her. Outside, she could hear the oinking of pigs from a nearby yard, and intermittent howls and cries from the street. The sounds made her think of Cosmo, locked up with the lunatics in Friern Barnet, and, really for the first time since he'd gone, she throbbed for him. How brave he was, and how lonely he must feel. How she missed him!

Her thoughts slid across to Mrs Pearcey. According to Ovilry, the prisoner was being held at Holloway Prison, not a mile away. Hannah imagined the conditions there were not dissimilar to her own this evening, or indeed to Cosmo's: bread and dripping for supper; a hard wooden bed in a sparse tiny room. Or perhaps Mrs Pearcey was in a shared cell with a gaggle of petty thieves and prostitutes who had smuggled in liquor under their skirts. Hannah envisaged a scene like earlier by the fire downstairs, of bawdy camaraderie, like a Hogarth etching. But even if she was surrounded by others, Hannah guessed, Mrs Pearcey must be feeling completely, utterly alone.

8

Women's lives are often very dull; but it would help to make them otherwise if wives would sometimes think over, during the hours when parted from their husbands, a few little winning ways as surprises for them on their return, either in the way of conversation or some small change of dress, or in any way their ingenuity would have suggested.

— Girl's Own Paper

On Wednesday afternoon, back at Camden Square, Hannah went down to the kitchen where Gwen was preparing dinner and asked her to go out to Camden Road station and buy the *Star*.

'I promised Cosmo I'd keep it for him,' she explained as the maid shrugged on her coat. 'He's away, you see, on a walking holiday, and he won't be able to find a copy in the Lake District.'

So many little lies she was telling at the moment — even when there was no need. Gwen wasn't beady like Ivy and rarely displayed any interest in the lives of the Teales beyond the bounds of her duties.

'Shall I bring it up to your room?' Gwen asked her, one

hand on the door frame. Hannah hesitated. It was cosy down here in the kitchen, unlike in the rest of the house.

'I might stay here,' Hannah asked, and then added meekly, 'if you don't mind?'

She knew she deserved the look of mild contempt Gwen gave her before the maid turned to stumble up the stairs. Alone, Hannah leant against the table, feeling self-conscious. She had been obsequious with Gwen, but the kitchen really was the servants' domain. In fact, the only time Hannah came in here was late at night, when the house was asleep, sneaking down to scavenge leftovers or to dig a spoon into a jar of blackcurrant jelly unearthed from the larder. She associated the kitchen with furtiveness and guilt, a place to be snuck into and out of as quickly as possible. It had been a long time since she had really looked around the place. In fact, had she ever?

The room was surprisingly dirty. Only the range and the pine table looked recently scrubbed. The surfaces not in everyday use appeared not to have been touched for months. The ochre walls were streaked by soot; the single, high window dim with dust. A couple of the copper saucepans sat on the range, for everyday use, but the vast majority of the pans and utensils were languishing on high, inaccessible shelves, looking sticky and tarnished. Her mother liked eating but didn't like fancy food, and had never been enthusiastic about entertaining. As soon as she'd had the excuse to give it up — when Mr Teale died — she had. The cook was dismissed, the bain-marie and ice-cream moulds retired.

Hannah spied a tin of Peek Frean biscuits on the dresser, buried under a messy pile of old post and circulars, and prised off the lid, but, devastatingly, the tin contained only lemon rinds. She took out one, idly using it to buff her nails as she wandered about. The scullery door was ajar, and she went in. If she rarely came down to the kitchen, she *never* came in here, this little room for the dirty work. Beside the sink sat a pile of tripe, looking like a grubby dishcloth, and the plates from lunch, still littered with bread crusts and boiled-egg shells. A bunch of lavender, long ago leached of scent, hung from the ceiling. On the shelf sat several bowls of solid, waxy fat – dripping for Mrs Teale to take to the refuge, she guessed. On the floor beneath the sink was a bucket of sand and another covered with a lid. She peered in to see that it was full of pink water, in which floated several pale wads of cotton. Sanitary napkins.

Flustered, Hannah replaced the lid and backed out of the scullery. The sight of the soaking fabric made her feel intrusive, but also something more unsettling than that. Looking across to the open scullery door, she felt that she had summoned thoughts of Mrs Pearcey, as if the murderess had been standing silently behind her all this time and as Hannah had peered into that bucket, had gently touched her shoulder.

She thought back to the testimony of the upstairs neighbour at Priory Street, who had entered the scullery on the morning after the murder to find the curtains soaking.

Buckets of blood-soaked water in dank little rooms.

From the street outside she heard the howls of a cat fight, felt the vibrations of a train passing underfoot. At the centre of the table was a board on which sat two brown onions, waiting to be chopped. In Hannah's newly heightened state, even these most ordinary of objects felt charged – direct echoes of that half-onion Hannah had seen on the dresser of the kitchen in Priory Street.

Had it been disposed of by now? Or was it still there, shrivelling imperceptibly by the second, overlooked by all those men trampling through the house, searching for more important things? Now, Hannah leant forward and picked up one of the onions, measuring its pleasing fullness. It occurred to her that she had never actually chopped one up. She had cooked before, of course, but only jolly things for recreation – jellies and petits fours, pancakes on Shrove Tuesday, feeble attempts at spun-sugar confections with their old cook. Who would voluntarily chop an onion?

She began to peel off a strip of its skin, using her thumb and forefinger with the same slow precision she applied to the horse chestnut leaves outside in the square. Once removed, she did another strip, and another, until all the papery brown skin lay on the table. Then she stood up and went through the dresser drawers until she found what looked like a reasonably sharp knife and, placing the onion on the board, sliced it down the centre in one decisive, satisfying action. She registered its stinging vapour and screwed her eyes shut, but too late to avoid the tears.

A monstrous crash came from somewhere close by. Her watery eyes shot open, the pain forgotten. What on earth was happening? The sound was horrific, loud and continuous, like an avalanche, and her first thought was that the house was falling down around her. But there was no obvious sign of upheaval; all the cups on the dresser remained calmly on their saucers. It was only when her eyes had fully cleared that she noticed the new darkness outside the high little window, and realised that it was just a coal delivery, dropping from the pavement chute straight down into the store beside the kitchen. It was a sound Hannah was familiar with, but only when experienced from several floors above the source, as a light rumble. It was twenty times as fierce down here in the bowels of the house, in a room separated from the coal store by only a single layer of bricks.

The barrage came to an abrupt stop, the delivery complete, and the sound of four sets of heavy hooves and scraping wheels signalled the cart moving away from the pavement. Quiet was restored. Hannah sat at the table feeling chastened, as if the coal delivery had been sent to abort her fantasy; her silly attempt to connect with Mrs Pearcey through an onion. Yet she also felt tingly and on high alert, as though the world around her was pulsing with significance.

From above came the slam of the front door, and a moment later Gwen was back in the kitchen, with the *Star*. She looked at Hannah and then at the halved onion.

'Don't let me stop you,' she said, and smiled, which was such a rare sight that it served to break the odd spell Hannah was under. Gwen dropped the paper on the table, before picking up the knife and continuing to chop the onion.

Hannah wondered whether she should take it up to her bedroom to read, in case her mother came down to the kitchen, but she didn't really want to go up to that icy room. Besides, Mrs Teale didn't come down here very much; she wasn't one to fuss around with endless lists or try to control the maids. She picked it up: the headline read HAMPSTEAD HORROR – TERRIBLE NEW DETAILS REVEALED! and the front page was filled with an illustration of the scene at yesterday's inquest, Mrs Pearcey looking pensive in the witness box.

Inside was Ovilry's account of the proceedings and to its right, underneath an advert for Bovril, there it was: a column headed WE TALK TO PHOEBE HOGG'S NIECE AND CONFIDANTE, written by *our correspondent*.

Leaning close to the tiny print, Hannah read her story. Unlike the account of the murder scene at Priory Street, the Lizzie Styles interview had made it into print barely changed, as it largely consisted of Lizzie's words, verbatim. By rights, Hannah thought, she should feel prouder of this one than of her first offering – after all, it was a literal report of the views of someone close to the case, rather than a heightened, lurid account from an opportunist blagger. Instead, reading it left her feeling as uneasy as she had felt when writing it up. As she had suspected then, seeing Lizzie's words in black and white – 'Frank just isn't a nice man', 'Life there was a perfect misery for Phoebe' – did indeed seem to transmute the woman's feelings and beliefs into facts, or at least something very close to facts. Hannah hadn't appreciated this power of newsprint before; that the simple act of publishing a statement gave it weight, regardless of context.

Still, she reminded herself, what Lizzie said most probably *was* true, wasn't it? And Frank was clearly not a nice man. So, in this instance, there was actually little to feel anxious about: the truth almost certainly aligned with the impression she had created.

Closing the paper, she wondered how, and when, and how much she would get paid for the interview. She had included her address when she had sent it to that Summersdale chap, but perhaps she was expected to go to the office and receive her fee in coins from that drawer of his, as before. When she could bear to leave the warm kitchen and go upstairs to the writing desk, she'd send him a note to ask.

She looked over to where Gwen was now rapidly chopping the onions into tiny cubes. No tears for her, efficient as she was in the kitchen arts. Gwen was a relatively new addition to Camden Square, and practised a blank, offhand obedience. Hannah knew nothing about her besides the fact that she was nineteen, from Lewisham, and – overheard from a conversation between Gwen and Ivy – that before coming to them she had worked for Jews, moving between their houses and doing all the things they couldn't on the Sabbath, like lighting candles and poking the fire. Gwen much preferred doing that, but it was just a weekend job and they couldn't keep her, so she'd been forced to come and work for the Teales.

'What do you think about this Hampstead murder?' she asked Gwen now, her eyes on the illustration of Mrs Pearcey on the front page of the *Star*.

'Well, it's not the Ripper,' Gwen replied. 'So, I'm not that bothered.'

'Really?' Hannah looked up. 'Even though the actual story is so horrible? A female murderer? A baby?'

The maid shrugged and wiped her hands on her apron.

'The woman next door when I was young, she killed her husband,' she said casually. 'Clubbed him on the back of the head with a bottle when he was toasted. Things happen, don't they, in houses?'

Gwen's attitude was the inverse of hers, Hannah thought. For Hannah, bad things happened in the street, and home was safe.

Onions chopped, Gwen took the board over to the range

and scraped them into a pan, to which she added some glugs of milk.

'Would be nice to get a gas range in here,' she said, over her shoulder. 'The Jews have one, you know?'

'I'll mention it to mother,' said Hannah.

'You look quite Jewish, you know,' said Gwen.

'I know,' said Hannah. 'I think someone on my father's side was Jewish, once.'

This was by far the most substantial conversation the two young women had ever had. Hannah watched Gwen move expertly around the kitchen, selecting utensils and lifting pans from shelves. She had a compact, rectangular figure and unusually wide-set eyes, of the kind that might well have been seen as very beautiful a century ago. Despite Gwen's indifference, Hannah felt a pleasing sense of companionship, down here together in the warmth. She thought of the shrieks coming up from the kitchen on the night of her engagement dinner, when Gwen and Ivy were preparing to head off to the Bedford.

How long had it been since Hannah had shrieked with anyone? She spent little time in female company these days, her mother aside. Emily was fully submerged in the domestic realm, and in truth, even before she got married, theirs had been a rather one-sided friendship, in which Emily had held forth with her strong views, leaving little space for Hannah in their conversations. Other school friends had similarly disappeared into their grown-up lives, ensconced with little-known husbands in newly built villas in Stoke Newington and Pimlico. In one fell swoop they had become married women, who lived life as married women should. Her dealings with them were now conducted entirely through occasional At Homes, where they would complain about the servants and gush about their children and serve biscuits from a silver basket given to them as a wedding present.

She felt a sudden, intense desire for closeness and collusion – even with Gwen.

'You know, Gwen, Cosmo isn't really in the Lake District,' she said to the maid. 'That's just a story. He's doing an assignment where he is going undercover in a lunatic asylum.'

Gwen glanced up at her, mildly interested.

'Only, it's a secret,' continued Hannah. 'My mother mustn't know, you see?'

'Brings back bad memories, I suppose,' said Gwen.

'How do you mean?'

'Oh, I thought Mrs Teale had gone away to one of those places. Ivy told me.'

'I think she might be confused,' Hannah replied. 'Mother does lots of work with unfortunate women and runs a refuge. Ivy must have thought it was that.'

Gwen shrugged and then ducked into the scullery, emerging a moment later with the tripe, which she threw down on the table.

'Where is the Lake District, anyway?' she said.

'It's in the North somewhere,' replied Hannah. 'There are lots of hills. And lakes, of course.'

'Right,' said Gwen, now concentrating on cutting the tripe into squares. Hannah waited but their conversation had petered out. She opened the paper again, this time turning to Ovilry's account of the inquest. He had indeed chosen to describe Mrs Pearcey with a negative slant; the prisoner, he wrote, had a *chilling, cold stare* and *a distinctly masculine bearing*. Oh, if he only knew that Hannah was responsible for the exclusive interview published next to his! Her earlier uneasiness about Lizzie Styles had dissolved away; now she smiled with her secret, at the delicious fact of being part of an exciting and important gang of news gatherers, even if no one else in the gang knew it.

For the next couple of days, Hannah continued with this routine, coming down to the kitchen in the afternoon, asking Gwen to run out to the newsstand, and then reading the latest on Mrs Pearcey in the maid's undemanding company. Curious as to what the other publications were reporting, she requested Gwen buy a variety of papers, not just the *Star*. Each of them carried their own exclusive stories on the Hampstead Horror; it wasn't just Ovilry – and Hannah – who had been scampering across London, following leads, charming and persuading, and writing the stories up with supernatural speed. Several of the reporters had returned to Priory Street, where apparently there were still so many gawkers the police had resorted to stuffing the keyhole of Number 2 to deter nosiness. The *Gazette* reported that the police had tracked down the boy who had delivered the fateful letter from Mrs Pearcey to Phoebe on the Friday morning, inviting her for tea.

There were some surprisingly positive reports about Mrs Pearcey's character. One neighbour described how the accused used to sit in the window of her house and cheerily greet passers-by. Another described how happy and proud it had made Mrs Pearcey to offer around the lettuces that she had grown in her garden. A man who lived a few doors down was quoted as saying, 'Once, a beggar came to my door – I'm telling you this even though I don't come out well – and I turned him away. The beggar said, "Well, thank God you are not all hard-hearted people, for the lady next door at Number 2 had some feeling."' Apparently, the kind Mrs Pearcey had given him threepence and some bread and butter.

But the stories weren't all favourable. Mrs Crowhurst, the widow who occupied the second floor of 2 Priory Street – and the one who had discovered the soaking curtains in the scullery – claimed to be concerned about 'goings-on' in Mrs Pearcey's quarters. On Friday evening, when Mrs Crowhurst's son, who lived on the first floor, visited the privy, he noticed the smashed glass outside the kitchen. His mother attributed the mess to a row Mrs Pearcey must have had with the man she called her husband, Mr Hogg. Hogg would take his dinner and tea with her once or twice a week, and on those days Mrs Pearcey would make a great show of the fact, saying, 'Well, I must go and get my husband's dinner ready, he will be in directly.' On the occasions when Hogg did not show up, Mrs Pearcey was unsettled and said things like, 'I wonder where he is that he does not come.' A Mrs Piddington, who lived next door, described how she had lent Mrs Pearcey a dress stand, and on that fateful Friday afternoon had been about to go round to ask for it back when she heard a terrible crashing sound coming from Mrs Pearcey's rooms. She and her husband assumed it was a marital row and so, although alarmed, resolved to keep out of it.

All these little details, thought Hannah, were like the pinches of flour Gwen added to her sauces: thickening up the story. Her earlier misgivings about her own contribution to the sauce now seemed foolish. The Lizzie Styles interview was essentially more newsworthy than many of these other reports; Lizzie did, after all, have an intimate knowledge of the victim, the accused *and* Frank Hogg. Her voice was more important than that of a neighbour who had once shared Mrs Pearcey's lettuce crop.

On Friday, several of the papers carried the information that the funeral for Phoebe and Tiggie Hogg would take place on the coming Sunday, the procession starting from the Clatworthy undertakers on Camden High Street.

Sunday. Two days' time. Should she go? There was no real justification for it. The crowd would be swarming with journalists, and they'd all be reporting on the same spectacle. The Hogg family would be inaccessible in their cortège. She couldn't imagine there would be any chance to be a renegade, to find a secret back door and get a scoop.

And yet . . . and yet. If she *could* find an exclusive story there, what a coup that would be!

And perhaps, even without the chance of getting a story, she had a duty to attend. The funeral of poor Phoebe Hogg and her innocent baby was an important moment in this tragedy she was caught up in. She should pay her respects, if nothing else.

She easily convinced herself: she must go. She could tell her mother she was having tea with Emily again, or perhaps use another one of her school friends as an excuse this time. It occurred to her that she still had her mourning clothes from when her father died. By rights she should have disposed of them after her year was up, but she had never got round to it, and there they still were, at the bottom of her chest. She smiled to herself at the serendipity, at how her laziness had been vindicated.

Hearing a sound from outside, Hannah looked up to the

high little window to see the legs of the postman passing by, followed by the familiar snap of the letterbox. Laying down the paper, she went upstairs to fetch the post. There were a couple of letters for her mother, which she left on the tray, and one for her, which she brought back downstairs to open at her new base, the kitchen table. Inside, tucked into a folded piece of headed note paper from the *Star* office, was a postal order for five shillings.

Payment for Lizzie Styles! Her pleasure at the sight of it was followed by a faint touch of pique. Why only five shillings, and not six, as before? She supposed it wasn't as big a scoop as getting into the murder scene . . .

'Oh, I forgot,' said Gwen. 'Something else came for you.'

Hannah looked up. Gwen was now at the dresser, holding a fistful of cutlery from the drawer, and with her other hand she pulled something from her apron pocket and handed it to Hannah. It was a creased, official-looking letter addressed to her; on the back, the return address read: *Colney Hatch Lunatic Asylum, Friern Barnet.*

Hannah frowned, and looked over at Gwen, who was now loading the dumb waiter.

'When did this arrive? Why didn't you give it to me immediately?'

'Yesterday, miss,' replied Gwen, stiffly. 'The postman handed it to me when I was on my way out of the house, so I put it in my apron rather than straight on the tray, and then it slipped my mind. My sincere apologies.'

She vigorously cranked the dumb waiter's wheel, before stomping upstairs to receive it. Hannah grimaced. It was obvious that her sharp tone had snuffed out their delicate little intimacy. And now she had a moment to think about it,

Gwen's simple explanation was surely the truth. What possible reason could the maid have for deliberately withholding a letter linked to Cosmo's secret assignment? Moreover, Gwen wasn't as literate as Ivy; it was quite possible that her reading ability was limited to recognising her employers' names on envelopes, and so she wouldn't have known where the letter came from, anyway.

Perhaps her engagement with the Pearcey case was changing her, Hannah thought; hardening her character, making her suspicious and interrogative. She would have to think of how she could regain Gwen's favour, but for now, she felt she was trespassing down here in the kitchen, as out of place as a dog in a church. She took the envelope upstairs to her room, lay on the bed and opened it.

Dear Miss Teale,

I'm writing to you in my capacity as the superintendent of the Colney Hatch Lunatic Asylum. A new patient here, identified as Charles Winterbottom, now claims that he is in fact one Mr Cosmo Walters and has been admitted under false pretences. He now wishes to be discharged. He has named you as his next of kin, able to both vouch for him and take responsibility should we agree to release him. Please advise me at your earliest convenience.

Yours,

Mr Simon Culpepper, Esquire

Hannah stared at the neat italics, before laying down the letter and rubbing her temples, as if this would ease the feelings of ambivalence it had produced. Of course, she felt awful for Cosmo, who was clearly having a wretched time.

She imagined him cowering in the corner of a slimy room with barred windows, limply kicking away the rats going for his ankles, gaze fixed on the door as he waited, fruitlessly, for the arrival of the warden come to release him.

Yet, she could not deny a sense of disappointment at his attempt to abort the assignment. Cosmo had said himself that the editor would only be interested in the story if he stayed inside for ten days. The American journalist had managed it – and she was a woman!

Surely, Cosmo was not in mortal danger. Mr Simon Culpepper, Esquire, wouldn't let anything terrible happen to him. And Hannah thought of herself on her parallel money-making mission. What risks she had taken! How far she had gone beyond the bounds of her normal life!

The letter had arrived on Thursday. Today was Friday. It was already a day old. If Hannah had not been down in the kitchen, and jogged Gwen's memory of it, the letter might easily – *easily* – still be there, forgotten, in her apron pocket.

As Cosmo's wife-to-be, her duty was to assist him. But perhaps by not immediately answering this letter and leaving him in there to fulfil his stated mission, she *was* helping him. He would thank her, afterwards, when his story was on the front page, the editor had promoted him, there was a guinea in his pocket, and the two of them were several steps closer to their six-roomed house in Canonbury. And in the meantime, Hannah could go to the funeral.

Hannah spent much of the following day, Saturday, in her bedroom, feeling out of sorts. She had taken the decision about Cosmo and the letter but could not fully digest it; it sat in her stomach, bothering her. Outside was uninviting, the sky iron-grey. Below her, the house was quiet. She tried to distract herself. No sewing octopuses onto nightgowns; she didn't have the blank-minded patience required for such work. A novel, perhaps? She scanned her bookshelf – Eliot, Dickens, Collins, Alcott – but none of her old favourites appealed. Instead, she picked out *The Beast Within*, the Émile Zola novel that her erstwhile suitor James had given her. It was the only one she didn't know, and besides, it seemed fitting for her current state of mind.

Getting under the covers, she started to read. Within a few pages, it was clear that the beast here referred to something far darker than a guilty conscience. The story told of a man who flew into fits of blind violence, attacking his wife when he believed she had been unfaithful, yet remembered little about the incident afterwards.

They crashed against the table and nearly overturned the stove, she read. *There were smears of blood and strands of hair stuck to the corner of the sideboard. They staggered back towards the bed, gasping for breath, dazed and sickened by the force of his onslaught . . . At such times his body took on a life of its own; he became the slave of the beast within.*

Hannah's skin grew hot as she read. The story's brutality made the drawing-room tussles in her magazines, with all their wrist-gripping and stern words, seem like pantomime. There were descriptions of animalistic sexual activity that were like nothing she had come across before. Hannah continued on for a while, horribly compelled, before laying the book aside and staring up at the ceiling.

The tortoise woman, from the refuge – hadn't she exhibited similar behaviour? Not as horrific as the novel's character, of course, but still – she had flown into a blind rage at that boy on the York Road, and then appeared not to remember it at all when Hannah mentioned it a few days later. Her mother had said the woman suffered from epilepsy.

Perhaps Mrs Pearcey was similarly afflicted. It would explain why, despite such overwhelming evidence that she had been involved in the murder, she was denying all knowledge of it. Had she just forgotten?

Hannah didn't know what to do with this thought. She lodged it in the back of her mind, in the shadowy space reserved for Mrs Pearcey. And then she put *The Beast Within* back on the shelf and picked up *Middlemarch* instead.

On Sunday morning, Hannah woke early, instantly alert, as if she'd been waiting all night for this moment. She lay in bed impatiently, blindly leafing through a magazine, until at last she heard the faint slam of the front door, at which she jumped up, crossed over to the window and pressed her cheek against the glass. She was just in time to glimpse the back of her mother heading off in the direction of York Road and the Foundling Hospital, before disappearing from view.

Hannah sprang into action. Over on the chair, her mourning dress sat, unearthed from the chest, a mound of crumpled, musty crêpe. She held the dress up at the window, inspecting it, although she knew it was in a poor state and there was little she could do about it. After all, she had worn it continuously for a year, after a hurried trip to Jay's Mourning Warehouse on Regent's Street on 21 June 1887, the morning after her father died, when the streets were still littered with confetti from the celebrations for the queen's jubilee. The dress had been retired and shoved in her drawer on 20 June 1888. The bombazine still carried flecks of pollen from a past summer, and the faint tang of perspiration. Traces of the Hannah from before: the limited girl who secretly devoured tawdry magazines and shared Garibaldis with Emily, who perched self-consciously on the bridge at Camden Lock, imagining herself as a romantic heroine who would be kidnapped by a passing bargeman; who practised the piano and attempted to enjoy sewing. The Hannah who hadn't yet met Cosmo; who hadn't heard of Mrs Pearcey; who wouldn't have dreamed of doing what she was about to do.

Now, she climbed back into the fusty, scratchy costume, drawing in her breath as she hooked the bodice. It was snugger than she remembered. Too many illicit sausage rolls and midnight spoonfuls of jam. She pinned on the veil. Then, without even looking in the mirror, she flew down the stairs and out of the door.

The morning was suited to a funeral, with brooding, low clouds and spitting rain. As she hurried towards Camden Town, veil down, Hannah noticed some men eyeing her with interest. A young widow – that most exciting of prospects.

Clatworthy's Funeral Parlour was halfway down the high street, almost opposite the Bedford. The Brown's dairy junction was as busy as ever, but as Hannah pressed through the throng, she realised that everyone seemed to be heading in the same direction she was. She overheard one woman telling another that she had walked all the way from Chiswick, starting at 4 a.m. that morning.

'I heard that he turned up at the undertaker's yesterday, behaving very strangely,' said another to her companion as they marched alongside Hannah. 'Demanding to see them. He was raving, apparently. I actually think he's going to go berserk today.'

'I don't think he's going to turn up,' replied her companion. 'He must know what everyone's thinking, that he's had something to do with it.'

The gossiping crowd was reminiscent of that at Priory Street and at the hearings – but those had the feeling of a day out, a jaunt. Today, the atmosphere was darker. The filthy weather aided this impression, but it seemed to Hannah that the horde really did have more of an angry, feral energy. It felt similar to the time she was caught up in a group of people off to a political demonstration. People elbowed past her with drawn brows and set mouths, looking as if they were on a grim mission.

About fifty feet away from the undertaker, the mob had grown so dense she came to a stop. Hearing a noise above her head, she looked up to see two women hanging out of an upstairs window above the bakery; now, she noticed that there were more figures at more windows, above the butcher's and the fishmonger's and the laundry. Over on the roof of the Bowman Brothers' department store, a group had gathered, waiting, hands on hips, silhouetted against the grey sky. All of the windows of the music hall were filled with onlookers. The road was as clogged as the pavement, and the traffic had given up trying to move.

A clock struck 10 a.m. The mood of the crowd was growing even more fractious, exacerbated by the rain that had started to fall. Squashed, her view restricted to the black coats and hats of those beside her, Hannah noticed a nearby lamppost and had an idea. Moving beside it, she hoisted herself up onto it, one foot braced on its base, to gain a few feet of height.

Several people glanced up at her, and who could blame them? A woman in mourning, clinging onto a lamppost! Clutching the cold metal, elevated above the crowd, she felt rather like a figurehead on the prow of a ship, her sense of power enhanced by the anonymity provided by her veil. Should anyone she knew glance up, they wouldn't recognise her. From this new vantage point, she could see the full extent of the crowd. It was vaster than any Hannah had seen before, and people were still packing in from all directions: from Kentish Town, Hampstead, Holloway and Euston. Surveying the scene, she felt an odd sense of pride and proprietorship. It was as if all the newspaper readers had materialised: all those people she had imagined in their drawing rooms, reading her words over their cod and boiled potatoes, were now gathered before her.

It was a turnout befitting a music-hall star or a minor royal. Yet the people were gathered here to pay tribute to a domestic servant and her baby. Two working-class females who, had this terrible thing not befallen them, would have lived and died without attracting any attention or interest from the world at large.

She wondered if anyone would speak about them at the ceremony, and what they would say. And then she thought about her father's funeral, for the first time in a long while. As he'd died at forty-nine, she supposed his life had been cut short, too. That event was a modest gathering of twenty at a church in Highgate: the immediate family, his brother, plus some colleagues from Temple and a few friends from the Garrick. The eulogy talked about his sharp legal brain, his bridge prowess and his geniality at the club – in short, a man who bore no resemblance to the father she knew. Or rather, she didn't know the man who was being described; these were qualities he reserved for others, outside his family. But it appeared that this was how the outside world saw him, and how he would be officially remembered. The man he was when at home with his wife and children was not important.

Then, Hannah was back in the moment, up on her lamp-post, because down there in the crowd, there was action. She stood up straighter, tightening her grip. From the Kentish Town fork of the junction there had emerged a number of mounted policemen, who were working together to push apart the crowd, creating a channel. Following in their wake were a hearse and several mourning coaches. The cavalcade started to inch down the high street. Hannah watched as the crowds swarmed around the vehicles, all of one mind, forming patterns like shoals of minnows.

And then she became aware of a sound. It was a deep, sinister, escalating noise, one she hadn't heard before. The only thing she could compare it to was the lowing of cows, as if a hundred beasts had escaped from the dairy and were making themselves known. Belatedly, she realised: it was the crowd, baying.

The hearse came to a halt outside the undertaker, and, within seconds, six men emerged, carrying a coffin piled high with wreaths. Following behind it were several mourners, their heads bowed. Among them, Hannah recognised the tall figure of Lizzie Styles, who climbed into the carriage parked behind the hearse. And then, the baying turned to booing, the sound catching like wildfire and rising in crescendo until it was unignorable, now accompanied by hisses, too. Somehow, the crowd had pre-empted the next person to emerge from inside. From her perch, Hannah watched as Frank Hogg raised his head and looked over the crowd. She was too far away to see his expression. The booing and hissing grew louder, and the onlookers pressed towards him. The policemen linked arms to hold them back, so that he could climb into the second carriage. Three figures, whom Hannah identified as his mother, sister Clara and brother Edwin, quickly followed him. As the coach started moving, the crowd surged forward again, and again the mounted police escorts used their horses to push them back. A further dozen policemen on foot surrounded the Hoggs' hearse, forming a human ring around it against the swell of protestors.

'What did you do, Hogg?' screamed someone. 'What do you know?'

Cries of 'Murderer!' and 'Liar!' and 'Evil!' bounced off the hearse as it ploughed northwards. Everywhere Hannah looked, she could see ugly, contorted faces.

The rain was falling heavily now. Hannah's shoulders were soaked through, moisture collecting in the tiny holes of her veil. Her fingers were white cold and aching from clutching onto the post. Suddenly, she could hold on no longer and slithered to the pavement. Straightening up, she asked the man next to her, 'Where are they headed?'

'Up to the cemetery at Finchley,' he replied impatiently, looking over her shoulder. The rain was dripping off his ears.

Finchley was where her father was buried, so Hannah knew it was a good five miles away. She frowned at the man as she computed what he was saying.

'So,' she asked, 'people are going to follow it all the way there?'

The man shrugged *of course* and set off to join them.

Hannah stayed where she was, leaning against the lamp-post, as the feverish procession moved away, past the Mother Red Cap, and veering right at the junction towards Kentish Town. She waited, unmoving, until it was out of sight, the booing and shouting gradually growing fainter.

Only when she felt she was sufficiently distanced from it all did Hannah start moving herself, heading back towards Camden Road. As she walked, she barely registered the rain or the pavement beneath her feet; she felt light-headed with shame. Why did she come? How had she nearly become the kind of person who joined a baying mob willing to walk for two hours in the rain behind a hearse, uninvited, to attend the funeral of two people they didn't know?

Her earlier pride in her contribution to the news stories had turned inside out. The *Star* had a circulation of, what, half a million? How many of those people heckling Frank Hogg had read her interview with Lizzie Styles, in which Lizzie had voiced her suspicions? How many of those boos was she personally responsible for? She felt as if she had been anointed with an unholy power, like being able to lift a coach with one hand, and had only belatedly realised the responsibility that came with it, and the damage she could inflict. She felt both in awe and horrified at herself.

By the time she reached Camden Square she was drenched to the skin, as wretched as she deserved to be. The rain was so strong that it was hard to see further than a few feet in front of her, or to take in much more than the sound of it beating down on the flagstones. But as she approached the house, she heard a cry from somewhere nearby. 'Mrs Teale! Mrs Teale!'

Hannah stopped in her tracks. Her mother was back? As she looked around her, peering through the torrent to try to identify both Mrs Teale and the person who required her, she started scrabbling around in her head for a reasonable excuse for being outside in the torrential rain dressed in mourning.

'I say – Mrs Teale!'

And now, looking over her shoulder, Hannah could see a man hurrying towards her from the eastern side of the square. Such was the poor visibility, it was only when he was a few feet away that she realised who the voice belonged to. At just the same moment, he recognised her.

'Hannah?'

Could this really be Cosmo? His face was scrunched up against the rain, and under his cloth cap she could see that his head had been shaved. He was wearing a raggedy linen shirt and rough blue trousers, far too big and bunched up around the waist where he'd tied them with string. And here he was staring at her, as if she was the odd-looking one.

'Who's died?' he asked. 'Not your mother?'

Was his tone one of curiosity, or shock? It was hard to discern anything in such sleeting rain. She shook her head, and for a moment they just stared at each other, both drenched, exposed and pathetic in their guises.

'Come inside,' she said.

Upstairs, Hannah directed Cosmo to Will's room and told him to help himself to any clothes he could find. Then, she retreated to her own room. She was reeling, but how much of that was due to the ugly funeral, or to Cosmo's surprise reappearance, she couldn't tell. She had had no time to contend with the first drama of the day before the second one had occurred, and now the events were smashed together, like a traffic pile-up. She tried to empty her mind, focusing only on the physical sensations of what she was doing: peeling off the sodden, rough bombazine, flinging it over the back of the chair, finding a towel, putting on her old day dress.

Eventually, she went down to the drawing room. The fire was getting going; Ivy must have just left. Cosmo was already there, leaning against the fireplace, warming up. He was wearing a garish green tartan suit of Will's, bought for a Burns Night dinner a few years back.

'That's a funny choice,' she said.

'Well, this is the one he gave me,' replied Cosmo.

'Will's here?'

Cosmo laughed. 'Barely. He was fast asleep but roused himself just enough to listen to my plea and to tell me he could loan me his second-best tartan suit.'

There was movement at the door; Ivy had come up with a tray of tea. Cosmo and Hannah waited in silence until she had left the room. Hannah realised that she had no idea how he was going to react to what she had to tell him.

'So, how was the asylum?' she began politely.

'Oh, darling, I can't begin to tell you how dreadful it was,' he said, and then proceeded to do just that as he paced around the room, tea sloshing in his saucer. He painted a vivid picture of the constant howling and groaning; the barely warm porridge; the strip washes and plank beds; his neighbour's bodily fluids; the constant air of menace and derangement; the at best ineffectual and at worst malign management. As she watched him speak, Hannah tried to conjure the sense of familiarity and fondness she had previously experienced in his presence, but it was as if her feelings hadn't yet caught up with the surprise of him turning up like this. He just looked so different, in Will's suit, eyes bleary, his head sprouting fine, pale stubble, the shape of his skull intimately exposed.

'I know I was meant to endure it for ten days, but it really was simply intolerable. No one could have. I asked them to write to you, to help get me out, but they clearly lied about doing that, too,' he continued darkly.

Hannah looked away towards the fire, the glowing caves between the coals. The jar of spills next to it, rolled-up pieces of paper – Cosmo's paper.

'Maybe the letter got waylaid,' she said, standing and moving over to the fire, her back to him. 'It does happen.'

'Oh, no, no,' he said. 'Them lying about sending it totally fits with my impressions of the place.'

Anyway, he continued, when Hannah didn't appear to vouch for him, he was so desperate he was preparing himself to write and tell all to his mother, even at the cost of the torrent of anxiety that would ensue. But then, just as he'd resolved to follow this plan of action, he was struck by another one.

'You see, I knew that jacking it in might mean the editor rejecting the article, and it all being a huge waste of time. So, I thought, how can I make it more exciting, and justify the story? It came to me. I would try to escape!' He paused for dramatic effect.

She stared at him. 'How on earth?'

'Well, I decided to climb into a laundry basket,' he said. 'One of those big ones. Bury myself in the foetid sheets and stay stock still, then get carried out of the building by the porters.'

'Gosh!' said Hannah, taken aback. 'And so, what happened?'

'Well – it turned out I didn't need to,' he said, with an embarrassed smile. 'Just as I was thinking of it, the warden told me that I was free to go.'

Hannah laughed at the bathos.

'What, so you just walked out of the gate, like a normal person?'

Cosmo nodded. She felt that he was caught between annoyance at looking foolish and not having had the chance to prove himself a hero, and his desire to be seen as easygoing and having a sense of humour. The latter impulse had won, just.

'Yes, a more straightforward exit, I must say!' he said.

Hannah felt a rush of affection for him.

'And how did you get back here?'

'On the bus. Luckily, I had kept back a penny for emergency situations such as this, hidden in my shoe. Fearful traffic coming down, though. The road was terribly jammed up near Highgate. Some sort of mass funeral procession.'

He squinted at her, as if just now remembering her earlier appearance.

'Wait – were you part of it? Was that why you were in mourning? Who died?'

At that, Hannah stood up and walked over to him, pulling her chair until it was right up beside his. She took his hand in hers, and he looked at her with surprise.

'Cosmo, now I have to tell *you* something,' she said. Now it was his turn to feel proud of her. 'You asked why I was dressed in mourning, and, well, it's a bit of a story . . .'

And then she told him everything, starting with lying on her bed and overhearing the maids on that Saturday morning – extraordinarily, just over a week ago. As she spoke, she watched Cosmo's expression slide from confusion to amazement and then, as he absorbed what she was telling him, to an emotion that was less clear-cut. He alternated between smiling and wincing. Occasionally he'd say something, but he spoke more to himself than to her, as if he were trying to sort it out in his own head.

'You went into the office and introduced yourself to Summersdale?' he murmured. 'You got a scoop over Ovilry?'

But it wasn't the same as it once was, when he'd repeated what she'd said in wonder. Now, his tone was far more muted and conflicted.

Still, she continued, telling him about her suspicions that Mrs Pearcey had epilepsy, supported by her encounter with the tortoise lady in Camden Town. Finally, she reached the end of her account – the unnerving funeral procession just that morning – and stopped talking. By now Cosmo had risen to his feet and was pacing around the room.

'I thought you'd be pleased,' Hannah said meekly.

'Oh, Hannah, I am, but . . .' He sighed. 'It's just – I don't know. It feels odd that you're . . . I mean, Fleet Street is no place for you. It just feels a bit . . . off. I don't know. You going to see Summersdale. What if he thought I'd sent in my wife, because I couldn't do the work myself?'

'I'm not your wife, yet!' she replied, surprising herself. 'And he definitely didn't know who I was. Anyway – what would it matter? Women are doing this kind of thing now – not many, I know, but some are. What about that girl in America, who did what you did?'

'Girl?' He frowned.

'It was a female journalist who went into a madhouse,' she explained, adding meanly, 'for a whole ten days.'

'Well, that's America,' replied Cosmo, too loudly.

She looked at him over by the window, with his stubbly head, his set mouth, in Will's stupid suit, and felt, for a moment, unloving. He sighed and went back to flop down in his chair.

'But the main point is,' he said, 'that it isn't the kind of thing you should be exposed to, this. Awful murderers. It's dirty work.'

'I did it for us,' she said quietly.

'I know! And that fact makes me so happy, darling, the idea that you're trying to build our future. It's just – oh, I don't know!'

He slumped back against the sofa, anguished, and looked up at the ceiling.

'I say – I haven't eaten for ages. Do you think there's anything downstairs I could have? Call one of the girls?'

Grateful to be released, Hannah went down to the kitchen herself, but neither of the maids was there. Hot with embarrassment and annoyance, she sawed at a piece of bread and scraped some hard dripping on it. Perhaps, she thought, this argument, this reckoning, was a good thing: an intimate interaction that most girls didn't experience with their fiancé before marriage. A chance to see her betrothed in a base form, exposed and real. When she brought the food back upstairs Cosmo was standing at the window.

'Bread and dripping! It's like being back at the asylum!' he said as she handed it to him, smiling to show it was a joke. She could see he was trying to make an effort to restore relations, and it made her feel more in control of herself.

'I know you don't approve of these sorts of stories, the ones best left to Ovilry,' she said, 'but I thought it was worth it. For us. For the house. I got six shillings for the first one, and five for the second. Anyway, of course I'll be stopping now.'

'Oh, really?'

'Yes, of course!' she replied, with feeling. 'To be honest, it hit me today, when I was outside the undertaker's, that it's a rather grotesque—'

'But it sounds like you're rather good at it.'

Wrong-footed, Hannah wasn't sure how to respond.

'What stage is it at now, the story?' Cosmo continued. 'With Mrs Peatey?'

'Pearcey,' corrected Hannah. 'Well, she's in prison. The trial will be next month, apparently. I think there are some more hearings next week, although it seems to me that they've got quite enough evidence. I suppose the thing the journalists will be trying to find out now is her motive. More about her, who she is. That's why I thought of the epilepsy. And whether Hogg was involved, or whether she did it all herself – which seems unlikely to me, even if she was in a fit . . .'

'Let me go into the office and discreetly sound out Ovilry,' he said. 'Find out what he's pursuing. I must admit, I rather love the idea of this anonymous correspondent continuing to outwit him.'

Hannah stared at him. 'You think I should carry on?'

'*We* should!' he said. 'You've done jolly well, but I'm back now.'

Before she could respond, he continued, 'I'll have to keep well in the background, because there'll be hell to pay if

Ovilry knows I'm on his turf. But as far as Summersdale knows, it's just a pretty little girl who is somehow scooping their official correspondent, isn't it?' He smiled to himself. 'And then, when it's over, I can reveal all and tell the editor who you are and that I was really behind it. And then, who knows? Maybe I'll get a promotion!' He sighed happily. 'Oh, I love it – like a puppet master behind the scenes directing operations . . .'

Then, finally, he looked at her properly. His face was transformed, triumphant.

'What do you think, Hannah?' he said. 'We can be a team.'

Hannah gazed at him, her glistening-eyed fiancé, and then down at her shoes. So tangled were her feelings, she knew she didn't have a hope of unpicking them now, in the moment. But sitting separate to that was her desire to please.

She nodded and smiled.

'I knew I'd picked the right girl!' cried Cosmo, and with that, he leant over and kissed her, on the mouth, for the very first time.

9

While a happy marriage is the ideal state, who could tell us how much the world owes to spinsters? Of one thing we may be very certain, viz., that the world would be much worse off if there were none of these self-denying creatures to carry on its works of mercy.
— Girl's Own Paper

Shortly after the kiss, Cosmo had left to go home to Kensington. Hannah had watched from the drawing-room window as he'd trotted off down the street, Will's green tartan suit incongruous in the wet gloom. He had left a dampness on her lips, and for a few minutes she resisted touching them. The actual experience of her first kiss – all three seconds of it – didn't feel as momentous, as soul-shaking, as she had been led to believe it would. If she removed the evidence, she was worried the event would have left no mark on her at all.

As Cosmo disappeared from view, Hannah had shifted her focus back to the room. The slice of wall between the two drawing-room windows bore the ghost of a print, the very faint outline of a square where a frame had once hung. The print had been there for her whole life, until her mother had started stripping the house for the refuge, but looking at the square, Hannah had realised she couldn't even remember what the image had been. How ephemeral it all was! Finally, she had wiped her lips.

On Friday morning, a letter arrived from Cosmo. Gwen made a show of bringing it to Hannah in the drawing room straight from the postman and gave a sarcastic curtsey as she retreated. Hannah had clearly not been forgiven for her sharpness over the asylum letter.

Cosmo wrote that he'd finally managed to have a word with Ovilry about the Pearcey case,

> *enquiring in a casual tone, as if just catching up on what I'd missed. I asked him what are the burning questions still unanswered and he said – did she have help? What was her motive? What is the direct evidence linking her? I think the first is the top line of enquiry – did she have help? I mentioned the epilepsy black-out angle, as if it had just come to me, but the editor wasn't that keen, I'm afraid. Not exciting enough. He thinks the readers will either want a confession from her or, better still, Frank Hogg's involvement. That man Hogg has a bad odour about him. Let's have a think how to go about it.*
>
> *Yours, Cozzy*
>
> *P.S. Mama says we really must meet with the vicar of St Mary's, to confirm the order of service.*
>
> *P.P.S. Good news – the editor says he'll print the asylum story if I say I DID escape in the laundry basket. After all, I very almost did!*

Hannah read the letter again before scrunching it up and lobbing it across the room into the fireplace. She was feeling irritable and out of sorts, and had done all week, ever since

Cosmo's reappearance. She knew she should be pleased that he wanted to work as a team on the Mrs Pearcey story. Not only did it show that he saw her as a real helpmeet, but it also meant that she could continue to be involved with the story. In fact, it allowed her to have it both ways, absolving her of responsibility. She could piously hold on to the revulsion she felt at the funeral and feel that if it were solely down to her, she would have ceased her involvement, at the same time as indulging her unsavoury desire to know everything she could about this grisly story, and to stick with it to the very end.

But the simple truth was that Cosmo's intervention had taken the wind from her sails. Mrs Pearcey wasn't *hers* any more.

Furthermore, on a practical level, she just couldn't think of how she – or how she and Cosmo – might get something incriminating on Frank Hogg. What had felt like a thrilling challenge when she was doing it on her own now seemed a hopeless undertaking. Those figures who personally knew Hogg and had a reason to be disloyal, like Lizzie Styles, had already been interviewed. If there was someone else who would provide some damning insight into Frank Hogg's character, she didn't know how to begin to find them. Besides, after her interview with Lizzie, she felt she wanted more than just someone's opinion on the man; opinion that might fill half a page in a paper but wouldn't make any difference in a court of law. They needed proof.

Even if she were to act as Ovilry and the rest had before, and grab a moment with Hogg on the street after one of the hearings, then really, what would Hogg say? 'Oh, very well. Out of all these other journalists beseeching me, I pick you to hear the truth. Yes, I did help my lover to murder my wife and child. Now, direct me towards the gallows!'

She sat down beside the fire and stared at the ashes of Cosmo's letter. The maddening thing was, she *should* have more insight than the others. She had met Mrs Pearcey. She had been inside her house.

She thought back to their meeting on the Prince of Wales Road, the morning after the murders. *What if there's more than one culprit?* Mrs Pearcey had asked her. Hannah had assumed she meant *victim* and had got the words confused. But perhaps she hadn't.

Still, that was no use. It was hardly solid evidence, just an ambiguous statement that she was interpreting according to her own suspicions.

She sat down at the piano and started thumping out a nonsense tune.

'Stop it!'

She looked up to see Will enter the drawing room and flop into a chair. His hair was all over the place, his eyes gluey.

'I think I've been poisoned,' he said.

'Where did last night take you?'

He gave a wave, as if to say, *Where didn't it?*

'Don't you ever have to do any college work?'

He glanced away and said, in a still-blithe tone, 'I think we might be going our separate ways, me and Oxford.'

'What? Really?'

Will nodded. 'Some people just aren't made for ivory towers. I need to be out in the real world.'

'But what will you do?'

'Producing, of course.'

'Does Mother know?'

'Not yet. I thought I'd tell her at Christmas. I'm sure she'll understand.'

'Such a waste,' Hannah said. 'Honestly.'

'You go to university, then!' he said. 'Go on. Tell Cosmo that you've decided to become a blue stocking instead of getting married.'

He looked around the room, searching for another subject for conversation.

'What's all that?' he said, indicating the pile of linen night-dresses on a chair, waiting patiently for Hannah to return to them.

'Wedding things,' she replied.

'Ah, yes, the great day approaches! Which of your friends are coming, again?'

Again? They had never had this conversation before, not least because Hannah hadn't officially invited anyone yet. She *must* put her mind to it.

'Well, Emily, of course,' she said. 'And . . . others.'

'Is Emily the one who lives on Gloucester Crescent?' replied Will. 'I like her. She's homely but there's something about her. A plain Jane with a twist.'

'For a start,' responded Hannah tartly, 'Emily is now married with a baby, and couldn't care less what you think of her. And anyway, she's too old for you, surely.'

'Oh, no,' Will said. 'I like older women. Far more interesting. Less coy and beseeching.'

'Is this really how you talk to a sister? You're not in one of your gentlemen's clubs now.'

'More's the pity,' he said. 'The Savile would never have such a feeble fire.'

He went over to the hearth and stood close, his lower legs

pressed up against the fireguard, inspecting his reflection in the mirror above the mantelpiece. Hannah picked up one of the nightdresses, extracted a needle from the pin cushion and sat down with them. She could at least *look* like someone who was knee-deep in wedding preparations.

But rather than sewing, Hannah watched Will in his self-absorption. She thought of Cosmo in this room a few days ago, stomping around in anguish at the thought that his colleagues at the paper might discover that Hannah had helped him in his work.

'What do you think of Cosmo?' she asked Will.

'Cosmo's a great chap! Even if he does wake me up to borrow my tartan suit. I'm sure we'll be great friends.'

'What about me? I mean, do you think he and I are well matched?'

'Gosh,' he said, nonplussed. 'Well, yes. Of course! I mean, well – you're nice. And he's nice.'

Hannah laughed, and Will shrugged and smiled, acknowledging the inadequacy of his response. It was quite possible, thought Hannah, that this reply was all he had, and that he had given no time at all to contemplating her character.

'I'm sure he can give you what you need,' Will continued. He moved away from the fire.

'What *do* I need?' Hannah asked.

'Oh, I don't know! What do we all need? Jolly company? A nice warm house? As few demands on us as possible?'

'I don't think Mother thinks much of him.'

'She generally doesn't think much of men, does she?'

'She never criticises you! I feel I'm always disappointing her.'

'She probably just thinks I'm a lost cause,' said Will. 'And

I generally think that parents are hardest on their children of the same sex. I suppose they see them in their own image. Father made it quite clear to me that I wasn't the son he had imagined.'

Hannah was taken aback by this uncharacteristic reflection.

'What did he—' she began to ask, but Will cut her off.

'Enough of this miserable talk!' he said, sitting back down again. 'I must speak to your father-in-law about investing in the play.'

'He's not my father-in-law yet!' Hannah replied. 'And I don't think he has spare funds any more.'

'Ah, well,' said Will. 'I'm sure I'll find the money somewhere. Now that Cee-Cee's starring in it.'

'So that's happening, is it?'

'Definitely,' Will nodded. '*A Needle in a Haystack* ended last night, so she's got no excuse not to be in mine.'

'Ended? I thought it had just begun.'

'Reviews were so stinking they closed it early.'

Presumably, there had been another one of those cramped, hysterical dressing-room parties for the closing night. Hannah thought of the blonde actress, Dolly, how arch and uninterested she had been in their conversation, and wondered why human nature made it so that we are desperate to be liked by people who make it clear they aren't at all bothered about us.

The memory of her encounter with Dolly merged with thoughts of Cosmo, and their need to find a story, some real evidence against Frank Hogg. Will's chatter faded into background noise, and she looked down at the white expanse of linen before her as the nascent thought took shape and gained weight. Then she stuck the needle back in the pin cushion, stood up, and told Will she had to go out.

'To see Emily, as it happens,' she said, feeling she must give some excuse.

'Can I come?' Will asked.

'No!' she said. At the door, she turned back to ask, 'Which street is Kettner's on?'

'Church Street,' he replied. 'Why? Is that where you're meeting Emily? Then I should come. It's not really a place for two women alone, I think.'

'No,' she said, half out of the door. 'We're not going there at all. I just wondered.'

Hannah knew Soho somewhat, because Mrs Didier, the family's dressmaker, was based there (she really must make that appointment for alterations!). But Mrs Didier's atelier was near Regent Street, whereas the map told her that Church Street was on the less familiar side of the neighbourhood, near Tottenham Court Road. The omnibus dropped her at Cambridge Circus, outside the vast, nearly finished new theatre. Builders climbed all over it, like flies on a cow. It was cold, and she could see the workmen's breath as she walked past into the dense enclave of streets.

This side of Soho seemed shabbier than the other, and far more foreign; a continental village, its narrow streets almost entirely composed of restaurants and food shops. It was nearly lunchtime, and the odour of garlic and hot oil seeped from doorways and windows as she passed boards advertising *Prix Fixe* menus. Outside a café, two pairs of grizzled elderly men played dominoes. As she passed, one of them exclaimed, '*Enfoiré!*' and forcefully flicked his piece over.

The foreigners here used to be almost entirely French, Hannah remembered, but now she noticed Italian businesses, too, offering the same food they had eaten in Naples – macaroni and ham and sliced melon – and the newsstand she passed offered Italian titles alongside the French ones. Clutching her copy of the *Star*, it was Hannah who felt marked as a foreigner.

She easily found Kettner's, an establishment occupying half a block, its façade embellished with hanging baskets of ivy. A menu by the door offered *oeufs à la Russe, sole à la Dugléré, tournedos à la Périgueux* and *crème pistache*. Hannah's stomach had a spasm of longing.

Dolly said she lived 'next to' the restaurant. Neighbouring it was an anonymous residential building, with sooty brickwork and mean little windows. Opposite the restaurant was an identical-looking place. Approaching the door of the first building, she saw there was no bell, and so rapped on the door with her knuckles. She waited, looking up, but there was no response, from Dolly or anyone else.

What now? She bet Dolly spent some of her time in the glamorous restaurant next door – perhaps they would know where to find her. Returning to Kettner's, Hannah pushed open the door. The foyer was thickly carpeted; at its centre sat an unmanned desk, on which lay a large, leather-bound reservations book. To her left and right were doors, through which she could see vistas lined with oak panelling and replete with tables laid with white tablecloths, cutlery, wine glasses and candelabras. The stage was set, waiting for the cast – those names in the reservations book – to make their entrance.

There seemed to be no one about here either. She called

a timid 'Hello?' and was about to retreat when she heard faint voices in the room off to her left. Walking in, at first the room seemed deserted, but she saw it was L-shaped and, continuing around the corner, came across two men sitting at a table. The table was laid for lunch, but the men weren't eating, just drinking red wine. One of them was much older than the other – in his early thirties, perhaps – while the younger of the two looked barely an adult. They were engaged in a deep conversation, and clearly did not work here, and would likely not be able to tell her where an actress called Dolly lived. But Hannah didn't immediately move on. There was something familiar about the older man – what was it? He had an unusual and striking presence – a large face with a prominent forehead and chin, and his hair was unusually long and swept behind his ears in a centre parting. He was still wearing his coat, an extravagant affair with a fox fur collar and a large ruby brooch. The younger man was dressed more normally. The older man was reading out loud from a piece of paper while the younger man listened, with intense attention, his head bowed.

'Those who find ugly meanings in beautiful things are corrupt without being charming,' the older man intoned. He had a performer's timbre: posh, slow and sonorous. 'This is a fault. Those who find beautiful meanings in beautiful things are the cultivated. For these, there is hope.'

He paused and looked over at the man.

'Will that do, Henry?'

The younger man laughed.

'I'm hardly going to criticise your writing, am I?' he said, in a far less educated voice.

'I suppose not,' said the older man. He smiled and picked up the carafe to top up their glasses.

Hannah was still staring at them. The older man glanced up at her, with pale, down-turned eyes; he seemed unbothered, or accustomed to being looked at.

'Are you lost?' he asked her, in a tone which suggested he might equally have said, *Will you get lost?*

'No,' she replied, flustered. 'I mean, I'm looking for—.'

'Mademoiselle, do you have a reservation?'

Hannah turned to find a waiter at her side. Suavely, he steered her back out to the foyer as she replied.

'Oh, no,' she said. 'I'm actually just looking for someone who lives nearby. I thought you might know her. Dolly?'

The waiter nodded.

'Mademoiselle Dolly. Oui. She lives next door.'

'Yes! But which room?'

'The very top one,' he said. 'On the right.'

Outside the residential building, Hannah again fruitlessly rapped at the door before she started calling Dolly's name up at the window. Eventually, she heard the sound of a sash being pulled up and a blonde head poked out.

'What is it?'

'Can you come down?' Hannah called. When Dolly remained looking down at her, she added, 'We met at the party at the theatre. Do you remember?'

The head disappeared, and half a minute later the front door opened. Hannah was expecting Dolly to look dissolute, wrung out from the closing-night party the evening before; in her wrapper, that eye make-up smeared. But rather, she was smartly dressed, in a demure green silk dress.

'Oh, yes, you,' she said. Hannah was gratified that Dolly remembered her, but the actress's tone was cool. 'What is it?'

'I wanted to ask you something. A favour.'

'I've actually got to go and see someone about a job,' said Dolly. 'The show ended early.'

'I heard,' said Hannah, and then it came to her, from nowhere. 'You should talk to my brother about that. He's putting on a play, you know. I think Cee-Cee is signing up.'

Hannah hoped Dolly wouldn't make the association between this powerful impresario figure and the drunken sop in his father's clothes she had met at the opening-night party. And she must not have, because her little face tilted with interest.

Hannah smiled, wondering, had she always been this sly? Had this dangerous power lain dormant in her all these years?

'But I actually wanted to talk to you about something else,' she said. She felt self-conscious there on the street, aware of passers-by, but knew she had to press on. 'Do you know this story?'

Hannah showed her the copy of that day's *Star*, with the headline: '*A GREAT DEAL NOT RIGHT' ABOUT MRS PEARCEY, SAYS NEIGHBOUR.* Dolly glanced at it.

'Who doesn't?' she replied, but her tone was curious.

'I have some . . . association with it,' said Hannah, wishing she had prepared her phrasing. 'I mean, I've met some of the people in it, and I've been to the crime scene and . . . well, I wanted to ask if you wanted to be involved in it with me.'

'How intriguing,' said Dolly, and although she was trying to sound nonchalant, Hannah could tell by the narrowing of her eyes that she was definitely interested.

'Shall I come up?' said Hannah. 'So we can talk in private?'

Dolly hesitated.

'No, it's a mess. Let's go next door.'

Letting the building's door bang shut behind her, Dolly led the way into Kettner's. The maître d' was stationed at the desk in the foyer now.

'You found her,' he said to Hannah.

'François, can we just have a quick drink?' Dolly said.

The man pursed his lips.

'Only for you,' he concluded, and led them to the right-side room, away from where the two men were sitting. He indicated an empty table.

'Please don't disturb the table setting,' he said.

'Of course,' said Dolly, charm personified, as they settled on the pink banquette. 'Two glasses of champagne, please.'

'This place is like my parlour,' she said to Hannah as the maître d' retreated. 'Now, tell me what on earth you're talking about.'

Hannah placed the newspaper in front of Dolly, as an *aide-mémoire*.

'So, what do you think about Frank Hogg?' she asked. 'Was he involved?'

'Oh, no doubt at all,' said Dolly. 'He's such a creep.'

'I agree,' said Hannah. 'But there doesn't appear to be much evidence.'

'I bet he couldn't bear the baby crying, and he was bored of his cow of a wife, so he persuaded Pearcey to help him bump them off.'

'But was it done so that he and Mrs Pearcey would be free to be together?' said Hannah. 'Because if so, that really backfired, didn't it?'

'I reckon he was tired of her, too,' said Dolly. 'So now

he's rid of both of them, and he's free to go off with his new strumpet. Trust me, I know these men.'

Hannah nodded, caught up in Dolly's certainty.

'So, I've had this idea,' she said. 'About how we could perhaps get some evidence.'

And then, in a low voice, she explained her plan.

It was a long shot, no doubt about it. Hannah didn't know which public house Frank Hogg frequented, if he went to one at all. Perhaps he wasn't even a drinker. In any case, he might want to avoid appearing in public while at the centre of the most famous newspaper story in the country. But she was buoyed by Dolly's reaction to the proposal.

'Of course he's a drinker,' hissed Dolly, her face up close to Hannah's. They had ordered another two glasses of champagne. 'And of course he'll be at a public house this weekend. He'll either receive sympathy from people there, or get into a fight to defend his honour. Either of those are better than staying at home cowering behind drawn curtains, in the company of a broken mother and suspicious sister.'

Dolly was adamant that they must go on a Friday night – in other words, that very evening.

'That's when these working men go drinking. All of them. Straight after work, with their wages hot in their pocket.'

'I don't know if he has been working this week,' said Hannah, thinking of his appearances at the hearings.

'Even if he hasn't been, he'll still go then, to see his friends. Trust me.'

Such was Dolly's confidence and gratifying enthusiasm for the whole idea that Hannah agreed to meet her at Kentish Town station at 7 p.m. that evening.

As they talked, the room had begun to fill up around

them with diners, mostly groups of smart men. The maître d' came over to tell them they had to leave.

'Put it on the tab, François,' said Dolly as they got up.

'Soon we will be able to bind that tab into a book,' replied the maître d', but he let them go.

Dolly was flushed and buoyant; a totally different person from the cool, wary woman Hannah had met next door an hour ago.

'Isn't this place heavenly?' she said, taking Hannah's arm as they stepped onto the street. 'Do you know, Oscar Wilde is *always* here?'

'Oh, that's who it was!' replied Hannah. 'You know, I seem to have a talent for meeting notorious people.' Then she started laughing and, despite Dolly's look of bemusement, found she couldn't stop.

When she got home, fizzing from it all – the champagne on an empty stomach; the boldness of her idea; her successful initiation of Dolly; her random brush-up against celebrity; oh, the glamour! – Hannah wrote a note to Cosmo describing the whole brilliant plan, littered with exclamation marks, and put it on the tray for the girls to post. Then, abruptly, she needed to lie down on her bed. When she woke, discombobulated, the first thing she registered was that her mouth was horribly dry. Then, she remembered the note. She rushed downstairs to retrieve it, but the tray was empty. She stared at the bare silver, stricken with regret. How could she have committed such a secret plan to paper, even if it was only for the eyes of Cosmo? She didn't have a clue as to the consequences if such a note was made public. If Dolly did get a confession from Frank, would the fact that the two of them had engineered the encounter render such evidence inadmissible in court? Was what they were doing actually illegal?

For a mad moment, she considered going to Fleet Street. She imagined herself running into the foyer just as that languid doorman was handing the letter to the messenger boy to give to Cosmo, and snatching it from his grasp. But it was too much of a long shot, as well as too exhausting an idea. Besides, her bedside clock told her that it was nearly 5 p.m. She hadn't the time, if she was meeting Dolly at seven.

Instead, she did the best she could in the circumstances. She wrote a second, terse note to Cosmo – *I beg you to ignore and destroy my previous missive* – and asked Ivy to run it to the postbox immediately. Then, depleted by the drama, she went to lie down again, just for twenty minutes.

Standing in front of her closet an hour later, Hannah wondered what to wear. Did the labouring classes put on their glad rags to go drinking, or just turn up in their work clothes? In any case, surely her best option was to play it safe. No butter-yellow silk tonight, stained or not. She reached for her dark-blue dress, the one she wore for shopping and as unremarkable as dresses got.

As she pulled off her nightgown, she realised to her surprise that she now felt rather relaxed, as if she had already paid in full for her overindulgence earlier in the day. Her head was still somewhat foggy, but it felt like a positive state of mind, one that blanketed over unhelpful thoughts and anxieties, allowing her to be only in the present.

She carried the candle over to the dressing-table mirror. Another miracle: she didn't look too seedy. Her skin was even, her eyes bright. She had entered a topsy-turvy world, where she slept during the day and half a bottle of champagne made her look prettier.

The big question, of course, was would Frank recognise her from their brief meeting on Prince of Wales Road? But with her new sanguinity, she didn't feel worried about that. After all, she needn't get close to him at all. Her involvement in this scheme only went as far as scanning a packed public house, spotting Hogg and pointing him out to Dolly, because Dolly could hardly rely on a newspaper sketch for positive identification of her target. Then, she would melt away and let Dolly take over.

So, all the risk was on Dolly, and her new friend hadn't seemed at all concerned. On the contrary, she gave the impression she had played a role like this a dozen times before. 'I'll get something,' she had reassured Hannah. 'I know how to get things from men.'

As the two of them had parted ways outside Kettner's, Dolly had mentioned Will's play and told Hannah to inform him she was available. Now, with her head straighter, Hannah considered whether she should feel guilty for giving Dolly a false impression of her brother's influence. She quickly decided she shouldn't. After all, Hannah hadn't actually lied about anything, and she certainly would tell Will about Dolly's interest. Moreover, Hannah felt that Dolly did not agree to help trap Frank Hogg because it might lead to an acting role further down the line. It was no means to an end. What appealed to her was the ensnaring itself. After all, Dolly was bored and unemployed, saw herself as fearless and seductive, and liked being in the thick of things. What better way to spend an evening than by toying with the man at the centre of the most sensational murder case in London?

Ready, Hannah crept downstairs. On the floor below, the doors to Will's bedroom and the drawing room were ajar, and she could hear Will and her mother in the drawing room. Her mother's voice was, as ever, too low to make out, but she heard Will say clearly, 'Oh, I wouldn't go that far, Mama!'

Hannah hesitated on the landing. Calm as she felt, she suspected that she did not have the required agility of mind to go in there and deliver a convincing reason as to why she was going out. Could she really conjure yet *another* appointment with Mrs Didier or tea with Emily at 7 p.m. on Friday night? And so she continued her silent descent down the stairs and slipped out of the front door.

10

The girl who degenerates into a genuine flirt becomes blind to the signs of the times and of her little world. A siren voice may lead her to think she is the queen of the situation; but the disillusion soon comes, and the young adventurer finds that she is the subject of a hard taskmaster, whose service she cannot escape.

– Girl's Own Paper

She had arranged to meet Dolly at Kentish Town station and walk to the public house from there. The location of Frank Hogg's workplace had been published in the papers; he helped out at his brother Edwin's furniture-moving business on Castle Road, which was just off Prince of Wales Road. 'We simply go over there,' Dolly had said, 'and find the nearest place.'

Hannah arrived at the station with ten minutes to spare and stood at the side of the entrance to wait for Dolly. It was dark, and the pavement was thick with pedestrians, commuters heading homewards and shoppers heading out, sliding around each other like eels in a tank. Noisy supplicants, beggars and sellers did their best to impede them. Beyond them, packed, swaying omnibuses passed by, alongside carthorses trudging with their necks low. Down Kentish Town Road, the banks of glowing shops stretched out of sight, a necklace of lights. Hannah was reminded of the evening of her engagement dinner, when the Teales passed through Camden Town at around this time on a Friday. Kentish Town was not such a major thoroughfare, but the end-of-day atmosphere was similar.

That evening, she had observed the scene from behind her carriage window, safely sandwiched between her relations. Now, she was out here, alone, on the stage itself.

It was a drizzly, blustery evening, the kind you didn't want to spend waiting on a pavement. A train's worth of passengers were disgorged from the station, and she straightened up, expecting Dolly, but by the time they had thinned out, she hadn't materialised. Maybe she wouldn't turn up. This was, after all, a mad idea, agreed upon by two near-strangers after drinking too much champagne. How long should she wait? A stray seagull was perched on a nearby lamppost, keeping a keen eye on an old man selling sausage rolls from a basket below. The coster had his own caw – *sausies, sausies, sausies, sausies* – delivered in a seamless monotone, as if the word had been worn down and smoothed by decades of continuous use. As always, the aroma of warm pastry made Hannah's stomach turn over – but now, she had the quiet, stunning realisation that she was free to just buy one. And so, without further thought, she did, walking over and paying a penny to the taciturn coster, who placed the warm, greasy slab straight into her palm. She moved away to eat it, close to the station wall, turning her back to the crowd. She may now be someone who bought a sausage roll on the street, but she wasn't ready to publicly devour it. Face inches from the oxblood bricks of the station wall, she took a bite, and another. Oh, the rare, pure joy of satisfying her greed!

'Lining your stomach,' came a female voice from behind her. 'Very wise.'

Swallowing, Hannah turned to find that Dolly had appeared at her shoulder. Behind her was a small audience, a handful of male passers-by who were staring at her. She was dressed to be given a second glance, done up like a pantomime dame, her blonde hair piled high and frizzy, a tiny ornamental hat perched on top, then those baby-panda eyes and small pink lips. Hannah and the other women around them were dressed for the dreary weather, interchangeable in their dark outdoor coats. Dolly was wearing a tight Astrakhan jacket with a fur collar, over a full red skirt, and high boots. A large brooch in the shape of a bunch of grapes – the grapes made from pearls – was pinned to her breast, and she was carrying a carpet bag.

'A sausage roll?' said Dolly. 'I want one of those.' Hannah pointed out the seller at the entrance, flattered that Dolly would want something she had. Spotting the coster, Dolly clapped her hands.

'Of course – Jackie!'

She skipped over and Hannah watched as she greeted him with a slap on the shoulder, his grumpy old face softening at the sight of her. The two of them talked for a minute, the exchange ending with the coster handing her the roll and holding up his hand theatrically to refuse payment even though, Hannah noted, Dolly hadn't even made an attempt to produce a penny.

'You know him?' Hannah asked superfluously, when Dolly returned to her, already tearing into the pastry.

'I do,' said Dolly, her mouth full. 'Had a stint playing at the Bedford. And some of my friends work around here.'

She abruptly stopped eating and threw the remaining half on the ground; the seagull promptly swooped on it. Then she tucked her arm through Hannah's.

'Shall we go and get the bastard, then?' she said.

As they set off, Hannah thought she detected the pressure of Dolly wiping her fingers on her coat sleeve, but she wasn't sure. They headed down towards Prince of Wales Road, turning heads and attracting hisses, Hannah feeling like a dowager chaperone as the actress clip-clopped along the pavement.

'I can't quite place the public house nearest Castle Road,' said Dolly. 'But I'm sure I've been in it. I think I've been to them all.'

'What,' said Hannah, 'every public house in Camden Town?'

'*And* Kentish Town.'

The wind had picked up; above their heads, shop signs creaked, and stray sheets of newspaper and wisps of hay scurried along the pavement. The pedestrians around them hunkered down in their coats. Dolly used her spare hand to keep her absurd hat in place, and drew herself tighter to Hannah. Hannah hadn't been clung to like this for a long time; not since the intense friendships of school. As the carriages and hansoms rattled past, she had the vision of her old friend Emily in the back of one of them, mewling red baby on her lap, heading home from a dull tea with her mother-in-law, glancing out of the window and spotting Hannah arm-in-arm with her exotic new pal. *Oh, Em,* she imagined saying, in response to Emily's hurt, *I'll always be so fond of you, but people change and lives diverge, don't they? It's only natural. Yes, she's an actress, but she's not what you think . . .*

Actually, Dolly was pretty much exactly how Hannah had imagined an actress to be, with her glamour and insouciance, her whiff of wantonness. Now, as they continued down the road, she was giving Hannah a guide to the public houses of her neighbourhood.

'So, you have the castles,' she said. 'Edinboro Castle, Dublin Castle, Pembroke Castle and Windsor Castle . . . Scottish, Irish, Welsh and English, you see? The railway bosses set them up because their workers were always fighting with each other, Scots versus Irish and so on, and missing work. So this way, each nationality had their own place and they didn't get into so many scraps.'

'Gosh,' said Hannah. 'I didn't know that.'

'Well, I suppose you wouldn't, would you?' said Dolly, but not in a nasty way.

Hannah felt she had much to learn from her new friend. As on their previous encounters, she felt keen to make Dolly interested in her, too. As they passed the hatters, she realised she had something to say – and that she, too, had a claim on the neighbourhood.

'My father died just there,' she told Dolly, pointing to the spot on the road where it happened.

'Oh, God!' Dolly replied. 'Who was he brawling with – Scots, Irish or Welsh?'

She laughed at her own joke. Hannah felt embarrassed.

'Oh, all of them, probably,' she replied awkwardly.

Her larkiness was wooden, but Dolly didn't seem to notice, and she didn't ask any further questions about Mr Teale. Perhaps death was a difficult subject for her, or perhaps in her world life was hard, and tragic events were quickly processed into humour.

A tall man hurried past them, and then must have turned back, as a moment later he reappeared at Dolly's shoulder.

'Will you come with me?' he said.

'Not a chance,' replied Dolly, and the man hastened away.

Dolly didn't remark on the incident; perhaps it was unworthy of comment. The two of them turned right onto Anglers Lane, past the false-teeth factory, which was closed and quiet now, just a thin trail of smoke seeping from its chimney.

'My pal works there,' Dolly said. 'I meet her from work and she comes out looking like a ghost, covered in this porcelain dust.' She bent down to stroke a cat that had appeared at her ankles. 'She says it's not that bad, though. They only employ women, so no creeps trying it on when the supervisor turns his back. She keeps on telling me to apply for a job.'

'Would you?'

Dolly gave her a look of disdain.

'Six in the morning till six at night, six days a week? A week's holiday at the seaside, surrounded by all the same people you work with? Are you joking?'

As they emerged onto Prince of Wales Road, Hannah thought of Mrs Pearcey in her sealskin factory, surreptitiously slipping a pelt under her skirt, holding onto it through her pocket as she said her goodbyes and left for the day. Then, back home in Priory Street, laying her stolen trophy over her bedhead, smiling at the thought of showing Frank Hogg when he came by that evening.

That sealskin was Hannah's secret. The stolen magazine, too. And the fact that she had actually met Mrs Pearcey, on this very road, just before Mrs Pearcey had made the fateful mistake of agreeing to accompany Clara Hogg to the police station to identify Phoebe Hogg. She considered, for a moment, telling Dolly everything, to feel the gratification of her surprise and interest, but she stopped herself.

They had now arrived at the top of Hadley Street. A hundred yards down sat a glowing inn, noisy even from here. And of course, now that she saw it, Dolly realised that she had been in the public house before.

'Ah, yes, the Trafalgar,' she said. 'It's all right. No rougher than the others.'

They walked past rows of houses, their windows so flimsy Hannah could clearly hear the clank of crockery and the whistle of kettles from within. The faint smells of fish, potatoes and cabbage seeped out; it must be just after the dinner hour. Peering over the half-nets, Hannah glimpsed front parlours just like Mrs Pearcey's – cheap floral wallpaper, a couple of chairs, a piano, the odd framed print, an aspidistra. She glimpsed women, or their top halves, at least: women with pink faces and tired eyes and messy hair, carrying things in and out of the room. No Gwens or Ivys to help out here. Had these women been at home all day? Or had they done twelve hours at the teeth factory before coming home, covered in porcelain dust, to shove a cod's head in the pot? She thought about asking Dolly but didn't want to invite her disdain.

She heard the sounds of children: thumping mulishly at the piano, laughing, quarrelling with each other. But no male voices. Presumably, having eaten their dinners, the husbands had now all absconded to the Trafalgar.

Outside the public house, they stopped. The din was formidable, even from here. Ahead of her, Dolly pushed at the door and a particularly loud burst of laughter seemed to intimidate even her; she hesitated for a moment, her hand flat on the wood, before stepping inside. The door banged shut behind her. Hannah stared at the panel of frosted glass, the dark, shifting shapes within, and reminded herself that she had been in this position before, trepidatious outside a raucous public house. But of course, at the Cock Tavern on Fleet Street she had been accompanied by Cosmo. A man. Her fiancé. And in that case, she hadn't thought that Frank Hogg might be inside.

'Scuse us,' came a voice from behind her, and without waiting for her to react, a hand reached over her shoulder and pushed the door open. She ducked aside as a trio of young men – traders of some sort, still in their dirty aprons – barrelled in. Hitching onto their momentum, Hannah caught the door before it slammed shut again and followed them in.

The arrival of the traders was met with a joyous 'Ey-up!' and they slapped some backs as they headed to the bar. Nerves humming, Hannah stood to the side of the entrance and scanned the crowd. There were actually fewer people in here than you would guess from the noise and she could see most of the faces in the room. Her gaze went only to the short, stocky men, looking for one with squinting dark eyes, and hair as stiff and greasy as a pigeon wing.

Hogg didn't appear to be here. Relaxing a fraction, Hannah looked around again, now taking in more of the room. The place was no glittering gin palace, but it was more decorated than the Cock, with a bit of etched glass behind the bar and some prints on the wall. The atmosphere seemed different, too. In Fleet Street, it felt like the newsmen were still at work, swapping stories, sniffing out competition, whispering secrets. Here, the mood was high-spirited and celebratory. It certainly didn't look like anyone was thinking about work. Graft was over; hats were off; sleeves were rolled up. Somewhere, on the other side of the room, a rough, jolly tune was being bashed out on the piano. The smell of sweat hit the same note as the fumes of beer.

The noise was solid, and it was impossible to pick out individual conversations, yet she thought she caught Irish and other non-English accents. Female voices, too. Yes, there were women here: she counted five of them. A few feet away from Hannah, a scrawny, middle-aged woman plucked the glass from her male companion's hand and took a glug, before her companion snatched it back.

'You're not welcome,' he said crossly.

A few men glanced over at Hannah, but the attention was no more than when she got on the bus or queued at the baker's. The other women here, she noticed, were more dressed up than she was — not to Dolly's level, but they had made some sort of effort to be noticed. A decorated bonnet; a red gauze handkerchief knotted around their neck; a spray of dried flowers pinned to their dress; low necklines, showing a sliver of corset.

Now, where was Dolly?

On cue she heard a call and turned to see Dolly beckoning her from the side of the room and pointing down to a table. Of course, she had managed to secure a seat.

'Is he here?' she asked as Hannah reached her.

Dolly looked tense; her lips were a tight red slash.

Hannah shook her head.

'Well, we'll just wait,' said Dolly. 'Every so often, you get up and scout round the corner. I suppose he could be in the saloon.'

The table she had found them was pressed up against a mirrored pillar, so only one side was usable. The two of them had to sit side by side, their backs to the room, awkwardly facing their reflections.

'It's actually quite good,' said Dolly, as Hannah squashed in beside her. 'You can see the door in the mirror, so you can spot him as he comes in.' Hannah looked up at the space above their heads and saw that she did indeed have a view of the entrance, beyond the crowd in the room. Just then, on cue the door swung open and she stiffened. Him? But no, it was a small person – so small she couldn't see them. It was as if a phantom had entered, until she saw a boy weaving through the crowd towards the bar holding a jug.

She looked down again, straight ahead, at their reflections, as if they were on an evening out with their doppelgängers. How extraordinary, Hannah thought, that she had imagined she looked good earlier, in her bedroom. Now, next to Dolly's small, vivid, painted face, she looked sallow and drained, like the women she had glimpsed over the nets on Hadley Street. No wonder she hadn't caused a stir when she came in.

They sat in silence for a moment, Hannah looking around her, taking in this rackety, alien environment. What now? The thought of alcohol made her throat seize up. Would Dolly be put out if she just had lemonade?

'Shall we get a drink?' she asked.

'*Buy* a drink?' said Dolly. 'No, no. *He* buys us one.'

He? Us? Hannah turned to Dolly. Had she forgotten this integral part of the pact? 'You mean, *you*,' she said. 'I can't be here while you . . . he knows what I look like, he might . . . I can't . . .' Her voice grew louder, panic rising like overflowing beer suds. 'Remember, I was just going to point him out and then leave immediately, and then you—'

'Yes, fine,' Dolly interrupted flatly. 'He buys *me* a drink. Not you. Don't worry.'

She was looking steadily at Hannah in the mirror with those panda eyes, her expression neutral. Hannah had revealed herself just now. They both knew that her panicked reaction had not been just about the possibility of being recognised by Frank Hogg, but at the thought of being aligned that closely with Dolly. Being seen as someone who accepted drinks from strange men, and who flirted with them. The kind of person who ate a sausage roll in public, without even turning their back.

Embarrassed, unable to think of what to say, Hannah stared at the space above their heads, a chastised sentry returning to duty. The room beyond them abstracted into shifting shapes and colours: pale and dark clothing; red, haw-hawing faces. Then, Dolly spoke up.

'Nelson lived in Kentish Town for a while,' she said. 'Emma Hamilton, too, after he died. That's why it's called the Trafalgar.'

'Oh, really! That's interesting!' Hannah replied, over-animated in her relief that Dolly had chosen to move on.

'Do you like Emma Hamilton?' Dolly continued.

Her tone remained innocuous, but Hannah now realised that this wasn't just polite conversation. Since when had Dolly shown any interest in Hannah's opinions – or, indeed, made polite conversation? This, then, was a test: a chance for Hannah to redeem or further condemn herself.

'Well, I don't know that much about her,' Hannah replied, careful to maintain eye contact in the mirror. 'But I know that Nelson was very fond of her, and from all accounts it sounds like she was quite the force of natu—'

'I love her,' Dolly interjected. 'She's my heroine. She came from nowhere and made her own way and charmed everyone, lived this fascinating life all over the place, meeting all these interesting people. She was *free*. A thousand times more impressive than these posh women who spend their lives shut away in these dead houses, having babies and moaning about their cooks. And everyone has the nerve to sneer at her! Worse than sneer.'

Her little hat wobbled as she spoke with feeling.

'You know, I agree,' said Hannah. 'I think you're quite right.' Her aim was to mollify Dolly, but she realised that she meant it. 'I think people like her actually *live*.' She smiled at Dolly in the mirror, hoping she would hear her sincerity.

Although Dolly didn't immediately return Hannah's smile, her face relaxed, and Hannah felt the moment had passed. Looking at them both in the mirror, Hannah was reminded of a parakeet her grandmother had kept in the kitchen, with a tiny mirror in its cage, so the bird felt it had company. Or perhaps just so it could admire itself. Who knew?

'You're so pretty,' she said to Dolly. 'You look like Sarah Bernhardt.'

Dolly laughed. 'I don't at all. Is she the only actress you know?'

Hannah shrugged. 'Well, you're pretty. That's all I'm saying.'

Dolly considered her reflection. 'It's probably just the paint.'

Hannah hesitated, then said, 'Do you have some here?'

Dolly squinted with bemusement and dipped into her bag, emerging with a tiny tin. Holding it conspiratorially down below the table, she twisted it open to reveal a scarlet paste. Hannah glanced around. People surrounded them, animated in their little clusters, but as the two of them were sitting with their backs to the room, no one was paying them attention. They might almost be alone. She turned back to Dolly.

'With my finger?'

Dolly nodded. Hannah stroked the paste with her little finger and, watching herself in the mirror, smeared it on her lips. The difference was barely discernible, so she went in for another dab, and another, building up the colour until it was startling against her skin.

'Oi,' said Dolly. 'Don't use it all.'

But she was smiling her approval, and Hannah smiled back, watching her new crimson lips stretch wide. How white her teeth looked! Her mouth, once something functional, now felt far more potent. They were right, the magazines, with their solemn warnings: a few swipes of this stuff was enough to make you an entirely different woman, alluring and bestial. She and Dolly were a pair of parakeets, dazzling against a background of plain, anonymous male torsos.

'Do you want to get married?' Hannah asked Dolly, in the mirror.

Dolly laughed.

'I didn't think it was such a silly question!' protested Hannah. 'I mean, even Emma Hamilton married, didn't she?'

'It's not silly,' Dolly relented. 'No, I don't think so.'

'Why?'

'Every man I meet who wants to marry me – and there have been *dozens* – expects me to give up acting. I don't know who I'd be if I didn't go on stage.'

'But what about children? Don't you worry you'll be fearfully miserable and empty without them?'

Dolly laughed again. 'From what I see, having them can be pretty miserable, too.'

'You ladies need a drink.'

Still smiling, Hannah glanced over at the figure who was now standing behind them, in the space between the two of them, his frame filling the mirror. She registered hands stuffed in the pockets of his trousers. A clean white shirt and braces. A blue spotted cravat knotted around his upturned collar.

Her smile fell away. Above that, a reddish-brown beard and squashed dark lips. One eye half-closed under a low brow. A greasy pigeon-wing of hair.

'Ta, but we're all right,' replied Dolly, giving him a quick, dismissive smile in the mirror.

'Haven't seen you here before,' said Frank Hogg.

Dolly didn't seem as if she was going to respond. But then – whether it was realising Hannah had frozen, or recognising his features from the newspaper illustrations – it only took her another second to cotton on. Twisting around in her chair to face him, she said, 'Well, actually, come to think of it, maybe I could do with a little *quelque chose*.'

Hannah didn't turn in her seat and kept staring at the mirror, her gaze now fixed on the frosted glass panel of the front door, as if by looking at it hard enough she could find herself on its other side. His odour was strong, like a horse's.

She shouldn't have sat here with Dolly. What was she thinking?

'You what?' said Frank Hogg, to Dolly.

'Oh, excuse my French,' said Dolly. 'I thought you looked the classy type.'

'I've never been accused of being classy,' Hogg replied, 'but I think that *quell*— whatever you said – is foreign for "rum". Am I correct?'

'Oh, so we do speak the same language,' said Dolly.

'I'm more interested in Spain, myself,' said Hogg, not moving. 'My friend lives there. Says life is good. Warm. Cheap. He says I can go and stay with him.'

Spain. The country chimed with something in Hannah's memory, but she couldn't think exactly what.

'Well, I hope you're not going tonight,' said Dolly. 'I want that drink.'

Fine, thought Hannah. *It's fine. He'll go up to the bar and get drinks, and I'll slip away.*

'You?' Frank Hogg said, to her.

She forced herself to turn to him but couldn't meet his eyes, couldn't bear to lift her gaze higher than that cravat. She now saw that there was another, similar-looking man lurking behind him. Edwin, his brother. Frank's own doppelgänger.

'Nothing for me, thank you,' she mumbled. And then, a notch louder: 'I must go, actually.'

She noticed that the people nearest to them had fallen silent, as if they were listening to what the Hoggs were saying.

'You can't leave us with her,' replied Frank. 'She'll speak French at us all night.'

Hannah gave a choked laugh and pushed back her chair.

'Would be nice if you stayed,' he continued. 'Else one of us will be a spare part.'

'Oh, I can't, I'm afraid,' said Hannah. Clumsily, she started to get to her feet.

'We've had a rough week,' Frank persisted. 'Could do with some cheering up. Get our gigglemugs back on.'

Gigglemugs. Now, Hannah *could* remember where she had seen that word before: on the back of that business card on Mrs Pearcey's mantelpiece.

'I've got to get going,' she said.

Her heart was racing so fast, she couldn't conjure even a vaguely plausible reason for leaving. Now was the time for Dolly to step in and back her up. To say to Frank and Edwin: *Don't worry, I can handle you both.* And then, to Hannah: *All right, sweetheart, go well.*

'Yes, you must stay,' said Dolly, her fingers gripping Hannah's forearm. 'I can't let you leave alone.'

Startled, Hannah turned to her, half risen from her seat. What was she doing?

'There's a madman on the loose around these parts,' Dolly continued. 'Didn't you hear? Tore up a woman the other day.' She lowered her voice to a stagey whisper, directed at Frank. 'They think it's the Ripper!'

In the mirror, Hannah saw an expression cross Frank Hogg's face, somewhere between a frown and a flinch, and it dawned on her what Dolly was up to. She sank reluctantly back into her chair, like a sigh. Around them, the clusters of drinkers were quiet, listening to every word.

'Where did you hear that, then?' said Frank.

'I read it in the papers,' said Dolly. 'Somewhere near here.' She shivered theatrically. She was giving the impression, Hannah realised, that she found it quite thrilling. 'Talking of which,' she continued, 'I could murder that glass of *quell* . . .'

Frank turned and nodded at Edwin.

'Wait,' he then added. 'Better get one for Alf, too. He's really extracting his pound of flesh.'

Edwin nodded and sloped off towards the bar. Frank remained standing there between the two women, rolling a cigarette with one hand. Even on the most basic level, the situation was uncomfortable: the two women at their small table, half twisted in their chairs; the man looming over them; the mirror reflecting it all. Hannah's instinct was to stand up, to not feel so trapped, but she felt she must take her cue from Dolly, who remained seated.

Down here, she was eye-level with his torso. The waistband of his trousers. One hand rested on his belt. Those short-fingered hands, which had been in such places, and done such things.

Frank wasn't speaking, just remained planted there, pulling on the cigarette. Dolly was inspecting her nails, affecting nonchalance. Hannah looked at herself in the mirror – the old her with the new flaming lips. The lip paint was her big mistake, getting her into this position in the first place. Putting it on, she had taken her eye off the door, and would Frank have been so insistent that she stayed if she had looked plain and un-Dolly-like? If she hadn't advertised her gameness? But perhaps the paint would also be her saviour, the barrier to Frank – or Edwin – recognising her from the Prince of Wales Road.

'Haven't you read the papers this last week?' said Frank now, breaking the silence.

Dolly looked up from her nails. 'What's that?'

'The Ripper. It weren't him.'

Hannah glanced up at Frank. He was focused on Dolly, and so she felt able to look at his face properly for the first time that evening. She saw the bumpy profile of his nose, the tiredness around his eyes, the broken veins, like tiny starbursts, on his cheeks.

'It was a woman who did it,' he told Dolly. 'And she's been caught.'

Now Dolly swivelled to face him properly, her pointy little chin tilted up to him, eyes wide.

'A woman!' she said. 'I don't believe it.'

Just then, Edwin rejoined them, holding two glasses of rum in each hand, and passed one each to Dolly and Hannah. Dolly took a gulp. Hannah copied her, but only pretended to drink, her lips tightly sealed against the noxious liquid.

'Look here,' said Frank. 'I'd better tell you — this is a bit awkward, either way, you see — but it was my wife what was killed. My little girl, too.'

Dolly gasped and clamped her hand over her mouth. Hannah did the same. But she was not just following suit; her shock was genuine. Of course, there was no revelation here, but — whether due to her heightened, nervy state, or the fact that she and Dolly were pretending with all their might to be hearing this for the first time — Frank's statement hit her in the chest. It was a bolt of pure horror, unmediated by everything she knew and felt about him and the case. For that moment, he was just a man, standing before them, revealing that his wife and child had been brutally murdered.

Frank grimaced, and made a single choking noise, like an aborted sob. Beside him, Edwin was granite-faced. Hannah realised he hadn't yet said a word.

'God,' said Dolly finally. 'What a terrible thing. I'm sorry I brought it up.'

She, too, sounded genuine. For a moment, Hannah wondered whether this might be the end of it. She and Dolly would offer their sincere sympathies, make awkward small talk over their drinks, and leave.

'S'all right,' said Frank. 'It's not like I can get away from it.' He had regained his composure. 'This morning, bloke from Madame Tussauds knocked on the door, asking me to sell 'em my daughter's pram and stuff like that. When the police have finished with them. Even her boiled sweet that was in her mouth, they want.'

'The ghouls!' cried Dolly.

Frank took a gulp from his glass; Hannah watched his Adam's apple move as the liquid slid down his throat. 'Might as well. Why would I want 'em? And money's never unwelcome, is it?'

Eyes fixed on Frank, Dolly cocked her head. It was only a slight gesture, but Hannah felt it signalled that if there had ever been a chance of Dolly feeling sorry for Frank, and leaving him be, that moment had now passed.

'And you're saying a woman did it?' said Dolly. 'But why?'

'I can't believe you've missed it in the papers,' he said. 'You must be the only girl in London who don't know the gory details.' He paused and turned to Hannah. 'The only *two* girls in London who don't know.'

Hannah smiled weakly and looked away. She clutched the glass tightly; beneath the table, her knees shook. The red ceiling and walls pressed in on her; she felt as if she was in an oven. The music had stopped; indeed, it seemed like all the chatter in the room had hushed. She could hear the sound of the barmaid washing up.

A man passing by had left a glass on their table, an inch of beer left inside. Frank Hogg leant over and dropped in his cigarette end; there was heard a brief fizzle as it hit the liquid.

'Well, I must get the papers then,' said Dolly. 'Except, well, they often get things wrong, don't they? Don't tell you the full story.'

Feeling movement behind her, Hannah looked up into the mirror to see that Edwin had stepped closer to Frank, and was whispering something to him. She looked down at the scratched varnished surface of the table, her knees shaking faster, out of her control.

'You don't say much, do you?' said Frank.

She looked up at him. Edwin was no longer at his ear, but had moved back to where he was standing, behind her chair. She could hear his breathing, smell his yeasty breath above her head.

'Funny, cos you seemed quite interested in talking to me last week. On the street. To my brother, too.'

'Oh, you can't know Amy,' cut in Dolly breezily. 'She only arrived in town this morning. We both did. Stop down in Deal usually.'

Frank didn't respond but kept squinting at Hannah. Adrenaline seized her, and in a sudden movement she tried to push back her chair and stand up but the chair, tucked in tight under the table, didn't budge. Something was in the way. She swivelled to see Edwin's leg braced against it.

'Talked to that silly girl as well, didn't you?' said Frank.

He meant Lizzie Styles. She thought of the figure in the window, watching them. All those bad things that Lizzie had said about Frank, which Hannah dutifully wrote down and then had printed in hundreds of thousands of newspapers distributed across London. Hannah closed her eyes, to be met with the vision of one of those vast rolls of blank paper she had seen on Fleet Street advancing on her, intending to flatten her.

'My mother was very upset,' Frank continued.

There was a coarse shriek of laughter from somewhere in the room. Around her, the hubbub of the crowd had suddenly got fiercer again; it felt as if everyone was now just shouting nonsense at each other as loudly as they could, just so they could not hear if she called for help. Again, she tried to push her chair back, and again, it didn't move. Her hands gripped the edge of the table, ready for another attempt. If she mustered all her strength and caught him off guard, Edwin might topple over and she could stand up – but then what? Frank would just grab her. Would anyone in here help her, or would they just stand and watch, scared of Frank – or enjoying the show?

'Come on, *monsieur*,' said Dolly beside her, ostensibly jovial, but Hannah could hear a quiver in her voice. 'I'm gasping for another *quell*. I'll come to the bar with you.'

Frank ignored her.

'We think you should come with us now,' he said to Hannah, 'and say sorry to my mother.'

Petrified, she looked at him square in the mirror. He looked back at her, slowly rubbing his fingers across his mouth.

'Hannah!'

At first, she thought the voice was inside her head, a bellow of despair at getting herself into this situation. But then, a moment later, Cosmo was crouched, panting, beside her chair. They stared at each other; he looked as incredulous as she felt. Then, he took her arm and pulled her to her feet. The two Hogg men must have stepped back or been pushed back by Cosmo. Hannah did not look at them, but registered they were still there, two dark edifices.

'I've been to every public house in Kentish Town,' said Cosmo. 'And there are a lot of them.'

He started pulling Hannah towards the door.

'Wait, Dolly!' she said, and turned back to the table, her arm outstretched to wrench Dolly to safety behind her. But Dolly was already on her feet and stayed right behind them all the way out.

After they burst out onto the street, Hannah made it only a short way before she had to stop, closing her eyes and breathing deeply, one hand clutching Cosmo's arm.

'Gosh, Hannah,' he said. She felt him trembling, too.

'He hasn't followed us out?' she asked, eyes still closed.

'Who? Anyway, no, no one has.'

Then came another voice, faint and female.

'I'll be seeing you.'

Hannah opened her eyes and turned to see Dolly setting off in the opposite direction to them, heading towards Chalk Farm.

'Wait,' called Hannah, but Dolly didn't stop, and Hannah watched as she trotted away, through the railway arch, as fast as her boots would allow her. Her little hat had slipped right down to the side of her head. Was she shocked and shaken, as

Hannah was? Annoyed that Cosmo had interrupted them? Embarrassed? As Hannah watched her disappear into the darkness, she realised that she would probably never know.

'What was she doing in there?' said Cosmo beside her. 'Offering private theatricals?'

'What?' Hannah frowned at him, and started walking briskly down the street. Cosmo caught up with her.

'Well, you mentioned an actress in your note,' he said. 'And she looked suitably showy. So I thought . . .'

'She was trying to get a confession from Frank Hogg,' she replied shortly. 'I told you that's what we were doing there, didn't I?'

Had she? In truth, her memory was a bit hazy about the exact contents of her note to Cosmo, exuberantly dashed off earlier.

'She put that stuff on you,' he said, in a quiet, hurt tone.

Hannah didn't know what he meant until he gestured towards her mouth. She started to rub at the lip paint, but then her hand fell away, a dead weight. She realised she was profoundly exhausted – too tired to explain, too tired to continue to defend Dolly, too tired to speak at all.

'Can we just be quiet for a bit?' she said.

He took her arm and they walked in silence for ten minutes, along Prince of Wales Road, and then onto the high street. By now, the shops were shuttered, and the crowds much thinned out. The drinking establishments were the only places with their windows still glowing, and those people still on the pavement looked as if they had just staggered out of one and were heading to another. A few sadder, quieter figures leant against walls or crouched in doorways. Hannah and Cosmo crossed the road and walked east, before she steered him left into Rochester Square, a cut-through to Camden Road. The square was a more modest version of Camden Square, and passing a lit drawing-room window, Hannah thought of her mother back at home, whether she would have stayed up, and if so, what Hannah might say to explain her unceremonious exit earlier. Hopefully, Cosmo would continue on his saviour mission, conjuring up some activity the two of them had attended, and which she had been late for when she had fled the house.

They walked alongside the fence of the square's communal garden, a dark mass of undergrowth. From somewhere in there, foxes squealed. Abruptly, Cosmo stopped and turned to face her.

'Oh, Hannah, I can't tell you how terrible I feel,' he said passionately. 'When I got your note I just . . . To think that I put you in that dreadful situation – indirectly, perhaps, but still – by asking you to help me on that story. That you were obliged to compromise yourself – besieged by men thinking who knows what? I am so deeply ashamed. I honestly don't know if I can forgive myself.'

Hannah opened her mouth to say something – she wasn't entirely sure what – but then Cosmo leant in and kissed her. It was not a kiss like the one before, in the drawing room. That had felt like a thank-you. This one was more like an attack, urgent and fierce. He clasped the back of her head as his tongue dug between her lips; his other hand gripped her forearm. Startled, she took a step backwards, finding herself up against the fence, and he came with her, mouth welded to hers. The metal railings dug into her shoulders. His hand was in her hair; he tried to reach her tongue with his, and she let him find it. His saliva tasted sweet and sharp, like lemonade. She put her hand on his neck, fingering the soft stubble at his nape. He put his leg between hers, and she felt the pressure of his thigh against her. Her body responded, pressing back, alive and eager, her breath quickening.

After some moments Cosmo released her and took a step back. He stared at her, panting heavily, with a pained, defenceless expression that excited her. Her mouth was wet; she reached up to touch it, but Cosmo took her fingers in his and squeezed tight.

'Just think,' he said, voice hoarse, 'soon we can do that all the time.'

He hooked his elbow through hers, and they continued strolling towards Camden Square, as if they'd just stopped to retie a shoelace. Hannah was silent, not from coyness or horror, but struck dumb by the animalism of what had just happened. She could only feel its effects: her insides fired up, her blood rushing, her cheeks roasting.

But wait – hadn't she felt similarly undone half an hour ago in the Trafalgar, face to torso with Frank Hogg, his breath heavy above her? Were these feelings sparked by Cosmo, her soon-to-be husband, or were they the lingering effect of Frank's menace? The two encounters seemed to twist around each other, like twines of a rope, and she felt sick at the connection, as if Frank himself had been watching them from the shadows. She must expose him to the light, make him an object of cold study rather than a lurking threat.

'That man with us, in the Trafalgar, when you arrived,' she said as they crossed Camden Road. 'That was Frank Hogg.'

'What – really?' He turned to her. 'There were a couple of lugubrious-looking chaps hanging over you . . .'

'Yes, that was him, and his brother.'

'I didn't realise. I thought they were just gawpers,' said Cosmo. 'So, what did Hogg say?'

Hannah paused.

'He said that he was selling things to Madame Tussauds. Things connected to the murders, like the baby's pram. Even the sweet she had been sucking.'

Cosmo whistled.

'Well, that doesn't make him look good, does it?' he said. 'That's a story! I'll tell the editor.'

But there was more than that, wasn't there? For the next half-minute, Hannah was silent as she went over the little things Frank had said that had snagged at the time, and that she had filed away to examine properly later. The mention of Spain. The cigarette fizzing in the glass. 'Gigglemugs'. Buying a drink for that man, Alf, who was taking *his pound of flesh*.

'What was the name of the man who gave Frank Hogg an alibi for the evening of the murders?' she asked Cosmo. They had now entered Camden Mews, their boots too loud on the cobbles.

'What?' he replied, nonplussed. 'I don't know!'

'Ovilry will know,' Hannah said, more to herself than to him, and noticed Cosmo's nose wrinkle with annoyance. She stopped and turned to him.

'You know,' she said, 'I think he did it by himself.'

'Why would you say that?'

'Just a few little things adding up,' she said, keeping her voice low, conscious of the hushed houses beside them. 'So, he asked his brother to buy a drink for someone called Alf, who wanted *his pound of flesh*. If this Alf is the casual labourer who helped him with an alibi on the evening of the murder, isn't that suspicious?'

Cosmo shrugged. 'Hmm. But even so, it's not *evidence* as such.'

'He threw his cigarette end into a glass of beer – and in the kitchen of Priory Street, I noticed there was a cup of tea with a cigarette end in it. So maybe that indicates he had been in the kitchen?'

'It could have come from anyone!' Cosmo replied. 'Maybe someone else in the house smokes?'

'Maybe,' said Hannah. 'But it seemed to be mostly women living there. And Mrs Pearcey seemed like a clean person. I don't think she'd have just left a cup of cold cigarette tea sitting there, if she had noticed it before that night? I don't know, it just seemed odd . . .'

'Hannah, that's not nearly strong enough,' said Cosmo. Although he, too, was speaking quietly, his tone was firm and authoritative, as if he was trying to prove that Ovilry was not the only person who knew things.

'And Hogg mentioned wanting to go to Spain. So, maybe that's his motive – he wanted to start a new life abroad and needed to get rid of his burdensome family first. And he was tired of Mrs Pearcey, too, so he decided to frame her for the murder, and that would take care of her as well.'

'But if that were the case,' replied Cosmo, 'then why would Mrs Pearcey still be covering for him? Wouldn't she be denouncing him from the rooftops, rather than not saying a word?'

Hannah didn't have a response to that. And she admitted that when Dolly had confidently put forward the theory that Frank Hogg wanted to get rid of them all, it had sounded more convincing. But she, Hannah, had been in Hogg's presence, and he had *seemed* evil, and capable of such a thing – hadn't he?

Again, she had a visceral memory of Frank breathing down her neck; how vulnerable she felt stuck seated there while he loomed above, his belt just inches from her face. The feeling of Edwin's foot jamming the chair as she tried to push it back. How every cell in her body had throbbed with alarm. Her attempt to expel Frank Hogg from her head felt unsuccessful; he was gripping on tight, with those strong, stubby fingers. She pulled in closer to Cosmo.

'I think I must stop this Mrs Pearcey business now,' she said meekly. 'Do you mind awfully?'

She was being manipulative, she knew, but she needed Cosmo to feel guilty. She wanted to remind him that, if it hadn't been for his suggestion that they work as a team to try to out-scoop Ovilry, she wouldn't have been in the Trafalgar in the first place. To revive his self-flagellation of earlier, which he had cut short when he kissed her. It wasn't entirely fair of her, she knew, but events that evening had been so intense and shocking, she needed to absolve herself of responsibility for them – for now, at least.

'Of course!' Cosmo replied in an anguished tone, clutching her tightly. 'You absolutely must stop. It's out of the question to carry on. No more of it now.'

They had reached her house. Hannah saw with relief that the drawing-room windows were dark; she wouldn't have to face her mother this evening. She found her latch key, and Cosmo gave her a chaste kiss on the cheek, before bidding her a whispered goodnight.

Upstairs in her room, she undressed, watching herself in the dressing-table mirror. Clearly, she was a different person now. Shaking out her hair, she smelt the smoke from Frank Hogg's cigarette.

11

By the fall of drops of water, by degrees a pot is filled. Let this be an example for the acquisition of all knowledge.
— *Girl's Own Paper*

No more of it now. Hannah's new life, free of Mrs Pearcey, got off to a slow start. For some time after the Trafalgar evening she felt contaminated. Frank Hogg's unsavouriness clung to her, like the foul odours ingrained in tannery workers, however much they washed. But as the weeks passed, his potency diminished, and she found herself able to view him, and the whole business, with a degree of detachment.

How much energy and time she had given to this sad, grubby story! It had been a period of madness. But no one else knew quite the depth of her involvement – and no one needed to now. It would be one of those things she would forget about herself; an extended moment when she had not behaved as she should have, like when the builder had exposed himself to her in the square when she was a girl, and rather than run away screaming, she had stood there, looking.

She could not entirely rid her head of the questions she had about the case, over Frank's involvement, and Mrs Pearcey's motivation for keeping quiet — not to mention the terrible possibility that an innocent woman might soon be led to the gallows. These were serious obstacles to her peace of mind, but all she could do was step around them, as you would luggage awkwardly left in the middle of a room.

As well as marking the end of her involvement with the Mrs Pearcey affair, the events of the Trafalgar evening confirmed to her how right she was to marry Cosmo. She no longer held him responsible for what happened with the Hoggs in the public house; indeed, she had only felt that way for a moment, when very shaken up. He may have encouraged her to hunt for stories on Mrs Pearcey, but it was she who had hatched that particular plan, and it wasn't his fault that the meeting had gone the way it did. And he had saved her! What better illustration of his devotion, and of the general protection afforded by a husband, than Cosmo swooping in to rescue her from that man? Before this, she hadn't thought of him as especially brave, but now he had shown his mettle. He had been tested and proved himself worthy. The *Girl's Own Paper* would approve.

Although, of course, the paper would certainly *not* approve of what the two of them then did in Rochester Square. In the days afterwards, Hannah had avoided reliving the encounter, in her bid to shake herself free of Frank Hogg, but when she finally did, she found, to her surprise, that she did not feel ashamed of her behaviour. Embarrassed at the possibility of being seen from those windows, certainly, but not ashamed. It occurred to her that she might have felt differently had she not met the non-traditional Dolly, or seen those couples clamped together in the theatre dressing room. But she had.

It was as if Cosmo had lit a fire in a cold, shuttered room inside her. For it to have happened just weeks before they stood together in their smart clothes at the altar in St Mary's may have been premature and improper, but she could not see it as an abominable act. In fact, she felt the two of them were essentially already married; that minute of intense intimacy had bound them together irrevocably.

But still, there was the actual wedding to contend with. Despite it being a modest affair, Hannah sensed that the preparations could easily expand to fill all the time available for them. For the next month, she needed to occupy a different character — of someone effective, no-nonsense and unreflective. And she would not dwell on what awaited her afterwards, at Milton Terrace — the unspecified period in that tense, over-stuffed waiting room before she was fully granted admission into her new life.

In her notebook, she tore out all the pages relating to Mrs Pearcey — the notes she had made on Crossfield Road, on Priory Street, and on the Lizzie Styles interview — and threw them on the fire. Now, the only writing it contained was her trousseau list. She wrote to Mrs Didier, asking for an appointment. Next, she wrote to Emily, formally asking if she would be her bridesmaid, and inviting her on an expedition to Pinkett's department store. Emily agreed to both, and the two arranged to meet at the bus stop in Camden Town the following afternoon.

Hannah secretly hoped that Emily wouldn't bring her daughter with her, and so was disappointed when her friend approached the bus stop, cradling the baby. When Emily drew closer, however, Hannah saw that what she thought was a swaddled infant was actually a huge white fur muff engulfing Emily's forearms. Emily extracted herself from it and the friends embraced, agreeing that a shopping jaunt was just the thing on such a chilly, miserable day.

'Bea has a sniffle, so I didn't want to risk it,' said Emily as the bus pulled up. 'Such a shame – I think she'd enjoy it, all the glittering lights and things to touch and people cooing over her.'

On the top deck there were no seats beside each other, so Hannah sat behind Emily and Emily twisted in her seat to chat, as the bus jolted them through the grey streets into town. They covered the same subjects they'd talked about when they'd last seen each other, over biscuits in Gloucester Crescent. Babies. Weddings. The quiet joys of domesticity. Emily didn't ask if anything new and extraordinary had happened to Hannah, and indeed, why would she? The old Hannah would probably have told the old Emily; clasped her hand and lowered her voice and said, 'Now, Em, you won't believe this . . .'

But they were not their old selves. Besides, how could she tell her Mrs Pearcey story without its shameful ending: Hannah unchaperoned in a public house, being intimidated by Frank Hogg, whose anger towards her might be half justified by what she had put in the newspaper? No, as far as Emily was concerned, the two of them seamlessly picked up from where they had left off, and all the dark, messy stuff in between hadn't happened at all. And that was surely for the best.

As the bus passed through Euston, Emily rummaged in her bag and produced a newspaper. Hannah felt a lurch at the sight of newsprint, but this paper was not the *Star*. Nor was it one of its tawdry siblings, but rather *The Times*, and Emily turned not to its front pages but to the announcements at the back.

'So, I read this in an account of the wedding of someone or other and thought it sounded quite delightful,' Emily said. 'For inspiration.'

She read aloud: *'The bride's travelling dress was of shot heliotrope voile, daintily arranged with a collar of cream embroidered muslin and point d'esprit net, and a pretty little sleeveless coat lined with heliotrope silk. The hat worn with this costume was of rustic straw most becomingly trimmed with branches of mauve lilac and draperies of heliotrope chiffon.'*

'That does sound nice,' said Hannah. 'But I don't think I need a travelling dress. We had talked about Lake Lugano, but I'm not sure we're going to be able to go on honeymoon. At least, not immediately.'

Emily pouted. 'Oh, that is a shame. Ah, well, you can concentrate on things for the house. Much more interesting than clothes, I think.'

Now was the time to tell Emily that there was no house, either, and that the newlyweds would be living with Cosmo's parents for the foreseeable future. But such was Emily's newfound love of the domestic life that doing so would likely wrong-foot her. All Hannah wanted at the moment was for the two of them to feel connected and on the same path.

The wind had picked up and she felt suddenly chilly, exposed on the top deck. She leant over Emily and put her arms around her neck in an embrace, and then, impulsively, slid her hands down and wriggled them into Emily's muff, so they sat, too tight, on top of Emily's own. Emily laughed with surprise.

They got off at Oxford Circus and walked down to the vast edifice of Pinkett's. The breeze was agitating the flags hanging from the building's façade, the flapping sounding like horses' hooves, as if there was a stampede overhead. Hannah and Emily joined the flow of people going through the entrance, which was flanked by two doormen dressed like toy soldiers, who looked as grave as if they were guarding Kensington Palace.

The first time Hannah had stepped into one of these places, as a child, she'd felt as if someone had somehow found out all her desires, even things she hadn't yet articulated to herself, and built a wonderland from them. A place where the black, white and grey of everyday life was replaced with duck-egg blue and coral, and embellished with gold leaf. She was used to shops displaying apples and potatoes and tins of bicarbonate. Here, the objects were gloriously non-essential – except, of course, that she now wanted them so much they seemed vital for her happiness. Dainty, ivory-handled fans, just the right size for her palm. Velvet coats as soft as a kitten, and silk stockings so fine they barely existed. Bowls filled to the brim with sugared almonds. Huge white feathers arranged in jars. Shelves of cut-glass ornaments and trinkets, a candelabra placed beside them so that the light glinted off a thousand tiny surfaces. Even the candles were things of beauty: new and just lit, not the guttered little stumps she was used to. The mingled scents of myriad perfumes and teas. The gentle hiss of the gasoliers and the tinkle of a fountain over by the entrance. The shop girls in their smart black dresses seemed barely older than her, and indulged her, dabbing her hand with lily of the valley talcum powder. While the historical dioramas at Madame Tussauds excited and intrigued her, the floors of Pinkett's and Harrods were unadulterated delight; an experience so indulgent it felt illicit.

The young Hannah had turned to her mother, mouth agape, wanting to revel in the gorgeousness together, but then she saw Mrs Teale's expression as she gazed around the floor. Her look was not one of revulsion, exactly, but somewhere between vacancy and distaste. Then she had noticed Hannah's deflation and smiled, trying to conceal her reaction. Back then, Mrs Teale wasn't so militant about things.

'Straight to haberdashery?' said Emily now.

To get there, they passed through the beauty section. There was a display of dozens of types of cold cream, arranged in a great pyramid. *Fairfax lotion. Baker's Wonder Cream. Otto of Rose Cold Cream. Parisian Snow Cream. Facial Powder of the Fairies. Liquid Bloom of Roses. Dr Leverton's Magic Cream. Dr Smythson's. Dr Jackson's. Dr Green's.* There was one endorsed by Sarah Bernhardt, which made Hannah think of Dolly. What was she doing now?

'So, who is Cosmo's best man?' asked Emily.

'Oh, I don't know,' said Hannah, distracted. 'I'm seeing him tomorrow, I'll ask him.'

Despite all her good intentions, she had lapsed into circumspection. She thought of her mother, desperate to shed her worldly goods. Then she remembered the pot of cold cream on Mrs Pearcey's dressing table: a home-made one in a plain, unmarked pot. If Mrs Pearcey had ever aspired to buying a real one from a department store, to endowing Dr Jackson and Dr Green with her shillings, that dream was over.

She and Emily wandered through the furnishings, with the great logs of fabric that were so large it took two shop girls to unroll them. Nearly every shopper there was female, of course. But now, Hannah noticed how many children there were, liberating the ribbons in the haberdashery section, rifling through the buttons, thumping the piles of fabric, trying to find the fun in this adult playground.

Emily spotted some chintz she thought would be nice for Hannah's nursery curtains – 'we have the same for Bea' – and went to inspect it. A shop girl slid over to attend, advising them that she was at their disposal, and stood with her hands laced behind her back and a fixed, patient smile. Now, of course, these shop girls were no longer older than Hannah. This one looked about eighteen, was fair-haired and plain, her chin bumpy with spots. Hannah wondered where they slept; above the shop, in giggly dormitories, smoothing each other's hair into buns each morning? How much did they earn, and what did they do with their money? Were they hoping to marry? Was this job just a means to an end?

She and Emily moved along to the next mound of fabric.

'Do you think it's nice, working here?' she asked Emily.

'Well, I don't think I'd like it,' said Emily. 'Whatever the staff discount. You know Caroline, from school? I hear that she was engaged to a perfectly nice chap, and then called it off, and is now a typist, living in a shared flat in Chelsea! I mean, of course, that would be better than marrying a monster, but . . .' She shrugged, as if both of them were unable to imagine being in such an unfortunate position, and then smiled. 'Han, do you remember?' She started singing: '*Miss Buss and Miss Beale, Cupid's darts do not feel . . .*'

She looked at Hannah to finish the rhyme. Hannah complied.

'*How different from us, Miss Beale and Miss Buss.*'

It was a ditty that they'd all sung at school, about the spinster women who had founded the school. Hannah smiled, and they continued their afternoon, looking at things Hannah couldn't afford with which to furnish her imaginary house.

After they grew tired of the shop, the friends travelled back to Camden Town and said their goodbyes outside Brown's dairy before turning their separate ways home. It was just past 6 p.m., and the evening newsboys were out in force. A few feet away from Hannah, one held a copy of the *Star* above his head, rotating between the traffic and the pavement to display his wares.

'Baby farm in Bermondsey!' he yelled. 'Baby farm in Bermondsey!'

Hannah stopped in her tracks. She had resolutely avoided the newspapers since the Trafalgar evening, not even buying one when, two days later, Cosmo told her that he had fed the information about Frank Hogg selling possessions to Madame Tussauds to the *Star* and they had made a small story out of it. But now, she felt strangely affronted that the case seemed to have been pushed from the front page. Why had it gone off the boil?

Surely, buying a paper could do little harm, she thought. It was just like sticking the tip of her finger in the jam pot. She walked over to the boy, bought a copy, then moved to the side of the pavement, leaning against the wall of the dairy to read it.

The first pages of the paper were indeed occupied with the story of a baby farm, but on page five, there it was:

HAMPSTEAD HORROR – NEW GRUESOME DETAILS. Written by Ovilry, of course.

Now, reading today's report, she understood why the Hampstead Horror had been relegated, at least temporarily, from the front. The story didn't contain any great revelations. It appeared that in the past few days there had been yet another hearing, at which the existing evidence was reiterated. Objects associated with the crime, such as the pram and bloodied clothing, had been shown in court. Inspector Bannister stated that he had climbed inside the pram himself, in order to test that it could hold an adult weight. A Priory Street neighbour claimed to have heard a child screaming, and the smashing of glass. A policeman said that the murder was carried out in *a most brutal manner and with the greatest amount of violence that it is possible to believe anyone capable of.* Ovilry asserted that *the police still suspect that more than one person is involved in the murder.*

One piece of new information was that a trial date had been set: 1 December at the Central Criminal Court. At the end of the hearing – as at the end of every hearing – Mrs Pearcey was asked whether she wished to make a statement, and replied, 'No, sir, I wish to reserve my defence.' Apparently, she 'smiled' at Frank Hogg when she passed him on the way out of the court. 'Friends' of the prisoner were quoted as saying that she had a 'buoyant disposition' and was feeling confident of an acquittal. How on earth could she think that? To Hannah, it seemed that these hearings consisted of a succession of little weights being steadily added to the guilty side of the scale, leaving the other side dangling empty.

Hannah folded up the *Star* and was about to stuff it in

her pocket, but then realised she didn't want to keep it and handed it back to the boy. She walked on towards Camden Road, through cold, dark streets, rubbing and blowing on her numb fingers, feeling baffled and disquieted. Why was Mrs Pearcey putting herself through all these awful hearings, mutely watching the evidence against her mount up, and not offering any defence or explanation of what happened that evening? Was she really trying to protect that low-life, Frank Hogg? Did she honestly think that he was going to somehow save her? Hannah felt as if the woman was on a cart trundling to the gallows, and at the moment, it was still moving just about slow enough for her to jump off and survive. Very soon, it would not be.

Still, this wasn't her business any more, she told herself, as she reached the front door and pulled out her latch key. Her concern was the fact that New Year's Eve – her wedding day – was now a month away, and, despite her resolution to make it the exclusive focus of her life, she still had dozens of decisions and arrangements to make.

Inside, Hannah went upstairs to her freezing room, lit a candle, pulled out her magazines from under the mattress and got into bed. She leafed through them, trying to fan the bridal flames. Each issue invariably included an article on the topic of marriage, and she knew them all: from the earnest edicts reminding women of the profound peace and satisfaction to be found in the domestic sphere, to the more wry takes on the subject, painting men as selfish monsters who must be humoured and manipulated.

She turned to an article titled 'Whispers to Our Wedded Girls by a Middle-aged Woman'.

> It is a great mistake for a wife to be always full of her own little concerns, to the exclusion of her husband's: to make it evident to him that she thinks her new bonnet much more interesting than his new book; that she cares much more about Freddy's cold, or Lily's chilblains, than his hoarseness or threatenings of gout . . .

She turned the page. Next, 'Some Successful Spinsters'. At the top of the list was Anna Sewell, the author of *Black Beauty*.

Hannah put down the magazine; it was no good. She could not be distracted by this froth, could not shake off the spectre of Mrs Pearcey, who would not be on anyone's list of successful spinsters.

Among the magazine haul was the one belonging to Mrs Pearcey, which Hannah had picked up at Priory Street. On the face of it, there was nothing to distinguish the issue from all the dozens of others spread around her, yet to Hannah it might as well have been glowing – a single hot coal in a sea of cold black ones. She picked it up and flicked through it, this time noticing that some of the illustrations of winsome young women had been carefully coloured in, presumably by Mrs Pearcey herself. It was as if the women had been made up, Dolly-style, with crimson lips and cheeks, bright blue eyes, yellow hair and darkened eyebrows. She kept turning until she reached the page with Mrs Pearcey's shopping list. This time, though, she carefully lifted out the scrap of paper, holding it up to the candle to examine it. *Onions. Pots. Bacon?* What could be gleaned from such a banal list?

Hannah squinted. Now that there was light behind the paper, she saw that there was writing on the back, too.

Turning it over, she found another list. The same round handwriting, but this time in black ink.

2 night dresses
2 day dresses
4 flannel squares
4 bibs
1 hood
4 long petticoats
Napkins

Bibs. Napkins. This was a baby list.

Hannah stared at the words as they registered. Her hand holding the paper fell heavily to the bed, as if it had been turned to stone.

There were two possible explanations. The obvious one was that Mrs Pearcey was with child. The other was that she *had* been expecting a child but the event had not come to pass. After all, who knew when the baby list had been written? The fact that it was slipped inside a current issue of a magazine didn't mean much. By that point, the baby list could have been obsolete news, the piece of paper useful only for scrap, used by Mrs Pearcey to write a shopping list on its blank side. Perhaps what was really on Mrs Pearcey's mind in the days before the crime was not bibs for a forthcoming child, but whether or not she could afford to buy bacon.

But wait. Wasn't there a third, more prosaic possibility? That the list was not personal to Mrs Pearcey at all. It had been ascertained that she lived by her needle, when she worked at all. Perhaps the list was just a paid job, a set of baby garments made up for an unknown customer at that sewing machine in the kitchen, in exchange for a few pennies.

The list could be everything, or nothing. She mustn't jump to conclusions. But Hannah couldn't help recalling the story she had overheard her father telling his friends in the drawing room, all those years ago.

Maddeningly, her mother was out. Hannah waited by the window in the drawing room, looking into the inky square. A light wind rustled the leaves of the few evergreen trees, as impatient as she was. In the end, Mrs Teale's clothes must have acted as an invisibility cloak in the darkness, as Hannah was only alerted to her return by the slam of the front door below.

She knew the rhythms of the house so well: the exact time it took for Mrs Teale to take off her coat and hang it up, check the letter tray, listen for the maids, and then make her way upstairs. As her mother reached the first-floor landing, Hannah was there.

'There was something I wanted to ask you,' she said, launching straight in. 'Do you remember years ago, when father had a colleague who fathered a child with a female prisoner, so that she could plead her belly and escape hanging?'

Even on the unlit landing, Hannah could see her mother flinch.

'I do,' Mrs Teale replied carefully, moving past Hannah into the drawing room. 'Why do you ask?'

'So, she wasn't put to death when she was convicted – but can you remember what happened after the child was born?'

Hannah continued, following her in. 'Was she hanged then?'

Mrs Teale walked over to the window, to stand in the spot Hannah had just vacated.

'No,' she replied, turning away. 'In fact, I believe the woman remained in prison for a while and then was pardoned.'

'Really?' said Hannah. 'So, she wasn't hanged, and then was just set free?'

'Yes. I believe that outcome is not uncommon in those circumstances. Out of sympathy for the child.' She was silent for a long moment, before turning back to Hannah. 'Why are you asking?'

'I was just wondering!' Hannah replied, nonsensically, already halfway out of the door. Climbing the stairs to her bedroom, she laughed out loud. At last, Mrs Pearcey's behaviour made sense. Frank had killed his wife and child, and she had agreed to take the blame, in the knowledge that, if convicted, she had a card to play. This was why she was staying silent as the evidence piled up around her. The fact that she had his child in her belly meant she would be given a helping hand down from that speeding cart.

Up in her room, Hannah paced about, too stirred up to rest. She glanced out of her little window at the night sky. Usually, the stars were obscured by the pall of smog over the city, but tonight, a few twinkled. She thought of Mrs Pearcey at her cell window, her hand resting on her stomach, looking out at them and smiling with her secret.

And now Hannah, too, knew. Perhaps she was the only other person who did, besides Mrs Pearcey and Frank. She supposed there was nothing she could do with this knowledge

– or, rather, nothing she *should* do with it. As she had agreed with Cosmo: *No more of it now.* But in any case, surely, Mrs Pearcey would soon play her hand. After all, the trial would begin in just two days.

12

A girl should keep no secret of her own from her mother. She is the adviser and the protector of her daughter, and she will know best what steps to take. Never let her find out by chance what concerns you so seriously, more especially when anyone else has been made a confidant.

– Girl's Own Paper

On 30 November, the day before her trial was due to start at the Central Criminal Court, Mrs Pearcey was put on a carriage from Holloway Prison and transported to Newgate, which adjoined the court. The notoriety of the case meant that great precautions were in place at the court to prevent overcrowding: barriers erected in corridors, and extra policemen on guard. On the first day, the courtroom was packed, with many 'fashionable ladies' come to spectate, armed with pocket flasks and sandwiches. The prisoner was escorted through the secret tunnel between the prison and the court, emerging into the dock wearing a black dress and brown cloak, with no hat, and her hair 'curled attractively' around her face. She spoke only to plead 'not guilty' in answer to the judge's question, and then sat quietly, her hands in her lap.

Hannah learnt all of this indirectly. Mrs Pearcey may have been dominating her thoughts, but Hannah had been keeping her promise, to Cosmo and to herself, to stay away from the details of the case, and had not looked at a newspaper since that Pinkett's jaunt, two days ago. But it so happened that on that first day of the trial, she was downstairs in the kitchen, leafing through a pile of the cook's old recipe books, still looking for ideas for the wedding breakfast, when Gwen and Ivy came down with the shopping, and an evening paper – the *Pall Mall Gazette*, not the *Star*. As Gwen peeled the potatoes for dinner, Ivy read aloud from that day's report of the trial. Hannah leafed through recipes, writing down random phrases such as *saumon à la mayonnaise* and *fruit jelly*, and pretending not to listen.

The usual troupe of witnesses were called to the stand in court. Inspector Bannister. Clara, who talked about Mrs Pearcey's odd behaviour at the mortuary, when they had identified Phoebe's body. The Priory Street neighbours. Mrs Sawtell, the wife of the police inspector, who claimed that on the day after the murders, when Mrs Pearcey had been at the police station, Mrs Pearcey had told her she had had 'words' with Phoebe. A man who worked with Edwin Hogg and had provided Frank with an alibi for the evening of the murders . . .

'Hold on,' interrupted Hannah. 'Does it mention that man's name? Is it Alf?'

'It doesn't say,' said Ivy, puzzled.

New evidence had been produced: a cache of incriminating letters had been discovered in Mrs Pearcey's rooms, under her bed. The newspaper correspondent noted that these letters seemed to form the large part of the evidence for the prosecution, which said that they proved her obsession with Frank Hogg.

Under her bed! These letters were not mentioned at the hearings. Did that mean they were discovered only recently? Were the letters quietly lying there, stuffed behind her copy of *Princess* magazine, when Hannah had sunk to her knees and peered into that dim space?

Ivy read out the letters, slowly, hesitating over some words:

'Frank, dear, you said, "if I thought I loved you" – what did you mean by that? Don't you know that I do? How can I prove to you that I do love you dearly? If there is anything I can do to prove it, I promise you it shall be done, you have more power over me than anyone on earth. When I say that, I say all. Do have a wee bit for me when I come to-morrow. I hope you did not get into any bother. Good night, dear.'

How disconcerting it was to hear Mrs Pearcey's private thoughts. Hers had been the one voice missing during this case, and here she was, exposed, being relayed in Ivy's affectless tone.

Ivy continued reading:

'My Dearest F. – Shall I see you about two to-morrow? Come if you can, dear, if you can't stop long. I have got such a bad headache or heartache. Hoping you are quite well, with best love from your ever loving M. E.'

'Dear Frank, – Thanks so much for the letter; it was so good of you to send it. I am thinking how selfish I am for asking you to come here to see me. Of course you don't want to be

bothered with me; but if you can come on Friday I shall be very glad to see you, as I am afraid to come to the shop. I might make mischief, so to prevent it I had better not come. People say ugly things some times, not nice to hear. So when I come into the shop again I shall be very careful, and especially if an inquisitive lady should come in — you know who I mean.'

'Dear Frank, the time has been so long to-day; every minute seemed an hour, waiting for you. Do try and come on Friday. So good-bye till then, with good wishes from M. E. In this false world we do not always know who are our friends, and who are our enemies. We all have enemies, and all need friends.'

'Can it be so, or does my sight Deceive me in the uncertain light? Ah! no; I recognise the face, Though time has touched it in its flight.'

'That last bit's odd,' said Gwen.
'It's from a famous poem, I think,' said Hannah.
'The trial is expected to conclude tomorrow,' Ivy read, laying down the paper.
'I mean, she's going to swing, isn't she?' said Gwen.
Hannah resumed blindly flicking through the recipe book, letting the pages riffle against her fingers.

The following day, the second of the trial, Hannah finally had her appointment with Mrs Didier. She took the box containing Emily's dress on the bus to Maddox Street in Soho, just behind Regent Street and Pinkett's. Mrs Didier operated from a basement, like most of these grandly named ateliers, which could fit four hundred times into a department store.

Mrs Didier had never been in the sweatshop business – Mrs Teale would not have used her if she had – but she used to employ four young seamstresses. Now, Hannah saw as she entered, there appeared to be just the one, a fair-haired girl who sat cross-legged on the table under the artificial light, nose almost touching her work, as she sewed a trim onto a scarlet silk. The table and her own dress were speckled with tiny pieces of red fabric. She didn't look up at Hannah. The studio's small window was open, but the place was nonetheless horribly hot and stuffy, insulated by the rolls of fabric lining the walls. A side table held a quantity of honeycomb lace, piled up like tripe in a butcher's window.

Mrs Didier looked tinier and older than ever.

'Where is Hervé?' asked Hannah, pleased that she'd remembered the name of the dressmaker's dog.

'Dead,' replied Mrs Didier bluntly. 'Long time, I've not seen you. Three years? I thought maybe you might have gone over there, like everyone else.'

She flapped her hand in the direction of Regent Street. Hannah thought of her infidelity at Pinkett's, just a few days ago.

'No! We just don't have much money, after father passed away, you know,' she said. 'But now – as I said in my note – I'm getting married! And my friend has lent me her dress, but I'm sure it's too—'

'Yes, yes,' replied the old woman. No congratulations or clamouring for details from her; she wasn't the sort. Hannah knew that was why her mother liked her.

Hannah went behind a screen to try on Emily's dress, which, as suspected, was several inches too tight and wouldn't fully fasten. She emerged, awkwardly stuffed into the strained satin, averting her gaze from the mirror, as Mrs Didier unspooled her measuring tape.

'I think I'm about the same size as I was before, with the yellow dress,' said Hannah, trying to regain some dignity. 'I wore it recently and it still fits.'

'Soon, you won't be,' said Mrs Didier, prodding her stomach. 'You'll need a new gown for *that*. I should make you one, to be prepared.'

Did Mrs Didier somehow know about all those illicit sausage rolls? Then, Hannah cottoned on to what the dressmaker was saying. Not her, too!

'Your mother was so huge with you,' continued Mrs Didier. 'I had to use six yards of muslin for hers.'

'That's funny,' said Hannah. 'As I turned out so short.'

'How is she?'

'All right, I think,' replied Hannah, holding her arms away from her body to allow access to the tape measure. She glanced down at the crown of Mrs Didier's head as the woman bent in front of her. Her hair was white, but with a yellowy tinge, like old snow, and so sparse her pink scalp was visible.

'She still in her weeds?' said Mrs Didier.

'She is,' Hannah replied, and then, because Mrs Didier's directness was emboldening, she added, 'Silly, really, when she didn't even seem to like father that much. It's hardly a Victoria and Albert situation.'

'Well, she wants to tell men to stay away, that she's not open for business,' said Mrs Didier. 'And who can blame her, after him? But there are a lot of men who target widows. She'd be better off with a beautiful new dress, I think. It'll look like there's someone who loves her, and who wants to buy her nice—'

'What do you mean, "and who can blame her, after him"?'

Mrs Didier was now over at the table, her back to Hannah, scratching some figures in a notepad. She straightened up, just slightly, before bending again over the pad.

'Just – you know what men are like,' she said shortly. 'Now, you'll let me make you a veil, at least. None of this ready-made department-store rubbish.'

Mrs Didier moved over to one of the piles of lace. The conversation was clearly over. For a moment, Hannah stayed put, looking across the room to the single, grimy little window, propped open with a wooden boot stay.

'Come and look,' ordered Mrs Didier from across the room. Hannah did as she was told.

After the appointment, Hannah wandered through the streets of Soho, in no rush to get home. She passed restaurants opening their doors for lunch; a man in a beret carefully pasting a poster on the wall, advertising a lecture at Conway Hall entitled 'What Is Anarchy?' She felt very hungry, and considered a pastry – or even ducking into one of the restaurants for a solo *coq au vin*; an unprecedented move – but then remembered the straining satin, and kept walking.

She thought about Mrs Didier's comments about her mother, and how she appeared to know her far more intimately than Hannah did. She imagined the two of them in that claustrophobic basement, bemoaning the indignity of thinning hair, and the foibles of their husbands, and whatever else older women talked about.

And who can blame her, after him? What had been so bad

about her father? Most probably he had been absent and off-hand, uninterested in Mrs Teale's feelings and thoughts. Not that her mother would have twittered on about the children's illnesses, or how the butcher was out of chops again, or any other trivial domestic matters – but Hannah thought she might have wanted to talk about the books she was reading, and what was happening in the world. Hannah had come across some men like that herself, who seemed to need to constantly remind women how much less important they were. From what she had seen of her parents' relationship, she guessed her father might have been one of them.

On Maddox Street, she stepped around a group of children who were mockingly dancing around a one-man band. Harmonica strapped to his face, the man played looking over their heads, pretending they weren't there. At Oxford Circus, she paused before the intersecting streams of traffic, the buses heading north that could take her home. The weather wasn't too terrible; cold, but with a clear winter sun. She decided to walk on, heading down Oxford Street.

What grumblings might she have about Cosmo, when she met up with Emily over Garibaldi biscuits in two decades' time? Hopefully not indifference. He seemed interested in her thoughts; that was what made her like him. But wasn't it true that anyone could pretend to be a certain way, at least for a little while? And even if they weren't pretending at first, people evolved, sometimes to the point of becoming entirely new characters. Everyone around Hannah had changed in the course of her knowing them: Emily, Will, her mother. So of course Cosmo would, too. And so would she.

What sort of people would they become? What would

she end up being maddened by? That little squint he gave to herald his jokes? His glibness? Or one of a hundred little habits, yet to be discovered and entrenched over a thousand dinners? It struck her, once again, what an extraordinary leap of faith it was to get married.

On she walked, down Oxford Street, one in a vast crowd. Around her, people marched ahead and milled about, got in and out of carriages, entered and left shops, their blank expressions shielding their private preoccupations. Would they go straight home after work, or nip into a public house? Would they marry that man, or this one? Should they go to the doctor for that niggle? Sausage roll, or *coq au vin*? At this exact moment in the city, she thought, a million decisions were being made, most of which were unremarkable, the low-stakes stuffing that filled one's day, but one of which might be seismic. Those people frozen in Pompeii, who made the decision not to go out fishing that day, or who couldn't be bothered to visit their friend in Rome. Tiggie Hogg's life, too, if her mother hadn't accepted that invitation to tea at Priory Street. Mrs Pearcey's, if she hadn't bumped into Frank Hogg.

Hannah spotted a newsstand ahead and veered towards it. There was the *Star*: HAMPSTEAD HORROR TRIAL LATEST! She stopped in her tracks; her blood fizzled. Was this it? Had the jury reached its verdict, and the prisoner revealed her condition to a stunned courtroom? She peered closer to read the opening paragraphs of the article but quickly realised that it was just a report of yesterday's events, which she had already heard, courtesy of Gwen and Ivy in the kitchen the previous evening. Of course it was. It was only lunchtime. Journalists weren't magicians, not quite.

Today's news wouldn't have hit the papers yet; it was probably still materialising.

All these tiny decisions were being made all around her, as unremarkable as the act of breathing. And taking place right now, two miles away, at the Old Bailey, was the biggest decision of them all.

Before she knew it, Hannah had changed direction and started walking towards the court.

It was just gone 2 p.m. when she arrived. Rounding the corner from Holborn Viaduct, she was confronted by a vast, terrible hulk of a building, which seemed to inhabit the whole block and had the presence of a fire-blackened brick dumped into a toy town. The walls seemed as tall as ten men, punctuated by tiny windows, right at the top. Smoke trailed from each of its many chimneys. Behind it, the dome of St Paul's loomed, sentry-like.

This, of course, was Newgate. Hannah hadn't been in front of the prison for years, and the sight shocked her as much as it had when she'd first seen it. The court was next to the prison, symbiotically attached. She walked along the awful wall until she found the entrance. The court building was less forbidding than its neighbour, with a neo-classical façade, and a small flight of steps leading to its entrance, embedded in a shallow semi-circular wall. A policeman stood guard. Pinned to the wall beside him was a typed list, the lettering too small to read from where she stood.

The man was young and sullen-looking, the strap of his helmet high on his long chin. For a moment, Hannah thought it was the same man who had been guarding Priory Street.

'Is the trial still going on?' she called to him. 'Mrs Pearcey?'

He shook his head. 'S'over.'

No more was forthcoming. The burning next question hung in the air, but Hannah felt that she didn't want to hear the verdict as a one-word answer from this curt official. Instead, she turned away. Now, she noticed that there were barriers leaning up against the wall of the court, and loitering around the entrance were a handful of men. They didn't look like pressmen or lawyers, or officials of any kind, but rather members of the public, dark people drawn to this terrible, gloomy place. They would probably know what had gone on in court – but Hannah didn't want to hear it from them either.

The wind had picked up. From the south, an omnibus approached, its sign stating that it was heading for Camden Town. Hannah thought she should get on it. But she let it rattle past and started walking.

The scene in the *Star* offices was very different from her previous visit. Now, the foyer was thronging and the atmosphere febrile, with people whizzing in and out in great haste, the grand entrance door not given the chance to close. The same stagey man as before was behind the front desk, arguing with a messenger boy.

'Well, go and tell your master what I said,' he instructed sternly, as Hannah approached. 'I predict he'll come round.'

He paused to turn to Hannah, eyebrows raised.

'Ah, it's you,' he said. 'Here to see Mr Summersdale?'

She smiled, pleased to be memorable.

'I'm actually here to see—'

'You know the way,' he interrupted, too busy for details.

Turning back to the boy, he continued, 'Tell him four shillings is out of the question.'

Hannah nodded thank you, and passed through the back door into the press room. When she'd last been here, it had been ghostly. Now, like the foyer, the vast space was humming with industry, with every desk occupied; row after row of men scribbling furiously or talking in urgent, important tones. Somewhere unseen, machinery clanked and sighed.

Hannah hesitated just inside the door. She looked around for Cosmo but couldn't spot him. Coming here was a mistake; everyone was far too busy, and Cosmo would be taken aback if he saw her. She would slip away before she was noticed.

Too late. A couple of men nearest to her glanced up from their work, and then there was a small ripple effect of looks, the men curious about the random woman in their midst.

'Well, hullo!'

A man had risen from his seat a few feet away and was striding towards her. Ovilry. Of course, he would have spotted her before she did him.

'Looking for your fiancé?' he said. He looked around the room half-heartedly. 'I think he's out – I don't know where. In some slum, somewhere. Or having lunch.'

'I actually wanted to talk to you,' said Hannah quietly, aware of the eavesdroppers around them, and feeling idiotic for being there at all.

'Well, you're in luck,' said Ovilry, in his loud, bumptious voice, 'because five minutes ago I was still on deadline and couldn't have stopped for anyone – even you. Fire away.'

There was a self-consciousness to his tone, as if he were performing for the benefit of his colleagues.

'It's silly really,' she said, almost in a whisper, 'but I just wanted to ask about the Mrs Pearcey trial. I know it'll come out in the paper soon, but – I just couldn't wait. What was the verdict?'

Ovilry laughed.

'Oh, it's not over yet.'

'Really?' She looked at him, askance. 'But the man at the court said it was.'

'For today, yes. But not the whole thing. They finished with the evidence, but there's still the summing-up. The judge said it was too late today, and sent the jury to a hotel for the night.'

Hannah felt her muscles softening with relief. She realised she wasn't ready for all this to be over. She'd had her own small reprieve, just for today.

'Will you tell me what happened in court?' she said. 'What was the defence?'

Ovilry glanced up at a clock on the wall.

'Look, I've got to get something to eat. Walk with me to the pie shop and I'll tell you.'

Without waiting for her reply, he headed to the door, plucking a hat from dozens on a stand. Hannah hesitated; this all seemed rather bold. But the fact that Ovilry had spoken to her like that in front of his colleagues, none of whom appeared at all shocked by his suggestion, made her conclude that it was all right. This was not an invitation to lunch, merely a conversation with a busy pressman. She followed in Ovilry's wake, and caught up with him in the foyer. Once out on the street, it turned out that the pie shop was directly next door to the office, so their walk took a matter of seconds. Because it was past lunchtime, there was no queue.

'Do you want one?' Ovilry asked her. 'It's not just eel. You can get cranberry as well.'

The detail felt oddly intimate. She hesitated, tempted as always, before shaking her head. He ducked in, and she stared at the window, at the display of eels plaited together artistically on a vast bed of parsley. Ovilry emerged half a minute later with a pie wrapped in paper and led her to the steps of the office.

'Shall we perch here?' he said, indicating the side of the steps, out of the flow of people. They sat, he taking the step below her, and he took a bite before beginning.

'So, in the main, it was the usual troupe of witnesses, saying the same old things. But the main new evidence was these letters they found in her rooms . . .'

'Oh, yes, I heard about these.'

'Banal, girlish things, which are not only the backbone of the prosecution's case, showing that she was obsessed with him, but also being used by the defence to show that Hogg can't be trusted.'

'How so?'

'Oh, for instance, Hogg claimed on the stand that he and Pearcey weren't intimate until after he was married – as if that made it somehow more respectable, rather than less – but then they read out a gushy letter from her from months before that, which suggests that they were. It's clear now that he was seeing Pearcey and Phoebe at the same time, and then Phoebe became in the family way, and he hastily married her, but continued his relationship with Pearcey.'

'Was he questioned about that? How did he react?'

'Very annoyingly! He's clearly been instructed to keep a lid on the histrionics. None of the weeping over the pram business like from the hearings. Now, he's just cold and vague. Just repeating "I might have" and "I do not recall", over and over again. He's coming across incredibly badly.'

A scruffy blond dog had approached them on the steps and stood staring at Ovilry's pie, nose twitching.

'And then today was the barristers' summing-up,' Ovilry continued. 'Fulton, the prosecutor, droned on in the manner of someone who feels his case is so sound he doesn't need to bother with theatrics. His main thrust was that there was a ton of evidence at her house, and she had a clear motive; she was obsessed with Frank and although she might have told herself that she could accept the fact that he was married, in reality she couldn't. And so, she wanted to remove the obstacle to them being together. And then Hutton – that's Pearcey's barrister – stood up and made a valiant attempt to defend her. He said that she had no real motive – Frank Hogg had never promised her marriage, and so what good would it do for her to kill his wife? And he reminded the jury that she was described as affectionate and kind by those who knew her, and how could such a woman perpetrate an act of such savagery? The evidence was circumstantial, and if there was any doubt whatsoever, they must acquit. Then the judge was going to sum up but decided it was too late, and he'd do it tomorrow.'

Hannah tried to digest all this, staring absently down at the steps. During their conversation, rain had started lightly spitting; droplets speckled the stone. Behind them, the bells of St Paul's tolled three.

'I hear that Hutton tried to get her to plead manslaughter or diminished responsibility due to madness, so as to get a lighter sentence, or the asylum,' Ovilry continued. 'But she refused. It's a terrible gamble.'

'Did she speak?' asked Hannah. 'Mrs Pearcey?'

'No. The accused aren't allowed to give evidence.'

Sitting there beside one of the few people as involved in the case as she was, Hannah felt a strong urge to let Ovilry in on her theory. Why she thought Mrs Pearcey was taking such a gamble. She didn't know if she could trust him – in fact, surely she couldn't – but the need to share overrode those finer considerations.

'So, the oddest thing happened . . .' she began.

'Well – hullo! What?'

She looked up, startled. Cosmo was standing a few feet away, paused in the act of climbing the steps, and looking between her and Ovilry with confusion.

'Hello!' said Hannah, flustered. She jumped to her feet.

Ovilry dusted the crumbs from his fingers and leisurely stood up.

'I was just telling your fiancée the gossip,' he said, and tipped his hat to Hannah. Then, in a low voice, so low that Cosmo couldn't hear, he said to her: 'You know, I think she's going to get off.'

He skipped up the stairs into the office. Hannah stared after him, mouth open.

'Hannah?'

Gathering herself, she turned to Cosmo.

'I came to see you,' she said quickly, blushing, stepping towards him.

Instantly, he was mollified, his face relaxed. 'Well, that's nice. Do you want some lunch? I've eaten, I'm afraid. If I'd known . . .'

'No, no,' she said. So, what was her reason for coming here? She grasped at the first thing that came to mind.

'I've just ordered my wedding veil,' she said.

'Oh!' replied Cosmo. She watched his expression as he considered how best to respond to this piece of non-news. There was a fleck of something caught on his moustache. 'Well, that's exciting! Obviously, you mustn't tell me anything more, so it's a surprise on the day.'

Touched at his efforts, she smiled at him. This boded well for their marriage, she thought, if he didn't sneer at small conversation. They chatted for a few minutes, confirming an arrangement to meet with the vicar at St Mary's in a few days' time, before Hannah excused herself to catch the bus home.

Arriving back at Camden Square an hour later, she was relieved to find her mother out at the refuge. After a dinner of bread and cheese, she took herself to bed but lay awake for hours, keyed up from her day. If Ovilry was right, and Mrs Pearcey was found not guilty tomorrow, then questions of culpability would naturally be directed towards Frank. How wonderful that moment would be – the whole courtroom turning to him, their suspicions of his repugnant character confirmed. There might not be enough evidence to try him, and he might escape the gallows, but he would be convicted by public opinion. Forever tarred.

And of course, if she was found not guilty, Mrs Pearcey could keep her little secret to herself.

Hannah had fallen asleep still grappling with the decision of whether to attend court the next day, but her unconscious must have decided the matter for her, because when she woke up the next morning, she didn't waste any time prevaricating; she just quickly got dressed and slipped out.

It was a drizzly, lowering morning. She'd never taken an omnibus to the city this early, along with all the workers, their faces set and glum, as if they, too, were facing the gallows. When the bus turned into the Old Bailey, she saw that the barriers she had noticed yesterday now lined the pavement, and contained a straggly but seemingly endless queue, stretching all the way down the street, past the point where the court building merged with Newgate, and around the corner. Getting off the bus, Hannah glanced up at those dim little windows in the prison and wondered if Mrs Pearcey was watching them.

Hannah walked down the queue, which seemed mainly composed of pairs of women – if not all 'fashionably dressed', as the papers claimed, then at least they looked respectable, and were indeed carrying flasks and sandwich boxes. In fact, in appearance they looked much as she would if she were off for a picnic with Emily on Hampstead Heath.

Hannah started to feel anxious. There must be a hundred people here already; surely, they wouldn't all fit in?

Then, a woman stuck out her arm as she passed.

'Eh! I was wondering where you got to!'

It was her almond-perfumed friend Moira, from the early hearings. She beamed at Hannah, as if seeing her had made her day.

'Come in here,' she said, and shoved the barrier ajar so that Hannah could slide in. The women behind them *tsk*-ed their disapproval.

'That's not fair!' said one. 'Some of us got up at 4 a.m. to get here!'

'Well, I live in Billericay, and I got up at 2.30,' countered Moira. 'And she's my friend.' She turned back to Hannah.

'You know it's cheating to come in just for the verdict,' she said good-naturedly. 'Like skipping the savoury and going straight for dessert.'

'I know, I'm terrible,' Hannah replied, trying to repay her friend's kindness by being as jaunty as she was. 'Will we get in, do you think?'

'Oh, yes,' said Moira. 'I've counted. We're fine.'

Hannah smiled. 'So, what have I missed?'

As Moira recounted what had happened in court over the past two days, most of which Hannah already knew from Ovilry, the queue started shuffling forward.

'Do you reckon she's going to get off?' asked Hannah.

'I do,' replied Moira. She said that she felt Hutton had done a good-enough job in convincing the jury that there were too many things that couldn't be accounted for, and that if there was even the slightest doubt, they had to acquit. 'And Hogg has come across very poorly.'

Within a few minutes, they were at the front entrance of the court, at the bottom of the stone steps. It was a different policeman from yesterday; older, more polite. He was counting them down under his breath, and just after Hannah and her friend were in, he barred the door. Hannah heard a furious squawk of protest from the women denied entry.

Once inside, even the voluble Moira fell silent. They were led in a crocodile down a series of dark, narrow corridors, passing several doors, each guarded by a solemn usher, until they reached one marked P. This one they were directed through, and found themselves in a gallery overlooking a double-height room, where they were directed to squash up together on hard benches.

Below them was an arrangement of mahogany pews,

desks and chairs, and the scene was one of quiet industry. In the centre of the room, half a dozen barristers in wigs and gowns looked at papers and spoke quietly to each other. To the side sat a few rows of ordinary-looking people; from her seat in the gallery, Hannah could only see the tops of their heads. A full pew must have been reserved for pressmen, because Hannah spotted Ovilry, already at work, head bent as he scribbled something. An empty pew was marked *Jury*. The judge's bench was also unoccupied. And so, too, was the large pew facing it – the dock.

The atmosphere was decidedly gloomy. The only natural light came from a set of windows above the jury box, beyond which Newgate loomed, its bricks just a few shades darker than the dense, foggy sky. Hannah noticed that a mirror had been fixed to one of the pews, angled towards the dock. She also noted that the judge's bench was the only one with cushions. Above it hung a coat of arms and a sword.

'Is Hogg here?' Hannah whispered.

'Down there,' Moira said loudly, pointing down to where the ordinary people were sitting. Hannah recognised Frank's greasy head. And now that she knew it was him, Hannah saw the rest of his family around him: Clara, Edwin, his mother. In another pew a woman sat, leaning forward, her elbows on her knees and hands covering her face like a child.

'Who's that?' she asked her friend.

'Her mother.'

Mrs Pearcey's mother? Hannah hadn't given a thought to her family. Peering down, all she could see of the woman was a dark parting. Hannah willed her to drop her hands, anxious to see her face, but just then a door below opened. Twelve men entered the court and filed into the jury box.

It was starting. Hannah sat straight-backed, riven with nerves. Then followed three loud knocks, at which everyone in the court rose to their feet. A tall, burly man entered, clad in voluminous scarlet robes, and sat down on the comfortable-looking judge's bench.

'Judge Denman,' whispered someone behind her.

Everyone remained standing, and the room was silent. Then a door at the back of the dock opened, and the public gallery craned forward as one, as the figure of Mrs Pearcey emerged. She was wearing what was presumably the same brown cloak as described in the paper; her head was bare, her hair curled. She sat down, alone in the dock, the one non-crowded spot in the court. In the murky air, she was the only person illuminated, and Hannah saw now that the purpose of that mirror fixed to a nearby pew was to reflect natural light onto the face of the prisoner.

The judge directed the rest of the room to sit, and then embarked on his summing-up of the case. Hannah was struck by the loveliness of his voice. It was deep, educated and sonorous, almost relaxing to listen to – completely at odds with his subject matter. He first outlined the prosecution's position, that the murder took place at Mrs Pearcey's house; that she did it alone; that she took steps to avoid discovery of the crime. He went through all the evidence, so familiar by now, piece by piece. He dismissed the idea that the blood in the kitchen could have come from a nosebleed or killing mice, as claimed by the defence. However, he instructed the jury to pay heed to all areas of doubt in the prosecution's account of events: they must only find the prisoner guilty of murder if that was their 'irresistible conclusion'. He also stated that what the prosecution claimed to be a 'confession'

– the statement Mrs Pearcey gave to Eileen Sawtell in the police station, saying she had 'words' with Phoebe that evening – did not qualify as one.

As he spoke, Hannah watched Mrs Pearcey's profile, lit by the shaft of light from the window. Teeth resting on her lip, her gaze as steady and unreadable as ever. Her face was like a theatre curtain, firmly closed to conceal all hint of activity behind it.

Denman then moved onto the issue of Frank Hogg. There was no reliable evidence that he had anything to do with the crime; however, the judge described him as a man with a 'vile and loathsome character', and that the jury should be hesitant to believe him because he was 'so bad'. Indeed, Judge Denman found it hard to believe that any woman could conceive a 'violent passion or lust' for a man like Hogg.

Such startling, strong words! Surely, this was a direction to the jury that Frank Hogg should be held responsible, at least in part, for the murders? Together with the rest of the public gallery, Hannah leant forward to look at Frank, but the position of her seat denied her the satisfaction of seeing his expression as he was denounced so publicly. Moira reached for Hannah's hand and squeezed it; the two of them exchanged smiles.

'However, I must clarify an important point,' Denman continued. 'Mr Hutton appears to have assumed that unless it was absolutely established that the prisoner had acted entirely alone, and perpetrated the actual injuries that caused the death of the deceased, then she could not be found guilty of wilful murder. But, gentlemen, that is not the law.'

Hannah's smile fell away, and she felt Moira release her grip on her hand. What was happening?

'Rather, it is enough that you should be satisfied that the murder could not have occurred without the prisoner being involved in some way,' Denman continued. 'To what degree is not the question.' So, he explained, if the jury felt that Phoebe Hogg's death would not have taken place in Priory Street without the prisoner's knowledge, or without her assistance in some way, then the prisoner must be found guilty of wilful murder.

'Wait,' hissed Moira. 'Does that mean—'

'Shh,' said Hannah, because at that moment it felt easier than saying 'yes'.

Denman further clarified to the stunned room that Mrs Pearcey may not have been the only person involved in the crime, but if she seemed involved, or had attempted to destroy proof of her involvement, and there was no strong evidence to incriminate anyone else, the law should apply only to her.

The implications of his words resonated through the court. Looking down at the dock, Hannah saw the prisoner shift position in her chair, bringing her right hand up from her lap to clutch the side of her head and leaning slightly forward. Having been so still and composed up to this point, this movement from her seemed unspeakably dramatic.

The image came to her of Mrs Pearcey standing before her on the Prince of Wales Road, clutching that pile of newspapers, pleading, *Help me*. Hannah had not helped her then, at the beginning of all this. And now, as the story neared its end, it appeared that her suave lawyer had failed her, too, in the most grievous way imaginable.

The St Paul's bell boomed – 1 p.m. The room was as silent

as in the aftermath of an explosion, the only sound the scribbling from the press box.

Denman broke the tension by sending the jury out to consider their verdict; they quickly filed out through the side door. Mrs Pearcey disappeared through the door at the back of the dock. Their swift exits from the court led to an intense release of pressure. The public gallery exploded with shocked, excited chatter as women unwrapped sandwiches and unscrewed flasks.

Moira exhaled deeply. 'God, what a twist,' she said. 'I suppose that's that, then.'

'But how can her lawyer not have known this?' Hannah hissed. 'To go down the path that Hogg had something to do with it, even if there is no direct evidence against him, and only now discover that even if he did, it doesn't actually make any difference? That if the jury thinks it likely she had anything whatsoever to do with the murder, or knew it was going to happen, she should be found guilty?'

It seemed to her the kind of error that should end a man's career. Yet, the judge had just given the lawyer the lightest of reprimands.

'Well, yes, that was a bit of a blunder,' replied Moira, taking a swig of tea. 'He should have known. But I suppose she didn't give him much choice except to use that defence. She hasn't got an alibi. She hasn't offered any halfway convincing explanation for all that evidence in her house. She's not playing the insane card. What's left, except that someone else was involved, too?'

Hannah looked down at the dock, at Mrs Pearcey's empty chair.

'Have you ever known a case where a woman has been

sentenced to death and then been reprieved, because she was with child?' she asked.

Moira froze, cup suspended in mid-air, and squinted at Hannah. 'What, you think she's going to plead her belly? Why would you think that?'

'I don't know anything,' said Hannah. 'I was just wondering.'

Moira seemed satisfied with this reply — after all, how could Hannah know anything that the court did not?

'So, there was that case, now, when was it . . .?' She cast her eyes to the ceiling, consulting her mental murder catalogue. 'A good decade ago. Here at the Bailey. Drowned her daughter. When she was convicted and sentenced to hang, she said she was expecting and got a reprieve.'

'What happened exactly? They gave it to her, just like that?'

'Well, no — she was inspected, of course, to make sure it was true.'

'Inspected?'

'Some women in the courtroom, matrons, they were asked to make sure that she was with child — to check for the signs — and when they were satisfied she was, they told the judge and then there was the reprieve.'

Hannah hesitated, embarrassed to expose her lack of knowledge.

'What are the signs they were looking for exactly?'

Moira gave her the patronising look of a wise matron to an innocent maid.

'The quickening,' she said. 'Movement. Kicking. You know.'

'So, they put their hands on her belly to feel for movement?'

Moira nodded.

'And does it always move? The baby? Even when it's just started?'

'You really have a lot to learn, don't you? No, it only starts to move four or five months in.'

'But what then if she's with child, but it's too early for the movement?'

Moira shrugged. 'They've got to feel it move,' she said. 'Otherwise, how will they know it's there?'

Hannah thought of Mrs Pearcey's hands concealed in her lap as she sat in the dock. Were they resting on her belly, trying desperately to detect movement; the little flutter that could save her life?

There was a loud rap from somewhere in the court, startling Hannah. The room fell quiet.

'They can't be back already,' said Moira.

But they were. The hushed court watched the side door open and the twelve men filed back in, heads bowed. Mrs Pearcey was led back into the dock. This time she did not take a seat but remained standing. Now, she had attendants: a female warden at her side, a male to her left and a policeman behind her. The judge nodded to a clerk, who stood up and addressed the foreman of the jury.

'Have you agreed upon your verdict?'

'We have,' the foreman replied.

'Do you find the prisoner at the bar guilty or not guilty of the wilful murder of Phoebe Hogg?'

The foreman was not a man for drama; he did not pause at all.

'Guilty,' he said, his voice clear and flat.

Hannah shut her eyes. She felt as if her head had been

shoved down under water: the sounds of the room were muffled; her chest highly pressured; her skin cold and tingling. What an unspeakable moment this was. How inhumane that a roomful of people could be subjected to this.

When Hannah opened her eyes again, the judge had placed a square of black silk on top of his wig.

'Mary Eleanor Wheeler, have you anything to say why the court should not proceed to pronounce sentence of death upon you?'

Hannah forced herself to look at her. Now, even Mrs Pearcey's worst detractors could not call her monstrous, or mannish; the woman standing in the dock looked like a chastened schoolgirl, her shoulders rounded, gaze downcast. Mrs Pearcey began to speak, but her voice was so weak that she couldn't be heard. The usher silenced the room, and the judge asked her to repeat herself.

She whispered, 'Only that I am innocent of this charge.'

'You have been found guilty after a most patient trial, and after a most powerful and able defence, and I must say that I feel it to be absolutely impossible to conceive that the death of Phoebe Hogg would have taken place without your having been an active instrument towards that death. I do not wish to add to the pain you must feel by saying as much to you. I do say, however, that I think it is one of the many instances that have come before me, even at this very session, of the terrible results of persons giving way to prurient and indecent lust. You have become a person of so little moral sense that eventually you have been an instrument, and a willing instrument, of taking away the life of a woman whose only offence was that she was married to a man upon whom you had set your unholy passion.'

Hannah had forgotten to breathe. Now, feeling light-headed, she inhaled deeply. The room was still and stricken, all except for the pew of pressmen, synchronised in their activity, their heads bent, scribbling away.

'Now,' said the judge, 'I cannot hold out to you any hope whatever that within a very short time you will not cease to live as an inmate of this our world.'

Mrs Pearcey lifted her head slightly, enough for Hannah to see that her cheeks were glistening. There was a sob from elsewhere in the room – Mrs Pearcey's mother now had her arms wrapped around her bowed head.

Denman continued, in that beautiful voice: 'You will have a certain time for preparation. God grant that you may use that time for your eternal benefit. You will be kindly dealt with, kindly ministered to, and I trust that you will use the short time upon earth that remains for you in readying yourself for another world. I now have nothing to do but to pass the sentence of law upon you.

'Mary Eleanor Wheeler Pearcey, it is the sentence of this court that you shall be taken to the place of lawful execution, and there you shall be hanged by the neck until you be dead, and afterwards your body shall be buried in a common grave within the precincts of the prison wherein you were last confined before your execution, and may the Lord have mercy on your soul.'

The court ushers echoed 'Amen'.

On that cue, Mrs Pearcey turned and walked down from the dock, refusing the assistance offered to her by the female chaperone. Hannah heard the soft thud of the door closing behind her, and there followed a long moment of collective dazed silence, before a clerk instructed the room to stand.

Hannah rose clumsily to her feet and watched as the judge swept out of the court, flanked by his officials.

At the Marylebone hearing, when the judge left the court, the room had erupted into spirited noise and movement, as when a teacher leaves a classroom. Now, it was different; people were much subdued, not just feeling the queasy elation of high drama, Hannah thought, but the sickening gravity of it all. She could also sense the profound deflation of the losing side. All that thought and planning, all those hours of carefully formed arguments, all those hopes and reassurances – all poleaxed in a stroke by that single, brusque word. On the floor below, the lawyers stood up and gathered together their papers, as briskly as if they were being evacuated. The table of pressmen leant into each other to exchange comments – Hannah watched Ovilry shake his head in response to a colleague – all the while still writing in their notebooks.

She leant forward to peer down at the rows of family and friends. From her angle she couldn't see much of their faces, but she saw that Frank Hogg's chair was already empty; he had been spirited away, along with his mother and siblings. A few people sat silently, staring at nothing. Mrs Pearcey's mother still had her arms wrapped over her head, and a woman beside her was patting her ineffectually on the back.

Hannah turned to look down at the dock, at Mrs Pearcey's vacated chair, the dust already settling on it. She just couldn't accept that the whole thing was over; she felt like the sole person in the room waiting for an encore. Somewhere in the building, back in her cell, Mrs Pearcey was surely now revealing her condition to the chaperones. Their eyes wide in shock, they were placing their palms on her belly, looking at each other and nodding slowly as they registered the tiny flutter. Calling for the judge. Backstage, out of earshot, there was a maelstrom of action; the doors would soon open again, the actors would emerge back onto the stage, and the true conclusion to the case would be revealed.

She kept staring down at the dock as the public gallery emptied around her, until an official put a hand on her shoulder and told her it was time to go.

Back at Camden Square, Hannah headed straight up to her room, but her mother heard her on the stairs and called her into the drawing room.

'I've been waiting for you,' said Mrs Teale. 'Come and have some tea.'

It was a relatively inviting scene in there for a change: the fire was roaring and Mrs Teale was reading beside it, the other chair positioned opposite, as if waiting for Hannah. On the side table sat a tea tray and a half-demolished plate of slivers of Cheddar atop Bath Oliver biscuits.

Hannah sat down and accepted a cup. She took a bite of cheese and biscuit, but it tasted as appetising as raw suet.

'Will you come to Somers Town this evening?' continued her mother genially. Her cheeks were flushed from proximity to the heat, and her hair was less severe than usual; she looked youthful and pretty. If Hannah didn't know her better, she might think she was excited about something. 'It's so cold, I think we'll have a full house.'

Swallowing her unwelcome mouthful, Hannah realised she couldn't even force herself to talk about anything else.

'You know that woman who killed her employer but then got off because she was with child?' she said. 'The one father's friend represented? Did she announce her condition at the trial itself, or was it later, after she had been convicted?'

Mrs Teale blanched and carefully placed her teacup back on its saucer and then down on the side table before replying.

'You've asked about that twice now,' she said. 'Why is that, Hannah?'

And then, at last, Hannah told her. Not everything – she didn't see the need to mention her own participation in the Mrs Pearcey saga: the chance meeting on Prince of Wales Road; the illicit sortie into Priory Street. All that was irrelevant now. But she laid out the whole story of the crime, from start to finish, as factually as possible, to the one person in London who was still unaware of it. Conscious of her mother's disapproval of such sensational interests, she didn't meet her eye as she spoke, but instead kept her gaze fixed on the fire.

Her mother listened without interruption until Hannah reached the end of the story, with that day's guilty verdict.

'So, you were there in court today?'

Hannah nodded miserably.

'And what makes you think that she is with child?'

'I just thought that it was a possible explanation for her lack of defence,' Hannah replied, after a pause. She couldn't mention the baby list or how she had got hold of it. 'Pleading her belly, so she would avoid hanging. But then, she didn't do that. So, I wondered whether she still could, or if it was too late.'

'You seem sure she is innocent.'

'I am!' replied Hannah, before clarifying, 'Well, I think he definitely had something to do with it. The man, Hogg.'

'But there's no evidence against him?'

Hannah thought of that cigarette end, floating obscenely in cold tea in the Priory Street kitchen.

'Well, they didn't bring up anything in court,' she said. 'But I think he actually killed them, and Mrs Pearcey is taking the blame. Maybe she knew about it and is keeping quiet – and if that's the case, then obviously that's terrible. But I think maybe she felt as if her life was small and drab and hopeless, and she fell in love with this awful person who somehow had this hold over her, and she felt compelled to do what he asked her to, and . . .'

Her voice rose in agitation.

'Just seeing her there in court, Mother – in the dock by herself, surrounded by all these men judging her – and there he was, not being punished at all. And she's not rich, and I think her lawyer wasn't very good, because she couldn't afford the best, and it just seems so unfair . . . or maybe she's a lunatic . . .'

Hannah felt herself getting tangled up and trailed off. Was she arguing that Mrs Pearcey was wholly innocent, or partly, or that she did actually do it, but only because she was insane? She didn't know. She stared into the fire despondently. After a long moment of silence, Mrs Teale spoke.

'Everyone has choices,' she said simply. 'My women, at the refuge – many of them have appalling backgrounds. You wouldn't believe how appalling. They are enmeshed with awful men. And several of them appear to be mentally unsound. But none of them have done something like this, or been party to it. Killing a woman. Cutting her throat. And then, for no reason at all, murdering her innocent baby.'

'But—'

'I'm not sure this woman is deserving of your sympathy,'

Mrs Teale continued. 'Come and help me at the refuge, and put your energies to better use.'

Hannah thought of what Mrs Didier had said, about how Mrs Teale had complained about her husband's minor foibles. And here she was, not condemning Frank!

'Frank Hogg is a really horrible person,' Hannah said forcefully. 'If you met him, you'd see. A *vile* person. He has a bad odour to him. He did it. I know it.'

'But that doesn't mean anything in itself,' said Mrs Teale infuriatingly. 'We women are supposed to be slaves to our intuition, but it's the facts that are important. Intuition is faulty. Lots of people look awful but aren't, or appear perfectly respectable but have done things that would really shock you.'

Hannah felt defeated; too muddled and emotionally exhausted to fight on. She felt aggrieved, too, that her mother had broken the agreement Hannah had entered her into: that Hannah would confide in her, and that she would understand. Hannah picked up another biscuit, snapping it in two, but not eating either half.

Outside, dusk was gathering. Mrs Teale went over to the window and whipped the curtains shut, the brass curtain rings clanking on the brass rod. She remained by the window as she turned back to Hannah.

'There's actually something I wanted to talk to you about.' There was a faint waver to her voice. 'It's hard to think how to put it gently, so I'm just going to say it. Do you really want to get married?'

Thrown, Hannah looked over.

'What do you mean?'

'Just that,' said Mrs Teale. 'You've been acting quite

strangely these last weeks, distracted and unsettled, and so I was wondering—'

'Why don't you like Cosmo?' Hannah cried. In her already heightened state, she felt suddenly on the verge of tears.

Her mother shook her head.

'We've been through this. I don't dislike Cosmo. You know that I don't like what he does for a living, but as a person he's . . . perfectly all right. It's more . . .'

She stopped, was silent for a moment and then restarted. 'I just want to let you know that if for whatever reason you don't want to get married, then you don't have to.'

'But what do you mean by that?'

'I can support you.'

Hannah frowned.

'I thought we didn't have any money.'

'We don't, at the moment,' replied Mrs Teale. 'Your father's annuity barely covers us. But I've been thinking about giving up this house – it's too big for us. And if I do, then there will be enough money for us both to live on.'

Mrs Teale had been looking at Hannah as she spoke. Now, she glanced out of the window, over the square.

'Your brother is at university and then will be off, doing his own thing,' she continued. 'We won't need two maids, so we can economise there, too. There's actually a girl at the Foundling Hospital I've been talking to, who says she can come and work for us. The dark-haired girl, Frances – do you remember?'

Hannah shook her head, trying to understand it all.

'But where would we actually live?' she asked.

'Well, there are the two rooms up at the top of the refuge,' she said. 'The one you sometimes sleep in? They're not bad, really – certainly no worse than your bedroom here. And so I thought – you've been showing an interest in the refuge recently, perhaps you would find it satisfying working there alongside me.'

Hannah looked at her mother's thin back as she stood in front of the window and gave a dry, silent laugh. Of course; she should have known that there would be such a condition attached to her mother's offer. She wasn't concerned about what was best for Hannah; she just wanted Hannah to join her in her joyless, martyrish existence. Hannah felt furious and exhausted, but had just enough wherewithal to know that it would not be a good idea to vent what she was really feeling in this moment. Instead, she put down the biscuit halves and stood up, signalling her intention to go upstairs.

'Thank you so much for the thought,' she said, in the tone one would take if a friend offered tickets to a four-hour-long opera, 'but I'm afraid I very much want to get married.'

Mrs Teale looked at her and nodded, and Hannah felt her close up again, like a tapped mussel shell.

13

Man, there is no doubt about it, is more or less selfish, he cannot help himself, it is a fault which to a certain degree is compatible with his position as a 'lord of creation'. He is the master, the head of his wife and household; his word is, or should be, law, and the wife's duty is to submit and carry out his will.

– Girl's Own Paper

Hannah's unease and frustration continued into the next day, when she met Cosmo at the top of Primrose Hill – their special place, where he had proposed. Cosmo arrived wearing a coat with a fur collar she hadn't seen before. She looked at him in the merciless winter light. His nose was red from the cold, but she could see he had made an effort for her; there was a sheen of wax on his moustache. She thought: *This is the face I'm going to be waking up next to for the rest of my life.* He smiled at her, a touch uncertainly: perhaps he was thinking the same thing.

From the summit of the hill, London was spread before them. This was a well-known vantage point, and there was a small group gathered. Near to them, a class of uniformed school children were listening as their teacher pointed out aspects of the city. Despite the cold, the girls had bare legs, their skin goose-bumped.

'Shame your father isn't here, with his special camera,' Hannah said, indicating the girls.

The comment surprised her as much as him. Neither of them had brought up Mrs Walters' outburst at their engagement dinner; Hannah had been unsure what to think of it. Now, she realised that although her tone was arch, this was a serious test. She watched Cosmo's face.

He winced. 'Papa's judgement can leave something to be desired,' he said, looking squarely at her. 'I suspect he's learnt his lesson now, with Gigi cutting him out of the will.'

His response was good enough. Hannah looked out over the London view. The dome of St Paul's dominated, as stark as a tombstone. Hannah thought of the bells clanging through the courtroom.

'It's odd, isn't it?' she said. 'My life with you is just beginning, and hers is about to end.'

It took him a moment to realise what she meant. 'Ah, so you heard about the Pearcey verdict.'

She nodded. 'Ivy mentioned it.' No need to tell him about her presence in court. *No more of it now.*

'Not entirely unexpected, but the whole thing is quite strange,' said Cosmo. 'It doesn't quite add up, you know? Motive and whatnot. What we need is a confession – or, at least, a full account – from her, but that's impossible. No reporters are allowed to get near her. They're barred from the prison, of course. Even Ovilry isn't trying.'

'Maybe she'll get off, somehow,' she said. She restrained herself from mentioning the secret only she suspected.

'True. There's still an appeal. Now, everyone is going with the epilepsy angle.'

Hannah frowned. 'Everyone?'

'I mean, her solicitor is petitioning the Home Office, and that's his main line of attack. So now the papers are going with it, too. Saying that, yes, she might have done it but she attacked them in a sort of . . . what's the word? . . . fugue state – that's it. So she can't remember what happened.'

Absorbing this information, Hannah felt both vindicated and aggrieved. 'I suggested that first, don't you remember? A while ago?'

'Oh, did you?'

'I did!' she said, indignant. 'I told you about that woman from mother's refuge, the one with the tortoise, who I saw having a huge row, which she then seemed to have no memory of.'

'Oh, yes, of course you did.' Then he squeezed her hand and turned to face her. 'Aren't you clever?' She watched his face brighten, his eyes shift over her shoulder, as he had a thought. 'Ah, now that's an idea . . . That woman – do you think I might interview her?'

'What – for the paper?'

'Yes! That might be just the thing,' he said, animated now. 'Can you put me in touch with her?'

Hannah looked away, down the hill. Dotted on the slope were a number of anonymous, bundled-up black shapes: a handful of dogs and prams. At the bottom of the hill sat the zoo, normally the source of exotic bellows and bird calls, but today it was silent. The animals must be under cover, curled up, dreaming of the warm homelands they had been snatched from.

What if an interview with Mrs Aversham did make a difference, she thought, and bolstered Mrs Pearcey's appeal? But that was a vague, abstract possibility. What seemed horribly real was the image of Cosmo, the blunt instrument, going into the refuge, loudly asking for Mrs Aversham and then crouching beside her, asking all sorts of intrusive questions. Describing her with hyperbole in his article: her stringy blonde hair, her broken fingernails, her wretched countenance, that poor tortoise . . .

She shook her head.

'I don't think so. I'm sorry.'

His mouth twisted with disappointment.

'Oh, really?'

She didn't want to say the truth in case it hurt his feelings.

'My mother would hate it,' she said instead – although this was also true, of course. 'Let's not give her more ammunition against you!'

Cosmo gave a hurt frown.

'I mean,' she said quickly, taking his hand, 'you know what she's like.'

It was a feeble response from her, but they both silently agreed to leave it there. They walked down the hill and had a cup of tea, and talked about their upcoming meeting with the vicar at the church in Kensington, the day after tomorrow.

The following day, Mrs Pearcey's solicitor, Freke Palmer, released a copy of the petition he had sent to the Home Office, and all the newspapers printed it, word for word. Hannah smuggled a copy of the *Star* back up to her bedroom, got under the covers and read.

The petition focused on the lack of premeditation, trying to cast doubt on the notion that Mrs Pearcey had asked Phoebe to tea with the intention of killing her. If there was no premeditation, the charge would not be wilful murder, and execution could be avoided.

The place and circumstances were as ill-adapted for the perpetuation of a crime as they well could be, the petition stated. Why would she use such weapons as a kitchen poker and a dessert knife for the job, if it had been planned?

Instead, Palmer suggested, the more likely series of events were these. Mrs Pearcey innocently invited Phoebe and her baby for tea. An argument ensued – the 'words' that Mrs Pearcey had mentioned to the inspector's wife at the police station – and Mrs Pearcey reacted badly, striking Phoebe. Palmer speculated that she had gone into some sort of a catatonic fog, which was why she couldn't remember anything. What appeared brutal was really just the effects of a deeply fractured mind that, in a moment of rage, entirely shattered.

To back up this theory, Palmer reminded the Home Office that at the inquest, it was stated that the blood spatters on the walls and ceiling of the kitchen of Priory Street were similar to the spray caused by a horse's hoof splashing in mud, thus suggesting that Mrs Pearcey had stomped around the kitchen in a daze. The blood-spatter pattern also called into question whether Phoebe Hogg was still alive when her throat was cut. If not, then maybe Mrs Pearcey cut her throat only in order to fit her body into the pram, rather than it being the cruel cause of death.

Hannah winced as she read these explicit details. This approach for sympathy felt like a terrible gamble.

Palmer then moved on to the motive. The prosecution's

case was that Mrs Pearcey murdered Phoebe out of jealousy, hoping it would enable Frank Hogg to be with her. But, said Palmer, there was no evidence for this. Mrs Pearcey could have married Frank had she wanted to – her letters proved she was 'passionately attached' to him and that he was equally attached to her. A single word, Palmer wrote, *would have taken him from her rival and secured him as her own husband*, but instead she *sent him back to a woman who had a better claim on him and saved this other woman from disgrace, and the child that was not yet born from bastardy.*

Almost as an afterthought, Palmer asked the home secretary to consider the affidavits of Mrs Pearcey's mother, John Pearcey, Charles Crichton and others, all of whom testified to Mary's epileptic fits, or sudden and violent *paroxysms of fury* of which she'd had no memory afterwards. He asked for commutation of the death sentence on one who was *almost a girl* at twenty-four years old and known for her *great kindness*.

As she read, Hannah put herself in the position of the home secretary presented with the petition and felt unimpressed. Why didn't they bring all this up at the trial? From reports she had read, not a single witness in court testified to anything being wrong with Mrs Pearcey's head. There were no mentions of fits, seizures or migraines. Pleading temporary insanity seemed highly convenient, now that Mrs Pearcey had been found guilty.

The illustration accompanying the report of the petition showed a scene of Mrs Pearcey being visited by her mother in prison, the two women collapsed in each other's arms. *Mother, I am innocent!* the caption read. As no pressmen were allowed into the prison, Hannah thought, presumably this was a piece of propaganda suggested by the lawyer.

She was about to put the paper under her mattress when, at the bottom of the page, under the report on the petition, she saw a headline instructing the reader to turn the page for *A TRUE ACCOUNT OF EPILEPTIC RAGE!*

With trepidation, Hannah did as instructed, to be greeted with an illustration of a woman in a state of contorted fury, being restrained by her wrists by a man. It was actually an almost identical scene to that illustrating 'A Fatal Promise', but in this version, the altercation was taking place on the pavement, not in a drawing room, and the figures were dressed in tattered, working-class clothes.

The article was ascribed to *our correspondent*. With a rapidly escalating sense of outrage, Hannah started reading:

> She can be found plying her trade on the streets of Camden Town, the district some call the tradesmen's entrance to London. Winding her way through traffic, she beseeches the public for charity, clutching a dehydrated tortoise, her only true companion. A more pitiful – and more harmless – spectacle cannot be imagined. But there is another side to this poor, pathetic lady, one a lot more disturbing. When angered, she can lose control of herself, and then not remember a thing afterwards. Like the murderess Mary Pearcey, she is believed to suffer from epilepsy. Our correspondent talked to her . . .

Furious, Hannah scrunched up the paper and threw it to the floor.

'I saw the *Star*,' she called to Cosmo when she was still some distance away. He was waiting for her outside St Mary Abbott's, hands in his pockets, looking up at the steeple. She marched towards him, the church-path gravel crunching underfoot. 'Did you think I wouldn't see it?'

He turned to her. His hat was pulled low and his scarf tied high around his neck against the cold, but she could still see he looked a touch embarrassed.

'Oh dear, I was rather hoping you wouldn't.' He exhaled a great cloud of breath, visible in the cold.

'Well, that's honest at least.'

'It was funny, actually,' he said. 'When we had finished in Primrose Hill and I was waiting for the omnibus at Camden Town, I just saw her there on the street, weaving between carriages, thrusting that poor tortoise in people's faces in the hope of a penny. She didn't mind talking at all.'

'But I asked you not to!' Hannah had been stewing with anger all night; it had propelled her across London this morning.

'Well, you didn't exactly,' he replied. 'You said your mother wouldn't like it. And so, I didn't go to the refuge, and I didn't put my name to it. Or hers, for that matter. I was very sympathetic to her, you know.'

Even under his scarf, she noticed his manner change, become more defiant, as it had done when Mrs Teale had criticised the press over dinner in Milton Terrace.

'It's for the greater good, Hannah,' he said maddeningly. 'It's to help support Pearcey's appeal. And to earn us some money. Your mother will probably never know – after all, she has made it abundantly clear she wouldn't go near a rag like the *Star*.'

Hannah felt even more upset at this disingenuousness on top of the betrayal. He stepped forward, and she turned her head away, towards the graveyard. She noticed dark shapes of figures, curled up around the tombstones.

'Look, I'm sorry I didn't tell you,' he said, touching her shoulder. 'I hate to see you distressed. And of course, I welcome and respect your opinion, more than anyone else's. But ultimately, well' – he paused – 'I made the decision.'

The timbre of his voice changed for those last four words. Hannah glanced back at him. He did seem quite commanding; framed against the wintry sky, in his big overcoat, youthful face largely obscured, he looked like he might have known battlefields. She had a vivid, unbidden memory of the sensation she felt in Rochester Square when, in a totally different way, he had acted like her husband, too.

Of course, she knew he was right. It was up to him to make the final decision in important matters. And now, as the wind left her sails, Hannah thought that, actually, perhaps she wanted to experience the peace that was supposedly her reward for surrendering to his authority.

She gave him an acquiescent smile, but then couldn't help adding, 'Shall we end it here?' Cosmo looked taken aback, and she quickly clarified, 'Chasing Mrs Pearcey stories, I mean. Both of us. *No more of it now* – remember?'

Cosmo nodded; she offered her hand, and they shook on it. The church bell chimed, breaking the moment, and she noticed that a bald, rotund vicar had appeared in the doorway of the church, looking at them expectantly.

'Shall we?' Cosmo said. Still clutching her hand, he led her into the church.

The vicar was pleasant but businesslike, and only twenty minutes later they were leaving the church.

'Well, he seems nice, doesn't he?' said Cosmo as they crunched back down the path. 'And that all seemed quite straightforward. Interesting that this is the tallest steeple in London.' He clutched her shoulder. 'Oh, I am looking forward to it!'

'Me too,' she said, smiling up at him. 'So much.'

She waited for what she hoped was a decent amount of time, as they made their way towards Kensington Church Street.

'One last thing about Mrs Pearcey,' said Hannah casually. 'If her appeal fails, how long will it be, until the thing is done?'

'Oh, not long at all, I don't think,' Cosmo replied. 'They're usually swiftly dispatched.'

She *was* to be swiftly dispatched. The following day, the papers reported that, should her petition fail, Mary Pearcey would be executed on 23 December, in just over two weeks' time.

No more of this now.

She had definitely meant it this time. But in the hours after meeting Cosmo at the church, her head was busier than ever with thoughts of Mrs Pearcey. And while before those thoughts hopped from question to question – *Why was she so obsessed with Frank Hogg? Was the whole thing his idea? How much did she remember about the night in question? Was it premeditated?* – now, they all circled around a single, horribly visceral image. The prisoner sitting in her cell, deep in the bowels of Newgate, her hands resting on her stomach.

It was not long before she had decided that her and Cosmo's joint promise to end their involvement in the case was unfair on her, Hannah. Mrs Pearcey meant nothing to Cosmo. She was just another story, one of equal weight to an asylum, or a dosshouse, or a baby farm, or any other subject that might be good for a few shillings. Asking him to stop pursuing her was like asking someone who was indifferent to dogs to promise not to pet one if they saw it in the street. An easy vow to make.

But Hannah had been face to face with Mary Pearcey. Frank Hogg had threatened her, his breath on her skin. She had been in the bedroom at Priory Street; she had touched the sealskin, the unwashed sheets. She had Mrs Pearcey's magazine under her bed. Her list. And she might have guessed her secret.

So, even if the core of the woman remained a mystery, Hannah felt – well, perhaps the term *affinity* was too strong, but she was certainly more intimately involved with her than Cosmo and Ovilry and all the others prowling around. And now that her execution was imminent, she felt duty-bound to help in any way she could. If Cosmo could cite the moral high ground in interviewing Mrs Aversham because it might help Mrs Pearcey avoid the gallows, then surely Hannah had a far greater claim on it by trying to reach the prisoner in her cell? It might be too much to hope for that Mrs Pearcey would betray Frank Hogg and reveal his role in the crime, considering she had failed to take this line in the trial. But then, who could predict the decisions made by someone facing impending death?

And if, as Hannah suspected, Mrs Pearcey was waiting to reveal her condition – either because movements could not yet be felt, or for the drama of leaving it until the very last minute – then perhaps Hannah could be the one to persuade her that now really was the time to bring it out into the open.

And how little time there was! Hannah felt sickened by the sense of urgency. The more she thought about it, the more certain she felt that the appeal to the home secretary would fail. Epilepsy, or insanity, or any mental problem that mitigated her responsibility for the crime, should have been disclosed at the trial, or any of the many hearings that preceded it. To air them now, belatedly, seemed shoddy and desperate.

If only her father were here. He would be able to tell her how the system worked, what happened once the judge had reached for that black silk handkerchief, what were the chances of reprieve. And, of course, he could fill in the details about the woman who had announced her pregnancy and been saved from the gallows. But he was not around – and she was certainly not going to bring up the subject with her mother again.

How would she get inside Newgate? She thought back to the phalanx of stern wardens guarding Mrs Pearcey at the court; those ominous black walls of the prison. Journalists were strictly forbidden from entering, Cosmo had said; even Ovilry wasn't trying to charm his way in. This situation was way beyond blagging.

But according to the paper, Mrs Pearcey's mother had visited her. Presumably, then, the prisoner could invite people into her cell. Up in her bedroom, Hannah opened her writing pad.

Dear Mrs Pearcey,
You don't know me, but we met on Prince of Wales Road on

the twenty-fifth of October. You gave me a newspaper and asked me to help you. I am sorry I could not help you then, but I would like to help you now. Could I come and see you?

She turned the page and tried again.

Dear Mrs Pearcey,
This may sound odd, but I've been in your house! I have seen your half an onion, and stroked your sealskin, and admired the shine on your aspidistra leaves. I feel as if I know you somehow – and I want to help save your life.

She turned the page.

Dear Mrs Pearcey,
I met Frank Hogg in the public house last month. I think he is a bad man, and I believe that he was involved in the murders of his wife and child, for which you have been held solely responsible. Tell me all about it and I will try my hardest to save your life.

And again.

Dear Mrs Pearcey,
I found a baby list hidden in your magazine, and I know your secret. Let me help you tell the world the truth, and save you from the gallows.

No, no, no. Her first attempt felt feeble. Considering what came straight before and just afterwards, what were the chances that Mrs Pearcey would remember their fleeting, inconsequential encounter? The second was too creepy and intrusive. The third was too bald and startling, and would probably have the opposite of the desired effect. If there was anything that the world knew about this mysterious woman, it was that Frank Hogg had an inexplicable hold over her. And the last seemed rather threatening, not to mention high risk. What if Hannah was wrong about the significance of that baby list? She didn't believe she was, but it was still mere speculation.

The first version would have to do. Hannah tore it out of her pad, sealed it in an envelope and addressed it to *Mrs Mary Pearcey (née Wheeler)*, at Newgate Prison. Then she went downstairs and asked Ivy to post it immediately.

No response came the following day, or the next. Hannah paced around the house. Occasionally, she went out to walk around the square, affecting nonchalance, as if this might conjure the postman. Who knew how long it took for letters to reach prisoners? The London postal service may run twelve times a day in the free world, but how did it work in there?

By day three, she concluded that either the letter had not reached the prisoner, or Mrs Pearcey had received it but ignored it, tossing it into a pile of similar unanswered pleas banked up in a corner of her cell.

She must not give up. There had to be a way in. Tucked up in bed one afternoon, trying to get warm, she closed her eyes and strained her imagination, trying to inhabit Mrs Pearcey in her current, unspeakable situation. What would get her attention? What would she want to hear?

And, just like that, it came to her. She pushed off the covers and slid down to the end of the bed to dig under the mattress for Mrs Pearcey's copy of 'A Fatal Promise'. Flicking through the magazine, she noted the grimy finger marks on the margins of the papers. Yes, Mrs Pearcey had read the story, perhaps several times.

It was a long shot, but it felt like the only one she had.

Dear Mrs Pearcey,
I find myself in a delicate situation, and would greatly appreciate your guidance. There is a man of whom I am excessively fond (his name is Captain Errol Cameron of Lochmohr – perhaps you know him?). I think I should like to marry him. However, my uncle has another idea, and has betrothed me to another. On the dying wish of his late mother, my Captain is similarly promised to another. This lady is no good (perhaps you know her, too? Miss Juliet Marling? I hope for your sake you don't!).

Anyhow, as you can imagine, it is all most difficult and I am wrung out from the emotion, and can no longer think straight. That is why I am appealing for your help. I am more than happy to come to visit, at a time of your choosing, and would be honoured for even just a few minutes of your time.

Yours, Bertie Verner, 28 Camden Square, London

For the next two days Hannah ostensibly went about her wedding preparation business, making sure to be out shopping at just the time the evening papers were hitting the street. Mrs Pearcey continued to occupy the front pages, with accounts of her pitiful existence in Newgate. At first glance, it appeared to the reader as if the journalist had actually had access to the prisoner, but on reading it became clear that the information came from another party inside Newgate. A member of staff, Hannah supposed. Or perhaps the details were being provided to the press by Freke Palmer, to elicit sympathy and remind readers that Mrs Pearcey was a human being.

The condemned, Hannah learnt, was eating heartily: bacon and eggs, chops and mutton. She was supplied with malt liquor and wine, and drank a bottle of ale before bed. She took a walk around the prison yard in the middle of the day, and often sang or recited scraps of poetry to herself. She liked to feed the birds from her window. She was tidy and obedient, and gentle and kind to those who guarded and tended to her.

It was also reported that, in order to raise money for her defence, she had authorised Freke Palmer to sell her personal items to Madame Tussauds. For £200, the museum had bought all the furniture and objects in her kitchen, in order to create a tableau of the murder scene. For good measure, they also purchased her piano, her pictures and the carpet from the front parlour.

Hannah imagined the Tussauds' stockroom, where these gruesome artefacts joined Frank Hogg's offerings: the bloody perambulator and Tiggie's boiled sweet. Did Mrs Pearcey even know he had sold these things?

In addition, the papers were still running stories about epilepsy, and accounts supporting the theory that Mrs Pearcey had committed the crimes in a fugue state. Reading them, Hannah felt renewed annoyance with Cosmo for 'forgetting' that she had suggested this idea weeks ago. One paper carried an interview with John Pearcey, the man whom Mrs Pearcey had lived with prior to her relationship with Frank Hogg. In it, he claimed that Mary had often complained about terrible headaches, and had once brandished a bread knife at him over dinner, *her eyes flashing*, before forgetting the incident ever happened.

In the middle of December, Hannah came in from shopping for collars at Bowman's and was shaking the snow from her hat when she noticed an envelope sitting on the tray. It was addressed, in neat italics, to *Miss Bertie Verner*. She froze, and the hat fell from her fingers. She listened. The house sounded empty. What luck that her mother hadn't reached the tray before her.

She picked up her hat, hung it up with her coat and then examined the envelope. The paper was thick, and the handwriting incredibly neat, like one might expect on an invitation to tea at Windsor Castle. She turned it over to read the sender address: *Newgate Prison, Old Bailey, London.*

She felt almost scared to open it. It was too extraordinary that Mrs Pearcey had responded – as if a fictional character had come to life.

She gently unpeeled the flap of the envelope, trying to preserve it as much as possible. Inside was a slip of paper, written in the same careful hand, authorising a Miss Bertie Verner to visit Mary Wheeler at Newgate Prison, for twenty minutes, the following day at noon.

Hannah's nerves woke her at 5.30 a.m. She had gone to bed in a state of heightened feeling, giddy from her success, and it was only now that she began to think about the implications of her visit. What would Mrs Pearcey be expecting from her, and how might she react when Hannah failed to deliver it?

The most benign scenario, she supposed, was that the condemned prisoner had appreciated the originality of Hannah's effort to contact her, and had invited her in for a twenty-minute chat about romance stories – a frothy break from her unspeakably grim reality.

At worst – if Mrs Pearcey really was insane, and her lines between reality and fantasy had blurred – was it inconceivable that she really would be expecting Bertie Verner? And how would she react to receiving Hannah instead? Tricked, of course. Then, Hannah would be the monster: lying to a vulnerable woman, taking advantage of her compromised state, fraudulently stealing a precious half-hour of the meagre time she had left in the world. Perhaps Mrs Pearcey was only allowed a certain number of visitors, and Hannah's visit would be blocking one from a real friend.

Hannah felt sick. Unable to stay in bed, she got dressed, hurried downstairs and straight out of the house, thankfully seeing no one. It was only just past nine, and so she had hours to go before the visit. She decided to walk into town, but the snow had fallen again overnight and was ankle-deep, and by the time she reached Camden Road, her boots were soaked through. Instead, she caught an omnibus, and sat on the top deck, watching the hushed, carpeted streets. The further into town they got, the browner the sludge on the pavements and roads, but at Hannah's eye level, above the fray, the snow was fresh, plentiful and unblemished. White eiderdowns covered awnings, and windowsills looked as if they had been trimmed with lace.

An idea came to her. She got off the omnibus early, at Oxford Street, and headed for Pinkett's. Admitted inside by a visibly shivering doorman, she went straight for the beauty department, and stood in front of the pyramid of cold creams.

Joseph & Sons. Atkinson's. Mitchell's. Dr Rooke's. Palmer's &

Co. For some reason she couldn't fully explain to herself, she didn't want to buy a pot with a man's name on it. She decided on the one advertised by Sarah Bernhardt, even though it was the most expensive, and asked the assistant to wrap it up as nicely as she could.

Clutching the parcel, Hannah left the store, and decided to walk the rest of the way. Here in the centre of town there had been attempts to clear the pavements, but still, her progress was slower going than usual. By the time Hannah arrived at the Old Bailey, she was no longer early: it was coming up to noon.

The terrible bulk of Newgate squatted before her, its darkness stark against the white sky. There weren't many people around. She supposed she'd expected a baying crowd, a reflection of the extraordinary interest the papers had in the case, but there were just a few loitering voyeurs, bundled up against the cold.

The prison's entrance wasn't obvious, and she walked along the wall until she found a door with a vast knocker. It was a heavy circle of wrought iron, like something to which you might tether a wild horse, decorated with just a few sober curlicues. No jolly lions' heads here. Staring at it, the phrase came back to Hannah: *As black as Newgate's knocker.* It was something her father used to say. The fact that she was now in front of it, a knocker so infamous it had become an everyday saying, took the wind from her. She forced herself to lift it. Her numb fingers were not prepared for its weight and she let it drop feebly. It barely made a sound, but almost immediately the door swung open to reveal a smartly dressed policeman, his bulk filling the doorway.

'Are you expected?' he asked.

She nodded, and fished the visiting order out of her pocket. He gravely inspected it, before nodding and stepping aside to allow her to enter.

The door closed heavily behind her. Although she was not strictly alone, with the policeman beside her, she had the same sensation as she had felt in the hallway of Priory Street: a sense of being sealed off from the world, and the desperate urge to turn on her heel, tear open the door and flee. As she had done in Priory Street, she made herself take one step, and then another, and another, into the building, heading away from light and life. The corridor was plain and panelled, lit only at its far end by a gasolier, under which another policeman sat at a desk. By the time she reached him, Hannah felt quite undone with nerves – she needed to visit the facilities; she wanted to vomit.

She passed over the visiting order, her hand trembling. The man inspected it. He was middle-aged, alert, with a very precisely cut moustache. His skin was yellow-tinged under the light. On the desk in front of him was a cheap birthday card, a cherub holding a bunch of forget-me-nots, with a pencil lodged inside it. He looked up from the form.

'Shouldn't you be a man?'

She stared at him, uncomprehending. Did he mean that everyone who had been to see her so far had been male? Did he think that Mrs Pearcey should only receive men, in these precious last hours of her life?

'Bertie?' he continued, waving the form.

'Oh,' she said. She had forgotten her *nom de plume*. She choked out a laugh. 'No, Bertie can be a girl's name, too, I think.'

I think? It was supposed to be her name – there was no *I think* about it. She was being the worst blagger of all time.

'Can I see your documentation?' the policeman continued.

'Oh, I don't have any.'

'Visitors must provide documentation.'

'I didn't know,' she said. 'I didn't bring anything.'

He nodded towards a sign on the wall, bearing two bald statements: *Visitors must provide documentation* and *Visitors are not permitted to pass anything to prisoners.*

Hannah stared at the sign, the white letters swimming. If she had known she would have to prove she was Bertie Verner, she'd never have taken this ridiculous path in the first place. She clutched the Pinkett's parcel, feeling the hardness of the jar within the layers of paper, like a fruit stone. There were two competing forces within her: frustration and profound relief. A large part of her wanted nothing more than to be ordered to leave this place, to walk back down the corridor and be admitted into the snowy, fresh world outside.

But. But.

'I'm sorry,' the guard said, nodding towards the exit. Interaction over, he opened the birthday card and picked up his pencil. She shifted on her feet, as if preparing to move, but stayed put. The half-completed message inside the card was visible. Upside down, she read: *My dearest wife, I'm sorry I could not spend your birthday with you, but I send all my love and good wishes for . . .*

And it came to her.

'I'm so foolish,' she said. 'I'm sorry to waste your time. I didn't know about the documentation, or that I couldn't bring anything inside. I have something for her, you see.'

'What is it?' asked the policeman, glancing up.

'Oh, just some very expensive cold cream,' she replied. 'I thought it might cheer Mary up. It's the kind of silly thing that pleases us women.'

She held up the Pinkett's parcel, glad for its ostentatious ribbons and fancy name stamp.

His eyes widened, just a fraction.

'I didn't realise it would be confiscated,' she continued.

It was as if someone else was talking.

'Visitors can't pass anything to the prisoner,' he said, but his tone was now less severe.

'If I left it with you, do you think there's a tiny chance it might be able to get to her, after it's been checked?' She paused, and swallowed. This was it – she was getting very close to the line. 'And if not, then perhaps you can think of someone else who might want it?'

She watched him, his fingers resting on the birthday card. Please, she thought, let him be imagining handing the parcel over to his dearest wife that evening after work; her astonished delight when she opened her unexpected present. How she would instantly forgive him for working on her birthday, along with all of his other minor misdemeanours.

There was a long moment of silence, during which she thought: could she be arrested for trying to bribe a policeman? Then he said, 'All right, I'll try. No promises, though.'

He reached for the parcel; she passed it over and watched it disappear behind the desk. He gestured down the corridor, towards another door.

'Go and see Mrs Golvestone, through that door. She'll take you to the prisoner.' He coughed. 'And next time, bring your documents.'

Mrs Golvestone, a pale, moon-faced woman only a little older than Hannah, led her down another dingy corridor, past more closed, unmarked doors. It was disconcertingly silent; Hannah had expected wailing and sobbing from the cells.

'It's so quiet,' she said.

'There are no other prisoners here,' Mrs Golvestone explained. 'Only her.' She was surprisingly cheerful and chatty for someone in such a sombre job. 'They're kept in Holloway and Brixton usually. They only come here when the court is in session, for their trials, and they only stay after if . . .' She delicately left the sentence unfinished.

'Has she had many visitors?' asked Hannah, still jangling with nerves.

'Some. Her lawyer obviously. And her mother. Her poor mother. She was in this morning. And then, recently, there have been a few doctors.'

'How is she generally?' asked Hannah, emboldened by the woman's indiscretion.

'Up and down,' she said. 'As you'd expect really. But she's always very polite to us. Here we are.'

They reached a door, and stopped. Hannah could not absorb the fact that behind the door, just feet away, was Mrs Pearcey herself. Mrs Golvestone now assumed a more businesslike manner.

'Twenty minutes only. There will be wardresses present at all times. Please be careful not to say anything that might upset the prisoner. Should we judge this to be the case, we will terminate the interview. All understood?'

Hannah nodded mutely, and with that, the woman rapped on the door with her knuckles and pushed it open.

14

Trashy novels and tales do great mischief: not only do they cause waste of time, which might have been far better spent, but, by giving readers false impressions of life, they make them dissatisfied with their honest lot.

— *Girl's Own Paper*

Her first thought was that the cell was bigger than she'd expected. She'd imagined a space like the box room at the refuge, but this was double that size, at least. Then, she registered something odd: the cell was bisected by a swathe of fine netting strung from the ceiling. On her side of this divide, where she entered the room, a woman sat at a table, clad in a dark uniform with a wide white collar and black bonnet. Placed closer to the netting sat an empty chair. On the other side of the netting were two women. One was sitting on the bed, dressed in the same uniform. The other was sitting on a chair, close to the netting, wearing a shawl, her hair hung loose and wavy down her back.

'My dear!' said Mrs Pearcey. 'Do sit down.'

'Hello,' replied Hannah.

Legs wobbly, she sat heavily in the empty chair. About five feet, and the netting, separated them.

'I must apologise for the smell of meat,' said Mrs Pearcey. 'I've just had my lunch. They bring it early in here.'

Her voice was light and musical, as if she were hosting an At Home. Hannah stared at her across the divide. Although the netting was not dense enough to obscure Mrs Pearcey's face, it blurred her features, as if she were wearing a veil. Hannah's memory filled in the tiny nuances of the face that she had studied in court; that had been so discussed in the papers. The sloping nose, the overbite, those pale, heavy-lidded eyes.

All that loose hair felt surprisingly intimate – provocative, almost. But Mrs Pearcey's posture was formal, her head upright and still, her hands folded in her lap. Perhaps this stance was a habit formed over all the hearings over the past couple of months. Because of the shawl, it was impossible to see whether her stomach was round.

'I brought you some cold cream,' said Hannah. 'But they confiscated it at the door.'

'Oh, you are terribly sweet!' said Mrs Pearcey. 'Really, you shouldn't have.'

Hannah opened her mouth to speak but found she was struck dumb by the unreality of the situation. She glanced over at the wardresses, one for each of them. The one on Hannah's side, at the table, was ostensibly reading a magazine, while Mrs Pearcey's, perched on the bed, was staring into the middle distance. Clearly, both of them were listening in. Beside the bed was a washstand, on which sat a plate and cup, and a small stack of books; Hannah was too far away to read the titles. A large clock hung above the table.

Behind the barred window, she could see a blank sky. The air was dense, cold and stagnant, carrying a whiff of carbolic soap as well as the lunchtime meat.

'Do you have a message for me?' said Mrs Pearcey kindly, as if prompting her.

Hannah stared at her. Did she?

'When I got your letter, I thought you had a message for me,' continued Mrs Pearcey. 'You wrote the story, in the magazine, with Bertie Verner?'

'Oh, no, I didn't write it,' said Hannah. Her mind scrambled at how she could possibly explain how she knew Mrs Pearcey was familiar with 'A Fatal Promise' without revealing that she had been rooting around her home. It was beyond her, and she heard herself say lamely, 'I just guessed you might have read it.'

Amazingly, this answer seemed to satisfy Mrs Pearcey, who nodded. Perhaps she felt that strangers now knew so much about her — so much of her private life had been exposed to the public — why not her reading habits, too? Emboldened, Hannah continued.

'My message is, I want to help you. This is a horrible situation, and I know people at the newspapers, and there must be something—'

'I like those silly stories,' Mrs Pearcey said, as if she hadn't heard Hannah changing the subject. 'My mother brings them in. She's the only one they let bring things in for me. But they can't publish them quick enough. I've read them all.

'Or rather, Mrs Williams reads them,' she continued, indicating Hannah's wardress, sitting at the desk. 'She'll read them to me at night, and Miss Gower will sometimes stroke my back.'

At the mention of her name, Miss Gower looked over and smiled.

'I like the ones set in foreign places,' said Mrs Pearcey. 'That one in France . . . where is it, Miss Gower?'

'Per-ping-non,' read out Miss Gower.

Hannah smiled. 'I haven't read that one,' she said. Though it was a relief to be chatting with relative ease, Hannah's gaze flitted over to the black hands of the clock over the table. Four minutes had already passed. Almost a quarter of their time already gone.

Mrs Pearcey must have noticed, as she said, 'Would you like to hear what happened on the day of the murders?'

Hannah looked at her, astonished. Surely it couldn't be this easy?

'If you don't mind,' she said, a quiver in her voice.

'Not at all,' said Mrs Pearcey genially. 'It's the least I can do, as you've made such an effort to see me.'

Hannah kept her eyes fixed on her, not daring to glance at the wardresses, or the clock, in case it broke the spell.

'I was at home until midday,' said Mrs Pearcey, 'and then I went to Great College Street to buy a mousetrap. I have a terrible mouse problem, you know. Or – I *had* one.' She smiled to herself, before continuing. 'I returned home, cooked my dinner, then went out at around 3 p.m. to a wine merchant, and some other shops. I was home around 4.10 p.m., and lit the fire for tea. Phoebe arrived shortly after, and wanted to know if I would lend her a shilling and mind the baby. I said no. We both then left Priory Street at the same time. I went to buy some fish and Phoebe went somewhere – I don't know where! When I returned from the fishmonger, I walked into the house at the same time as my neighbour,

Mrs Crowhurst. Phoebe was behind the door with her pram. And I thought perhaps Phoebe was entertaining someone, and so I left the house again.'

'Wait,' said Hannah. 'You're saying that Phoebe was meeting a stranger in your house – and you left them there together?' What was this?

'Perhaps,' replied Mrs Pearcey. 'That might be what happened.'

Hannah glanced over at the wardress on the bed; she was sitting slackly, her gaze inattentive. In that moment, she realised that the women had heard this story before. Hannah wasn't the first person Mrs Pearcey had told it to.

Mrs Pearcey continued, in her light, detached tone.

'At 6.15 p.m., I took the tram from Camden Town station to Euston Road, then a bus to Oxford Street, and from there I walked towards Marble Arch, and back up Regent Street to Great Portland Street. I stopped to watch a Punch and Judy show, then I had supper at an Italian restaurant and afterwards took the bus from Great Portland Street back home to Priory Street, arriving home at 8.40 p.m. Just as I arrived home, the postman came by with a letter from Charles Crichton. I left the envelope on the kitchen table and left the lamp lit. A few minutes before 10 p.m., I left the house again, walking to Castle Road to see if Frank's van was there, but I didn't see him. Then I returned to Priory Street, and went to the Eagle public house, just next door, for a whisky. I stayed there for about twenty minutes, and then went home. I went into the kitchen again and the lamp was still burning. Then, I went to bed and slept soundly for the rest of the night.'

She stopped, having reached the end of the story. Hannah

swallowed. How on earth could she respond to such a tale, which didn't make sense or correspond to any of the evidence presented in court? For a start, the absurd notion that Mrs Pearcey had walked in and out of the kitchen after the murders, without noticing anything awry?

But Mrs Pearcey didn't appear to require a response. She just smiled placidly, as if pleased that she had discharged a duty. Hannah looked over at the clock: eight minutes gone. Over at the desk, the wardress briefly covered her face with her hands, not quite hiding a yawn, and the gesture made Hannah think of Mrs Pearcey's mother in court, hiding her face for very different reasons.

'Your mother has been to visit you?' she asked.

'Of course.'

'She must be feeling very sorr—'

'She is not to blame for anything,' replied Mrs Pearcey firmly. 'I had a wonderful childhood. A good Christian upbringing. There is nothing back there' – and here she waved a hand behind her back, to indicate her past – 'of any interest.'

Hannah nodded, feeling a rising panic. She was getting nowhere. Those horrible, ticking seconds!

'I want to help you,' she said. 'To save you.'

'Yes, everyone's trying to do that. I had some doctors come in earlier, trying to see whether I'm mad. But, you see,' she continued, 'I'm not sure I want to be saved like that.'

'What do you mean?'

'Well, let's say they decide I'm mad – then what will happen? They may pack away the noose, but instead they'll lock me up in an asylum for the rest of my life. With the murderers and criminals. Sinners. The worst people on earth. Death would be better, wouldn't it?'

'Well, I don't think—'

'And the thing is,' Mrs Pearcey continued brightly, 'I feel I'm already dead. My body, that is. I've always felt my body is dead, even when I was a child. Like I was hauling around a carcass, making it move through the world. It has never felt like mine.'

There was a pause. *This is the moment*, Hannah thought. There was no time for delicacy.

'But are you not expecting a child?' she asked, and held her breath.

Even through the veil of the netting, Hannah saw Mrs Pearcey's eyes widen in surprise. She gave a snort of a laugh.

'Why would you ask such a thing?'

Hannah noticed that both of the attendants were dead still. Now they were paying attention. She thought, for a second, of evading the answer – 'Oh, I was just wondering, that's all' – but she didn't have the will to lie. Besides, she owed it to the woman.

'I found a baby list,' she said, her voice as low as she could manage, while still reaching the ears of the prisoner. 'In your magazine.'

Mrs Pearcey was still frowning, confused.

'I went into your house, and I found your magazine,' Hannah elaborated, almost at a whisper. 'The one with the "Fatal Promise" story in it. And tucked inside was a list of baby clothes and so forth. And so I thought . . .'

'Ah,' said Mrs Pearcey. 'Yes.'

She shifted in her chair, and just by that slight movement, the light on her face changed, and Hannah could no longer read her expression behind the netting. Her impulse was to say something, anything, to fill the silence and relieve the awkwardness, but she suppressed it. Precious seconds passed loudly by. Hannah wondered whether the clock's intrusively strident tick was by accident or design.

At last, Mrs Pearcey spoke.

'It was for the little *niña*,' she said. Her voice was different, low and leaden.

She pronounced the name oddly, *Neen-ya*. Nina? But then, as Hannah was opening her mouth to ask who she was referring to, Mrs Pearcey went on, in a much brighter, perkier voice.

'You're getting married, I see?'

She gestured at Hannah's hand. Hannah realised that she had been twisting her ring from nerves.

Hannah nodded blankly, in no mood for small talk. She was still trying to digest the fact that Mrs Pearcey was not with child – and who was this Nina?

'Will you be a good wife?' asked Mrs Pearcey.

'Me? I don't know,' Hannah replied distractedly. 'I hope so.'

'Well, if you're not going to be, you mustn't do it.'

Her voice was loud now.

'I can't be a good wife. I know it,' Mrs Pearcey continued. 'I tried, but I couldn't do it. John wanted to marry me. Charles did, too. And Frank – especially Frank. Everyone's saying that I wanted to marry Frank, and I was jealous of Phoebe for marrying him, but it wasn't true. He wanted to get married but I said no. I couldn't be his wife.' She paused, and added dreamily, 'Frank was my partner. My eternal, cherished partner.'

Then her smile dropped, and her tone sharpened.

'She wasn't a good wife to him.'

Now, Hannah was on full alert. 'She' must mean Phoebe Hogg. Finally, was this it? Was Mrs Pearcey about to reveal something? She felt the wardresses pay attention again; like a mute Greek chorus.

'What do you mean by that?' she asked carefully.

'She just wasn't very good.'

'Can you explain why?'

'In all sorts of ways,' replied Mrs Pearcey obliquely. 'She wasn't a good mother, either. The poor little *niña*.'

Hannah glanced up at the clock. Sixteen minutes gone.

'I thought the baby's nickname was Tiggie, wasn't it?' she said, trying to keep a desperate edge from her voice. 'Not Nina?'

'Oh, that was our name for her,' said Mrs Pearcey. 'Me and Frank's. It's Spanish for girl child.'

Now, she leant forward and peered at Hannah through the net.

'I know you,' she said.

'Yes!' said Hannah. 'We met on the Prince of Wales Road, the morning after . . .' She stopped. 'You were carrying some papers, and I tried to buy one from you.'

'Yes, that was it,' said Mrs Pearcey, back to her At Home voice. 'How funny that you're here now!'

Hannah smiled in agreement – *Yes, wasn't it funny!* – while again reliving that brief conversation. *Help me*, Mrs Pearcey had said. And, *What if there's more than one culprit?*

'Three minutes left,' said the wardress on Hannah's side.

And then, feeling the air tightening around her, her mind concentrated by the prospect of wasting the next few minutes with small talk or awkward silence, memories and clues began to cluster together, like pins to a magnet. Frank mentioning in the Trafalgar that evening that he wanted to go and live in Spain. The Spanish phrase-book in the front room of Priory Street, inscribed *From Your Eternal Cherished Partner* – and wasn't that what Mrs Pearcey had called Frank, just now? The cigarette end in the cup of tea. Phoebe being a terrible wife and mother – or so Mrs Pearcey had been told. The baby list for Tiggie, whom they nicknamed *niña*, the Spanish name for a girl child. She thought of Frank's breakdown in front of the pram at the magistrate's hearing, and Lizzie Styles saying how much he loved Tiggie, but that he could at times be unintentionally clumsy with her.

'So very cold, isn't it!' Mrs Pearcey said now. 'I wonder if it'll snow again tonight.'

Hannah looked up at the clock and was astonished to see that only a minute had passed since this theory had come to her. Two minutes remaining. Mrs Pearcey was sitting there placidly, expectantly.

'Can I tell you what I think happened on that night?' said Hannah, and she went on before Mrs Pearcey could answer, talking low, and so quickly that her words backed up against each other. 'I think that both you and Frank were there. You had asked Phoebe to come over, and you were going to tell her together that you were going to live in Spain. You were going to take the baby with you, because Frank had said that Phoebe wasn't a good mother. That's why you had the list of things to buy and pack for Tiggie.'

She paused to take a breath. Mrs Pearcey was sitting stock still, looking at her. Hannah went on, thinking aloud, fleshing out her theory.

'And then there was an argument, and something happened

– and I don't think you meant to kill Tiggie, did you? You loved Tiggie—'

Now, Mrs Pearcey interjected.

'I didn't kill the baby,' she said.

'So, Frank did – didn't he?' said Hannah. 'But it wasn't on purpose.'

Silence. Mrs Pearcey continued to stare at her, her expression – from what Hannah could see of it – as unreadable as it had been in court. And then she leant forward, until her face was close to the net. Hannah mirrored her, until they were just a couple of feet apart. She didn't dare look at the wardresses.

'We were in the kitchen, all of us, and he was holding her, the little *niña*, and she was screaming,' said Mrs Pearcey, speaking so low that Hannah could only just hear her. 'And so he put his hand over her mouth to stop it, because of the neighbours.'

Hannah nodded, agog.

'And Phoebe kept going on and on, saying we couldn't take her away,' Mrs Pearcey continued, in that stricken whisper. 'He kept his hand on the baby's mouth to keep her quiet, and he was arguing with Phoebe, and it was all getting so heated. He didn't mean to. It was *her* fault – Phoebe's – for getting hysterical, for going on and on.'

'And then?'

'And then I noticed Tiggie wasn't moving, and then we looked at her and we all had a terrible shock.' Mrs Pearcey paused and swallowed before continuing. 'But then Phoebe started saying that she was going to tell the police that he'd done it on purpose – smothered the baby, that is – and that he was going to hang. Can you believe anyone could be so cruel as to say something like that?'

Now, she looked straight at Hannah, waiting for her reaction. This was the most sincere and heartfelt Hannah had yet seen her.

'That's terrible,' Hannah whispered. She sensed her agreement as to the awfulness of Phoebe was required in order for Mrs Pearcey to continue.

'And I saw *red*, and I—'

'It's time.'

Hannah looked up to see that both attendants were now on their feet, one standing behind Mrs Pearcey, the other beside Hannah's chair.

'Just one more minute,' said Hannah.

'I'm afraid not,' said her attendant, without a smile. Hannah wondered how much of her new steeliness was down to frustration at being shut out of the conversation.

'Well, you know the rest,' said Mrs Pearcey, back to her normal, light voice.

The woman put a hand on her shoulder and Hannah reluctantly rose to her feet. She wouldn't hear the end of the story – but actually, was there any need for it? Mrs Pearcey was right. She knew the rest. Except – if Frank Hogg killed Tiggie, why was she taking all of the blame?

At the door, Hannah turned back to Mrs Pearcey.

'You know, I met Frank Hogg not so long ago,' she said. 'At the Trafalgar.'

'Really?' said Mrs Pearcey. 'How was he?'

Her voice was full of warmth and excitement – a tone fit for news of a lover.

Hannah shook her head. 'You know,' she said, 'he really doesn't deserve your loyalty.'

'Visit's over,' snapped the wardress, gripping Hannah's upper arm and pulling her to the door.

'If you see him again,' said Mrs Pearcey, still in that bright, excited tone, as if she hadn't heard Hannah's words, 'please ask him to visit me.'

Hannah emerged back onto the Old Bailey, that infamous, deathly knocker bumping against the door as it closed behind her. She stood on the steps in the rare, lucid light and took in her surroundings. London, hushed and sanitised by the snow. The dome of St Paul's, streaked with white like a poorly iced cake. But still, everywhere were signs of life. A bundled-up man scuttled past, head down and hands jammed into his pockets, cursing as he slipped on the cobbles. A woman coster at the corner shrieked, *Pots, pots, pots, pots,* carrying her basket of baked potatoes on one forearm, as lightly as if it were a shawl. On the road, piles of horse droppings steamed.

Finally, she started to move, slowly, in the direction of Fleet Street. She could feel and think of nothing except the pure, profound relief that she was free, out here; that she was not Mrs Pearcey.

In no time at all she had reached the junction of Ludgate Hill and Fleet Street, and stopped. Just down there was the *Star* office. What an entrance she could make, clutching her scoop. She imagined entering that vast roomful of men, and them all looking up at her from their work, bemused or distracted, Cosmo rising from his chair in surprise. Then, as they learnt why she was there and what she had for them, their expressions would change, and they would cluster around, their eyes brightening, jaws tightening; that look she now recognised of a pressman in the presence of a juicy story. And Cosmo would be proud of her, wouldn't he? Never mind *No more of it now*. That promise was a weedy one, made before anyone could conceive that Hannah would do something so bold, and get what the whole of Fleet Street was desperate for.

But, standing there at the top of the street, she didn't feel triumphant. It was as if her initial swell of joy at being free was now subsiding, leaving behind a gritty residue of questions and emotions. She decided she must try to understand those unsettling twenty minutes before revealing them to anyone. And so, she turned around and started walking away from Fleet Street, in an unfocused direction.

So, she had got a confession, of sorts. *I saw* red . . . *you know the rest*. Mrs Pearcey had killed Phoebe Hogg in a fit of rage, after Phoebe had threatened to have Frank arrested for killing Tiggie. The violence wasn't premeditated, but the death wasn't an accident. There must have been a point during the frenzied attack when she had realised that she was fatally injuring Phoebe, and yet she hadn't stopped. Assuming she was telling the truth, strictly speaking there had been no miscarriage of justice: Mrs Pearcey was responsible for the death of Phoebe Hogg.

But then, there was Frank and Tiggie.

If anything was made clear during their conversation in the cell, it was that Mrs Pearcey was still obsessed with, and unswervingly loyal to, Frank Hogg. If Hannah was to write a front-page story in the *Star* claiming that Mrs Pearcey had revealed Frank Hogg's role in his daughter's death, the prisoner could just deny it. After all, it was Hannah's word against hers. Even the wardresses didn't hear.

Besides, such a revelation wouldn't help Mrs Pearcey now.

She had been charged with the death of Phoebe alone; as far as Hannah knew, the baby had been mentioned only in passing during the trial, just an addendum to its mother. Hannah had a vague recollection of someone – Moira? – telling her that by law a person could only be tried for one murder at a time. If so, then presumably the police had decided to go with Phoebe, as there was such strong physical evidence against Mrs Pearcey for her death, with the murder weapon and blood splatters, and far less for the poor, smothered baby.

Of course, Hannah could not discount the possibility that the confession was an invention, and neither death happened the way Mrs Pearcey said they did. Perhaps she wanted to distract Hannah from the real truth, or perhaps she just made something up for her own perverse amusement. It was clear she could be a fantasist; she had had no qualms about telling Hannah that detailed, nonsensical account of what she was doing the night of the murders. Perhaps the woman even believed her own lies, and it was just second nature for her to shape memories to suit her purposes.

And there was something else bothering her. If indeed Mrs Pearcey was telling the truth about killing Phoebe, then Hannah felt oddly cheated. After all those weeks giving the mysterious, distant figure of Mrs Pearcey the benefit of the doubt, Hannah felt she had been denied the chance to reconcile this strange but personable woman, sitting just a few feet away, with someone who committed such a heinous act. The strain of listening to Mrs Pearcey's whispered admissions at the end of those twenty minutes, and the abrupt termination of the interview, meant that Hannah hadn't been able to properly study her in light of her confession. She had not looked Mrs Pearcey squarely in the eye, knowing she was a murderer.

Perhaps the whole thing had been pointless. When Hannah had left Newgate, those twenty minutes with Mrs Pearcey had felt like a large snowball in her hands; now, it was melting fast.

She had been trudging the streets blindly, but now paid attention to where she was, and found that a homing instinct was taking her north, back towards Camden Square. She kept going, keeping pace with a cart making its laborious way along the road, carrying a load of snow-covered spheres: cabbages, pumpkins, cannon balls?

Whatever the truth of Mrs Pearcey's situation, she thought, what *was* undeniable was the horror of it. The unspeakable reality of a person locked in a cell, halfway towards burial, the tolling of St Paul's the only sound able to penetrate the thick, unyielding walls. The solicitousness of the wardresses, who would feed you, read to you, stroke your back, do anything for you – right up to the point when your executioner appeared at the door, and that stroke turned into a grip on the shoulder. Above all, the inexorable progress of those clock hands on the wall. How easily the minutes slid by, and what choking desperation Hannah had felt to somehow fill them fruitfully! Those twenty minutes felt like a terrifying insight, a microcosm of Mrs Pearcey's time left in the world.

Unless, of course, she was saved. And, surely, there was still *some* chance of that. Palmer's petition to the home secretary. Visits from the doctors. The pro-reprieve sentiment in the newspapers. And, secretly, Mrs Pearcey must have hope, too. Surely, a person could only make a statement to the effect that they would rather be dead than in an asylum when, despite what you told yourself and others, despite all the evidence mounting up around you, you still didn't really, truly believe that it was going to happen. That someone was going to pin your arms behind your back, put a noose around your neck, and then push you into the unknown. Someone or something, somehow, would intervene to stop such unthinkable horror coming to pass. You might hold on to that belief until the very last, until you felt the rope tightening around your throat.

In that final moment of clarity, would she feel the urge to publicly confess, to expel the darkness inside her? Or would she take it all with her, down through the trapdoor?

The air around Hannah now hung with the thick, metallic scent of blood; she was approaching Smithfield. Outside the market, dozens of carts were lined up, waiting for their cargo to be dispatched and carved up inside. The equine undertakers stood patiently, their nostril breath dense in the cold air.

As she passed by, Hannah wondered whether she was guilty of a lack of imagination. Perhaps Mrs Pearcey truly didn't want to be saved; would prefer to be killed next week rather than live for decades in an asylum. Who could really know what was going on in that head? And why was Hannah so keen to understand her? Mrs Pearcey had committed an appalling crime, either from madness or an unfathomable obsession with a hideous man. This was not a case of 'There but for the grace of God go I'. The only things she and Hannah had in common were their age, and their penchant for cheap magazine stories.

And now, something Mrs Pearcey had said – possibly the most innocuous and insignificant thing she had uttered in those twenty minutes – came back to Hannah. She had mentioned that she had run out of reading material, just when she most needed distraction. Hannah stuck with this thought, the only one she could fully relate to, as she drifted down the sludgy pavements of Farringdon.

Passing a food shop, she saw three young men having an animated conversation in Italian. Their overblown gesticulations and larky maleness reminded her of Cosmo and his friends in the Cock Tavern, and as she watched them, an idea took hold. It was quite brilliant. Her mood brightened; she even laughed out loud. Seized by a kind of euphoria, she picked up her pace, now heading for Bloomsbury.

Having never before been to the Reading Room at the British Museum, she wasn't aware that one needed a special pass to get in. This, then, was the second time that day when she had to try to gain entry to a London institution without the required documents.

The man at the front desk had an appropriately intellectual air, with round wire glasses and thin hair swept back off a high forehead. He didn't look like the sort to be open to a bribe of cold cream, even if she had some to hand. Her only option was the truth, or near to it.

'Could I please just see if my friend is inside?' she asked. 'I have an urgent message for him.'

The man rubbed his nose.

'Who is your friend?'

'Mr Timmer,' she said.

'Full name?'

She hoped he wasn't going to ask that. She'd been pleased enough to have remembered his surname. 'You know, I don't actually know.' She smiled at him, trying to be charming. 'We're not *that* good friends. But I do have an urgent message for him.'

The man ran his finger down a ledger of names.

'Yes, there is a Timmer here,' he said. 'I will pass on the message.'

'Please,' she said. 'Please, let me. It's – delicate. It needs to come from me.'

He looked at her for a long moment, to make it clear what a great favour he was granting.

'Five minutes,' he conceded.

She thanked him, and moved towards the heavy double doors beyond the desk. On entering the room, she stopped. Its shape shouldn't have been a surprise – everyone knew the famous Reading Room was built as a dome – but still, she wasn't expecting such scale and grandeur. She could be inside St Paul's. Above the stacks, ten-foot-high windows encircled the room, admitting celestial levels of light. At the centre of the room, ground-level shelves were fashioned in concentric circles, and rows of green-leather-covered desks ran off from them like sun rays. At each of these desks, lit by a dedicated lamp, sat someone, reading or writing. The contrast with her experience earlier that day, at that other inner sanctum, could not have been more startling.

Hannah walked timidly down the rows of desks, looking for Timmer. Astonishing how many women there were here; it felt like every other bent head was female. Many of them looked arresting, with undone – even short – hair and loose clothing, and handsome, intelligent faces. More than this, she was struck by their manner: their expressions of fierce concentration, and the easy, unselfconscious chatter between them, arms slung over the backs of their chairs. They spoke in hushed voices, but even in passing Hannah could hear the confidence in their tones. She felt she had infiltrated a secret society.

Then, she saw him. Timmer was at a desk, a pile of paper in front of him, a pencil in his hand, but rather than writing, he was sitting with his long legs wrapped around his chair, gazing at the girl at the neighbouring desk. She was one of these fascinating creatures, with wild, mousy hair and a strong profile, sucking the end of a pencil as she studied a book, seemingly oblivious to his interest.

Hannah touched him on the shoulder. He started, and then blinked with surprise as he registered her.

'What, hello!' he said. 'I didn't know you came in here!'

'I don't,' she replied. 'I'm here to ask you a favour.'

'Oh dear,' he said. 'Are you worried I'm going to take Cosmo on a wild pre-wedding jaunt and leave him covered in feathers in . . . Maidstone or something? Honestly, I was just planning a quiet little oyster supper . . .'

She shook her head. 'You can do anything you want with him. I wanted to ask if you would do something for me. Write something.'

'What, like a speech?'

'A story,' she said. 'Like the silly ones from women's magazines. You know, with a beautiful heroine caught between two men, and dastardly uncles, and vengeful widows, and altercations in drawing rooms . . .'

'I know them very well,' he said. 'In fact, I used to write them, until the *Star* offered me marginally more respectable employment.'

'That's what I thought!' she said, pleased she had

remembered correctly. 'So, could you write one for me? Very quickly? The juiciest, most dramatic one you can imagine. Set somewhere foreign.'

He smiled quizzically.

'What is this? Who's it for?'

'I'd rather not say,' she said, before realising that this was the last thing one should say to a journalist. 'I mean – to be honest with you, it's for me, and my bridesmaids. A silly thing.'

'Shh.'

The handsome, wild-haired girl at the next desk had a censorious finger to her lips.

'Some of us have essays to write,' she said, in a deep, posh voice. She was in her late twenties at least, and, Hannah noticed, not wearing a wedding ring.

Hannah grimaced in apology, and lowered her voice.

'As a wedding present?' she said to Timmer. 'And don't tell Cosmo? I'm embarrassed about being so low-brow.'

Timmer smiled, and sat forward in his chair.

'Why not?' he said. 'I'll see if I've still got it. I used to bash them out in two hours, back in the day.'

They arranged to meet outside the Reading Room when he was finished. It wasn't worth going home, and so, as she waited, Hannah wandered around the museum. The place was swarming with school children. In the Egyptian gallery, Hannah sat on a bench and watched several groups being herded by their teachers from sarcophagus to sarcophagus. They looked around ten or eleven years old. Some were clearly from respectable schools, smartly uniformed and ostentatiously attentive to their teacher, their pencils constantly poised on their pads. Another group clearly saw this more as a day out rather than an educational opportunity, and were more interested in joshing with each other and testing the acoustics in the gallery than the wonders of the ancient world.

Hannah found the sight of the children incredibly moving. Each seemed full of potential and the innocent solipsism of youth – the antidote to the black hole of Newgate. She wasn't so interested in the boys, but she observed the girls as they passed by her bench, noting her first impressions of each of them. One was awkward and diffident, at the back of the group, socks falling down her stick legs. Another was attractive and self-aware, with long, honey-coloured hair held up in two perfectly even ribbons. This one looked studious, peering close to read the inscriptions beside the statues. That one was furtively taking a bite of a sandwich. And that one appeared to be thinking of something that wasn't anything to do with the Ptolemaic dynasty, squinting sadly as she stared up at the roof of the gallery.

As she watched the girls, their ambient chatter filling the space, Hannah felt consumed with empathy. She felt that she had been all of them, once. What lay in store for them? When Hannah was that age, the answer was simple. But these girls were a new generation, and their horizon was now wider. Most of them were still destined to be wives and mothers, Hannah supposed, but now there were reading rooms, and colleges, and secretarial courses, and shop girl jobs, and digs in Chelsea. The knowledge they were gaining at school, these facts about Ramses III, might not just be used to help them provide their husbands with stimulating conversation around the dinner table, but for their own pursuits.

A new, small group now entered the gallery, and Hannah

recognised the severe black-and-white uniform of the Foundling Hospital. Among them, she spotted the small, dark-haired girl that her mother always spoke to after the Sunday service – the one Mrs Teale was considering taking in as her maid, in her future, pared-down living arrangements at the refuge. Frances, that was her name.

Hannah studied Frances properly, for the first time, noticing her thick eyebrows and sallow skin, similar to Hannah's. She wondered whether this had something to do with why, out of all the Foundling girls, Mrs Teale had chosen her to nurture – or was Hannah flattering herself? As she continued to watch Frances move around the gallery, part of an obedient crocodile, eyes swivelling to wherever the teacher directed them, the thought illuminated another memory, and then another, like a long row of candles, each lit in turn by its neighbour.

Her arms stiffened, braced on the bench, as the realisation came to her. It was simultaneously monumental and unsurprising, as great realisations often are. *Of course.*

Later, thinking back on it, Hannah wondered whether that moment was a legacy of her meeting with Mrs Pearcey at Newgate a few hours earlier. That conversation in the cell had been the performance of her life; she'd had to think on her feet and make rapid connections like never before. Sitting on that bench in the British Museum, observing the Foundlings, her mind was still fired up, ready to join the dots.

Two hours later, she returned to the Great Court and waited self-consciously at the bottom of the stairs leading up to the Reading Room, until a flushed-looking Timmer trotted down to her and thrust a small sheaf of paper into her hand.

'Two hours, three minutes,' he said proudly. 'The old muscles haven't completely atrophied. It's not terrible, actually.'

She thanked him profusely, and again asked him not to tell Cosmo, before briskly heading out of the museum. She could visit the Post Office in King's Cross on the way home, and send the story straight over to Newgate; Mrs Pearcey might even receive it the next morning. As she walked down the street, she skimmed the first page, and saw that Timmer, in his role as Cosmo's best man, had been having fun. The story was titled 'The Uncertain Bride', and the feisty, passionate heroine was one *Miss Hannah Teale.*

Hannah winced. How could she send a story to Mrs Pearcey featuring herself as the heroine? It would seem wildly egotistical, odd or insensitive – or all three. But then she remembered – Mrs Pearcey didn't even know her real name.

On 21 December, two days before Mrs Pearcey's execution date, came the news that the petition had failed. Under the headline HOPE OVER FOR MRS PEARCEY, the *Star* published the letter received by Freke Palmer from the Home Office: *I am directed by the secretary of state to say that, after medical inquiry and the most careful consideration of all the circumstances in the case, he regrets that he has been unable to discover any sufficient grounds to justify him in advising Her Majesty to interfere with the due course of the law.*

The paper reported that the Newgate chaplain was the one to break the news to Mrs Pearcey, at which *she turned in her chair and passed her hand over her brow.* It was now certain that, on the morning of 23 December, she would hang.

Hannah had bought a newspaper from a boy at the junction in Camden Town. The snow had returned, and the normally grimy high street was white-washed, fit for a biscuit tin. The street's everyday unsavoury odours had been snuffed out, and the costers had changed from their usual offerings to a fragrant festive range: eggnog and gingerbread and strings of dried orange, as well as fir trees, a clutch of which leant against the wall of Brown's dairy, as if inebriated and in need of support. The public house was glowing and packed; Hannah could hear faint traces of a singalong to 'Little Annie Rooney'. The butcher's window was crammed with plucked, pink turkeys, a rather unsettling sight *en masse*, while above them, rows of still-feathered geese hung like clouds. The obsequious fishmonger had attached a sprig of mistletoe to his hat, and used it as an excuse to give a sloppy kiss to every female customer, including Hannah, who had ordered a side of salmon for Christmas Day.

Leaning on the wall of the dairy, Hannah read the details of the home secretary's letter on the front page of the paper. Readers were invited to discover more details overleaf, but Hannah was wearing gloves and could not turn the page without taking them off. She put one gloved finger between her teeth to start removing it but stopped: she realised she didn't want to read on. Indeed, the prospect of more details made her feel queasy. It wasn't hard to imagine what the news would be, fed to the journalists by those gimlet-eyed wardresses, or concocted by the journalists themselves. Readers would learn how Mrs Pearcey reacted to the news that her fate was sealed. How she would spend her final hours. What she would be offered for her last meal. It was all horribly prurient and inhumane. Hannah handed back the newspaper to the boy and walked towards Camden Square, resolving that she would not read anything more about this case, and would do her utmost not to discuss it with anyone. Not even Cosmo.

The timing made this resolution simple to keep. Cosmo and his parents were spending Christmas in Norfolk with one of his sisters, and wouldn't be back in London until Boxing Day. She'd be safe in Camden Square. Her mother wouldn't bring it up, of course, and Will wasn't overly interested in that sort of thing – not interested enough to feast on the gory details. And the house's chief gossips, the maids, had gone. Mrs Teale had granted them a generous week's holiday, and they had taken the train back to unknown parts of the country to be with their families.

Christmas at Camden Square had become a modest affair since Mr Teale's death, with just the three of them, and presents limited to one carefully chosen book per person. On the day itself, Hannah and her mother would cook a roast beef lunch for the women at the refuge, and then the three Teales would have their own dinner in the evening. But there were still things to do – food to buy, bookshops to visit, charity boxes to assemble – as well as a few remaining wedding tasks, such as buying the rice to be thrown after she and Cosmo emerged from church, and chair ribbons for the reception.

Hannah did what was required of her, but in a detached way. Half of her mind, at least, was locked in an airless cell at Newgate, veering between states of hysteria and frozen horror, simultaneously holding out hope that someone would intervene to stop the inevitable, while knowing they would not.

★

At 8 a.m. on 23 December, execution day, Hannah was in her bed, eiderdown drawn up to her nose, staring at a dead daddy-long-legs suspended from the ceiling. She'd barely slept; each time she had approached oblivion she had jerked awake, as if her consciousness had decreed that she must be present, to share these torturous final hours with Mrs Pearcey, three miles away in her cell. She could picture the scene – one of few people in London who accurately could. She could see the prisoner on that narrow bed, under that rough brown blanket. Hannah imagined her lying on her side, facing the wall, away from that terrible, inexorable clock. The wardresses sitting beside her, taking turns to stroke her back, exchanging glances at each other over her hunched body, silently turning to check the time. On the table, an empty bottle of ale, an untouched plate of meat and potatoes. The netting had probably been taken down now; there would be no more visitors.

But of course, it was impossible to fully imagine what the prisoner was feeling. Lying there, Hannah had drawn on her memories of blind terror – all from childhood nightmares of ghosts and imaginary threats – but felt ashamed in doing so, knowing anything she could conjure would be grossly inadequate.

Outside, a few miles into the city, she heard the faint toll of a single bell.

Cosmo came to visit Hannah at Camden Square on Boxing Day evening, straight from his sister's. Mrs Teale was at the refuge; Will at the theatre.

'It was good fun, actually,' he said, sitting down and

accepting a glass of port. 'Lots of little sprogs running around. And guess what? Her husband says he'll give us ten pounds as a wedding present.'

Hannah, who was standing at the fireplace, gave a quick, nervy smile. Cosmo peered at her.

'My darling – are you all right? You look a bit peaky.'

She had purposefully neglected her toilette that morning; no pinched cheeks or powder. For this meeting she wanted to look completely natural, without contrivance. But it was true that she *did* feel peaky – nauseous at what she was about to say, at the tenor of the conversation they were about to have. She went over to him, knelt beside his chair and clasped his hand.

'Darling Cosmo. I must say something. Several things, actually.'

She hesitated. Good news first.

'So, Mother says that we can live here, after the wedding, until we get our own place.'

Cosmo's eyes widened, and he opened his mouth to speak, but she pre-empted him.

'—but without her! She's going to live in the refuge.'

Cosmo smiled, amazed. 'Well, that's a turn-up!'

'My brother will be here, too,' said Hannah. 'For a while, at least. Until he finds fame as a theatre producer.'

Will had announced his departure from university on Christmas Eve. Over dinner on Christmas Day, her mother had proposed the new idea: that she would leave the house to the two of them.

Cosmo looked only momentarily nonplussed. 'Oh!' he said. 'Well, why not?'

'He's going to borrow all your suits,' Hannah said. 'He's quite annoying!'

Cosmo smiled indulgently. 'It'll be fun!'

She mustn't let Cosmo get too relaxed, Hannah thought.

'But wait. Darling,' she said. 'You may not want to live here.'

Cosmo's smile faltered.

'I mean – you may not want to marry me,' she went on. She heard her portentous tone and realised that a part of her was excited by the drama of the conversation; the power she was wielding. An emotional exchange in a drawing room; a test of a fiancé's love – the scene was straight out of a magazine.

'Impossible!' he said. His eyes were slightly bloodshot from his days of indulgence in Norfolk. 'There is literally nothing you could say that would make me think that.' He forced a chortle. 'Even if you said you were madly in love with someone else, I'd say – let me win you back!'

She laughed, too. 'No! It's not that at all.' She held his hand again, and took a breath. 'What I mean to say is – I don't think I want to have children.'

Cosmo reared back and stared at her in astonishment.

'Not straight away, I mean,' she clarified quickly. 'Sorry.'

She winced; she had got swept up and overstated her case. The sense of drama was extinguished. She watched Cosmo's face as he tried to rally.

'Well, yes, of course,' he said. 'I mean, no hurry, is there? So, when are you thinking? Six months? A year?'

'I don't know,' she said. 'That's the thing. What I'm sure of is that I'm not ready now, and there are things I want to do first. That's all I can say.'

'What sort of things?'

'I don't know yet . . .'

'Darling, you know that I'm fully in favour of hobbies, don't you?' he said. 'I think it's vitally important for women to keep their minds active.'

'Not a hobby,' she said. 'Something else. Something – in the world.'

'Do you mean *a job*?'

Hannah shrugged. 'Perhaps. I don't know.'

He was so transparent, struggling to keep a neutral expression. She wondered if he was remembering an earlier conversation in this room, when she had told him about her involvement with the Mrs Pearcey story and he had been agonised over the fact that she had been into his office, trespassed on his turf.

'Charitable work? Like your mother?' asked Cosmo hopefully.

'Perhaps,' said Hannah again. She knew he wanted her to say, *Not journalism, of course*, and she almost did, to make him happy, but resisted. 'I don't know what I'm even capable of. But I'd like all sorts of things to be possible. The only thing I'm quite sure about is that I want to *do* something before having children. I can't tell you when I might be ready. And I completely understand if you'd rather marry someone else.'

Cosmo now stood up and started pacing around the room, uncharacteristically quiet. Hannah knew she must give him space to think, but she didn't seem able to stop talking now.

'That's the thing,' she continued. 'I love you but I don't know you, inside out. And you don't know me. And so, I think we must go into this open-eyed, and knowing as much about each other as we can, for it to be a success. Don't you think?'

He was now looking out of the window, his back to her and hands stuffed in his pockets.

'Certainly,' he said, without looking round.

His short response made Hannah chatter all the more.

'But of course, I mean, we can't predict or control the future,' she said. 'And how we will both turn out . . . I mean, who knows? You might do – something and I . . . well, I might go mad and end up in an asylum. Who knows?'

Now he swivelled to look at her, and gave a nervous laugh.

'Why would you say such a thing?'

Hannah was surprised herself. She hadn't intended to go down this road but now realised she wanted to continue.

'Well, Mother did, you see. Yes, even my mother! The most sober woman on the planet.'

'When was this?'

'About fifteen years ago,' Hannah said. What a release it was, airing this. 'My father did something awful, and she went mad. Just for a little while. She was in an asylum. Everyone seemed to know, except me and Will. We were told that she had gone to Italy for a few months, and the cook looked after us.'

'What awful thing did he do?' asked Cosmo. 'Your father?'

'He was a barrister – you know that. And he had a client, a maid who murdered her horrible employer. He got her with child, so she could plead her belly and escape hanging.'

Cosmo stared at her, astonished, as well he might.

Since Hannah's moment of realisation sitting on the bench in the Egyptian galleries of the British Museum, she had clutched this knowledge to her. She hadn't told Emily, or Will. She certainly hadn't told her mother. Saying it out loud now solidified it, although since the thought had come to her, she hadn't once doubted that it was the truth. All the pieces fitted together perfectly, like a cleanly broken saucer. Mrs Teale's reaction to the story about her father's 'friend' and his client pleading her belly. Her coldness to her husband during the last years of his life. Her complicated reaction to his death. Mrs Didier's remark about his awfulness. Gwen's throw-away comment in the kitchen about Mrs Teale having been in an asylum, which Hannah had initially assumed to be a mistake, but had confirmed with Ivy in a private conversation before Christmas. The truth behind Mrs Teale's 'trip to Italy' was apparently an open secret, passed down to them by previous servants at Camden Square.

'And what happened?' asked Cosmo. 'To the girl, I mean?'

'The maid? She was given a reprieve, apparently. I don't know what happened to her then. Disappeared off somewhere, I suppose.'

'And the child?'

Now, finally, Hannah paused and considered before speaking. She glanced at her pale, undefined face in the mirror above the fireplace.

'I don't know,' she said.

Finally, she was holding back. She was sure that she *did* know what had happened to the child. It explained Mrs Teale's attendance at the Foundling Hospital since her father's death, and her particular interest in the welfare of a small, dark-haired child. The same girl who was shortly due to be put out into the world, and who her mother wanted to employ at the refuge. The same girl who shared Hannah's colouring, and who Hannah had observed as she had threaded her way through the Egyptian obelisks in the British Museum.

She didn't want to reveal this suspicion to Cosmo; she had said enough. She felt no loyalty to her father or guilt about exposing his misdemeanour; he didn't deserve discretion. But the fact of her mother wanting to help this girl, Hannah's half-sister, the product of an incident that caused her so much pain, seemed too tender to reveal.

'Gosh, Hannah,' said Cosmo now. 'Well, that's a thing.'

He flopped into his chair and picked up the glass of port.

'Please don't say anything about it, ever,' said Hannah. 'To your parents. Or my mother. Promise. But I wanted to tell you, because . . .'

She stopped, as she was about to say *because you're going to be my husband*, but now realised that he had never fully responded to her declaration at the start of the conversation. As it stood, Cosmo was still deciding whether he wanted to marry a woman who didn't know when she would want children.

Cosmo drank down the rest of his port and put the glass on the side table. Then, he reached for her hand.

'Because – I'm your husband,' he said. 'Or at least I will be, jolly soon.' And he pulled her down onto his lap.

On the following day, 27 December, Hannah was due to collect her wedding dress from Mrs Didier. The snow had all but disappeared, just a few grimy banks left in the kerb. The sky was a delicate, fresh blue. She decided to walk into town through Regent's Park, passing by the zoo's Giraffe House in the hope of glimpsing one of the new calves, and then catch the omnibus home from Soho with the dress.

Camden Town had a denuded, post-Christmas atmosphere. Already, fir trees lay abandoned on the pavements, some still pathetically festooned with paper chains, callously dumped as soon as their moment was over. Half of the shops were shuttered, although the lights of Brown's dairy were still on; people always needed milk. Peering into the public house as she passed by, heading towards Mornington Crescent, Hannah saw that it was still fairly busy, but now the drinkers were mainly solitary and muted, recovering rather than celebrating.

At the junction, as ever, there was a newsboy, a stack of papers wedged under one arm.

'Last riddle of Mrs Pearcey!' he called, waving a paper above his head. Hannah saw it was the *Star*. 'Last riddle of Mrs Pearcey!'

She stopped. Riddle? Hannah knew what had happened that night in the kitchen of Priory Street, and why. She had been admitted into Mrs Pearcey's inner sanctum, and learnt the truth. She had solved the case. Hadn't she?

She had resolved to avoid all further details of the story. That terrible, single toll of the bell at Newgate, on the morning of 23 December, was the end. *No more of it now.* She looked at the boy as he moved away from her, weaving through the thin traffic, but after a few minutes, she dug into her pocket for a penny and called after him.

She opened the paper while continuing to walk towards Regent's Park, as if reading it on the move somehow diluted the act.

The paper described Mrs Pearcey's final meeting with her lawyer, Freke Palmer, two days before her execution. It was bitterly cold in her cell, and so the meeting took place in the chief warder's room, which was warm and well lit. Palmer told the journalist that she had entered the room with a *certain amount of cheerfulness*, remarking on the bad weather. She first wanted to talk about the few possessions of hers that remained after the Tussauds sale, and who would get them. They weren't worth much but had sentimental value. She wished a ring to go to her mother, and a Bible to her sister.

And finally, the paper reported, the prisoner made a very odd request. She asked Palmer to place an advertisement in a Madrid newspaper, which read: *To M.E.C.P. Last wish of M.E.W. Have not betrayed.*

There was no mystery behind the M.E.W. – that was her real name, Mary Eleanor Wheeler. But the first set of initials did not match anyone known to be involved in the case. And where did the idea of Madrid come from? There had been no mention of the city, or of Spain, at any stage in the case.

Was this, then, the article posited, proof of the involvement of another party?

Palmer said that when he had asked the prisoner the meaning of this strange message, she claimed it was not connected to the crime, but rather to a marriage that had taken place between her and a certain gentleman, whose name she had sworn not to divulge. They had been married in Piccadilly, in the presence of his valet. She thought this man might now be in Madrid, hence putting the advert in the papers there.

It was all most baffling, the paper concluded. The woman called herself Mrs Pearcey but had never been married to John Pearcey. And now she was claiming to actually be married to someone else entirely, now living in a far-off land. And this mystery man was the person she wished to reassure of her loyalty, in her final act upon this earth.

Offering another theory, the newspaper pointed out that

the initials M.E.C.P. *nearly* matched those of the prisoner's assumed name, Mary Eleanor Pearcey. Bearing in mind that she was known to have mental problems, perhaps for some secret reason she was sending a message to her younger self, to her previous, innocent iteration. But why would she do that? And why put it in an advert in a Spanish newspaper?

It was, the paper concluded, a complete mystery: a fittingly perplexing endnote to this most tragic and confounding of stories.

Hannah tucked the paper into her pocket and kept walking. She was now deep in Regent's Park; such was her absorption in this news, she had forgotten about her planned detour to the Giraffe House.

Marrying a gentleman in Piccadilly, in the presence of his valet. Wasn't that a scene straight out of a magazine story? The mysterious foreign gentleman, stopping off in London and sweeping a random sealskin-factory girl off her feet before disappearing back to the Continent.

Yes, Hannah felt certain of it. Mrs Pearcey had concocted an intrigue as an explanation for the cryptic advert, in order to distract from its true meaning. A dramatic flourish that would leave the world guessing and cause a stir from beyond the grave. She was more than capable of such a thing, given her casual relationship with the truth. Take the ludicrous account of the day of the murders she had told Hannah in the cell.

And the true meaning of the message? A complete mystery to most. But not to Hannah.

M.E.C.P. What was it that Mrs Pearcey had called Frank Hogg in the cell? *My Eternal Cherished Partner.* That phrase was also inscribed in the Spanish phrase-book in Priory Street. It may have been a present from Frank, given in anticipation of their new life together in Spain. Perhaps she and Frank used the phrase for each other.

Have not betrayed, the advert read. So, Hannah had been right in her theory of what happened that night, and Mrs Pearcey's whispers to her in the cell, fleshing out the story, were not an attempt to mislead. She had assumed the blame for Frank's role in his daughter's death, alongside her own culpability for his wife, allowing Frank to remain free to go off to Spain and start the new life that the two of them had planned to have together.

Knowing Mrs Pearcey even the little that Hannah did, it made a warped kind of sense. What grander gesture could there be, what greater act of devotion, than saving the life of your beloved? Of granting him his dream future, even though you were no longer around to share it? It was an ending fit for the greatest romantic heroine, as well as the one thing left in her power after she was taken into custody. It ensured that Frank could never forget her; even if his head was turned by a sweet little *señorita* in Spain, he would always be in her debt.

And now, as Hannah strode through the park, the noises from the zoo growing faint behind her, she understood what she hadn't before: that Frank had appeared to love Mrs Pearcey, too, once. He had an affectionate nickname for her. He trusted her to bring up his daughter. It seemed they were both looking forward to a life together in Spain. Once, their relationship must have been genuine and true, and it was only when things went terribly wrong that Frank's weakness and self-interest came to the fore. Then he had used Mrs

Pearcey's love for him to persuade her to take the blame for them both.

Hannah had now come through the park and emerged onto the Marylebone Road. Ahead of her, on the other side of the busy thoroughfare, lay Soho. But instead, she turned right.

Even for Madame Tussauds, the queue was gargantuan, stretching all the way down the pavement and around the corner, composed of clumps of shivering families. Hannah considered going to the front and seeing if she could blag her way in, but decided against it. Those days were behind her. Obediently, she joined the back of the queue, and from listening to the conversations around her, it became apparent that everyone was there for one particular exhibit.

'I only want to see her,' said a woman standing in front of Hannah, to her companion. 'In and out, and then we can go for cake.' 'Do you think they'll have done the baby, too?' said another. 'I heard they took a cast of Pearcey's head when she was still alive.'

A Tussauds employee walked up and down the queue, reassuring the customers that they would all eventually get inside, and stoking their excitement for that moment.

'Every artefact from the case is here!' he called. 'Even the boiled sweet from the baby's mouth!'

He reminded them that the Chamber of Horrors, where the Mrs Pearcey exhibit was housed, cost an extra penny in admission.

The queue inched forward until finally it was Hannah's turn to pay over her money and join those cramming into the museum's lobby. The volume and intensity of the crowd, the air of anticipation, reminded her of the atmosphere outside the real Priory Street. Everyone was moving towards the same door marked *Chamber of Horrors*, and such was the mass of bodies there was little choice but to be swept along with them. The rest of the museum's exhibits, the Napoleons and Runnymedes, stood unnoticed and unloved.

Once inside the Chamber of Horrors, Hannah fought her way to the front of the buzzing crowd gathered before the exhibit.

She stopped, stock still. There, part-obscured by the jostling figures in front of her, was the kitchen at 2 Priory Street. There was the range, the dress stand, the sewing machine. The table, and the wicker chairs – one broken. There was the window, with its green blind, the broken panes at the bottom. Behind the glass, a painted screen stood in for the garden. The rag rug. The colander. The only things missing were the half-onion and the cold cup of tea, a cigarette floating on its surface.

And there stood Mrs Pearcey. Hannah could only glimpse her head and shoulders; people kept pushing in front of her, and it was impossible to get a proper look. So, instead, she moved to the further end of the tableau, where there was slightly more room, and found herself face to face with Frank Hogg.

She gasped; the sight was genuinely startling. He had sold some belongings to the museum, she knew, but she was not expecting his waxwork. He was standing slightly apart from the main tableau, arms hanging awkwardly at his sides. His likeness was uncanny, capturing his low brow, his raisin eyes, that greasy pigeon-wing hair – even his expression, the wounded and self-pitying look she remembered from the Trafalgar. She imagined him posing for the artists in the Tussauds backroom, looking in a mirror to arrange his features before the cast of his face was taken, carefully untying his cravat and handing it over.

Mary's eternal cherished partner. This was how a man could achieve immortality without even dying.

Beside her, a man turned to his companion.

'I read it's even his real beard,' he said. 'He shaved it off and sold it to them.'

So, that was it. Hannah peered closer at the waxwork's face, at the red bristles stuck into the wax. Those same bristles that he had rubbed his thick fingers against, a few inches from Hannah's face in the Trafalgar. Now, he was in Spain, starting a new life, clean-shaven.

Repulsed and entranced, she gazed at him, as if this Frank, at least, might offer a clue to the unfathomable hold he had over Mrs Pearcey. She remained, eyes locked on him, until she was barged out of the way by others eager to get close.

The crush in the small room was uncomfortable, the loud hum painful to the ears – but Hannah couldn't retreat just yet. She pushed her way back to the main tableau, the kitchen, manoeuvring herself until, finally, she was right in front of the model of Mrs Pearcey. The murderer was positioned by a fire screen with her hands folded at her waist, wearing a drab, dark-blue dress and a white apron. Unlike Frank's waxwork, Hannah thought her likeness was unfair – her face too thin, her overbite exaggerated. Her hair – a ratty brown, with none of the auburn tinge it had in real life – was piled up on the top of her head, and her marble eyes were blue and cold, staring into the middle of the room.

'Ugh!' cried a boy beside her. 'She's so ugly.'

'Well, she is a monster,' said the boy's mother placidly. 'What do you expect?'

Hannah kept looking and realised that actually the model makers had captured something of the real Mrs Pearcey, in that blank, dead stare. Hannah hadn't articulated it to herself before, but during her visit to Newgate she had felt there was something profoundly missing from the prisoner. An absence at her core.

Someone else behind Hannah was talking about Mrs Pearcey's mysterious last message, to M.E.C.P.

'I heard that it's the initials of Jack the Ripper,' the woman said. 'I always knew he had something to do with it.'

Hannah stepped away from her spot in front of the waxwork, and immediately two others pressed into her place. Detaching from the Chamber of Horrors crowd, she wandered to the exit through the other deserted galleries, passing by those poor, ignored royal children and religious elders, and the perpetually grumpy King John.

She thought again about that conversation she'd had with her mother here, all those years ago. *Do people in history know they're in history?* And she understood, now, that there were two types of history. The type made up of the single acts with huge repercussions: the Runnymedes; the murders. But then there was the quiet, everyday, undramatic kind, made by people who spent most of their time thinking about what to have for dinner, but who also made their own decisions and took small actions and lived just a little bit differently from their parents. Together, those decisions and actions accumulated, and gathered weight. They had an effect.

At the exit, Hannah emerged out onto Marylebone Road. Before her, a rackety battalion pressed into London, from

Tyburnia, Paddington and beyond, all classes of people in all kinds of transport – omnibuses, hansoms, carriages with drawn velvet curtains and footmen swaying on the back, goods carts – getting in each other's way but continually pushing forward, intent on further swelling the largest city on earth. Overhead, the clouds were moving fast and unimpeded. Weaving through the traffic, Hannah crossed the road and strode away from Mrs Pearcey and Frank Hogg, towards Soho, to pick up her wedding dress.

Author's Note

Mrs Pearcey is a work of fiction but Mrs Pearcey, the murderer, was a real person. As depicted in the novel, her crimes caused a huge sensation at the time. Not only were they particularly shocking – the killing of a mother and baby in an age that sanctified motherhood – but, highly unusually, the accused was an attractive young woman. Reports on the case filled the newspapers from the day the bodies were discovered to her execution two months later, and even beyond, when it was revealed that one of her last acts on earth was to ask her lawyer to post a cryptic advert in a Spanish newspaper, reassuring a mysterious someone that she *had not betrayed*. Shortly after her death, Madame Tussaud's mounted a tableau of the murder scene, and apparently 30,000 people turned up on the first day.

However, unlike, say, Dr Crippen or, of course, her contemporary, Jack the Ripper, Mrs Pearcey's notoriety has faded, to the point where she is not well known today (although, at the time of writing, the pram she used to transport the bodies is still on display in Tussaud's Chamber of Horrors, tucked away behind Dennis Nilson's TV). I think this is largely because of her opaque character. She gave no help whatsoever to anyone trying to understand how or why she could do such a terrible thing. She didn't confess, or give any rational explanation for her crime. The accepted motive of sexual obsession was unsatisfying as Frank Hogg, the object of her obsession, was, by all accounts, a rat: unprepossessing, shifty and uncouth, the opposite of the Victorian masculine ideal. How could a young woman sacrifice her life for such a specimen?

In short, although she was likely guilty, the whole awful case didn't quite add up. This is what attracted me to fictionalising it: I wanted to fill in the gaps, in Mrs Pearcey as a person and the crime as a whole: to give it a resolution, and meaning, that real life didn't provide.

The great Hilary Mantel described the act of separating fact from fiction in historical novels as like trying to return mayonnaise to oil and egg yolk – but for those who are interested, here goes. Broadly speaking, the facts of the Mrs Pearcey case included in the novel – the timeline, locations, suspects and witnesses, testimony and evidence presented in court, the outcome – are true, taken from contemporary newspaper sources. That said, these reports weren't comprehensive, and I don't think fact-checking was a huge thing in those days. Most of the colourful, gossipy details, such as Frank Hogg donating his stubble for his Tussauds waxwork, are also true – or, at least, *I* didn't make them up.

Hannah is a wholly fictional character, and her engagement with the story, encounters with the real people involved, and the conclusions she reaches, are imagined.

Lastly, although the geography of Camden Town today is largely unchanged from the time of the story, its stations then were not as we know them now. In 1890, Camden

Town underground station had yet to be built, and a dairy stood on that spot. Camden Town railway station was situated where Camden Road station is today, while Camden Road station was located further northeast along Camden Road, and no longer exists. Some of the area's streets have also been renamed since then. Notably, Priory Street, where Mrs Pearcey lived and Phoebe and Tiggie died, is now Ivor Street, perhaps due to its infamy.

Acknowledgements

I feel immensely fortunate that this novel found its home with Francesca Main, who is not only a genius editor but a joy to work with. Thank you too to Katie Espiner and the wonderful team at Phoenix: Lucinda McNeile, Holly Kyte, Jo Whitfield and Naomi Morris Omori who whipped the manuscript into shape; Steve Marking and Sofia Hericson who designed the book's brilliant cover; Harry Taylor, Hennah Sandhu and the Orion sales team who got it out there.

Huge thanks, as ever, to my agent Antony Topping and all at Greene and Heaton.

There are many good non-fiction books about Victorian true crime, but only one comprehensive account of the Mrs Pearcey story: *Woman at the Devil's Door* by Sarah Beth Hopton (Mango Books). I am grateful to the author for her research, bringing together the contemporary news reports on the case.

Love and thanks to my family – Horatio Mortimer, Deborah Moggach, Tom Moggach and Larushka Ivan-Zadeh – who read early drafts and gave invaluable advice, and to my son Kit, who may read it one day.

And to the friends who helped me, in all sorts of ways, to write this book: Adam, Alex, Ben, Caroline, Catherine, Charlotte, Chris, Claire, Craig, Damien, Eliane, Fiona, Gudrun, Josh, Laura, Rachel, Rebecca, Sathnam and Susannah. Also, Simon Booker: R.I.P.

RAISING READERS
Books Build Bright Futures

Dear Reader,

We'd love your attention for one more page to tell you about the crisis in children's reading, and what we can all do.

Studies have shown that reading for fun is the **single biggest predictor of a child's future life chances** – more than family circumstance, parents' educational background or income. It improves academic results, mental health, wealth, communication skills, ambition and happiness.[1]

The number of children reading for fun is in rapid decline. Young people have a lot of competition for their time. In 2024, 1 in 10 children and young people in the UK aged 5 to 18 did not own a single book at home.[2]

Hachette works extensively with schools, libraries and literacy charities, but here are some ways we can all raise more readers:

- Reading to children for just 10 minutes a day makes a difference
- Don't give up if children aren't regular readers – there will be books for them!
- Visit bookshops and libraries to get recommendations
- Encourage them to listen to audiobooks
- Support school libraries
- Give books as gifts

There's a lot more information about how to encourage children to read on our website: **www.RaisingReaders.co.uk**

Thank you for reading.

---

[1] National Literacy Trust, Book Ownership in 2024, November 2024
https://nlt.cdn.ngo/media/documents/Book_ownership_in_2024

[2] OECD. 2021. 21st-century readers: developing literacy skills in a digital world. Paris, France: OECD Publishing.
https://www.oecd.org/en/publications/21st-century-readers_a83d84cb-en.html